I0737969

A MYTHOS GRIMMLY

Edited by Jeremy Hochhalter
Additional Editing by Jaime Will

Published by Wanderer's Haven Publications, LLC
P.O. Box 212, Timnath, CO 80547 United States

First Edition : August 2015
ISBN : 978-0-9966938-0-6

To receive advance information, news, competitions, and exclusive offers online, please sign up for the Wanderer's Haven newsletter on our website: http://www.whpublications.com.

In memory of J.F. Gonzalez

Many thanks to the authors and Kickstarter supporters who made this anthology possible.

Table of Contents

<u>**Foreword**</u>

I believe that all stories begin with, *"Once upon a time…"* We may not say it, it may not be in the print, but those four words transport us to another place. It may be the past, present or future. It may be real or imaginary. That is the magic of such a phrase.

It is, however, only at the beginning of a fairy tale that we expect to see such a phrase. Modern takes on these stories are far lighter (Disney-fied) than their darker origins, but all versions of these tales are thematic. Morality tales meant to help us understand the difference between right and wrong, and the consequences of our choices. Cultures all around the world have such stories, passed down through the years.

Today, modern culture expects another phrase to accompany these tales. "And they lived happily ever after." For in these stories, the prince always rescues the princess, the knight always slays the dragon, and the evil queen is always defeated.

You will find very few of these happily-ever-afters within this book. Here, these morality tales have served as food for other beings, maddening dark things that live in the shadows and the strange geometries outside of our senses.

In the early 20th Century, H.P. Lovecraft penned many horrific tales that would come to be known as cosmic horror. While he was not a particularly successful author during his time, his works would grow in popularity in the following decades. Indeed, legions of "Lovecraftian" authors now enjoy expanding on his work, and creating their own terrifying tales along the same lines.

Very rarely does the hero escape unscathed from these tales, and so we come to the crossroads where fairy tales and cosmic horror meet. A Mythos Grimmly was conceived as an anthology where stories told to us as children came together with tales of unknowable entities, horror on a cosmic scale that the human mind cannot fathom.

So while there may not be happy endings for all, there are always new beginnings. It is here that I leave you alone to travel through the worlds that our authors have brought you to. And, as with all stories, we begin…

Once upon a time…

The Arkham Town Musicians

– Christine Morgan –

Now, it happened that there were, in the village of Dunwich, a series of strange events and dark atrocities, centering primarily around the Whateley family, and culminating on that most dreadful night when an inhuman voice shouted an unspeakable name from the height of Sentinel Hill.

But this is not an accounting of those events.

For it happened that there was, also, a poor and humble farmer who had been on occasion in the employ of the Whateleys. His cattle, in the end, met the same grim fate as most others near-abouts – missing at best, sore-ridden and sucked dry of every drop of their blood at the worst.

The farmer himself, left further impoverished and shaken all but to madness by what he had witnessed and the tumult following, soon drank himself to an early grave. He was by no means the only Dunwich resident to do so.

What went forgotten was that the humble farmer had also, for many years, kept as well as his cattle a few donkeys to help with his labors in the fields.

Or, a breed of creatures that might have been donkeys once … might have begun as donkeys … but had, over time … changed.

Whether it was from feeding off what grew in Dunwich, or

whether something else had responsibility, some hideous cross-breeding that introduced unnatural bloodlines, perhaps as a result of the arts of which old Wizard Whateley was said to have been a practitioner, the farmer could not know. Nor did he care to guess.

Only one of these creatures was left behind when the farmer died. Though he did not altogether resemble a donkey, it was as a donkey he thought of himself. And so, as a donkey he shall be called.

After all, he did the work of a donkey. He had the general shape of a donkey, with four strong legs that reached the ground in addition to the myriad centipedal limbs protruding in rippling rows from either side. Where his skin was not mottled pinkish-yellow, the hide was as coarse and grey-brown as any other donkey. If the two long whiplike tentacles that sprouted from his withers were unusual, bristling with hair and ending in reddish sucker-mouths, his tail and stiff mane and upstanding ears were perfectly ordinary. And if the end of his muzzle splayed out into fleshy pink tendrils such as might be found on a star-nosed mole, what of it?

He was still a donkey, hale and healthy and hearty, and proud.

But, in time, the donkey had grazed the grass of his pen down to bare stubble, which seemed disinclined to grow back. He had long since finished the oats and corn stored in the hay-shed where he slept. It occurred to the donkey that he could not stay here much longer on his own.

"Dunwich is done-for," said the donkey, and brayed a laugh at his joke. But he quickly sobered. "And what of myself, then? My master is dead, and his masters as well. Hard-working though I am, I doubt I would find much welcome among the neighbors. They would not take me in even for all my tireless strength. I am a donkey, yes. But I am, after all, no ordinary donkey."

He kicked down the fence of ramshackle wooden sticks and freed himself into the wider world. There, he found more grass, brown and sour and dry.

"For that matter," he said, "why should I want to go on toiling at thankless work on a farm? Why should I plod in the mud, pull a plow, draw a wagon? Did I not just say how I was, to be sure, no ordinary donkey? Why, then, should I labor as one?"

The donkey ambled at his leisure through the blighted fields. He glanced about with interest at the domed hills surrounding Dunwich, and peered down toward the dark, tangled hollow of the glen.

"No, indeed," he told himself, "I am meant for greater and better things than this. I shall go forth from Dunwich to make my own way in the world! Perhaps I might become a musician. Yes! Yes, and why not?"

Here, he hee-hawed at the top of his voice, and found the sound pleasing. He stamped time with a hoof, and when he slid his hairy wither-tentacles one against the other, they gave off shrill, rasping notes like violin strings or a grasshopper's legs.

"Why not?" he cried again. "But these country-villages are no place for such a celebrity as I am bound to be. In Arkham-Town, however, I surely will find my fortune and fame!"

So saying, and very satisfied with his plan, the donkey set out.

Past scattered houses that wore a uniform aspect of desolate age and squalor, he went, and past the huddled cluster of the village itself until he reached the tenebrous tunnel of a covered bridge where his hoofbeats clop-clopped with hollow echoes.

The road then curved, dusty and sometimes flanked by crumbling walls of briar-bordered stone, through a landscape of sloping rock-strewn meadows, luxuriant weeds and brambles. In forest belts, the trees loomed too large and whippoorwills chattered. Chimney-ruins and ancient rough-hewn columns poked up through the undergrowth. At boggy places, fireflies danced in abnormal profusion to the strident but dissonant croaking of bull-frogs.

"They," said the donkey, scoffing with a snort, "are no musicians, that is to be sure!"

He brayed forth his own song, shaming the bull-frogs into silence from their raucous rhythms. He trotted over yet more crude wooden bridges of dubious safety, which traversed deep gorges and ravines.

Not far ahead, knew the donkey, was the junction where Old Dunwich Road met Aylesbury Pike. And only a short while further on from there were the crossroads by Dean's Corners.

Ahead, at a spot where water trickled from a cleft boulder to form a pool by the edge of the road, the donkey saw a figure hunched over and lapping at the water. It seemed to him to be some sort of dog, or at least as much dog as he himself was donkey. In truth, the donkey had not known many dogs before; they had been scarce in Dunwich and unwelcome, for it was said they always set off with a terrific baying in pursuit of Lavinia Whateley's strange son.

This dog, if dog it was, had corpse-colored fur and loose skin that fell in rugose folds and wrinkles. His hind paws were paws proper, but his front ones gripped the rocks at the edge of the pool with long, narrow fingers. His face, when he raised his head, was oddly squashed of countenance, with an immense dripping scoop-shovel of jaw from which arose yellowish tusks.

"Good afternoon!" said the donkey, greeting the dog in all good manners and politeness. "How do you fare on this day, Brother Dog?"

"Wretchedly," the dog replied, giving its head such a shake that its jowls wobbled and droplets of water sprayed about.

"Wretchedly?" the donkey cried. "What a shame! Do you not have your freedom?"

"Oh, I have my freedom," grumbled the dog in a growl. "I, who was a huntsman's most faithful companion, I, who might have run pack-mates with the Hounds of Tindalos, I have all the freedom anyone could ever have, and two extra!"

"Then how is it you seem so displeased? I have only just gained my freedom, and could not be happier!"

"I'm sure that is fine and well for donkeys," the dog said. "But I did not gain my freedom. Neither did I choose it. I was, as I said, a huntsman's most faithful companion. Long years I went by his side into the dark woods. I faced any beast of the forest without fear, even the young of the Black Goat! I was ever loyal, and stalwart, and true!"

The donkey tipped his head, the centipedal limbs waving all down his sides in consternation. "Did your master, the hunstman, die? Mine did --"

"No." The dog snarled, grinding his yellow tusks against his sharp upper teeth. "He married. And his wife, you see, could not stand the sight of me in the house any longer. She feared what I might do to the children. As if I – I! – would bring them any harm!"

"The huntsman did not send you away!" said the donkey, aghast.

"Oh, no," said the dog. "He offered to, but that was not sufficient for her. What if it comes back? she said to him. Even if you led it far into the woods and left it, it could find its way! And so, he, the huntsman, my own trusted master, took up an axe and made to split open my skull!"

At this, the donkey gaped, then snuffled a breath so that the fleshy tendrils at his muzzle flapped and wriggled. "What did you do?"

"What could I but run? I would not have bitten him, despite his murderous intentions. So, now, here I am, with no home and nowhere to go."

"It is well that we found each other then," the donkey said. "For I am on my way to Arkham-Town, where I mean to become a famous musician. With a voice such as yours, so rumbling and resonant, you must make a fine singer yourself."

The dog considered this for a moment, and agreed that a famous musician sounded to him like a fine thing to be. They fell in most readily together, and soon reached Aylesbury Pike.

The air took on a fresher fragrance, bereft of the odour of mould so prevalent in Dunwich. Wildlife scampered unseen in damp drifts of fallen leaves. The day was crisp, the sky clear, though heavy clouds built over the hills. They saw no riders or wagons or other traffic, no one at all, until they came to the crossroads.

There, a signpost pointed in the direction of Dean's Corner, a sleepy but tidy and well-kept little village. Another arrow indicated Aylesbury itself, the distant smokestacks of mills and factories lost in a murky haze.

Most interesting of all, however, was the small mound of recently-turned earth where the roads met, marked with a rough wooden cross jutting up askew at an angle. But it was not the cross, nor the grave, that interested donkey and dog so much as what sat nearby.

It was a cat, large and queenly, of regal bearing. Her sleek coat was of many colors – umber, cream, russet, mahogany and gold. Her eyes were brilliant emeralds. She had a tail like a plume, and gloriously long, curling whiskers. Around her neck, on a silken ribbon, hung a bauble of Egyptian design.

The donkey greeted her as politely as he had done the dog. "Good afternoon, Sister Cat! How do you fare on this day?"

She gave a great yawn, showing ivory teeth. She gave a great stretch, back arching, needle-claws digging into the dirt. Then she sat primly again, licked her forepaw, and smoothed her curled whiskers.

"I am in great distress and despair, Brother Donkey," she replied. "Your companion does not mean to give chase, I should hope. I'll scratch him to the bone, if he does."

The dog grumbled. "I am a hunter, no chaser of cats."

"Good," said the cat. "For I am a cat of Ulthar, and will bring deadly punishment on any who try to do me mischief."

"We mean no such thing," the donkey assured her. "Brother Dog and I are merely traveling to Arkham-Town. But what do you do here? Whose grave is that you sit beside?"

"That of my mistress."

"She must have been tiny," observed the dog.

"It is only her head."

"Her head?" cried the donkey. "Where is the rest of her?"

"I will tell you," said the cat. "My mistress was, on her mother's side, kin to the Whateleys of Dunwich. Do you know of them?"

"Indeed," the donkey said. "I came from there."

"Well, after what happened there, her neighbors decided that she must be a witch. They set upon her, and beat her to death with sticks and with staves. Then they used the blade of a shovel to chop her head from her neck. Her body, they threw into the river. And her head, they buried here at the crossroads, so that even if her spirit somehow returned, it would be unable to find its way home."

"Barbaric!" the donkey declared, and the dog woofed his agreement of this assessment.

"They would have done the same to me, if they could," the cat went on, "for all it is forbidden to kill any cat of Ulthar. But I eluded them, and avenged my mistress."

"How so?" asked the dog. "You are only a cat."

Her ear flicked disdainfully. "I caught yuggoth-mice, which feast upon the pallid mushrooms in the deep groves. I carried their slick, bloated corpses to the village, and dropped one into each well and rain-cistern."

At that, the dog and the donkey exchanged an impressed look. Clearly, the cat was not one with whom to be trifled.

"And what will you do now?" the donkey asked her.

The many-colored cat uttered a sigh. "With no warm hearth to curl up by? With no mistress to put down dishes of milk? I have been sitting here all this day, asking myself that very same thing."

"Why, then! You must accompany us to Arkham-Town! Brother Dog and I are on our way there to become famous musicians. We have definite need of a soprano!"

"Famous musicians?" The cat preened. "I should like that very much, I think! Yes. Let us be off at once!"

So they were off at once. Though, as the cat had to frequently stop to wash her face or groom her magnificent coat, they made rather less good time than they otherwise might have done.

It was coming on toward dusk when they first heard the eerie, warbling cries. The noises sounded something like the hoot of a barn-owl, something like the dawn-crowing of a rooster, and something like nothing ever voiced by the throat of any earthly creature.

Along the road there ran a ragged line of stout old fenceposts, the fence itself now long gone. Atop one of these, the unlikely trio saw as they drew closer, perched the source of the cries, holding on by the grip of scabrous orange-brown talons. Matted-looking feathers stuck out in uneven clumps from black, rubbery flesh. A stinger-tipped tail waved from its hind end and it flapped wings of leathery membrane for balance.

Where a face should have been found, there was none, nor mouth, nor beak. How it therefore uttered such a voluble and incessant din, they were at a loss to wonder.

The donkey attempted several times to hail the winged creature as they approached, but it must not have heard, for it paid no notice until suddenly and with a tremendous start of surprise it broke off mid-crow.

As mouthless and faceless as it was, that it was eyeless also came as no shock, yet somehow it seemed to fix them with a piercing stare. Upon closer inspection, its aspect was that which might result had a chicken been mated with a night-gaunt. A reddish coxcomb on its head suggested it was male.

"Good evening," the donkey said. "How do you fare this day, Brother …?"

"Rooster," came the answer provided. "Or, near enough, for such have I lived as. And this day, Brother Donkey, I do not fare well at all, thank you for your polite inquiry."

"Why do you crow so full-lunged at this hour?" asked the dog. "The sun has all but gone down."

The rooster's leathery wings hitched in a helpless shrug. "What else can I do? What else have I known? I crow because I can, because I can do nothing else, and because it is only by purest good fortune I am still able to crow! Another day might have seen me silenced once and for all!"

They of course asked him how so, and what he meant by that, and why. To this, the rooster gladly responded.

"Until yesterday," he said, "I belonged to a chicken-farmer who lived in the hollow. Such a brute he was, in-bred, degenerate of nature and intelligence! He, not realizing my true nature, mistook me for a common cock and put me in with his hens. My presence alone so terrified them that, from thenceforth, they would lay far more than the usual number of rare double-yolked eggs."

No one chose to reply further to his remark as to his true nature, only musing to themselves that their initial supposition must in fact be not far from the case.

"Such eggs, of course, fetch a fine price at market," the rooster went on. "As for myself, it was no unpleasant living … I had, of course, as many fresh-laid eggs to eat as I wanted, and the occasional pullet or cockerel when I fancied warm blood and tender meat. I was required to do nothing more than crow with the dawn, and drive off any intruding foxes to the hen-yard – which, believe me, was no difficulty at all."

"No, it would not be," said the dog. "Foxes are slink-thieves and cowards. You must have scared them stark-white."

"Then, yesterday, the farmer's brother came visiting. A brute no less ill- and in-bred, though possessed of a slightly craftier cunning. When the oddity of the double-yolked eggs was boasted of at supper, this brother devised a notion to increase their profits even more. They resolved to rent their prize rooster around to other farms, sure that their neighbors would pay handsomely to share in the bounty."

"Ah," said the cat with an air of understanding. "The other farmers, however, might have recognized your night-gaunt lineage."

"Precisely so, Sister Cat. My neck would have been wrung in a trice. I made my escape this morning, before sunrise and without crowing, while the farmer and his brother slept. I only paused here to rest my wings, when the thought came to me that I had no other prospects and would likely not survive the night. I commenced, therefore, crowing for all I was worth, so as to get some final use from my voice."

"Your voice would have much use if you joined our company!" the donkey said. "We three are musicians, going to Arkham-Town to seek our fortunes. With such a practiced throat and lungs as yours, I have every confidence you will be a great success!"

Without hesitation, the rooster gave his most ready and enthusiastic assent. Because his wings were still tired, he rode perched upon the donkey's broad back.

The trio now a quartet, they resumed their travels, a jolly party in the highest of spirits. But such high spirits, it is sad to say, could not last long. The heavy clouds that had been building over the hills soon spread dark over the valley. Rain pattered down. The road went muddy.

The four quickly became miserable, the cat most of all. They trudged with heads down, squishing in mud, splashing in puddles.

The donkey tried to keep them in cheer with glowing accounts of the fame and prosperity they would find in Arkham-Town.

"We will have a fine house," he said. "A fine brick house with a slate-shingled roof. Rich cream for you, Sister Cat, instead of milk. Rich cream in a silver bowl, with a cushion by the fire! For you, Brother Dog, prime cuts of red beef, and all the ham-bones you can gnaw. I will have oat-mash with honey for breakfast, and a bed of softest new-mown alfalfa!"

"What of me?" asked the rooster, who, being able to fold his leathery wings over his head and ward off the rain, fared somewhat better – though no less miserably – than his other companions.

"Oh, whatever you should like!" said the donkey. "More eggs and hens, if that is your will. Sleeping until well past noon rather than having to wake to crow the dawn."

In this manner, they went on a while further, until the dog with his keen hunting eyes spotted a glimmer as of light from a window, off in the distance. It appeared to come from within a stand of tall trees, and a narrow track led that way from the main road.

"Let us seek shelter," said the cat, her proud fur coat soaked and bedraggled.

"Yes, perhaps it is an inn," the dog said. "We might find lodging there."

"We'll sing for our supper," said the rooster.

Since the rain was growing steadier, and no other options presented themselves, the donkey wasted no time in agreeing. Single-file along the narrow track they proceeded, wending through the woods, catching yet more tantalizing glimpses of warmly lit and beckoning windows.

Upon reaching the building nestled amid the trees, they discovered it to be not an inn but a quaint little farmhouse, old-fashioned, neglected, and in some need of repair. Its barn had collapsed, its garden was weedy and overgrown. The roof sagged, cracks ran up and down the wall-plaster, and the lights that had guided them hither shone through missing shutter-slats over windows lacking glass panes. But, to the wet and weary travelers, it might as well have been a king's palace.

Low sounds as of chanting came from within. Moving shadows sometimes passed in front of the windows, blotting out the light … which, by its flicker and hue they judged to be candle-glow.

"Sister Cat, you are stealthy, and Brother Rooster, you can fly," said the donkey. "Go see what's what, then come back to us."

They did as he directed, returning shortly with the news. Instead of the elderly farmer and his wife that might have been expected in such a place, several people – a dozen or more – crowded the house's single main room.

"They wear robes," reported the rooster.

"And carry candles and chalices," said the cat.

"Their leader is a bald man with a wispy grey beard like that of a goat."

"He holds a book with a Greater Sigil branded into the leather."

"And stands at a round stone altar."

"Lined with chalk, and sprinkled with ashes and salt," the cat concluded.

The donkey's wither-tentacles twined about each other with a bristly rasp. "Aha!" he cried. "Cultists! They've remade this old farmhouse into their church! How splendid! Do they have a church-choir?"

"None. Only the chanting." A fat raindrop struck the cat on the nose and she flinched. "We must do something!"

"Indeed we must, and indeed we shall!" The donkey started for the nearest window, from which one shutter hung by a hinge and the other was missing altogether. "You stand upon my back, Brother Dog," he instructed. "Let Sister Cat stand upon yours, and our winged brother perch upon hers. Then we shall give them a taste of our choir, and they will be bound to welcome us!"

The others deemed this a good plan and readily took their places. With his fingerlike fore-paws, the dog clutched the donkey's thick hide. The cat stepped up daintily and hooked her fine needle-claws in the dog's fur. Lastly, the night-gaunt rooster fluttered to perch on the cat's shoulders, head bobbing this way and that, wings spread.

"On three," whispered the donkey, then stamped time softly with his front hoof.

And, on his count of three, the company of musicians burst into song.

"Eee-yaw, eee-yaw, fthagn!" brayed the donkey.

"Yog! Yog-Soth! Yog-Soth-Oth!" barked the dog.

"Ia! Ia!" cried the cat, in her high and piercing meow.

"Cthu-hu-hu-hu-lu!" crowed the rooster at the top of his lungs.

All their voices together raised such a harmony the likes of which the cultists – or indeed any other living soul on this earth! – had ever heard. They spun from their altar. They dropped their candles and chalices. Their leader squealed like a girl, letting the book with the Greater Sigil on its cover fall with a hefty thump onto the pattern of chalk, salt and ashes. With a flapping of robes, bumping and stumbling over each other, they all dashed for the door and fled through it, scattering into the rainy night.

"I think they did not care for our music," the dog said, after a startled moment of some disappointment.

"Their loss, then," declared the cat, "for they obviously must lack any proper sense of refinement, culture or appreciation."

"Even so, and good riddance," the rooster said.

"Ah well," said the donkey. "As we are here and the hour is late, let us make ourselves comfortable. We may pass the night here nicely enough, I daresay."

It was so decided, and the four musicians went inside. They

found the place small but cozy. They feasted on the remains of the cultists' supper, laid out on a table, and made merry drinking each other's health from a jug of good wine.

Though the candles had gone extinguished, embers glowed warm in the hearth, and the cat settled herself quite happily there to groom. The donkey found hay strewn in a side-chamber, and while it was not new-mown alfalfa, he made a good bed of it. The dog, finding the bone of a leg-of-mutton still thick with meat-scraps, stretched out long and gnawing contentedly in front of the door. The rooster flew up into the rafters to perch on a roof-beam, holding fast with his talons and folding his leathery wings around his body.

Now, it happened that the cultists had run for some considerable distance in their fright, before they stopped and re-gathered themselves, and were greatly chagrined.

After all, they said to one another, had not they been gathered there for the very purpose of effecting a summoning of some eldritch creature? Was that not the entire sole aim of their ceremony? How foolish of them, then – and how shameful besides! – to scream and flee when the object of their ritual itself should appear to them in answer!

They must, they decided, return. They'd left in such a state of panicked rapidity that they had even left behind their book, an ancient tome acquired at considerable risk and cost from the library of Miskatonic University. Gaining access there again would be next to impossible, particularly since the events of the preceding August, when one Wilbur Whateley was said to have met his messy and unfortunate end within those hallowed halls.

Yes, they must return. Of that, there could be neither doubt nor dispute.

However, when they again approached the farmhouse, there arose doubt and dispute aplenty over whose task it should be to go in first and investigate. The windows were dark, the structure itself seemingly silent and unoccupied.

Of the creature that had manifested at the window – such a sight, even half-glimpsed! Conical and misshapen in outline, tapering to a height taller than that of a man! Many-headed, many-limbed and many-eyed! Worst of all, of many gaping mouths from which had issued those hideous, screeching ululations! – there was no current and obvious sign.

It must have, the cultists assured themselves, gone back to whichever realm from whence it had come. They should, should they not, be pleased by this development? Surely it was a sign of the Old Ones' favor!

Indeed! And indeed! And indeed thrice more!

Yet none were eager to volunteer, regardless of the threats or inducements offered by their leader – who could not, he explained, of course, himself go ... the precise reasons for which he somehow neglected to fully articulate. In the end, they set to draw lots, with whosoever drew the short one being the first to enter.

The man who drew short was reluctant but had no other choice. He went on tip-toe to the farmhouse, peered into the darkness, listened to the silence, and finally climbed in through a window.

By then, of course, the four musicians, exhausted from their day's adventures, had gone to sleep. They did not waken as the cultist, oblivious of their presence, groped about until he found one of the dropped candles. He then crept toward the fireplace, thinking he might kindle a flame to its wick from the embers.

That was when the cat, curled there with her fur nicely dry and groomed, woke and opened her eyes. The cultist, seeing them shining there in the gloom, mistook them for coals and poked the unlit candle at the cat's face.

She, anything but amused by this indignity of treatment, sprang with a fury of spitting and hissing onto the man. Her needle-claws sliced his cheeks to ribbons and a darting bite of her ivory fangs nearly tore off his nose.

The cultist, screaming, stumbled backward and trod on the dog stretched in front of the door. The dog, likewise, sprang up in a fury. His powerful jaws took a swath of robes, and a chunk of buttock with it.

Shrieking now, in agony and terror, the man crashed into the table. The rooster, who'd been perched on the roof-beam just above it, dropped down to seize him by the collar. The rooster's whip-thin tail coiled, tickling, around the man's neck and stung him with itching welts.

Well into a panic, beset on all sides, the unlucky cultist ran for what he only guessed might be safety ... the side-chamber where the hay had been strewn on the floor. Instead of safety, he was met with a strong kick from the donkey's hind legs. The force of that kick propelled him clear through a wall, leaving a great ragged gap in the plaster. He ran for his life – or hobbled – as fast as he could.

The other cultists, who'd been waiting, heard the sudden terrible commotion with great apprehension. Their comrade staggered into their midst, so much plaster-dust caked in his hair that they first thought it had gone white from fright. His face was furrowed with gashes, his backside bleeding profusely. Welts rose up red and inflamed on his skin, and several ribs had been broken.

He babbled at them from a frantic state of madness, babbled of devils and monsters, witches with knives for hands, beasts that bit like bear-traps, snakes that had vicious crab-pinchers at one end and scorpion-tails at the other, hulking indescribable horrors with hard hooves.

The cultists decided as one that they wanted no more of this. Casting off their robes, beating themselves about the heads in repentance, they ran every step of the way to the next town and its church without stopping, pleading for God's forgiveness with all of their might.

But, as for the donkey, the dog, the cat and the rooster …

Well, the four musicians decided the little farmhouse suited them quite satisfactorily, so that there was no more need to finish the long journey to Arkham-Town. They settled in, singing whenever they pleased, until the place got the reputation for being most dreadfully haunted so that the nearby folk stayed well away.

This made the quartet happy, for they had discovered they did not need fame and fortune after all. A roof, a well-stocked larder, and good company were more than enough.

And if no one has yet killed or banished them, then they must live there still.

The Magical Fruit

– Jayaprakash Satyamurthy –

There are human beans and then there are alien beans. How was I to know I was getting the alien kind? Sure, they came in all sorts of pretty colours, but everything does these days. I handed the milk glands over to the old man and I took the jar of beans from him. It glowed, it did, shining soft and strange in the dewy morning and now I could get home and have stew and then sow the rest of the beans. Maybe they'd even take root and grow.

Ah, but mama, mama didn't care for what I'd done. Mama was furious, her round face turning all red, tomato-headed angry mama cursing me, cursing me for being my father's son and he his father's and so forth. I am almost sure papa was mama's brother, so I guess all the papas all the way back were dorks. Were all the mamas tomatoes? I will probably never know. I also don't know where papa went, but whatever. Mama says it would take forever to name all the things I shall never know.

Speaking of names, she called me some pretty ripe ones and I was torn between feeling bad and being kind of impressed. Mama had a way with words. But I wasn't taking it anymore. I clunked her over the head with the jar, same way I'd seen her clunk papa back in the days when papa and mama and baby - that's me - made three. Only, once I'd clunked her she stayed clunked - all the red tomato juice flowed out of her round head, mama swayed back and slowly sat down on her heels, then her upper body toppled over and her legs spread out in front of her.

I'd done it now. I'd clunked mama, but good, and now I was all by myself in the old farmstead. So I buried old mama behind the empty shed, turning up the remains of some old skeleton when I did so. That was a bit scary, but the place was old, had been in my family for a long time, so who knew? Then I buried some of the beans in the patch where we grew stuff for the kitchen, nothing great but it was all that would grow. Then I took the rest of the beans and I made myself a delicious stew, filled the jar the beans had come in with moonshine from the still in the cellar and drunk myself blind and unconscious.

Next morning I gathered myself up and stumbled out towards the outhouse and that's when I saw it. Ever since I can remember, only small, crooked things have grown here. Or anywhere. I can tell they're small and crooked because mama and papa had a book of pictures of this very farm, from before. But even if they didn't, I think I'd know just looking at them.

But I am forgetting to tell things in order. That was when I saw it, so different from anything else that had grown in my lifetime, even me. Tall, straight, strong, reaching up into the grey skies where it went on until it was lost in the haze.

Sometimes when papa was still around we'd go to the township, and it was pretty blasted and bleak there too, all the houses looking like they were just old and tired and wanted to die and the people not much better. Small, twisted people; we were not much better, but it seemed the open spaces around us kept the air just a little bit cleaner. Still, township was where trade happened, where we could hand over a few lumpy, glowing taters and string beans and get clothes and things for the house in return.

I was thinking about that when I saw the huge beanstalk

growing in the farm that was now mine alone. The beans - so big, so many, in such bright, tempting colours. I'd seen nothing like it and I wagered that none of the townsfolk, uppity though they'd act when we used to bring them our produce, had either. Their eyes would go wide and round and they'd beg for the stuff. I'd be able to ask for anything I wanted - new milk glands that I could hook up in the kitchen, maybe my own meat vat. Maybe a bikercycle that I could ride around on instead of having to hump papa's handcart around.

First, I'd have some bean soup for myself. So I went up to the great big wonderful thing and cast about for a cluster of low-hanging beans. I noticed ridges in the stalk, or trunk or whatever, ridges and little sticky-out bits, like handles. I reached out and pulled on one of those bits. It remained stuck to the beanstalk. So I slid a foot into one of the ridges, then hauled myself up to a higher handle. Soon, before I even knew what I was doing, I was climbing up the beanstalk at a fair clip. Well, this was exciting. I'd once stood on Watchout Hill and seen the countryside stretch out in all directions, like a dirty hanky spread out all over the world, but my beanstalk went even higher. I wondered what I'd see. Maybe a better place, far far away.

I was sweaty and hot after a long while climbing, so when I saw an alcove coming up, I grabbed a few beans and then pulled myself into the alcove for a rest and a snack. These beans were a lot bigger than the ones I'd traded from that man; they were just the right size to hold in the palm of my hand, the way I'd seen papa hold mama's boobs once. Now you usually boil beans in some water but these felt nice, soft but not too soft, like I could bite into them, so I did. The bean was chewy, with a firmer outer bit and a pulpy inner bit that was like nothing I had eaten before. It actually had a taste, for one thing, and it felt good, like it was giving me energy even as I was eating it.

This must have been what food was like, before the world became so feeble. So feeble and ruined that even dungbrains like me who were born and raised in this world know it's a terrible place.

Stronger now, I climbed again. I knew I was planning to go to the town, but climbing the beanstalk seemed a lot more exciting. I was full of beans, alien beans, full of alien beans and raring to go. I must have climbed most of the day, stopping now and then to rest and eat, because the sun was descending into the hills far away to the west, almost lost in the murk. The days were never very bright, and it should have been too dark to see more than a few inches in front of my face by now, but the stalk itself gave out a glow, a weird glow, no colour I'd ever seen before. I felt strength growing in me as the sun's light faded and the glow of the beanstalk grew brighter. I felt my limbs shift, I knew they were thinking about changing. I didn't know into what, but I was open to suggestions.

My climb was finally at an end. I had reached a sort of plateau right at the top of the stalk. It was a wide, flat space, more or less circular, and right in the centre of it was a house. Not a house like the falling-over shack I lived in, or like the sad old heaps in town, sad old buildings that knew they'd lived on too long and should give up pretending they were still anything but heaps of junk. This was a big, beautiful house, grown from the same greeny stuff as the stalk itself, long, square house with two floors, lots of windows with see-through thin leafskins across them, the edges all wisping into beautiful green-yellow curly bits.

The glow was stronger than ever. It seemed to spread out across the sky and the weirdest thing was that a light just like it, in that same colour I'd never seen before, seemed to be answering it, streaming out of an old dead well not too far from the farm.

On the beanstalk plateau, holes were opening up in the surface and many plants and trees were starting to poke out of them. They didn't look like the things I knew, or the things I'd seen in old pictures, but they looked strong and healthy. Slowly, these things grew fruits, or nuts or things I didn't have words for, and these exploded, sending seeds or spores flying through the air far and wide to fall on the earth below.

Wherever they fell on the blasted, ashy ground, they started to grow and each of them cast the same glow around itself.

All this was fascinating. I had been seeing so many new things since that day, just a day back but it seemed a lifetime ago, when I had met that crooked old man and he'd traded me the jar of beans for those old milk glands. Crazy old man, too, kept muttering to himself about ten thousand years of transformation, time for fruiting, or maybe he said fruition. I stopped thinking about him. So many new things, but they were feeling less and less strange.

Right now, I wanted to see who or what lived in that house, so I walked right up to the big door in the middle of the ground floor and banged on it. It made a pulpy thudding sound. I waited a bit and then tried again. As I stood there, I could feel my bones moving inside my skin. I'd had a few growth spurts just a few years back, near the end of my boyhood, but these were faster, and without the pain. I put my hand out to bang on the door again, and I saw that it had become longer, with more joints, more fingers than I remembered. My skin was changing too, becoming glossy, smooth, and with that same glow all the plants and the beanstalk itself had. I felt the top of my head slowly narrowing and lengthening.

I was not surprised by all this. There are human beings and there are alien beings. And now I knew which I was going to be. I saw the thousands of years since my people had sent that first seed of change, to transform this land. Saw the slow spread of the conditions we needed to live in, the soil changing, becoming grey, ashy, the water changing, the light changing. Saw the long millennia of what the humans called cataclysm, saw the ages of seeding.

As the door opened, the last vestiges of the human whose form I had infiltrated and subverted actually joined with me in exultation. I think he/me knew that the human order was done. Thoughts of a pinched, meagre life, hungry and weak and so used to it you would never even know how frail and tired you were, of people made mean and wicked by the sheer grind of it all, of inbred bloodlines spawning weaker and weaker people, of the hatred and twisted love, the incest, the murder, the ugliness. Then, thoughts of strange action from a distance changing all that, changing the world, changing you. Changing into me.

I walk through the halls of my palace. I am the first; there will be many more. But right now, I am the first man on this new earth, and I am ready to ascend my throne, to gaze out over this world, now my world. The light, so bright, so natural and right. The pretty colours all glowing. Colour, at last. Life, light and a world, a new world to create.

Ginger Snap

– Michael Wentela –

What his fate would be, he did not know; but he felt that he was held for the coming of that frightful soul and messenger of infinity's Other Gods …
– H.P. Lovecraft
The Dream-Quest of Unknown Kadath

ONE

I am not the monster they think I am.

I am an average, everyday guy, with an average, everyday job, and an average, everyday life. But they're going to make me out to be something I'm not; they're going to make me out to be an inhuman monster, a soulless and brutal and amoral killer.

But that's not me. I'm just an average, everyday guy.

"So … Brendan – do you mind if I call you, Brendan, or do you prefer something else?"

I kept my eyes on him, sizing him up. What kind of detective was he? What kind of cop was he? What kind of man was he?

The detective was tall and lean, with a ruddy complexion on a narrow face and unkempt brown hair longer than most male cops. The face and hair made it difficult to pin down an age, but I put him in his mid-thirties. His clothes – a white button-down pinstripe

Oxford shirt with a red and blue geometric print tie, jacked down at the neck, and wrinkled khakis – hung off his frame as if he had lost twenty-five or thirty pounds but hadn't updated his wardrobe. His manner was easy and his smile genuine, but it could have been an act, given that his slate-blue eyes were hungry and calculating.

I shrugged. "Whatever you want is fine with me."

"Brendan, I'm Detective Colson and my partner over there is Detective Rainford. We need to ask you some questions, is that all right with you?"

I glanced quickly at the female investigator, Detective Rainford. She was short and very attractive, with skin the color of milk chocolate and a figure that in the 1950s would have been called statuesque. Her dark hair had a lustrous sheen and was stylishly pulled back, while her navy business suit had been tailored to accent her shape, and the white blouse was open at the neck with perhaps one button too many left unfastened. A simple gold cross on a delicate gold chain hung just in the start of the valley that defined her cleavage. I turned my attention back to Colson.

"Is that one of the questions?"

He smiled, but it was the kind of smile a person gave before they punched someone in the face.

"If you want it to be, sure," Colson said. "I know you've been read your rights and you don't have to answer any questions, but I guess I didn't realize we had a limit on the number that we could ask you."

I knew I had been set up – I was the patsy, served up on a shiny silver platter with all the trimmings – but that didn't mean I had to go down willingly.

"We can do this however you want, Brendan," Colson said after the stare down ended with him glancing at Detective Rainford. "The choice is yours."

Colson was the only cop who had spoken so far in the interview room, but I didn't think he was the one in charge. I turned my attention to Rainford and said, "Ask away."

"Brendan Lockhart, age thirty-seven, of 2001 Winchester Terrace, how long have you lived there?" Colson asked.

Ignoring the question, I held my gaze on Rainford and her dark brown eyes. They were warm eyes, the kind that someone could get lost in and not want to find his way out. They held no compassion for me, however. In her mind, I was nothing but a monster in human form, already tried, convicted and on death row. I smiled and turned back to Colson.

"A little more than eleven years, but I'm sure you already knew that."

He grinned at me, but it wasn't a friendly expression. "What do you do for a living, Brendan?"

"I'm the senior copywriter and editor for Braddock & Haynes. They're a marketing and public relations firm."

"How long have you worked there?"

"Almost seven years, the last three in my current position."

"And do you work downtown?"

"I have a work area there, yes, but my job responsibilities allow me to work from home a great deal of the time.

"That must be nice."

I gave him a one shoulder shrug. I was far more productive in my home office, away from the distractions of the corporate world, but I also worked far more hours than the forty I got paid for.

"What do your duties entail at Braddock & Haynes? What do you do?"

"Where is this going?" I asked. "I'm sure a quick Google search can tell you what a copywriter does. The title alone should tell you it's a person who writes copy."

Colson glanced at Rainford from the corner of his eye before putting his stare back on me. "Does your job entail taking photographs?"

"Sometimes, yes."

"Really?"

"Really. I often use photos to help me describe what I need to describe. The visual images help me put words to them."

"That's interesting, and I can see how that would work," Colson said. "It helps the creative process. It gets the creative juices flowing. Is that what it does?"

I gave him a two-shoulder shrug. "If you say so."

"Hey, I'm just trying to understand all this," the detective said, apologetically. "Me … I'm not creative at all, and I can't take a decent photo to save my life. The reports I write up are pretty boring, straight to the point without any catchy prose to liven them up. I'm sure Detective Rainford will attest to that, she's the poor soul who has to read and sign off on them. Isn't that right, Detective Rainford?"

Her affirmative nod was barely perceptible, but her eyes never left me.

"Do you consider yourself a good photographer, Brendan?" he asked.

"I would say … good is a relative term."

"What do you mean?"

"Photographs that you think are good, Detective Rainford may not think are very good at all, and vice versa."

"So … it's in the eye of the beholder, is that right?"

"Yeah, pretty much."

"Why pictures of the girl?" Colson asked. He leaned back in his chair but kept his eyes squarely on me.

I knew I had to tread carefully on this one. Why did I have more than three hundred digital photographs of Maddey on my camera? I couldn't say for sure, I'm not certain I knew, but all of them were candid shots taken without her knowledge or permission.

"I wanted to help her," I answered after rattling ideas around in my brain for what seemed like fifteen minutes. Hell, none of them even sounded good to me.

"Help her?" The detective smiled at me. "Really? You wanted to help her?"

"Yes, help her."

"How were you planning to do that by ... by taking pictures of her?"

"I ... I gave her money ..."

Each detective arched eyebrow in surprise at that one.

"... for food. I gave her money for food. I even bought her a meal one night."

"Really?"

"Yes, I ..." I stopped mid-sentence because I really wasn't helping myself. I decided to shut my mouth before I swallowed my entire leg along with my foot.

"Now, why would ..."

"Tell me about the girl," Detective Rainford said, interrupting Colson and joining the conversation for the first time since I was escorted into the room. "When did you first meet her?"

I took a deep breath and exhaled slowly. I glanced at the video recorder, red light glowing like a solitary crimson eye, in one corner of the brightly lit chamber.

The windowless interview room was small, almost claustrophobic. The two detectives sat with the door at their backs on one side of the battered table that was bolted to the floor, while I sat on the other, nothing but a blank wall behind me. The air was warm with hints of sweat, urine and fear. It smelled of ... desperation.

How much should I tell them? How much could I tell them without sounding like a raving lunatic? It had happened to me, and I had a hard time believe it.

I glanced at Colson. His cold eyes told me he wouldn't dial 9-1-1 if he saw me on fire. I was something that repulsed and disgusted him. I was less significant than a piece of chewed gum stuck on the bottom of his leather hikers.

So I turned my attention to Rainford, and her eyes held more promise. I could tell she genuinely wanted to hear what I had to say, but I held no illusion she would believe my words.

I sighed out loud and begin to tell my story.

TWO

He usually ignored the street urchins in this part of the city, rarely looking at them and never making eye contact as he passed, but Brendan Lockhart knew she was different from the very first time he saw her.

He could tell she was not the same as the other ragamuffin kids hanging out on the sidewalk just by looking at her, watching her, studying her. Lockhart saw it in the easy way she glided along the concrete and asphalt in the neon-lit night, the confident manner in which she approached targeted passersby to ask for a couple dollars, the clever way she appeared passive but took no crap from anyone else.

He trolled down the street twice in his car before he parked it several blocks away and took to his feet.

Lockhart's heart hammered in his chest and his knees felt weak – he hoped he didn't collapse face down on the concrete – as he rounded the corner. He spied the red hoodie a few blocks ahead, took a deep breath, exhaled slowly and began to walk.

As he walked, dodging the odd-out pedestrian heading in the opposite direction, he tried to formulate a reason to talk with her. None of them sounded plausible in his mind, all sounded contrived and a couple came off downright creepy.

He stopped and idly checked out the window displays of some shops as he headed toward her, but he had no clue what he actually looked at. The street contained a mish-mash of eclectic and esoteric stores that catered to a diverse clientele, but Lockhart repeated the process until he was about a half block away from the teen.

Absently staring at an unknown display, his mind churned out scenarios of how he could approach her, what words he could use to break the ice.

"Hey," spoke a female beside him.

Lockhart turned to the sound. He hid his surprise when he saw the teen-aged girl in the red hoodie beside him. "Hello," he managed to say without tripping over his tongue.

"What exactly are you looking for?" The girl nodded her hooded head toward the display.

He glanced at the display and did an embarrassed double take. Lockhart had stopped in front of a shop that sold products of an adult nature.

"I … I …I was actually looking at the artwork in the window," he managed to say.

The paintings on the large panes of glass were pretty good, done in the style of Vallejo and Frazetta with numerous scantily-clad damsels in peril, muscle-bound heroes in loincloths and ominous mythical beasts.

"Sure." She was skeptical of his answer.

"I'm an artist, a photographer," he said, which was a half-truth. "I'm always searching for ideas or inspiration."

"What kind of ideas or inspiration are you trying to get from this?" she asked with a sly smile.

The teen stood about five-foot-six and was skinny, almost scrawny. She was cute, with fair skin; her eyes were the color of pale emeralds and there was a dusting of freckles across her narrow nose and high cheek bones; her lips were thin and pale, but her teeth were improbably straight and perfectly aligned. She had applied her mascara with a heavy hand, and her fingernails were painted black. The teen's red hoodie was a zip-front from Aeropostale, and she wore a black T-shirt beneath it; her skinny blue jeans were too long and folded into cuffs at the bottom, while her scuffed black combat boots were laced only halfway but tied.

Lockhart shrugged. "Ideas and inspiration often come from the most unusual places," he said.

"Is that so?"

"Yes."

"What do you take pictures of?"

"I take photographs of architecture, landscapes, animals, people – you know, all the usual things."

"Do you make a lot of money taking pictures?"

He laughed. "I do all right," he said. "I'm not rich, if that's what you mean."

The teen shrugged. She turned her eyes out to the street for a moment, watching a couple of vehicles pass by, and then focused on him. "Do you have any money you can give me?"

Lockhart stared at her, those green eyes captivating and haunting. "That's what this is all about then, right? You want money from me?"

The girl shrugged one shoulder and made a face at him.

"Are you going to buy drugs with it?"

"I don't do drugs." She quickly pushed up both sleeves of the hoodie, showing him the inside of her freckle-dusted forearms. They were smooth and pale, without track marks or scars.

He studied them for a moment. Her arms appeared delicate and fragile. "What's your name?"

"What's yours?" she countered, pulling down her sleeves.

"I'm Brendan."

"Well, I'm Maddey, but everyone on the dirty boulevard calls me

Ginger."

"Ginger?"

Maddey pulled the hood down from her head to reveal dirty red hair tied off in a ponytail that disappeared into the back of the sweatshirt and some loose strands tucked behind her ears adorned with multiple piercings. "Does it make sense now?"

"Sure does." He stared at the teenager, trying to get a bead on her. "Where do you live?"

"Why?"

Lockhart smiled at the way she answered a question with a question of her own. "The street can be a dangerous place. There are a lot of bad people out here …"

"Are you one of those bad people?"

He chuckled. "No, but it's not like I'd say yes if I was one."

"I s'pose you're right about that." She grinned. "I stay at the shelter on Brigham Street. It's not the Hilton, but it's a relatively safe roof over my head."

"Good."

"Why, Brendan, are you worried about me?"

The man shrugged and reached into his pants pocket, pulling out a ten dollar bill. "No, it's just that I know they don't openly allow booze or drugs in there, not to mention people who are drunk or high, so if I give you this money, you probably won't go out and buy a bottle."

"I could smuggle it in."

Lockhart studied her face and decided she was teasing. "I don't think you'll do that."

"You're right, I won't."

"Okay." He handed her the bill, and she stuffed it in the front pocket of her jeans.

"Thanks."

"You're welcome." Lockhart turned to leave but stopped. "Be safe, and it would probably be a good idea to head to the shelter now, so you can get a bed and not have to sleep on the floor."

"What? No strings attached to the money? Nothing I … have to do?"

He shook his head. "Nope, no strings attached."

Maddey arched an eyebrow. "I don't get you, Brendan."

The man shrugged. "Just call me a Good Samaritan, doing a good deed."

"Okay," she said with a nod, "I will."

"Take care, Ginger." He turned and began to walk away.

"See you around, Brendan."

Lockhart waved and smiled. You can count on that, he thought.

For some reason, he just couldn't shake the girl from his thoughts over the next several days. No matter what he tried as a diversion, she crept back into his head like a heavy mist in the forest.

Lockhart tried to immerse himself in his work – whether at his high-tech office in the downtown high-rise building or his well-appointed one at his residence – his mind aimlessly wandered back to the pretty red-haired teen. On more than one occasion he hammered away at the keyboard of his laptop, watching the words appear on the monitor, only to have his thoughts drift back to Maddey. Several minutes later he found himself captured in the spider web of a daydream, with fingers hovering inches above the keyboard and an incomplete sentence on the flat screen.

Fending off her intrusion into his head was a lost cause.

Three nights in a row he drove to the rough-edged neighborhood where he had first seen her. It was an area of the city that at one time had been staunchly middle class but had almost imperceptibly slipped to near poverty. Lockhart cruised the street where his encounter with Maddey had taken place and the roads adjacent to it, surveying the neon-lit and trash-covered cityscape, hidden behind smoke-tinted windows.

Three nights in a row he went home frustrated and disappointed.

A couple of nights at home with good, but fruitless intentions, Lockhart had surrendered to his curiosity and was back at it. This time he was armed, and his weapon of choice was a digital camera with a massive 75 to 300mm telephoto zoom lens.

He trolled the car down the street, and his heart skipped a beat when he saw her wearing the same red hoodie and blue jeans, talking with a handful of street kids near a tiny green space park. Lockhart took several deep breaths and let them out slowly in a futile attempt to slow his racing heart, to reclaim his swooning head and to dry his sweating hands. It had minimal success.

Lockhart, biting his lower lip, drove the non-descript, black sedan past her and the others who ranged in age from teens to early twenties and continued on for a couple of blocks before he doubled back. He found a discreet curbside parking spot that enabled him to keep an eye on Maddey while it kept him mostly hidden from view.

Over the next three hours he sat in the less than comfortable seat and watched her interact with the kids who came and went with no regularity. Through the tinted glass, Lockhart snapped away with the camera and imagined the conversations they had, the raunchy jokes they told, the street-level news they shared, and the gossip they passed along.

He envied them and was jealous of the time spent with her. They were precious minutes he could never get back, they were seconds lost forever to time. Lockhart wanted to send the street kids away, to scare them off so he could have Maddey all to himself. He wanted to talk with her, tell her jokes, share the events of the day with her, and pass along gossip. But he couldn't do any of that while the other kids hung around.

His idle fascination with the red-haired teen-aged girl had become something different, something approaching a less than innocent obsession.

He tried to stay away from the street, and for a couple of days he had managed to chase thoughts of Maddey from his head, at least during waking hours, but then he found himself in his car and unexpectedly in that dicey neighborhood. He hadn't consciously planned it but somehow ended up there.

Lockhart spied the teen a half block ahead, and his heart fluttered behind his rib cage. Still in the red hoodie, she was alone and leaned against the brick façade of a smoke shop. He wheeled the car to the curb and climbed out, locking the doors with the key fob and walking toward her.

The teen gave him a megawatt smile when she saw him. "Hey, Brendan, what brings you to my neighborhood along the dirty boulevard?"

If you only knew, he thought but said, "I just needed to get out and stretch my legs. I've been spending too much time sitting behind a desk."

"Oh, and here I thought you missed me." She smiled shyly and glanced away from him.

"Yeah, sure," he responded. "That was it."

"Liar," Maddey said, but there was no malice in the word.

They spent the next ten minutes talking. She had told him that she was fourteen years old – turning fifteen in a few weeks – and that she had fled the home her mother shared with a loser boyfriend. The loser boyfriend had verbally abused and threatened her, occasionally smacking her mother around, but Maddey had baled on the less than happy home before she became the target of the physical abuse … or worse.

"Have you got a few bucks you can spare me?" she asked after a momentary lull.

Lockhart pondered the question for a moment. "Why don't I buy you a meal?"

"You mean like a date?"

He laughed. "No, I mean like me buying you a meal."

"Your Good Samaritan project again?"

Lockhart shrugged. "No, I ..." He couldn't finish the sentence because he didn't know what to say, and he certainly couldn't tell her the truth. "You seem like a good kid who could use a break."

She smiled at him. "Okay. There's a little burger stand a couple blocks over. The food is decent, not expensive, and there's a patio where you can eat."

"Let's go."

"And if I wanna call it a date, I can."

Lockhart laughed again. "If that's what you want."

He smiled when she took a ravenous bite from the cheeseburger; the teen ate as if she hadn't had a meal for days. Lockhart wondered what she had done with the money he had given her.

Maddey grabbed several fries, stabbed them in a small cup filled with ketchup and stuffed them in her mouth. She washed it down with a swig of Coke.

She raised her eyes and caught him staring. "What?" she asked somewhat embarrassed.

"Nothing."

"What are you smiling at?"

"You."

"What about me?"

He thought for a moment and said, "You have a healthy appetite."

She plucked a couple more fries from the box and popped them in her mouth. "Hey, a girl has got to fill up when she can," Maddey said after swallowing the food. "You never know when you'll get your next real meal down here on the dirty boulevard."

"There's that phrase again. The dirty boulevard?"

The teen gave him an incredulous look. "Oh, c'mon, you're joking, right? Really? It's in the old Lou Reed song. How can you not know that?"

Lockhart shrugged. "I guess the dirty boulevard is a pretty dangerous place."

Maddey picked up the burger but didn't take a bite. "You're down here, so what are you then? The Big Bad Wolf?"

He smiled. "Are you Little Red Riding Hood?"

"I could be," she answered with a grin that was far from innocent, "if you wanted me to be."

Lockhart started to say something, but the words caught in his throat. He tried to cover it by taking a bite from his cheeseburger and chewing.

"What?" Her lascivious smile grew even wider. "Did I shock you? You know, a girl's gotta do a lot of different … things to survive on the dirty boulevard."

He swallowed his food with a noisy gulp.

"I could be your Little Red Riding Hood if you wanted to be my Big Bad Wolf."

Lockhart stared at her, green eyes taunting him, but said nothing.

"What? Don't you like girls?"

After a moment, he answered, "Girls, no. Women, yes."

She smiled again, but this time it was the innocent version. "I'm just teasing, you know." Maddey took a bite from the cheeseburger and chewed for a moment before washing it down with a drink. "I didn't mean anything."

The conversation returned to less provocative word play as they finished their meals. After bussing their own table, they stood on the sidewalk.

"Thanks for supper," she said.

"You're welcome." Lockhart smiled. "You be safe out here on the dirty boulevard."

Maddey grinned. "I will." She quickly stepped forward and kissed him on the cheek. A heartbeat later, she was walking away.

"Wait."

The teen stopped and turned back. "Did you change your mind, my Big Bad Wolf?" She hit him with the lascivious grin again.

He blushed in the neon. "No." Lockhart dug in his pocket and pulled out some bills. "It's not much, but ..."

She returned and took the bills, folding them and stuffing them into a front pocket of her tight jeans. "Thanks."

"You're welcome and be safe."

"I will."

He watched the red-haired teenager walk away.

Lockhart had no intention of following her and couldn't explain why he did. But there he was, covertly watching – stalking? – her from a distance as she wandered away from the neon-lit streets and avenues for ones shrouded in darkness.

"What are you up to?" he muttered as she slipped through a hole in the chain link fence that surrounded a four-story brick building. It had been a garment factory and warehouse in a different era, but that had been decades ago. Now it was an abandoned and dilapidated structure that had been unoccupied, much less actually used, for at least a quarter century. Even in the faint illumination from distant street lights, he could tell.

He approached the fence but didn't enter the grounds through the hole. Instead, he hid as best he could and watched the teen as she stealthily moved to the boarded-up front doors. Maddey glanced in all directions before she pulled the door open and slipped into the darkness that loomed around her like the maw of a prehistoric beast.

Just like that, she disappeared.

Curiosity burned in him like a raging forest fire – Why had she come here? What was she doing inside? – but Lockhart couldn't summon up enough courage to pull aside the snipped piece of metal fencing and slip on to the grounds. Mentally berating himself for his cowardice while at the same time applauding his discretion, he walked toward his car, frustrated.

THREE

Over next several days, Lockhart obsessed and brooded about Maddey and why she had gone to the abandoned building that night. It wasn't the shelter she told him she sleeps at. He had to know – needed to know – why she went there and what she was doing. He couldn't chase those troubling thoughts from his head, no matter what diversion he tried. Her behavior that night seemed more than odd to him, but the ambiguity only fueled his curiosity. Not knowing bothered him, so he took matters into his own hands.

Armed with a flashlight, he ventured to the brick façade structure, which had numerous huge windows on all sides of each floor, but only a handful of them were broken or cracked. The company name painted on the side of the building had long faded to oblivion and was indecipherable. It looked worse in the daylight, but it didn't deter him. Lockhart slipped through the hole in the fence and proceeded into the building.

He started at the top and worked his way down, but, during his less than thorough search, he found each floor was pretty much the same, empty. All the equipment had been removed years ago, and the floors were wide open areas broke up only by brick support columns. Dust, dirt and other debris littered the creaking wooden floorboards. Far out of code electrical conduit was suspended from the high ceilings, while long dead power outlets dotted the floor. He found no visible signs of inhabitation by anything other than rats, there was nothing in the open work areas or the various offices. Lockhart was confused and disappointed as he walked from the main area of the ground floor toward the entryway.

Standing in the lobby, the receptionist's desk long removed, he had planned to leave, to walk out of the building and into the afternoon sun when he saw an unobtrusive door hidden in the dark recesses of a corner. What the … he thought as he clutched the knob and pulled the door open. It moved silently, and Lockhart found himself atop stairs that led to the basement.

"Oh, boy," he muttered, "the basement. I hate basements."

His body and consciousness seemed separate entities as he stood before the wooden steps that disappeared in the darkness. Fear swirled like a river eddy in the backwaters of his mind, but his obsession for Maddey was the current that pushed him forward. He snapped on the flashlight and began to descend.

The further Lockhart climbed down the stairs, the stronger the odor became; a smell different from the stale, musty air of the building above. It was subtle and faint at first but became more pronounced with each step. It was an earthy odor like freshly turned topsoil but with a stale hint of decay and decomposition.

At the bottom of the stairs, he surveyed the basement, which was also a wide open space with brick support columns; deteriorating cardboard boxes and wooden crates were stacked here and there. The darkness was thick like India ink, and the flashlight's beam seemed insignificant against it. The air was chilly and damp, about ten degrees cooler than outside and felt like a wet blanket; gooseflesh erupted on his skin.

He crept forward and the light found some clothes strewn about on the floor. He thought nothing of the mess, other than someone wasn't very careful about where they tossed things. He wondered if

Maddey actually stayed here and why she lied about it.

Lockhart walked further into the basement, his light shining on nothing but dust-covered debris and discarded litter – most of it looked old, as in decades old – that had gathered around the collapsing boxes and sturdy crates.

He muttered under his breath as each step propelled him forward. It was just idle babbling about why the teen would stay here and why he'd decided to go into the basement in the first place. More than anything, it was supposed to keep his mind from thinking about other things, troubling things.

Lockhart thought he heard something and quickly tracked the light in the direction of the sound. However, the disjointed beam found nothing as it jumped here and there.

"I must be crazy."

His nerves had frayed, and his mind played tricks on him. Cold sweat pooled in his arm pits, the small of his back and on his hands. He heard the blood pound through the veins in his ears in the crypt-like silence, while the flashlight beam flickered in his trembling hand. Lockhart took a deep breath and exhaled raggedly, hoping it would steady his nerves, but it didn't. He continued forward, putting one foot in front of the other.

He wondered if Maddey actually came down to the basement, much less stayed in it. Discarded clothes aside, he had seen nothing to indicate someone, let alone the red-haired teenaged girl, had been down in the basement. There were certainly no signs anyone lived there.

The light's beam searched the ground before him and revealed some small bits of white sticking up from the dirt and debris. They were small and narrow like pale twigs, and he wondered aloud what they were. However, he couldn't bring himself to stop and examine them closer, unsure he wanted the answer.

Lockhart heard another noise and followed with another spastic whirl of the light. Again he found nothing as the possible source.

He laughed, but it was a hollow sound like the lid scraping on a concrete tomb.

The man stepped deeper into the basement and saw more white on the floor, but there was no mistaking what they were. They were bones. With his mouth hanging open he studied them in the flashlight beam, but could find nothing to distinguish what the origin of the bones may have been. Lockhart had seen evidence and heard rats scuttling around in the walls, so he surmised that's what the bones were. Or at least that's what he told himself. He hesitated when the beam found larger bones that had been stacked into several small, intricate piles.

"What the ..." he muttered. "That's ... that's crazy."

But it didn't deter him. He rounded a series of crates stacked higher than he was tall, and, in the open space, there was no mistaking what his flashlight had uncovered. He gasped in stunned and unbelieving surprise.

Scattered about the dirty concrete floor were a number of unclothed corpses – the remains of both male and female teenagers – strewn about like life-sized dolls in a child's bedroom. There were more than a dozen, randomly placed here and there. None of the bodies appeared to be recent kills; they were dried and withered in decomposition.

Lockhart stared in shocked surprise. He knew he should have looked away, but he couldn't tear his eyes from the sight. He couldn't believe what his eyes beheld. He refused to believe it, but his body began to tremble in fear because the physical evidence was spread out on the floor in front of him.

He yelped in terrified surprise when a hand fell on his shoulder.

FOUR

As his heart leapt into his throat and his bladder threatened to spill, he spun quickly and ungracefully on his heels, barely managing not to drop the flashlight. In the haunted house lit gloom, he saw who had touched him.

Maddey smiled at him. "My … what big eyes you have," she said playfully.

"Maddey, it's you." He laughed out loud, but it was a mirthless and hollow sound. A different and inappropriate emotion slipped into his body. "You nearly gave me a heart attack."

"My … what sharp teeth you have," she said, ignoring his words.

"Wh … wh … what are you doing down here?"

She glanced down and giggled childlike. "My … what a big – "

"Maddey!" He tried to recover some of his composure. "Maddey. Ginger."

"You shouldn't have followed me, Brendan, especially down here," she said. "You were better off if you didn't know. Much better off."

"No, Maddey, this … this just can't be. It can't be. I know you, I … I … I know you. You're just a kid, a lost and scared runaway."

"You know nothing!" Her green eyes flashed to reptilian yellow and back to green again.

"Who … what are you?"

"I am … the Haunter of the Dark, the Crawling Chaos," she said softly as if savoring the words that revealed her secret. "I am a messenger from the Other Gods. I am the screams of your nightmares. I was old when this world was young, and where I go, others vanish never to be seen or heard from again."

"I … I …I don't believe you. That's crazy, Maddey … just crazy talk. You … Ginger, you need help. I can get you help, we can get you help."

"I don't want help, you fool!" She laughed at him. "I am what I am.

And this is what I am."

Right in front of him, before his terror-stricken wide eyes, she shifted into some of her thousand shapes:

a yellow-eyed cross between a nude, hairless woman and a serpent, with reptilian facial features and smooth dark green scales instead of skin, narrow torso with barely noticeable breasts, the plain of its stomach a few fades shades lighter in color than the rest of its body, a nearly imperceptible slit between its legs and those legs that led down to clawed lizard feet;

a lithe and androgynous-looking bare-chested Egyptian pharaoh, with a heavily painted face and sun-bronzed body, attired in royal garb;

a three-eyed ram-headed male, complete with thick, curled horns and a tuft of hair on its chin, a smooth white-skinned and well-defined torso, an enormous penis dangling between furry and muscular legs like the hind legs of a mountain goat with cloven feet;

a smiling, gap-toothed Haitian voodoo priest, with weathered skin the color of tar, dark eyes set deep in full cheek bones, a broad nose that topped a thick-lipped mouth, a bushy beard sprinkled with gray, a thread-bare but well-tailored silk three-piece suit and a well-worn top hat on his head;

a tall figure in a black robe with a dark hooded cowl draped over its lowered head, and when the figure raised its gray-skinned head to reveal its face, it had no eyes, nose or mouth;

an improbably tall, blue-skinned humanoid dressed in silver gossamer clothes that seemed to float around its torso caressed a smooth and glimmering glass and metal alien object in its hands;

a pallid-skinned and brown-haired male, whose black eyes were flecked with red, smiled and revealed elongated fangs, pearly-white and razor sharp, where his canines should have been;

an octopus-like creature, its smooth and slimy skin white-gray with hints of green, wriggled more than three dozen tentacles, each of them with a mouth filled with jagged but needle-like teeth;

a beautiful goddess, with an angelic face, long brown hair, gold skin that sparkled and shimmered, full breasts, a narrow waist and long legs, danced naked around a bonfire to music only she heard;

an unclothed male creature with dark skin, oily and smooth, a bullet-shaped head with lobeless pointed ears, lifeless black eyes, a reptilian nose, slit for a mouth and pointed chin, bat wings folded along its back, freakishly long and multi-jointed arms that ended in sharp clawed hands, a long barbed tail that lashed ceaselessly back and forth from its backside while a smaller version bobbed in the front, and long inverse jointed legs that ended with narrow feet, tipped with black claws; and,

lastly, the waif-like red-haired teen-aged runway girl in the dirty red hoodie with the twinkling green eyes and smile of sunshine stood before him in the beam of his flashlight.

Even though he had seen the phantasmic images with his own eyes, his brain refused to comprehend them. He couldn't comprehend them. "We have to get you help, Maddey. We have to go to the police, we can get you help. We have to call the police."

"No, we don't."

"Yes, Maddey, we do. We have to call the police."

"I've already called them, on one of your cell phones." She pulled something from a back pocket of her skinny jeans and showed him the iPhone, his personal phone.

Confusion swept across his face. "Wh … wh … what?"

"They're on the way here."

"Good. That's a good thing, Maddey, a real good thing. We'll get you the help you need." He reached out to take her by the arm, but she slipped away from him and sashayed toward the stairs.

"Maddey – Ginger – don't do this. We can get you help, I'll be there for you. You don't have to run anymore."

She laughed a sweet child-like giggle and continued to amble toward the steps.

"If you run, the police will catch you. Eventually, they will catch you. You know that, don't you? You can't run away from them."

Maddey giggled again. "But, Brendan, I'm not running away from them." She gave him the sweet, teenager smile that tormented his sleep. "I'm running to them." The teen danced to the stairs and bounded up them.

It took a long moment for the words to penetrate his thick skull and reach his brain, but the implication of what she's said – and done – hit him like a kick in the groin. "Uh … oh, hell!" He ran after her.

Lockhart flew up the stairs two at a time and ran through the lobby and burst out the front door. Outside the fence, he skidded to a stop on the sidewalk once he saw a police officer with an arm protectively around Maddey's shoulders, tears running down from her green eyes. She pointed a shaky finger at him, and the cop's partner drew a service weapon and screamed for him to freeze. He tried to speak, to explain, but only got screamed at again to put his hands up and get on his knees.

Slowly, he did as commanded.

FIVE

Humiliated, Lockhart had been handcuffed and placed face down on the sidewalk. He had breathed in dirt and concrete dust for nearly forty-five minutes, while cops and crime-scene technicians walked around the scene, some actually stepping over him. A crowd of gawkers had gathered but was held at bay by yellow crime-scene tape, while the press shouted questions to the police, the technicians, Maddey – and him.

He was roughly hauled to his feet and spun to face the officer in charge of the scene, a police lieutenant. He tried to speak, to explain.

"She's not what she seems to be. She's … she's …"

"So, what is she?" the lieutenant asked. "Why don't you tell me what she is? Are you going to tell me she's responsible for all those bodies in the basement? Is that what you're going to tell me? Is it? IS IT?"

"She's …"

"I'll tell you what she is. She's a fourteen-year-old runaway, who is the luckiest girl in the city tonight. She fortunate she's not in the basement getting defiled by … by you."

"No. No, she's …"

"SHUT UP!" The lieutenant turned to a nearby officer. "Please get this worthless piece of human excrement out of my sight."

The cop gruffly took Lockhart and placed him in an unmarked squad car, while the press yelled questions at him and the bystanders called for his head. His mind couldn't comprehend what had happened to him, it was too farfetched. He gazed out the squad car window and saw Maddey standing with a female officer.

He stared at her, willing her to glance in his direction. The teenager turned and saw him in the police vehicle. Lockhart gave her a pleading and imploring look that said you have to tell them!

Maddey returned a slight, wry smile before she winked at him.

A Wisdom That Is Woe, A Woe That Is Madness

~ E. Catherine Tobler ~

The tower rises from the edge of the cracked salt sea, a single tree wasting to sticks at its stony side. Surprise washes through Ismail at the tower's sudden appearance; his well-handled map shows the tower over three mountains more, nestling within the heart of a black, bramble wood. He expects to slice his path through thick vines bursting with thorns thirsty for a taste of him; to be clawed bloody before he stumbles gasping against an old, splintered door. No such obstacles greet him; his sword--the mark of every questing prince--rests unused in its leather scabbard.

The salt sea is cracked to the merciless sky above. What water the basin once held is long gone, the ground buckling into ripples of pale salt flowing outward even now as if something yet falls into their midst. Ages before, when water cloaked the sea, it was a rock, ever-growing rings of water lapping outward to the salty shore. A palm-sized black stone rests unmoving within a salt crater as if to say it was indeed so.

There is only this: the salt and the tree, the tower and the sky, until a shadow defines the dreadful height of the tower across the crusted ground. Ismail knows within his bones, this is the place he has sought for ages and for ever.

He moves forward, always within the breadth of shadow, lifting his eyes to the tower's pinnacle, but the highest point is lost within the dazzle of the sunlight. If there is a window, he cannot see it. The sunlight scoops his vision into its burning hands and Ismail stumbles to his knees within the salt. The water bottle he carries falls free and with a slosh spills its wet abundance into the salt; when vision returns, Ismail presses his fingers into the dark puddle, the salt as thirsty as he. Melting salt clings to his fingers and he wipes them down the length of his golden robes, thinking this worse than black brambles. All his water, lost to the salt. At least he could cut brambles, make them bleed in turn.

Ismail staggers to his feet. The tower's shadow lessens the day's heat, but sweat still soaks his skin. His robes are greedy for the moisture and, when he reaches the tower's door, wet. He stinks of his journey, wants to scrub himself clean in the salt, but seeks the carved words across the door's lintel, words to give proof of this place. He does not see them at first and panic sticks an icy hand into his gut until he spies the faintest shadow against the stone. He stretches, digging his fingers into the salt crusting each carved letter.

What is not killed is not dead.

Salt feathers down Ismail's wrist, tracing his sweat-damp arm. His fingers linger within the last word, pressing hard as he envisions they who built this place, they who raised the stones at the edge of the salt sea. Those who bound the princess within and cursed her to as empty an existence as there might ever be; those who branded her a monster for they could not dare understand the wonder and power within her small hands. They who could not stomach the way eyes strayed to her when she walked through the market; they who knew a threat in her smile and step. Centuries gone, the stories said--and no more than stories, so many others proclaimed, but here, here, proof beneath his fingers pulsing with his heart. Here she is. She in her tower, in her desolation, at the edge of a broken salt sea.

Ismail weeps at the idea of it, salted water coursing down his cheeks. It is water he cannot stand to lose, but he sobs uncontrollably, until his knees buckle and fingers slip from the words within the stone. He presses himself against the door; this door is not old or splintered, and its paint, the color of a twilight sky, still smells fresh, shines bright. A fabrication of the desert, he thinks, and kneels at its threshold. Nothing is as he believed, but for this place, anchored in all of time.

"Princess, I have come," he whispers in a voice torn ragged by the dry air.

But if there is a princess, she does not reply.

———

The tower: three storeys, pale rag- and mudstone rising from a jumble of debris at its base. The white tower rakes the sky in solitude when once it might have been part of something larger, though not something necessarily better. The white tower is the only object visible from the river, clouded horizon unbroken by tree or hill. The memory of walls intermittently marks the scrub grass.

Within as without, the tower once housed something larger, something more. Every upward step is notched, a large body violently dragged up or down; it is impossible to say which direction and perhaps, in the end, it was both. Hall and chapel stand empty, echoing, and the uppermost tower room also yawns vacant, a mouth swallowing the sodden roof spilling itself inward. Rusting rings and chains notched into the walls, the ages-old scent of bodies once kept; bodies in protest, bodies in revolt. Anger stains the floorboards, recollections of people etched into walls alongside marks of years.

———

Ismail spreads his map in the light of the fire, smoothing rivers and planets and stars flat so he can discern ground and not sky upon the page. It would not be this world, they all said.

His map said the same, until it curled in on itself and edge touched edge. Ismail made careful folds within the aging and yellowed paper, creating a cube, a triangle, and connected points that should never have connected. The map became a living thing within his hands, showing skies he could never have imagined existing. And this small speck, this lifeless rock, solid beneath bottom and foot now, crusted with salt, marked with a tower. It should not have been.

A meager dinner from his pack, but it isn't a lack of food keeping Ismail restless. He glances toward his ship--gleaming, white, pristine--resting beyond the last soft ridge before the jagged mountains. He wants to run for it, climb in and fly away because in the night that rises when the sun sets, the tower fluctuates. He believes at first it is only the angle of the light; the slow dwindle of sunlight into moonlight, and then a curious combination of both, until one swallows the other.

The light shifts from warm to cool and sharpens the tower's edges. Each corner attains a strange precision in the faint moonlight, obsidian stone chipped into a perfect cutting edge. Ismail is certain the stone would flay fingers--sandstone, he thought earlier, but not now. In the rising dark, he finds the brambles earlier sought, writhing from the ground in long lengths of salted fury, passing over the sharp walls with the whisper of skin against leather.

Ismail slides backwards in the salt, meaning to move away from the tower's base, but he never gets far; he cannot remove himself from the tower. The creeping black is always close to hand, his cheek grazing one of those sharp edges as if he had moved forward after all. He looks at the sky to gain a bearing, but there is no sky to be found; what hangs there is hideous, devoid of stars and moon, and Ismail reels as if struck. He smells blood and presses his fingers to his wounded cheek. The tower grows with a groan of cold iron.

The obelisk: no wider than shoulders, rising one hundred feet above its gneiss rubble base, from a barren granite island anchored in the center of a salt water lake whose shores are not easily viewed from the island unless one stands within the obelisk. A ragged doorway, unintentionally cut. No stairs, but rotting pegs, a stutter-step ascent.

The room beneath the marble capstone, perfumed with bay laurel, smothers; no one stood upright within its confines, only sprawled to gaze upon the world through thinning opaline walls. Words worn into the base of the capstone by incessant fingers: non occidatum, non mortuum.

—

The brambles are not black, but coated in salt as the ground; the lengths crawling the length of the tower and seeking purchase against Ismail's very own feet are pale and heavy with strange designs borne of the salt sea air. The brambles are barbed, humpbacked, and swollen with pearled crystals that, even with the sudden absence of light, glow. They light a strange pathway up the tower, shambling along its metal girth, reading for the golden light fracturing the buckled roof Ismail had not seen under the afternoon sky.

Ismail shouts at the sight of the light, at the sight her

she whom he has sought

she whom the say does not exist

she

she

spilling—

She, in a river from the window germinating in the tower's iron side. She, as strangely shaped as brambles, ungainly from her time within closed walls. She, eclipsing the naked sky with beauty and being.

Ismail does not stop to wonder what has occasioned the opening of the window, if it be the brambles rending the tower or another force at work. Surely if the princess could have pushed the iron panels wide, to welcome the day, the night, the air, she would have. He shouts again, calling to her so he might be heard above the rush of the salted brambles, and she, gazing down upon him as one might a lover long expected, looses her hair.

Her hair spills like a flood of ink against the salted brambles, dark and fine, and tangled just so Ismail may climb if he wishes. Small, fragrant hands find his own within the tresses, pulling him up and up; diminutive, soft feet balance beneath his, shoving him up in the way of circus performers. It is effortless this climbing, until Ismail realizes his sword has been left behind, resting beside the fire he can no longer see from this terrible height. Ismail looks down once, over his shoulder. He resists the cupping hands and pressing feet and at his resistance, they allow him to fall.

If he does not need them, they do not need him.

———

The lighthouse: Thick square base, rising into a sturdy octagonal core, giving way to a gentle circular apex. Four hundred and fifty feet of salted limestone blocks standing in ocean air, some sealed with molten lead, some cracked by the movement of earth over time. Anchored by the weight of years.

Within the circular room, a furnace to be fed at night so brilliant firelight might stream into the harbor, into the beyond. Flooring worn by feet, the dark, sweat-outline of a single body against the curve of a wall. Ships crossing the waters day in and out, ships coveted but never boarded.

The molten lead, the salted rock.

———

The night swallows screams.

Silent, Ismail plunges toward the ground, a flurry of hands and legs, until he catches a bramble. It is fire in his hands, scorching salt licking a wound into his palm, down the length of his arm. The night feeds on his screams, grows dense around him, and the black tower expands under the force of his fear. A tendril of hair brushes his cheek and Ismail lunges for it, abandoning his quest for his sword if it means reclaiming the touch of those small hands, the support of those small feet.

Each bears him up again and again, and Ismail's heart slows, his breathing calms, and he tells himself he does not see the barren sky above the buckling tower roof, sees only her pale and heart-shaped face within the black night of her hair; hears only her soft and breathless voice saying oh my prince, at last you have come; at last, at last.

He tells himself it is he who pulls himself into the tower; he disregards her support, her hands sliding under his arms to haul him across the window's sill. The sill is coated with the dust of a hundred years and it sifts around him in a cloud when she settles him beneath the window. Her hair moves in the dust like thick-bodied snakes, only glimpses of her figure: slim and pale as bones, teeth.

He trembles and cannot speak, does not dare for he finds every word inadequate as he crouches within her presence. Her shadow befalls him, though she glows within the tangle of her boundless hair, raking down cheeks and arms until the darkness of her puddles in his lap, the scent of cloves rubbed to warmth between fingers. He does not dare reach for her, though his hands beg to be knotted into the black, to find the small hands that once sought his, to taste of a palm, a wrist.

It is she who touches him. Her hands are strangely cool, soft as pink lilies as they enfold his own. His own: calloused, blackened, and ragged from the search that has found an end here. The she who should not exist, smiling as the crescent moon through the cascade of her nocturnal hair.

—

The peel tower: honeycombed travertine, eaten away by the years, but standing yet. It is the only structure for miles, existing only to hold its prisoner and the iron basket into which she climbs every night.

Every night that is to be, regular as the stars raking the sky above: she presses hands and feet against the iron eating the prints out of her skin, identity taken and taken once more. The shadow of her hands and feet edge the bowl, erased not by fire or time; no wind will carry these shadows away, nor melting snow or fracturing ice. Every night ever to come, she climbs into the iron bowl and burns herself to illuminate the darkness.

Every morning, she climbs out of her own ash. Reknits herself.

That which you do not kill is--

"...not dead."

—

Ismail weeps. Ismail believes himself unworthy. She bandages his hands within lengths of her hair and the cool, licking fire of her soothes him; eats into his flesh and gives him something he didn't realize he was missing. He cannot put a name to this something: companionship, touch, the proof he was not wrong.

He was not wrong.

"You," he says.

He swallows his other words, for speaking them in her presence seems like a curse. You are not dead, he means to tell her. I will take you from these walls. He lifts his eyes but cannot find hers for all the twisting hair. Maybe there is a gleam within some small parting; maybe it is green or black or something more like the color of uncertainty. But no, she is certain. He is not.

In her certainty, she waits. He can feel her watching him, even if he cannot see her eyes. Ismail longs to brush her hair from her face, so he might gaze upon the beauty the stories have spoken of, but he does not. Only looks at her as she is, hunched and draped, skin like moonlight flickering here and then there.

"You are not dead," he manages to say.

At this, she moves. She crosses the room and still the hair which binds his hands does not slither free. These tresses are so long, they might encompass the entire room. Vines, he thinks; roots.

"You are not dead and I will take you from these walls."

Across the room, jeweled curtains part. Ismail cannot see hand or foot, but she stands before the parting fabric and he presumes she has moved them; has parted the draped brocades and silks with her pale-lily hands to reveal the grandest room he has ever seen. Within this room there stands a bed, mounded with pillows and promise, spread with more silk, the colors of fire and frost and the forests of his home. His throat tightens at the sight of these colors and a sound escapes him.

Rest, he thinks. We should rest before we go.

But she has only ever rested. Waited.

—

The fleetfoot: obsidian stone cages a pendulous body in constant motion. The fleetfoot is never still, picking its way over night-drenched ground, over star-knotted river. On eight thread-thin legs the fleetfoot steps on no ground twice. Fleetfoot carries with it a prisoner and the night wind, the morning sun distantly towed on a string of silk. So distant, the fleetfoot never knows the touch of light.

The fleetfoot leaves small craters in its wake, eight in a pattern if you know how to look. Prints left in long grass fields and muddy lanes, so children would know it passed in the night. Livestock has been lost to its steps, squashed where they stand without other reasonable explanation. Children in these parts dream of pressed pig liver, flattened cow tongues. They marvel at the discovery of a chicken's egg balanced on muddy crater rim, shell so thin the morning sun turns it into a globe of glowing gold.

———

The splendid bed is as hard as nails. Ismail cannot understand how beauty is so dreadful against his tired limbs. He tries to sleep, to pass the night away before they take leave toward his ship; he cannot for the way the bed presses into every ache he possesses.

"Princess, how do you..."

But how did she do anything, let alone sleep in such a dreadful space. The pillows are as stone and the promise he felt upon first entering the room is long fled. He holds to the hair that wraps his hands still, seeking some relief, but neither is there any to be had here. It is cold and dry as the princess moves in a deeper part of the tower.

"Princess, we should--"

The night swallows his words. Ismail tries to tell her they must leave, for surely even the narrow cockpit of his glorious ship would be more comfort than this cold place she has known. He looks beyond the bed's draped frame, seeking the jeweled curtains, the window opening into night, but these things have both gone. The walls are sheets of iron alone, windowless, and the jeweled curtains have melted into rust, rot, ruin.

"Princess?"

She swells from the floor in a violent black wave and within the parting folds of her ebony hair, she smiles, but she has no face.

She has no face.

———

The black bramble wood before the iron tower: there is no record of any such place.

——

Ismail turns his shoulder into the pillows, means to roll free of the bed, but he is well and truly caught.

Of course, he knows he was caught long before: on a distant world of topaz seas and granite skies, where, upon a rotting parchment, he found the first mention of the first tower. That which you do not kill is not dead, what is allowed to live lives yet. In a small library, in a nook of scrolls, the laughter of a librarian echoing as Ismail was assured it was only a myth. Only a story, words inked onto paper by someone tired of their own small life. Words constructing a window into a place that never existed, never could exist.

But these places did exist, scattered across a universe so vast Ismail feared he would never be able to search them all. One by one they fell to his explorations, until this place--

the ages-old scent of bodies once kept; bodies in protest, bodies in revolt

One never searches every place, Ismail knows. The dark rises before a journey can find completion, and places and items are missed in the headlong pursuit of a thing long dreamed. When one comes to the point where all vanishes into a single prick of light--

"Prin--"

There is no light and when she leans over him, no face. She isn't wholly right, not the right word, not the right flavor, but he knows no other. Her body is curved and pleasing and to him this says she, she, she spilling.

She spills across him--the nail-hard bed ceasing to matter for there is only the rising pain of her as her blackened hair becomes the sea, becomes the tide carrying him out of the room, to a distant shore where stars gleam in the colors of death. Stars do not burn black, Ismail tells himself, but here they do, reflecting every wonder of her within their aspects. Every prick is a scream, pulling Ismail into her arms, pulling her inside of him.

"Princesssss."

She hisses from the place a mouth should be. But there is no face, the word misshapen as it pours from her. It is a thing mutilated, a skin turned inside out. Ismail's mouth cracks open because he means to tell her yes, he came for her and will take her away so she never knows another moment in this awful place, but that crack, the soft and wet oval of his mouth, is ransacked.

Strands of her flood into his mouth, bursting past lips and tongue. She is a comet shooting down his throat, exploding through stomach and into bowels. Ismail's screams are a balm across the broken shape of her. His unbound hands open and close upon a black sky he can no longer see. There is only her shape above him, moving ceaseless as fleetfoot taught her. Rest is death, waiting is death, and what is not killed is not dead.

———

The pagoda: thirteen levels of iron, wind bells beneath every eave, never silent. The second pagoda to occupy this location, the first of wood having been burned to the ground by lightning, by comet, by self-immolation. None can agree as to the method, only to the destruction, to the ash still circling its base. Without windows, unending iron stones packed into wall, into dome.

Its uppermost level, a square iron room. Within the center of the floor, the shadow of a figure from a nightmare, limbs spread wide then balled close. The yes-no motions of a body struggling, succumbing. The imprint of coiling hair.

All thirteen levels: the echo of a bone smile in a not-face.

———

And why would they lock a princess away?

The librarian asked Ismail in the closeness of the scroll nook, in an effort to show him how foolish his entire theory was. Princesses didn't need locking way, did they? Princesses were dainty, princesses knew their place.

Her place, now, is the hollow of Ismail's stomach. She is a solid weight inside him, resting, for the journey inside has exhausted her. She is not still, however; the tendrils of her spread through him, up his wide-flung arms and down into his shaking legs. She is fire and salt inside him, and she pushes as if she means to be born--but she has not died, will not die--

Ismail screams and the sound of it startles even him. He breaks from the fugue that has held him, tumbles to the floor, and spits a stream of iron stones. They splatter out of him and he is incoherent in his confusion. The iron burns his tongue and he thinks for one sweet moment he has dreamed the entire thing. He is sitting beside the librarian yet, and has only to reach out to clasp his hands.

Ismail stands on steady legs, looks around the ruined room, and tells himself that is all this is: a dream. The bed lies in ruin, the curtains rotting to threads, the iron walls flaking with rust. If she was here, she is here no longer. Just as in every other tower. He smooths his hair and beard, rubs fingers over unbroken lips, and tells himself he is alone as he has been since the start of his journey. He will not find her because she does not exist. They all said so and he was foolish to ever think, to ever believe.

His doubt gives her a stronger hold inside him. Ismail buckles to his knees, falling into the endless umbra of her. She stands before him, an immoveable, inescapable darkness. This shadow has a perfectly fine edge--Ismail can see the rotted light of the room just beyond it (just beyond her) but he knows he has no hope of reaching it. He cannot move for she will not allow it. Only allows him to bend more fully into her.

You will take me from these walls, Ismail.

She speaks without mouth, without voice, as another heartbeat inside of him. Her gruesome hand presses to his heart as Ismail stares into the unending gloom of her, watching black stars poison the heavens, corrupting every world they erupt over. One slides into another, causes a burst, fragmenting skies, unhinging her terrible nature.

What is not killed is not dead, but should have been.

Black stars inside his collar, burning with unseen fire as they sink into his bones, his marrow. Ismail should scream and quake, but he moves beyond these things, the nest of her atrocious hand already becoming a home, the thing so dearly sought.

—

The horologion clock tower: octagonal, crumbling and rust-stained marble, once buried but excavated by two calloused and eager hands, its full and empty height revealed once more.

A vane atop its roof spins under eight winds (angel wings standing in relief upon the stones circling beneath the roof) but always tells the truth of time within its longest shadow: time is ever fleeting and what is not killed, cannot be not dead.

Within its vacated heart, a water clock, but the water flows no more.

—

Ismail flings his arms wide, then balls himself up tight. If he sleeps, he sweats through his robes the whole of an endless night, pressed against the curl of one wall. In a fever, he climbs into the wreck of the bed, which seems an iron bowl, and begs for her to burn him to ashes.

She refuses.

She--

Ismail's bones cry her secret name as a chorus, Nyar, Nyar

breaks him as she might a tray of painted ceramic, with fists gone to hammers, and under her assault, Ismail shatters.

In her hands, he becomes something More.

Muscle and bone are trivial in their mortality, he reaches beyond both things, flexible without the need of contrived joints and pulleys. He can do anything with this body, fashion it into any shape he likes, and he finds he likes many. In many guises he walks through the rows of those yet sleeping, those who need waking. His fingers long to stir them from their slumbers, but she tells him no, tells him wait, and he waits, for what is time? It matters little to them, they who are so very powerful beneath the vast skies.

Black stars in black heavens, and Ismail knows he has never seen anything so beautiful until he finds himself once again seeking her face, but she has none. Never needed one when she could inhabit all. The flicker of moonlight skin through parting hair teases him closer, until his hands close into her, until she wraps around him in answer, presses him down into the rot of the room, and subsumes everything he once called his own. No longer--he is something More: concave and convex, capable of filling and being filled, flowing within and without, filled though empty.

He rises newborn and understands what is left to him, what she will bid him do. And though he understands, he weeps for the last time, knowing he will soon no longer be capable of such mortal things.

——

Chimney: Fifteen hundred feet of refractory bricks, drawing air and gas into perfect toxic exhalations against skies foggy or clear. The flue, once again no wider than shoulders. Deep grooves within the flue's inner stone walls, worn by two feet still relatively mortal.

Then.

Soot and flesh cake every stone, burrowing into crevices where the two soon become one and the same. Words traced unseen into the mess--was nicht umgebracht wird, ist nicht wirklich tot.

———

The salt sea cracks beneath his feet, ancient rings of power further destroyed as he moves away from the iron tower. His shadow on the ground is her shadow on the ground, hair spooling in his wake, stroking the stars down from the sky. His mouth holds the curve of her mouth, pleased and terrified both. He does not look back, for the tower has become an abomination to him; it only kept him from wandering, only kept him from spreading. The line of the tower runs down his spine, long to harden to metal, but sensation and tower no longer draw his attention as they once did. He moves ever forward, toward his trusty ship and once there, takes again to the stars.

They are imperfect in their brightnesses against the black of the void, but this will soon be repaired, as would everything be. He never once looks at the planet he leaves; it too is full of imperfection, of doubts, despite it being his birthplace. He never once looks back, only guides himself toward the horrible glow of the system's sun (a radiant egg perched on the rim of a mud crater), and sets his engines to overload.

The blow is staggering. But his body is no longer his body, and there is no agony even as he is ripped asunder. He becomes the stars, becomes the meteor, the bright burst streaking through all the night skies. He finds himself lodged in places he has known before, his hands pressed against a marble capstone where they will imprint words, his belly echoing the hollow metal curve within a fleetfoot, his feet pressed pale against a burning iron bowl. His prints are eaten from his skin, his body (concave and convex, filled and filling) made and unmade in a hundred thousand nightmares across a thousand million universes. The children cry his name in writhing terror until he is nameless in all his towers, until he bids them: seek me, for that which was not killed, is not dead.

—

The black bramble wood before the iron tower: Clawed from the earth when the stars rained down, brambles as black as the world behind eyes when closed. Every bramble thorned, awaiting the kiss of a prince's blade, a kiss that may never come. A river from the window in the tower's stony side: loose hair, a cupped hand.

I Am...

— John Claude Smith —

"Many a book is like a key to unknown chambers within the castle of one's own self."

—Franz Kafka

I am…

Waking in fire.

I feel eternally in flame.

My breath rises from singed lungs, climbing my esophagus, exiting in clipped bleats from a throat scarred by smoke. I feel I am gagging just to breathe. I feel I am drowning in fire.

I am drowning in fire.

Somebody says, "Calm down, Miss. Calm down. I'll get the doctor."

I am in a hospital. As my eyelids flutter open, my vision is blurred, though the room is dark. Perhaps my perception is skewed by the darkness; a cloying, pervasive darkness. Yet, I sense I've not used my eyes in a while.

How long? I do not know.

The skin of my face and neck sings a song of severe distress. My brain takes the flood of input and swerves toward shutting down, but I stall it. I hold my breath and stall everything. Though my nerve endings attempt to scatter, seek refuge in the internal sanctuary of blood, viscera, and possibly soul, it is to no avail. This song must be endured. This pain. This experience.

Even with the chorus rising up in chattering, masticating timbres, gleefully gnawing on the chaos-filled realm of gray matter that is my brain, my mind—these spiraling, absurd thoughts--I am able to raise my left hand to my face, to feel the soft, coarse texture. Gauze, not skin.

Then, I remember:

"I told you never to enter this room, Elizabeth. Never."

Stafford was furious.

My arms ache, twisted behind my back. I am tied to a hard, wooden chair. I stamp my feet on the ground, try to move. My exertion is muted: the heels of my shoes barely scratch the hardwood floor. Rope cuts into my shins. My message of frustration nothing more than indecipherable scribbles in dust.

I realize instantly the futility of the act. For what purpose was the effort expended? Escape? I am tied to a chair, with a madman who I thought I loved having done the tying.

"What are you doing?" I say. "Why are you doing this to me?"

He laughs. It is not joy that fills the laughter. Something more devious, perhaps more lunatic.

He is a lunatic.

I should have known this from the beginning—dyed blood red hair; blue-tinted beard braided down to mid-chest; a jumble of indistinct tattoos up and down his arms, his neck; intensity that simmered always, as if to strike with cobra-quickness; occult interests that bordered on obsessive--but that lunacy was part of the attraction. Especially the occult interests, something I'd just gotten into, while he knew things, lots of things draped in obscurity. That said, all of this was a harbinger of the level of lunacy that abounded within his broken brain.

"I told you never to enter this apartment. There are things you should never know. Never witness."

The apartment, part of Simmons Terrace, a complex in the battered part of town. The complex: a gift from his dear old dad before he passed. Number 234, second floor, far end of a worn green carpet hallway. Flickering light playing Catch Me If You Can with the moths, hanging askew from a sconce screwed into the wall, and missing some screws. Painted brown wooden door, smudged doorknob, cold to the touch; so cold it hurts, but that didn't stop me from inserting the strange key.

Entering a room of dust and secrets.

A room of mystery and promise...

"Miss? Elizabeth?" The voice is deep, cautious; it wears kid gloves.

"Yes," I say. My voice is rough. Charred, I expect.

"How do you feel?" A light jab with the kid gloves, searching for answers that seem more than obvious to me.

"Not well. Not right." Strength is woven into the words. I scoot back, sit up taller. Prop myself up with pillows.

"Careful," he says, as my vision begins to clear.

"What time is it? What day?"

A hushed utterance is passed between the doctor and nurse. Though the room is dim—my vision adjusting, from dark to dim, but light is sparse--I can make out a Mickey Mouse barrette in the nurse's hair. Bug-eyed, it stares at me.

The doctor, a man with silver-trimmed temples and stern eyes, says, "Two thirty in the morning. August sixteenth."

I emit a groan of despair. A tone that scales my throat, its talons digging deep as it exits. I've been gone, for lack of a better word, since the sixth. When the incident happened...

"I know, but..." Was I to lie to Stafford? Would he know I was lying?

"No buts. I told you time and time again, never to enter this room. You promised you wouldn't, yet here we are. After all my warnings, I had to leave, if only for three days. I left you the keys in case a tenant needed help or lost their keys, and pointed specifically to this one"—holding up the strange one (one of these does not go with the others) (mysteries and secrets; hush, hush)--"and to this apartment, and said, no. No. Never enter this apartment." He paces in front of me, swinging what looks like a leather strap from his right hand, occasionally slapping it into his left, for emphasis.

As he has just done.

I pause, no words to say to appease him. Taking in the empty room, it is as it was when I entered. Bereft of anything of substance, of life. Not of this earth, I thought then and think again now. A different plane, perhaps.

Except for the spirits of his former wives and girlfriends, who huddled in a scrum of knotted limbs, skin-eating decay, and filth in the far corner, watching. Evidence my perception that this is a different plane, an intersection between, well...simply between, confirmed by their presence.

There is no use tip-toeing around the obvious.

"How bad is the damage?" I say, expecting the worst, but the doctor's expression crinkles oddly, confusing me. "Well?"

He inhales deeply. The nurse turns away, stares at the door. As if she would rather be anywhere but here.

"The...damage..." He stops, turns and looks to the door as well. What the hell, he's a doctor. Give me the lowdown so I can move forward.

Is there moving forward from this?

"Tell me," I say, trying to sound strong, but my voice cracks. It's a tiny crack. The kind of barely noticeable crack that ends up breaching a wall, and the water flows; and annihilation smiles.

"Fourth degree burns over your whole head, part of your neck and chest. You were rescued before it spread further."

Though he states the ugly facts, there's an avoidance woven into his words that is the perfect partner to the crinkled expression he still wears.

There's something more, I'm sure.

"What else?" My eyes moisten as I say this, uncertain if this event has altered too much of what I wanted from life. From my goals; my new goals. If this outward scarring would inhibit what I need to know.

I am sobbing now, body quaking, uncontrollable.

"There, now. Just rest." This patented and pulled up from the black bag of by rote phrases signifying compassion bandied about as they seek their own means of escape. The doctor nods to the nurse, who approaches with a syringe.

"No. Tell me what else is wrong," I say, though the word "wrong" is chosen more for their comfort than meaning it is in any way elucidating the situation. I am not sure of anything at this point. What's right or wrong or been altered besides my flesh, and does that really matter? Though I want answers, I don't want to inspire more questions from them, or anybody.

I say, "Fuck," as I sense the tranquilizing fluid the nurse had injected into the IV spread like lava in my veins. More heat. More fire.

I drift off within seconds to their soft putty faces wearing masks of caring.

The dream is more a memory, continuing with the incident...

I watch Stafford squat down and pick up something.

I cannot tell what it is until he points it at me and squeezes. The shock of the smell, the bitter tang of the taste—lighter fluid.

"What's this?" I say, spitting fluid from my lips. He continues to drench me in the liquid. It burns before it is lit.

"No! What are you doing, Stafford? Honey..."

"Honey? You know what I am doing. Ending this as I have done before. Those who lose my trust, lose everything. That is the only way to keep the knowledge at bay. Humanity cannot know—"

"I won't tell anybody," I say, fighting with lies, but not exactly. I need to know more, learn more, but right now is not the time to fend for my heart's aspirations. Right now, I need to find a way out of this situation.

"It doesn't matter, Elizabeth. You know, and that's one too many. You know too much after looking...in there," he says, eyes angled down to my lap, where the ancient book rests, the substantial weight holding it in place. "I've had enough of trying to protect humanity from its power. I've had enough of being its caretaker." He stops, laughs again. Rats scatter from the scrum of dead wives and girlfriends in the far corner, scamper along the floorboards. The dead wives and girlfriends dissipate; perhaps the rats carry their souls, trapped in this room forever.

"No. Please. I just—"

He squirts what remains of the lighter fluid all over the book and drops the empty can to the floor. It clanks, muted and hollow; the room echoes in response, but there's no more noise from either. It settles stiffly next to a bright red fire extinguisher.

At this point, all I am is perplexed. What exactly does he have planned?

He reaches into his pocket and says, "I warned you this would not end well if you broke your promise." He lights a match.

There's not ending well and there's catastrophic. This was well beyond either.

I scream.

Voices rise from beneath me. The Henderson's from 134. Newlyweds.

Stafford tosses the lit match to the floor. It fizzles to a whisk of smoke. He takes the strap, whatever it is, and approaches me. He presses it over my eyes, pulling tight, tying it into knots at the back of my head. I can tell it is knots by his grunts, the effort he exerts.

"What is this?"

"I want you to remember what you've done," he says, close to my right ear. It is not a whisper. I almost jump at his words, flinch from his presence.

Confusion teethes on my thoughts. It seemed his intentions were to kill me, so what would there be to remember if I were dead?

And what of the fire extinguisher?

I hear the snick of another match come to life. As well as a heavier snick: the cocking of a trigger.

I hear the voices below me, Vicki and Chuck who likes to be called Charles but everybody calls him Chuck. Their inflection wears a cowl of disorientation.

I scream again, sensing part of Stafford's path, but not all of it. Not wanting to know all of it. Not wanting to know what I already know of his lunatic ways.

The voices remain distant, as if deciding on a plan of action. That's when I remember the best way to get somebody's attention.

"Fire," I yell, moments before the match ignites my face.

Waking again, this time in a fog of fragmented memories and shadows culled from a Boschian nightmare.

The world I'm sure Bosch lived in. Or perhaps Stafford.

A world I expect I will need to get used to.

One would think there would be curiosity at the damage, but not having seen what Stafford did to me, I contemplate what I can deal with. Having spoken to his dead wives and girlfriends, the coven of rotting spirits and minds gone to shit, I learned much about Stafford. Much about why the room was meant never to be explored.

I did not understand the whole of it, and sense was made flimsy by this lack of understanding. Yet one knows when one is supposed to be at a certain place, at a certain time, in the broad scope of the world one lives in. A moment to swing the pendulum toward a truth I have searched for years to understand.

I was not looking for what I found, but what I found is the key to who I am. I know it, whether I can explain it or not. Hence, my physical condition is only a hindrance if it impedes me from finding out more. I wonder if Stafford's single shot sayonara and the message he intended would cripple my newfound quest.

I had a seed of perception, but did not understand how to nurture it until I found the book.

"It holds secrets," Darlene had said, needles dangling from her skeletal arms; from the mist of her being.

"It opens doorways that should never be opened," Kay said. Sweet Kay, tracing Stafford's warning with a fingernail in the plume of her corroded breath.

"He'll take you before you learn how to use it," Maria said. Clever Maria, a voice adorned in snippets of the knowledge. She knew something.

"What is it?"

"It is the key," she said, stepping forward.

"It is pure evil," Doreene said, cowering as she did. She was barely there.

"Evil is not what it is, foolish child," Maria said, tsk-tsking Doreene, and the rest of them. "I will never understand what Stafford found appealing about you. Such a wilted flower. I suppose compliancy was all he really wanted from us."

"Shut up!" Doreene said, with the force of a blown dandelion.

Turning her attention again to me, Maria said, "It is our only path to freedom —"

"Not with what it awakens," Darlene said. Maria turned to face her, stare with intent. Darlene faded, though I knew she was still there.

"All you have to do is open it and read… Perhaps you are the one who is meant to awaken…" Her statement incomplete, yet the path she portended was clear.

These thoughts waver as I notice a figure sitting in the darkness of the room.

I wonder if the room is always dark, and why. And who fills the indistinct blob of the silhouette, when she speaks.

"Darling," she says. Mother.

I am…

Light made of heat made of stars going supernova in the condensed, concentrated realm of my head. The head of a lit match, hypnotic as it shimmies, made flesh.

It is a heat that turns flesh to liquid, to melting wax. Visceral turbulence etched with splintered nails like branding irons into my face; ripping, tearing. Deep down the trauma hounds feast on the patches of gristle and blackening bone. The skull beneath the bubbling epidermal lava. Not much to turn to fat there, but tidbits they lap with eager tongues.

Insatiable.

It is a living thing.

Fire is a living thing, even after it has left the body and had its way with mutilating what once might have been considered normal, average; not beautiful. It remains a ghost in the system, haunting with feverish efficiency. Cruel and consistent.

Its voice is a single droning tone, a piercing thought, riding the tip of the blackened fangs of the hounds as they scrape bone.

My voice wails in unison with the charring chorus.

I hear Stafford say, "If you really want to be its caretaker, be my guest. But know the consequences of—"

His voice is muffled by the red cry and sunburst enunciation beyond excruciation that wraps my head in its wail.

Caretaker? What kind of joke is that? I want more from the book than to just watch over it.

There is pounding out there, beyond my burning prison.

"Come in," he yells. "I had intended to save her, but you can have the pleasure, if pleasure is to be found in..." He falls silent as the sound of ruptured wood cracks at the force of a mighty weight.

There is a pop and thud and an aural chaos that is woven into the scorching thread that kneads my face in blisters that pop and skin that melts and—

--a flush of something cool, like an arctic belch, vomiting powder over my head; this hurts as well, a different pain. Not healing, just shifting.

Seconds slide by, the voices become clear as a Vicki says, "Is she alive?" while Chuck, who likes to be called Charles, but who gives a fuck right now, says, "She's alive. But he's not. Watch your step. Blood." "Oh, shit..." "Call 9-1-1," and I realize the siren wail that resonates with acute lucidity all around me—as the flame was, now this sound—is my voice, my throat shredding, hacking metal-on-metal razorblade symphonies in conjunction with the expression of such immersive horror...

"Darling," my mother says again.

"Yes, Mother," I say, though it is garbled by my dry throat. Or is it in transition? Perhaps this is my new voice? What languages will it teach me to speak?

"I thought I'd lost you."

She is not looking at me. This annoys.

"Well," I say, my timbres clearing and in league with the annoyance, "You obviously haven't. Why don't you take a look at your pretty girl and give her a big hug."

"Darling, I…" But she gives up, the fight not even worth the effort. As she's always done.

I don't care. I poke her as if she's dead, which she has been for me for years. Never there when I needed her. Never there at all. Dad having left upon my birth, she's the only parent I've ever known. Which means my definition of parent is devoid of meaning.

Dear old never-known dad probably left more of himself in my genes than she has. Thankfully.

"Come on, mother. How about a kiss," I say, even though my lips are probably nothing more than mangled pink flesh poking through gauze. It probably looks perverse to her, yet I really do not care.

I reach up to make sure there is gauze. There is. What's she so goddamned afraid of? That's when I realize the gauze is freshly applied. There was moistness and patchy hardening before I went to sleep. Was she here to watch the sideshow exhibit as it danced around, curtsied and tipped its motley hat?

The façade of mother she flaunts for others wears thin on her only daughter. I'm not into games. I'm into discovering who I am now. Uncovering who I am now…

I swing my legs to the side of the bed.

"Darling, what are you doing?" Her care is more out of discomfort than genuine empathy.

I start to unravel the gauze.

"Darling…Beth, darling. I-I should call a nurse." She rises from the chair, the plush blue cushion sighing at her retreat. As she passes in front of me, I reach out and grab her arm.

Contact.

She yelps, a tiny sound: a Chihuahua's tail pinched under heavy heels.

I hold tight.

"Baby, you're hurting me."

"Fuck you, mother," I say, the last word an abomination.

"Let me go," she says, and I release her. She continues to the door, looking back as I pull off the last of the gauze. "Oh, my..." Her face is much as the doctor's when I asked about damage.

There's something here I do not understand. Now is the time to get a clue.

The door swooshes closed as she exits. I hear the tap-tap-tapping of her expensive boots and her whiny voice fade as she rounds a corner.

I rise, gather my gumption as well as my balance, joints popping and muscles straining, and wobble what one might view as drunkenly toward the bathroom.

I step inside and flick the switch.

The light causes my eyes to water, yet I do not close them. There is too much to take in. The doctor's and my mother's confusion made...not exactly clear, but finding its footing.

I wonder as to why I was not in a burn unit. Perhaps my strangeness defied protocol.

I think about my absent father and the shadow that is my mother.

I think about my true parents, the only one's who could have created the masterpiece that is...me.

I laugh. The sound rises with the tenacious grind of a train seeking refuge from Hell. But it's not refuge I seek. It is completion.

I am...

Almost there.

Almost me.

I scrounge through the brown bag that sat on the floor next to the woman who called herself my mother. Mother, sweet mother, left clothes, shoes. As if she thought I was leaving anytime soon.

The details here do not matter. What matters is my quest.

Quickly dressing, I gather the strength to tumble out the window, my legs acclimating to the task, and sprint away.

Darkness is my shroud, my features muted by light and shadow. I may look curious to the few stragglers and homeless, but the image will fade as they slump in beds made of concrete and dream of strange creatures.

I will be the strange creature they thought they saw before Morpheus takes them to the places their personal demons frolic.

My breath is harsh, pluming amidst the two A.M. chill. Sunrise is hours away. My pace is swift. I will make it to the apartment well before the sun's gleaming stare points me out to others, who will pray I am a nightmare of which they want to pinch themselves in hopes of awakening into the real world.

Not a very promising choice, I think, veering toward Stafford's choices, and wonder as to his fear. All he had researched, a lie. With what he owned, the book that burned perhaps to ash along with my face, why did he not pursue its gifts?

Then I remember inhaling the deep, pungent aroma of ink and old pages, parchment allusions made tangible with what I have learned. Even through the thickening smog of my own burning flesh. I wonder what remains of the book. I wonder if any of it is salvageable, and if it is even there, in that apartment. Would the police or the fire department have taken it away, the grotesque scene one in need of answers they would never get, even with what remains of the book, if anything? Did the book burn to ash, never to be deciphered again?

Were these questions and more never to be answered?

Perhaps my physical condition was one to answer questions...or inspire more.

Would his ex-wives and ex-girlfriends have answers for the questions ricocheting in my reeling thoughts?

Was I so close to something, a true revelation and not just the opening of the door the hospital mirror presented?

Would I be left adrift, this monstrous creature no one would lay eyes on without feeling bile rise and tickle the back of their throat?

Too many questions, with answers doubtful.

I only knew the apartment might hold another key, this one invisible and to be slipped into the lock of the mind, helping me figure out my present predicament.

I think back to Stafford again, and his denial of the book and the gifts it held. I remember him saying his father was the one who was into the dark stuff, the black arts. I remember him and his knowledge, never something he embraced, more a necessity. Keeping it at bay. Keeping something at bay. I had loose threads in need of braiding. My interest only over the last few years, leading up to him, and this. Yet I know I have a stronger internal foundation as to why I have this interest now. He, on the other hand—I sense he was afraid of things, of his father's legacy of forbidden knowledge, yet that knowledge sat in the back of his brain, rocking to and fro, waiting, waiting.

He chose punk rock aesthetics, the red hair, blue beard, anarchist's attitude, but had not the heart to truly embrace it all. Surface level, like the tattoos. He was a lunatic, but it was a lunatic by choice, not a part of his essence.

My essence, well...

I thought of my spare minutes with the book and know it was mine, all mine. As Maria had suggested. Meant for me: its history and its promise. Welcoming me as a parent to a child.

No, not the book, but those who wrote it. Those whose dark wisdom bled onto those pages.

I think of what I am doing, and why am I here, tearing the yellow police tape from the door and turning the knob.

I knew it would open.

The key was with Stafford. It might have dropped and scattered amidst the chaos. The dead ex-wives and ex-girlfriends might have hidden it. These thoughts filter through me as I step through the door and gently close it behind me.

Breathing deep, the taint of burnt flesh and burnt paper--burnt old paper--tweaks my nostrils. Not strongly, it's been over two weeks since the incident. But enough to bring tears to my eyes.

I brush my wrist over the less damaged skin around my eyes, courtesy of Stafford's insistence I see what I am to see but not what he expected me to see, and lightly thumb the layers and layers of the flesh of my face, and wander to the middle of the room.

I turn in circles, waiting for something to happen.

"Why am I here?" I say aloud.

"You've come home," Maria says.

"Not home. This is Hell." Doreene, frightened, yet hiding in the darkest part of the room. She steps out and reconsiders options when she sees me more clearly. No light in the room but the moon peering through cracked glass.

She begins to weep.

"What's happened to your face?" she says.

"Yes, what's happening to your face?" Darlene, roaming along the periphery; perhaps the periphery of this world and another.

From happened to happening. I wonder…

I am…

In transition?

"You know what's happening, don't you, dearest?" Maria says. Her voice is vinegar-laced, joyful.

"I am…not sure."

"Perhaps not," she says. "But you have an inkling of what's happening, don't you."

"The book—"

"Yes." Not a question, a statement.

Shadows thicken where the others gather. Not Maria. She wants what I have, but does not court jealousy in anticipation of what I am…becoming.

Then I realize there is no book to be found here. Not exactly…

"You are beautiful," Maria says, stepping back, eyes wide in awe. She starts to chant. Her wish one for true resurrection, out of the spirit realm and into the flesh. Her understanding is distorted. To be as she is and to welcome the possibilities of discovering her true self—oh, what bliss she would experience.

As I am swiftly learning.

My final statement, one of triumph. A statement mocking Stafford's misguided damnation, as if he had the power to distribute such a thing. My true name revealed as the leaves of my face flap wildly.

(I am...)

Maria buckles to her knees in rapture, palms raised to the black heavens awaiting trespass through me. "Yes! Yes!"

(I am…)

As if another match has been flung to my head, thoughts spark and smolder through me as I read the leaves…

(I am…)

--the passage of eons, words and rituals, chants and spells scribbled in blood, ink, and fever sweat hallucinations; seeing too deeply, yet not enough…

(I am…)

--my absent fathers, human and…not, mad poets and mad geniuses and mad creatures culled from the rim of forever, the wasteland dwellers, both here and…out there…

(I am…)

My voice, a howl, a tolling bell, the time has come--now!

"I am--"

That is not dead which can eternal lie.

And with strange aeons even death may die
   "--The Necronomicon!"

The Apprentice, the Muse and the Mancer
~ Michael Griffin ~

I'm hiding behind Mancer's big shelf, watching them through gaps between books. Across the workshop, Mancer is collaborating with Taia. *My muse*, he calls her. Taia's movements are strange. One moment she swirls effortless, the next seizing postures which require strained effort as she contorts in place. Her perfect white skin glistens with perspiration, and her long straight hair, also perfect white, flails around her like a bright halo.

Mancer's attention is split between Taia's movements and his paper before him on the desk. His pen hand moves as if sketching, and while it's true he's interpreting form and outline, he's not drawing, but writing. More accurately, he's scratching letterforms, designing sigils, muttering words under his breath. Sometimes he tries spoken words in sequence using different intonation or inflection, playing one sound against the next like a singer, while his muse poses, her every movement synchronized to his speech.

Taia's paleness is revealed through her dress, made of thin rings of black metal, like a weightless suit of chainmail. Tiny loops jingle against one another, catch against the skin beneath, and slide free.

The portal window behind them looks into an abyss of water, dark and very deep. The only light out there is that which escapes this room. When something out in the water nears the glass, it steals a fragment of light, and as if startled to discover luminance where none is expected, swims away. Why Mancer situates us here, so far below, I don't know. When I've asked, he repeats his mantra: _Never question._

I assume the point is to be near whatever ineffable godhead he's striving to attract.

Taia spins, arms and legs so thin, whirling untouched by gravity, like a body suspended in perfectly clear water. Feet naked, nails bare, unvarnished pink. Those few aspects of her not absolutely pale are like this. Pink eyes, pink nipples showing through the garment. Other parts I barely glimpse, more hidden.

I want to see her eyelashes, closer. First I believed she had no lashes, but she has them. They appear to be white, as they would be.

What kind of creature does this make her, this pure lack of color? Very strange. I think she's beautiful.

Pressing myself closer, I angle my face, jam my nose against some musty tome, trying to see through the corner gap in the shelf. There's no space, no way to get nearer. I slide down, lower myself, look under. The cabinet is raised up on legs, and there's a deep gap beneath. I see Mancer and Taia directly. See her moving, sense the lightness and texture of her.

Silently I slide forward, press myself through, belly crawl into the room. I'm small, still not fully grown, and the space is wider than expected. Taia, there before me, separated by nothing. She moves as if wrestling with something invisible. I can't stop myself straining ahead, hoping to better see her movements, every detail of her, closer. Candlelight flickers, wild yet delicate, dancing as the muse Taia dances, responding to the rhythm of Mancer's incantation.

I wriggle forward, lift my head, and realize I'm exposed, fully out from under the shelf. I'm in the room, too close, and unhidden.

Mancer stops. The final note of his incantation resounds, echoes away.

I stop, try to wriggle back.

Taia freezes for an instant, then flits back, disappears into the shadows against the far wall. Her eyes reflect the candle, which flickers now only in response to the motions of Mancer's eyes. His eyebrows raise and spread, antennae surveying the room.

"What are you doing?" Mancer's voice booms.

Don't reveal fear. "Just... curious." My voice holds steady, mostly.

"Is this the aim of apprenticeship?" Mancer inhales, exhales luxuriantly, as if bored. "Spying, in secret?"

"I couldn't help.... Only wanted to see." Stop. Better he doesn't know.

"You were watching her, Taia. My muse. Is Taia your muse, also?"

What is she to me? I barely know her, have never spoken to her. There can't be any name for the way I think of her. "I have no muse. I have nothing my own."

Mancer's eyes reveal none of the sympathy I hoped for. "What do you imagine Taia is to you, then?"

My only hope is that she's left the room, is seeing none of this. I can't help squinting into shadows, hoping not to find her, but there, eyes flicker, visible in the dark. Shame burns my cheeks.

"My question."

"To me? Nothing," I stammer. "I only wondered. Was curious."

"So here we return to the beginning." Mancer's eyes widen like yawning mouths, even as his focus and his hands shift to straightening vellums, aligning pens. The candle's flame stops, frozen mid-flutter, then straightens, lengthens. "To satisfy your curiosity. That must be why I granted you apprenticeship."

My eyes sting. I look down, blinking. "No, Mancer."

"Why then? What reason?"

"So I could learn, and perform tasks that are beneath you."

"Then you haven't completely forgotten." Mancer smiles.

Crinkles form beside his eyes. A vertical crease divides his brow.

"No. I remember." I steal a glance, find Taia still lurking. "I'm sorry to disappoint you."

"Sorry. Well then. My work reaches an important stage. Recent outcomes lead me to dare hope I finally may be nearing... my own greatest desire."

"How can I assist, Mancer? I would love to do more than you've asked of me. I'm capable..." I stop myself.

"Truly? Capable of more? Is that your desire?"

I hesitate, already second-guessing. Maybe admitting the truth will only convince him I already forget my place. "I could."

"You could. Maybe I should sit back, rest these hands. We could exchange stations. I could occupy myself with lesser things, while my apprentice drives my work forward, boldly. A boy, not a man, makes manifest my own lifelong ambition. After all, any one can speak the words." He gestures at the workbook, his scrawling.

"I didn't mean--"

"Didn't mean. Never intended. Was only curious. Let me explain the best way you might help me. Not by exercising curiosity. Not by contemplating ways to prove greater capability." Forcefully his fingers screw shut an ink jar, the lid straining as if about to snap. "Do nothing more than finish the list of tasks I've given, otherwise leave me alone. Stop spying. Stop leering at Taia in her work. Stop muttering in imitation of incantations overheard."

"I haven't--"

"Of course you have. I'm tempted to let you discover what would happen, should you succeed." Mancer stands abruptly, as if he's just remembered something. "But enough. I go, seeking consult with my old teacher. See that by the time I return tonight, your tasks are complete. Think of nothing else. Only these tasks."

I turn my face, trying to hide the dejection I realize must show.

"But wait," Mancer says, as if he's remembered something more.

"There is another thing. You wanted new duties."

I brighten. Hope surges, too much to conceal.

"Fetch water." He indicates the bucket at the edge of his workbench. "Take this to the well."

"That?" I approach, lean in. "But it's a bucket of water, already full."

Mancer gestures. Force extends well beyond his outstretched palm, a motion making physical his intention, which strikes invisibly even as his palm remains yet two steps away. The bucket upends, water spills, soaks me down my front. My thin tunic sticks, all I'm wearing, gone transparent to my skin, as if I'm naked. My narrow chest, sunken belly, thin arms, and more below dwindling in the chill, fully revealed.

A laugh from the shadows, light yet womanly rather than girlish.

Mancer is already gathering oddments, ink-soaked corks, jagged razor blades, hollow needles. Mostly, scraps of paper, herb-infused and leaf-permeated, jars of special purpose inks, heat-carrying or whispering, invisible or truth-divining, these varieties and more. All this he sweeps into the many pouches and compartments of his hide pack, striped green and black. Usually it's my wish to study what he's doing, his tools of work, but this time I can't bear to see, don't want to know.

I jump, ready to hurry out, then turn and snatch up the empty bucket.

Taia's watching.

I run, wind through halls, dark ways so familiar I could race them blind, to my corner closet. I have no door to slam, can only exchange wet garments for dry, and take the bucket out to the shallow well, endlessly refilled from membranes trickling down the outer wall.

By the time I return the filled bucket to Mancer's desk, the workshop is empty and silent.

Though I quickly dry, sitting in my closet, I remain angry, feeling disrespected. I sit at my bench facing inks and pens and cut squares of parchment, linen and vellum, knowing I should resume my work. My hands take up the implements, yet I'm too preoccupied to focus.

Why won't Mancer listen? He can't judge my capabilities, because he refuses even to consider them. Certainly he's never tested me. I could be helping so much more.

And Taia, the more I know of her, the less I understand. Mancer seems to consider her an equal, a crucial partner in his work, while I toil down here in this closet, ink-stained hands itching, eyes strained bleary in the dark. Can't possibly accomplish any transcribing work yet, so I sort and clean nibs, then grind pigments for ink. I move without intention, still obsessed. The workshop. Taia and Mancer.

By now, he must be gone. What's she doing now, alone? I know nothing of what life she may have beyond her servitude to a decrepit would-be summoner. How does Taia occupy herself?

I'm not accomplishing anything, just sitting here halfhearted with distraction. I stand, survey my closet, then walk out the door and creep back down the halls, peering around every corner. This compulsion to see, I can't help it. This time, I'll stay back. Careful. No risk.

As I approach Mancer's workshop, I hear Taia moving, shuffling lightly within, like a muted chime.

Well hidden down the dark hallway, I watch her move, sort of dancing like before, now posing with a practiced quality, like rehearsal for a more meaningful upcoming performance. She's alone, no sound of Mancer's scratches and murmurs, yet still she moves with an urgency, occasionally straining, or moving faster than I can follow. She spins, pink eyes focused upon the spot where Mancer usually sits.

What's this she's doing? What music does she hear? If not music, some rhythm must give timing to her movements. Closer.

She's caught up in herself, unaware of me. Brow knit in focus, lean muscles tense. Long white hair sticks to her forehead, as before. Closer still.

She turns, her eyes seize me where I stand. She laughs, aware I'm watching.

I start to run, stop, look back.

Her look isn't scolding, seems more curious. Bemused.

"Is he gone?" I whisper.

She squints at me, studying me, not as a friend would, but with a teacher's judging scrutiny.

"You can't stop yourself, crossing bounds." Taia stretches her spine left, right. "He's right, you know. An apprentice must understand his role."

I want to protest, though I know she's right. "I finish my work."

She considers. "If you're capable of hearing anything I ever say, let it be this. Everything you know is wrong."

"What, about you?" I ask.

She shakes her head, laughs, as if I'm a silly child. Yet she's the tiny one, so slight. It's true, I don't understand. That's why she interests me.

"How old are you?" I venture. "What brought you here? What do you do for the master?"

Taia raises arms, bends at the waist, then spins, jumps and lands in a new pose. "None of this is for you."

"You're much too young to be with him." It's out of bounds, I realize, but can't stop myself. "You're more suited to... someone our age."

Her eyes narrow and she laughs outright. It's clear she's thinking of something else, more than what I suggested. "You're always reaching, trying to grasp at what you think you see, but your hands close on nothing, because you don't really see. Because of this, your concerns are meaningless. As for me? I'm ageless."

I protest. "Ageless? You can't be even as old as me."

"My appearance?" she asks, as if she hasn't considered this. "That's nothing. How old are you yourself? Fifteen?"

I consider exaggerating, or lying, but instead jut my chin defiantly, and nod.

"Fifteen." Her eyes go distant, searching. "I can't remember fifteen."

"But you're small." My hands indicate parts of my own body, corresponding to hers. "Your breasts, your..." I point between her legs. "Your body isn't yet developed, like a woman's becomes."

She shrugs. "I prefer this. It's conducive to work."

"Let me see your true appearance. If it's so different."

That same laugh, as if indulging a child. "I would show you, if I believed it might finally change you."

I feel her scorn diminishing me. "But I want to see!"

"But I want to see!" she mocks. "I've told you, your desires are based upon misapprehension."

She lectures me like a baby, though I still can't believe she's more than fourteen, at most. I believe what my eyes show me. It hurts, being dismissed. I'm the only one living here who's always excluded. The way she treats me, it's worse than Mancer. He's an old man. To him I'm a child. She's still mostly like me. She's not even looking at me anymore, having resumed her movements.

"You know something," I venture, "I've worked more words of my own than Mancer realizes."

Her eyes narrow, like a sprung trap. "Ha! You admit your secret. I'll let Mancer pursue it, then, unless you tell me. Be specific."

I'm caught. Why did I have to boast? The only thing left is to tell, perhaps hope to impress her with my capabilities. But I don't even know what to name the work I've done. What have I really accomplished? My experiments haven't really summoned anything. The more I think about it, the less sure I am the murmurings were even functioned.

Backing up, I look away. After a few steps, I turn and race back to my closet.

Swerving from frustration to anger, I try to resume work. There has to be some way to prove I'm more than they perceive. Obviously Mancer's never seen me as anything but a child, but he's wrong. I understand his work. I've held on, believing my time would come. A chance to show I can help. But he won't see, Taia either. They can't imagine me as anything but what they see.

I want to reveal what I've learned, practiced in secret. It's not much, yet. I have to extend myself, take chances.

I'm working with new parchment, copying scribbled poetry from tattered scraps in Mancer's jagged hand into clearer characters on good parchment. It's boring work. I'm not permitted to focus on the words, to think about what I'm reading. It's tempting to recite little bits, to prove myself capable, but it's forbidden even to consider the intention bound up in the words.

Still in secret, some part of me keeps track, even memorizes portions. If I read it to myself, under my breath, he'll never know. I've done it before.

How can I to do this? I have to try.

"That's what I have to do," I say to myself. "There's power in it. Speak out loud."

I have ambition, hope. I admit that. What's wrong with wanting more? Why else do apprenticeship, if not to gain knowledge, attain power, and finally move ahead? I want to impress Mancer, of course. What apprentice wouldn't? Probably he was like me, once.

Also I admit, I want to impress Taia. She's close to my age, despite what she says. Maybe not younger, as I first guessed. Her appearance intrigues me. I enjoy watching her, feel curious drawn to her thin, colorless form, her weightless white hair.

I want more than just to peek at her from a distance, while she dances for him.

"Say it, then," I challenge myself, aloud. "Say what I intend. What I desire."

Speaking such words seems transgressive. Rules broken, boundaries crossed. Unrecoverable.

"I want Taia to learn about me. I'll do whatever I must."

I try to sort the ragged scraps of Mancer's notes, prepare to transcribe them according to Mancer's rules, my primary duty, to render his sketches in clean, careful ink work.

I recall words I've spun in secret. They're not much. I have to go much farther. Am I even capable?

I allow my mind to focus on the words before me. Saying them in my mind has no effect, but then...

I speak aloud, read the lines from the paper.

A spark sizzles from the tip of my pen. Ink burns, tingling smoke.

I set down the pen and repeat the passage, holding index fingers inches apart. Heat wavers, distorting the air, then flame jumps the gap. The corner of a vellum scrap burns. I swat it with my palm.

Choose another, and speak. Words come to life, the ink dances, glitters, streams from the jar to my index finger, flows back again.

This isn't enough. It needs to be more, stronger than anything I've memorized, or even thought about before. No more casual tricks.

I stand, hesitate in the doorway to my humble closet, and set out. I take the winding path, past the locked closet, down dark hallways, beyond a row of carven wood mockups of strange ceiling-high creatures, sea-dwelling monsters, or perhaps gods.

Finally I reach the storage area near Mancer's workshop. Taia may yet be working, but I know how to approach in stealth, and find what I need without being seen. The rear of the bookshelf, the vantage point from which I watched before. Crouch, come up under, and there. Mancer's primary workbook, distinctive brown leather with an expandable binding laced with cord, so that my newest pages can be added in, as needed.

It's worth the risk. Think of all I want for myself. For Taia.

Is it really true? I'm going to do it, surprise them. I'll bring whatever Mancer's seeking, bring it near, bind it for him. He'll see.

I open the book, flip ahead as I carry it to the bench. Not many earlier pages are tabbed, and Mancer has only recently begun to express confidence about the nearness of his goal. Though I have obeyed the rules prohibiting me from reading what I copy, most of the time, I've seen enough to know it's been only within the latest dozen pages where something changed. As I copied these works for him, Mancer checked my efforts impatiently and with extra focus the very moment I finished. Among these latest pages are sections of words, strangely accented according to his specific instructions, and calligraphed in varying sizes and colors. It's as if his recent work is inspired by an entirely different foundation of myth and language. I can only surmise how these might be read, how Mancer himself would render them in voice. Imagining this, I can't help but picture Taia's movements. I visualize her clearly.

From experience I know the written words are valueless, except when spoken. My finger traces the lines. I rehearse them in my mind, soundless, heart pounding, until I feel ready to attempt my first summoning.

I mutter words, under my breath at first, feeling the weight of them as I proceed through the line. Tongue forceful, lips heavy, burdened with the significance of what I'm saying. What I'm trying to bring.

A spark whirls in the air before me, surprises me with sizzling brightness. It jolts me back. I stop speaking, and the effect vanishes.

I resume, from the beginning. Nothing happens. Too hurried. Intonation is important.

Starting again, I bear in mind the rhythmic, syncopated emphasis I've heard Mancer employ. Like emulating a favorite singer.

There's a loud pop, followed by a quavering in the air, separate from my voice. This time, nothing visual happens. Even the sound fades.

I slam my fist on the table, anger bursting within. So frustrating. I don't have time, can't wait. Have to show them.

"It's not just speaking the words." I try to remember how he explained it, repeat it in his voice. "Not just how the words form in the mouth, not just the spaces between. Most important is the carrying of intention through the act of speaking. The conveyance of willpower, within to without."

I realize I don't even know what Mancer's looking for. Am I really prepared to find it? I can't be sure, feel like giving up. Anger surges again.

I turn pages back, forward. Nothing here. This can't be it. Then I notice another book, beneath this one, mostly covered by loose papers on the desk. What's this? I've always believed Mancer makes me transcribe all the notes he makes. I've never seen this other book before. Thicker, paper far heavier and older. The cover is worn black, adorned with strange symbols in gold ink.

I set Mancer's book aside, and explore this other. Without thinking, I start to read. To whisper.

Not loud enough. Needs to be louder, but she'll hear. Who cares? Let her hear what I can do.

I raise my voice. The words build. Let her watch me, as I bring them down.

One line, another. In the air, a humming, a crackling resonance. A spark of visitation, something coming. Beneath me, the table vibrates. Nothing solid is visible, but I feel hands, fingertips tracing my skin. The air whirls, like fluttering birds.

I'm shoved back, jarred by unseen force. Still I read on. I'm struck across the face so hard, my teeth clack together. I fall to the floor, face down.

"No!" I cry, thinking I'll have to start again, now that my lines have been interrupted. Quickly I jump up, continue.

Above me, a shape moves, hovering. It's hard to discern its exact outline. Another emerges from behind it, then a third, all of them quavering and shimmering in the air. They spin and whirl, as if aware of me, as if watching. In a sort of aerial dance, they seem to be trying to position themselves between myself and the open book.

The incantation is complete. These things are here, but what next? I don't know how to contain them, or get rid of them.

Taia's going to hear, I think. That very moment, her footsteps come, lightly shuffling. The jingle of delicate metal rings.

She enters, seems to float into the room weightless, unconcerned. "What are you doing? You're..." She sees, runs closer, and freezes.

"Listen," I say.

I resume reading, this time with a difference. As I form the words, I watch Taia, just as Mancer always does.

A loud bang, then a series of bass-drum booms. A wind swirls, tugs my garment, ruffles my hair, as if the very air is expanding in pockets and rapidly contracting again. Like invisible lungs, breathing in the air.

I stop reading, and the overpowering sounds subside, replaced by whispers. The voices are nothing like my own, nor Taia's. Ghostly words, fragments of speech from another place.

Sudden flashes of blinding, nauseating brightness, alternate with sickening tangible dark, like an incoming tide of black. A smell, like something dead or rotting, nausea and seasick disorientation. I feel myself pulled, the harrowing tug of madness.

Wings flutter, still barely seen, brushing my face. Hands too, fingertips grasping, not separate but in the same space, as if some creature possessed of both hands and wings exists, invisible beside me. What is this? I try to shove it away, but my hands barely managed to find anything solid. Somehow, these things are able to see me, to strike me, yet when I try to fight back, I find nothing. My efforts are useless. I focus instead on the book, try to flip through other pages, seeking clues. Anything might help. I should've been more certain before I began. This isn't what I wanted. With all this fluttering around, it's getting hard to read.

Taia approaches, pink eyes focused not on me, but something past me. She approaches, swings backhand, seems about to strike me. I trust her. I feel an impact, the thing knocked away. Taia, no longer graceful like a dancer, but a different kind of poise now. Forceful and strong. A fighter.

I realize there are more openings, gateways all around me in mid-air. "The way is open!" Shapes swoop in, shove me aside. I stagger.

"Shut it," Taia screams.

"How?" Frantic, I search pages, too panicked to focus. I didn't know, shouldn't have tried. All these pages, what can it be? I barely recognize, don't understand. How can I pronounce these bizarre symbols?

Taia fights, movements fluid as her dance, striking hard, kicking high. To my eyes, her shape is changing, no longer so thin. Limbs fluid, transforming to something else. She swings backhand, strikes. A shape stills, and falls.

Another flies at my head, attacks, digs in fingernails. Frantic, I try to pry it off. I grasp, worthless, unprepared. My training, not physical. Can't defend myself, can't focus enough to make sense of these pages. I scramble away, toward the bookshelf.

Behind, Taia fights for us both. Her arms flail, deadly fists swinging.

As I crawl beneath the shelf, I realize I've lost the book, dropped it behind me. I turn, try to reach. Something grasps my wrist and pulls, drags me into the room. I can't quite see what it is, even as it's lifting me to my feet.

Taia's fighting several at once, whirling in wild-eyed desperation. One of her limbs is seized, then others, constraining her. She can only struggle, mouth contorted in agony. Nothing like herself. Experienced, as if she's done all this before. Also, even as she fights them, I see she's angry, angry at me. I want to help her, try to pull free, but the fluttering thing knocks me down, grasps my ankle, pulls me back. She tried to save me, now I should help her. We might not make it, maybe neither of us.

Just then footsteps approach, not the fluttering of intruders from the gates, but tangible steps, familiar. Mancer rushes in. With a clap of hands, he strikes the midair door. It shuts with a pop. From within his cloak, he draws a thick wand, heavy as a half-staff, and swings it, whirling fast as Taia did before. He strikes one, another of these squalling, half-visible demons.

"Why are you killing them?" I cry. "Aren't they what you meant to bring?"

Mancer swings without looking, again and again. His arms trace fluid arcs of a routine practiced a thousand times before, trajectories planned long before this incursion. When he finally stops swinging, the workroom is quiet. No murmuring, no whispered words, no atmospheric fluctuation.

Mancer hides the half-staff and folds his hands, instantly calm.

Taia joins his side. They're both angry.

Mancer glares. "This isn't what I sought. I told you before, you lack sufficient knowledge to understand, let alone assist. What paths you opened, I tried long ago. I realized my failure, and worked harder. Much trial and error, thousands of hours refining technique. I strengthened, learned. You are still not one tenth what I was when I began. I seek something deeper."

I look to Taia, the muse. She'll tell him I meant well.

Her eyes narrow. No help.

Mancer grips my shoulder, fixes me with his eyes. "I can forgive ignorance or error, but not curiosity. Some things should remain unknown." He turns to depart, stops, turns back. "Except by me."

Relieved, still half-stunned, I start back to my closet. Taia follows, grasps my shoulder. The gesture feels protective, not exactly the sort of contact I hoped earlier to experience with Taia, but now it's just what I need. Comforting.

"I thought that would be our end." I pause, trying to keep my voice from breaking. "I'm sorry." I want to say more, admit how ashamed I feel. I thought I possessed knowledge and skill adequate to handle whatever might come, but I wasn't prepared. I thought I was capable enough, smart enough, to deal with anything.

"You're still a child," Taia says. "It's arrogant and stupid to believe what your child's eyes tell you must be true."

I want to ask her to explain. Everything word she says, always a puzzle, always leaving me craving explanation. Maybe that's what I like about her, that hint of something held back.

I stop outside my door. "Why will Mancer let me remain? I failed."

"Because he sees. Finally your mind is where it should be." Taia's eyebrow lifted. "You were inept, humiliated. Now you'll be less reckless. Realize your smallness, how far removed from the kind of power and attainment necessary to approach... such things."

"But--"

"Now your apprenticeship begins."

I think of something else. "Why not let me see you, the way you really look? Now that I realize how different we are."

"I should let you see." She appeared to consider. "Maybe you would finally leave me alone."

I almost promise, but stop myself. I think she knows. "I want to see."

Usually I can't stop myself staring. Her body, her colorless skin. Now I find her eyes, brilliant pink, white lashes.

Taia seems to study me. It must be the first time we've seen each other this way.

She flips back white hair, which settles near-weightless over her shoulder. "The most useful lesson is understanding the multiplicity of truths you'll never, ever gain." Taia's shape doesn't change, but she leans in, looks at me closer.

Eye to eye, noses almost touching. I feel her breath, see deep into her eyes, see behind them. There I learn with perfect clarity how much more there is, levels deeper than I will ever know. So far removed from the possibilities I understood this morning, emergent into a world entirely changed.

Taia leans in, kisses me with her pale, bloodless lips. I jump, startled. How much has changed?

Mysteries remain. It's better to wonder, to imagine, than to know for sure. I return to my closet, the tiny, dark place where I sleep and work, and learn to live.

Normally she would cut the lancing pain from the sudden rush of blood past too-cold cell membranes with a smoke, but there wasn't enough atmosphere for tobacco to burn, and she was too fresh from cryo to drop nicotine straight. As her heart shuddered lazily back to life, Julia made due with a long drag of reclaimed body moisture, apple flavored and pharma tainted. She floated in the center of the pilot-tank, breathing softly in the cloistered monochrome gloaming of the data feeds wallpapering her photonic-crystaline cell. Augmented reality systems were only just coming online, shimmering out of the darkness like the defrost-cocktail bubbling in her guts. The holo emitters lit up, and the bootlog faded into the soft opalescence of the AR's basemode. Muscle memory played phantoms of the Huntsman humming to life on the other side of the meter deep well of light that surrounded her. Julia blinked frost from her eyelashes and extended her arms. A dynamic regalia of luminous red rings appeared around her wrists, spiraling softly as she navigated menus to find the quaint bakery skin she had picked up from a Galilean bard. She had paused by his tiny stall, a single note in the cacophony of the Callistoan central market, transfixed by the heady aromas of a bakery in full swing wafting from the bard's ARcore. She had wanted it instantly, made the excuse to herself that maybe it would help 'Granny' forgive the things she had said before heading upsystem to the Jovian worlds. She couldn't decide between disgust at her father at mapping his dead mother into an AI persona, or herself for wanting to assuage a machine's bruised ego. The real Granny would have loved the bakery, and that was all that mattered. Julia spun radiant indices until she had the bakery skin and the AR, pressed them together and slapped the lambent amalgam with her palm.

In the implied distance of the holointerface, the Huntsman's operations and systems files assembled themselves as a thousand buns, rolls, muffins, and pastries of every kind. Gauges and datafeeds glistened like sugary trifles in the parade of overstuffed bake cases that marched between dark hardwood pillars. Julia's long empty stomach clenched as a panoply of scents bloomed into being. She turned to face away from the delicious procession and sucked saccharine apple-ish ichor. The forward view screen was a vast plate glass storefront, beyond which the barren depths of the outer solar system clawed at the illusion of light and warmth in the little faux bakery. She had awoken right on target, coming into orbit above her home, but they were radio silent and running dark. In the penumbral abyss between Pluto and Charon, the twin docking beacons of the research station shone brighter than the forest of stars. It was the only sign of life among the stark, polyhedral silhouettes of the station pods in the inky, glacial surface of the little moon.

Julia turned back to the wall of delicious lies and stepped behind the counter. She scanned the grid of buttons on the polished brass mechanical cash register until she found one marked 'COMMS' and stabbed it with her finger. The bake case to her right shuddered, suddenly rearranged into a dozen trays of cupcakes, grouped by band from red velvet optical and infrared down to double-vanilla geomagnetic noise. There was silence for several light-hours. The closest radio signals registering this far out were oort-water mines and the Voyager museum.

"Charon Local 337," she croaked into the comm. "This is L2RH - Huntsman requesting approach vector and docking permissions." She held her breath while the seconds counted off and the station grew in the darkness beyond the storefront. Something was wrong.

"Charon Local 337, please confirm?" Julia moved down the line of bake cases, reading off their burnished copper nameplates until she found the diagnostics. She opened the case, a wicker basket suddenly weighing at her left elbow. She plucked specialist arbiter protocols from a rack of cream-frosted diagnostic expert-systems and dropped them into her basket. Overhead, the selected systems flashed red on a luminous holo of the Huntsman and the two dozen cargo containers she was towing. Julia had always loved the Huntsman, even when it had been nothing but the inert guts of a type 2 Myrmidon. It had been beautiful when they found it spinning derelict out from the plane of the elliptic, with its long sleek cannon and the jagged thruster fins bristling from the pilot-tank's casing. Julia had spent half her youth helping her father rebuild it, listening to his stories of the Jovian civil war. Cargo manifests streamed illegibly at each virtual container as the research station's customs bot validated her haul. Julia paused to squint at the manifests.

"If your customs protocol is online, you've gotta be able to hear me." As Julia bounded back to the communications display, her basket chimed the completion of diagnostics. She found an animated readout sheet among the empty, crumb speckled muffin cups and wrapping papers. Everything checked out, though bio-med flagged her rehydration and muscle response as below normal defrost rate. She threw open the bake case and grabbed the active cupcakes from the laser comm array and slipped them in among the their chocolate-caramel cousins on the UHF tray. Candied systems-integration data streamed down their frosting.

"Charon Local 337, this is L2RH - Huntsman requesting

approach vector and docking permissions." Juliet forced a level tone. Imagined catastrophes teemed at the edges of her thoughts. "I just pulled six days of cryo Granny! I can't handle this." She blurted into the comm.

A third blaze joined the docking beacons as 337's target acquisition laser painted the nose of the Hunstman, pouring autonav data and permissions into the ship's computer.

"Finally." Julia ran her hand along the AR display, gathering up the image of bake cases and bread racks like cloth. She flipped it to basemode, then threw it into the thin air, scattering instruments and indicators. With a few deft gestures, she brought the data suite and tactical systems to fore. Active sensors lit up everything larger than a grain of sand and closer than fifty thousand kilometers. Astrometerics wove the data into her sensorium and the pilot-tank evanesced, leaving the illusion that she was floating in space, slowly spinning towards the hangar pod as she decelerated. There was nothing of significance on the scan. Even the navbouys within a couple of light minutes were quiet. She grabbed the navsys image of her approach, spread it wide with both hands, and pinned it to the air at port. "Bridge command, what's your status?"

As she asked, flood lamps bloomed in the docking bay. The Pluto Special was still dry docked in the shuttle berth, leaving just enough room for the Huntsman in the auxiliary docking harness if she ditched her cargo first. She glanced up at the holo of the pods, laid out in twin rows opposite the tapering length of Huntsman's cannon, each one a month's provision. She tried to position the ship so they would lock onto the outer hull of the station and not just float past, then disengaged the tractor beam.

"Bridge command is currently unavailable." Granny's venerable growl was distorted by the format transition. Julia ground her teeth, fists clenching at the mockery of her grandmother's voice. Too late she realized the AR wouldn't read the gesture as anger. The

Huntsman lurched forwards as aft thrusters burned at full. It's tail fins caught on the docking harness. The cannon skipped off the hull, spinning the ship up, half out of the harness before Julia could open her hands and counter the thrust. But the ship wouldn't move. Its gun was trapped in the airlock gantry. Several thruster fins were tangled in the actuators of cargo loading arms.

Julia closed her eyes and prayed for strength. "Look, just put my father on the line." She snapped and started checking the seals on her suit manually before waving the skin of the pilot-tank aside. When the front wall of the pilot-tank had irised away, it was clear she was in real trouble. The beam emitter at the end of the Huntsman cannon would have to be cut free of the airlock's frame.

"Jacob is currently in the reactor pod."

Julia roared into her helmet as she floated towards the airlock, her fingers trailing down the barrel of the Huntsman's gun . "Look, put me through to a person will you?"

Granny huffed dejectedly on the comm. "I don't think you should talk to me like that anymore." her voice rasped. "It's disrespectful."

"I doesn't mater what you 'think'. You're not real! Just put a human on the line."

There was a moment of disapproving silence on the line, then Granny growled. "No such crew person is available."

"Where the hell is the crew?"

"All registered crew members are in the reactor pod."

Julia froze for a moment as she tapped at the control screen for the outer pressure seals. A tremor welled up from her guts. "What?" From inside bulbous gauntlets, her fingers shook against the cold, dead screen as she tried to enter her authorization. "Granny, why isn't the airlock door responding?"

"The better to prevent unscheduled contact during quarantine."

Julia's heart raced. "Qu.. Quarantine?" The word struggled out of her. Anxious moisture filmed between her skin and the cloying mylar lining of her suit. "There's no broadline about a quarantine." Julia had grown up knowing that life this far out was tenuous. This was the first time it had ever really seemed true. "Am I cleared to come aboard?"

"I don't think that's such a good idea, class 1 isolation protocol is in effect." Granny whined worriedly. "I can't promise you'll be safe, baby."

"I'm not your fucking baby!" Julia shrieked. "My suit is tight. I've got maybe an twenty minutes of atmo left!" She took a deep breath, tried to stop shaking. "Just let me in."

"I'm just trying to keep you safe is all." Granny muttered despondently as the airlock cycled down and the hatch spun open. "I can't help being worried about you..." her voice trailed off to a sad murmur on the comm. Julia clambered in, yanked the emergency atmo rations from the inner wall, and used her reflection on the inner door to aim as she integrated the two white spheres into the thick red metafabric of her suit. When the outer door sealed itself, the station's atmo filtered into the airlock, bringing a haze of bone white fluff drifting in with it.

"Granny?" A film of the stuff formed on Julia's visor. "Why is the station quarantined exactly?"

"Surface mission 22-997 introduced foreign elements to the life support core."

Julia pinched a tuft of the stuff from the filter on the air duct. "Foreign elements?" It was a terrifying prospect, thousands of new diseases had torn through colonies as humanity expanded into alien worlds.

The inner airlock door cycled open. "A fungus like organism." Granny grumbled on the comm. "It calls itself mi-go." The inner airlock door opened.

Julia floated down into the vertical access shaft that ran the length of the station. Linear constellations of emergency lighting ran down the three meter wide tube until they vanished in a well of darkness at the base of the station. "Wait. Calls itself...?" All the hatches Julia floated past were sealed from the outside. "Granny? We had Xeno contact in-system?"

The reactor pod's blast door was sealed, only a sliver of golden light shimmered at the tiny view port. Granny's voice dipped to a whisper. "The mi-go told me that it has inhabited Yuggoth longer than humanity has had culture."

Julia's suit bleeped irritably at the radiation levels and the heat coming off the reactor pod. "What's Yuggoth?" There were muddled life signs readings in there as well, enough to account for the whole crew and then some. "Granny? Why are the crew all sealed in the reactor pod?"

"The better to isolate the infection until the process is complete"

Julia pressed the palm of her gauntlet against the access panel for the reactor pod door controls. She flexed her hand slightly against control relays embedded in the fingertips of her pressure glove. The screws holding the panel in place spun themselves up from their sockets and lay down, magnetized against the hull.

"Huntsman?" There was a chime inside her helmet as a tiny icon in the shape of her ship appeared, like an inverted cartoon t. "Send a quarantine order on the broadline. Unknown xenophange." Julia pulled the main power feed. "Oh, and download Granny. Run some diagnostics on that crazy old bitch." She prized out the wires she was looking for from the rat's nest behind the panel. "But, use an isolated processor." She clipped the two wires she was looking for and tapped the ends together.

The door jumped open. A thick haze of moisture and long alabaster filaments of the pasty fungal spore-fluff poured out like vomit. Julia sucked her breath in sharply. Inside the reactor pod, the circular walls and deck around the reactor were coated in a squirming film the color of bruised flesh through which foamed technicolor masses of fungal polyps oozing heady oils. It enveloped every console and surface, blocking out light and life support. Only the reactor glowed. It was white hot, burning like a tiny sun. It should be erupting, boiling them into an expanding cloud of vapor. Instead, lightning arced from that weird furnace to three pinkish crustacean-things about the size of a man. They hovered, revolving around the shinning orb. Their bodies bristled with limbs, several curled inwards though twin bundles of membranous flesh jutted outwards from each creature's back; they billowed like light fabric on the wind in the streaming light pouring from the reactor. Each creature was crowned by a convoluted ellipsoid swathed in quivering antennae. They seemed lethargic, or sick, in their furtive gesticulations.

Julia's hands started to shake. Her chest ached. Thoughts spilled through her mind in sickening, dysphoric waves. All was silence save the echoing of her ragged, scattered breaths inside her helmet and a kind of high-pitched tone that seemed to be getting closer. Her vision dimmed as a ring of fog consumed her peripheral vision. She slumped against the doorframe and swallowed hard.

Beneath where the alien-things spun softly, there was a ring of deck plating around the reactor that was clear of the putrid, fleshy mass. Circumscribed around the clean plating was a half-meter wide arc of ruddy red, as though some great brush had painted it there. At the leading end of the arc there was a man on his knees, facing away from her. He was stuck to the deck as though gravity were normal and naked from the waste up, his brush-tip pants soaked through with sanguine ink. Arranged neatly on the crimson smear was a length of lumpy, purple-pink tubing that coiled between looping symbols like cursive text. There was no sign of the other crew, only the scattered biosigns from the squishy pink membrane. On her visor the kneeling crewman's dog tags registered. They were displayed floating next to his head. It was her father.

Julia whimpered. She started to rush towards him, but fell forwards as her center of mass shifted towards the deck. What felt like .7G dropped Julia to hands and knees. Her boots and gauntlets squelched through the membrane, spattering gory yellow mush across her torso. It was like puss erupting from an infected scab. She puked into her faceplate. Salty, panicked tears peppered the thin spray of bile. For a few ragged, sobbing breaths she closed her eyes, telling herself it was a dream, that she would wake up in the pilot-tank, groggy from a bad defrost cycle any second. The high pitched ringing grew in her mind, unfolding into a crowd of babbling thoughts demanding that she stand and run, fight, anything. Julia opened her eyes and tried to focus on the spew riming her faceplate. She stood cautiously, her head swimming and looked again at the man.

Her father leaned forwards, the muscles in his back tensing viciously. He lurched upright again, his palsy redoubled. There was a wet sucking sound and he gasped desperately. He heaved once, then began to lay out a fresh length of the tubing in the shape of another glyph. In a daze, Julia waded towards her father, blubbering between limp lips. As she stepped around him, the high tone grew from a whimper to a wail inside the helmet. His face was taut and empty, his eyes a solid glaze of cataracts. In his hands he clasped the grisly length of hose where it emerged directly from his belly. His intestines were uncoiling from a gash in his abdomen.

There was a sound suddenly like a woman screaming as Julia shut down the optical feed on her helmet. Sensor systems painted ghosts of the horror on her visor in hard green wireframes, nightmares pressed down into data points and rendered as simple polygonated shapes. The scream was still going as Julia slung her sidearm towards the thing kneeling in front of her. She scrabbled at the trigger, strobing the room with muzzle flares and a bright, cordite stink. The thing in front of her pulsed with each impact, tilting ever backwards until it flopped to the deck. She stood rigid and quivering until, sometime later, the scream died away.

Julia was hoarse and shaking. There was a ragged rasping to her breaths as she heaved again. There was enough regurgitated apple-sweat in her helmet now that she had to wait for the suit to vacuum it clear before she could take a breath. A bright yellow trefoil flashed on her HUD along with a readout of a near lethal radiation spike. Her sensor systems ran haywire, registering movement all around the reactor, but no image rendering. For three thundering heartbeats she could not make herself clear her visor. The fuchsia shelled monstrosities were already skittering towards her on their many limbs when she did. Their many antennae fluttering; their foremost claws opening.

Julia shrieked. The shaking of her hands set off her sidearm. It flashed twice. There was a burst of chitin and viscous white foam among the many grasping limbs and the murderous crayfish creature fell aside, it's hairy bean of a head more than half exit wound. For an instant the other two creatures paused.

Something in Julia burst. She turned and sloshed through the meaty filth, fighting the aberrant gravity of the reactor pod as fast as she could. She was sprinting by the time she reached the hatch and leapt into the access shaft. In the sudden microgravity her momentum carried her into the far wall. She tried to deflect herself down the access shaft too late. Something popped in her shoulder and she spun down the long meters to the airlock. With each rotation she could see those membranous bundles on the backs of the mi-go expanding, flapping to accelerate them towards her.

"Huntsman!" Julia shouted into her comm.

The tiny icon chimed into being, her only friend in the world.

"Huntsman, fire on this location."

The icon flashed red. Below her dozens of pink husked digits flexed excitedly as the fungal shellfish closed in.

"Emergency override Red Cap." Julia gasped. "Fire damn you!"

There was a light brighter than anything, then the world vanished. Her whole body rang with displaced whorls of electrons. The beam struck like lightning, infinite and overwhelming and then gone. The force of it's passing bounced Julia off the wall. There was no sign of the creatures, only the alternating views of Huntsman waiting above through the peeled and melting remnants of the airlock and the freshly punctured reactor pod below. Within the reactor, a new light bloomed, roiling up the access shaft in syncopated shockwaves that sent Julia reeling into the Huntsman. She just managed to mag-clamp one foot to the ship as the weird gravities below amplified and shifted, pulling everything down.

"Huntsman!" Julia screamed. "Go!" She clamped a hand to the hull as the ship fired its thrusters at a full burn. Loader arms melted in the heat, the last of the airlock gantry tore away as the still searing emitter assembly of the ships cannon slipped free and crashed into the Pluto Special. The shuttle spun away as the Huntsman shoved it's way out of the docking harness and into open space.

Julia scrambled forwards and fell into the pilot-tank wearily. For an instant she was floating alone in the beige nothingness of the tank. Then, the AR left her huddled on the rough oaken floorboards behind the shiny register in the little bakery. Julia clutched at herself and shook, taking long, slow breaths of her dwindling atmo. There was someone there then, an old woman, kneeling next to her, running wrinkled fingers through her hair and shushing her softly.

"It's all right now baby." Her Granny crooned. "I've got you."

Julia couldn't hate the AI here, in the AR while it held her gently, stroking and cooing as her real grandmother had countless times. She could only snivel and gasp as she sank into Granny's virtual lap and let the program snuggle her close.

"I got you a present Granny." Julia mewled incomprehensibly.

"I see dear. It's just like the bakery your grandfather had on Io. Thank you." Granny sighed. "Rest, we're going to have to freeze you again now baby, there's still isn't enough air."

Julia could only nod in acceptance and stare out the plate glass at the store front where a new star was briefly born in the icy skin of Charon. As her metabolism slowed and the cold embrace of emergency cryo crept up from her bones, pushing the pulsing vision away, into the emptiness, Julia imagined that among the twinkling radians of hard radiation she could see hundreds of streaming limbs flailing fervently at the emptiness of the void.

The Lost Book of Grimm
– Michael M. Hughes –

The Lost Book of Grimm: Hermeneutics, Intertextuality, and Psychocthonian Extrusions into Objectivity

Michael M. Hughes, PhD, Independent Scholar

The 2008 discovery of *Das Verfluchte Buch* (popularly known as *The Lost Book of Grimm*, but more accurately translated as the *Damned* or *Cursed Book*) has provided an enormous amount of new primary material of interest to scholars across a wide array of disciplines, including linguistics, philology, anthropology, and folklore. Despite the near-uniform rejection of the manuscript's legitimacy by leading Grimm scholars upon its discovery in the archives of an anonymous private collector, the recent authentication (via Furnow et al., 2010) leaves no uncertainty that this collection of "damned" folk tales was compiled by Jacob and Wilhelm Grimm for their own personal collections, but considered unsuitable for publication. As the first philologist to work from the original text (now in the special collections of the Humboldt University of Berlin) I have unearthed links between the *Verfluchte* manuscript and an obscure pagan cult (most notably chronicled in *Unaussprechlichen Kulten* by Friedrich Wilhelm von Junzt (1839), Düsseldorf edition). My philological/ anthropological exploration of the "unspeakable" or "nameless" cults received a chilly reception from academics (Ribeiro, 2010; Knowles et al., 2012; Wells, 2013) but has not, in my estimation, been refuted.

Several tales in the *Verfluchte* stand out as particularly unsettling. *Tolheit des Raben*, or "The Madness of the Crow," is the story of a young farmer's son, Otto, who meets an anthropomorphized talking crow in the woods. The crow promises to teach the boy the secrets of nature, and in one darkly poetic passage, compels him to consume a brew composed of a number of psychoactive plants (*die Heilkräuter*) (*Hyoscyamus niger, Solanum ducamara,* and *Mandragora officinarum,* among others associated with witchcraft and sorcery) to "open his eyes" to the underlying reality of the cosmos:

> "Now eat the plants I have brought to you, which will open your eyes," said the crow. The boy made a fire and boiled the crow's gifts in his pot [*der kleine Kochtopf*], then drank it all down because he was thirsty for knowledge, having been mocked as stupid [*dumm*] by the children of his village. Then the woods grew dark, and the sun and stars turned black as coal, and the boy fell to his knees weeping. "There is nothing," he cried. "No secrets. Nothing but emptiness." [*Keine Geheimnisse—nichts außer Leere.*]

When the boy is discovered wandering outside his village, the peasant woman who finds him screams in horror—his eyes have been pecked out by the crow, leaving only empty, black sockets. The story ends with the boy finding happiness, however, working in his father's fields as a living scarecrow.

Other stories hint at the presence of a secretive (occult, i.e., "hidden") cult, which I have linked to the organization known as the *Unaussprechlichen Kulten,* or unspeakable cult (as explicated, however cryptically, in von Jundst). Although the historicity of this cult has been challenged (Hanegraaf, 2009; Kripal, 2012; Leonard and George, 2013) I have shown indirect but compelling evidence of its continued existence and traced its migration from Europe to the United States (Hughes, 2013, *Journal of American Folklore*). The account of my brief, personal contact with an alleged cultist in December of 2012 was redacted from the paper without my consent (and, it should be noted, the editorial board of the *Journal of American Folklore* has refused to address my letters of complaint).

The first and most blatant cultic signifier occurs in *die Frau des Schneiders* ["The Tailor's Wife"]. Hilda, a pretty, fair-haired tailor's wife, discovers her newlywed husband performing occult rituals *[die Rituale]* in a hidden room beneath his shop. Philologists and scholars of German have so far been unable to translate the names mentioned in the ritual, and it has been suggested (Woermann, 2012) that Jacob and Wilhelm Grimm simply spelled them phonetically because their source(s) related the names in what the brothers believed to be meaningless syllables. It should be noted that one of the names, *Gatanoto*, is remarkably similar to *Ghatanothoa*—an entity described in *Unaussprechliche Kulte* and—tellingly—in a modern ritual communicated to me by my cultist contact (Hughes, 2013, unpublished personal correspondence).

Hilda's sudden onset of mental illness, while dismissed by Paula Hessel (Hessel, 2011) as a "typical exaggerated caricature of feminine psychological fragility filtered through Wilhelm's de rigeur misognistic gaze" is, in fact, a common fate of other characters in the *Verfluchte* who also fall prey to instantaneous or accelerated insanity —including young Otto (see above), the unnamed girl in *Die Frau, die mit den Fröschen spricht* [The Girl who Spoke to Toads], as well as an entire village populace upon the discovery of ancient standing stones in *Die Leute vom Schwarzen Stein* [The People of the Black Stones]. Insanity is, in fact, *the* major recurring trope in the *Verfluchte*.

My unpublished 2013 paper, in which I sought to verify and correlate the similarities between the ritual fragments mined from the *Verfluchte*, the *Unaussprechlichen Kulten*, and a modern version communicated to me privately by the alleged member of the extant cult, was largely unsuccessful. However, in a moment of insight, I intuited that the *Verfluchte* was not simply a collection of folktales— rather, it was a magical grimoire *disguised* as a book of common folktales (and note Wilhelm's playful homonymous clue in Grimm/ grimoire). This critical exegesis has occupied my studies (and precipitated my decision to leave the confining restrictions of the academy for independent research).

My experiments provided remarkable experiential verification of the *Verfluchte Buch's* practical efficacy as a grimoire of little-understood magical [cf. Crowley's "magick"] technologies. The reconstruction of what I now understand to be a primordial ur-ritual—pieced together by mapping the intertextuality between the *Verfluchte, Unaussprechlichen Kulten,* and the modern text—facilitated contact with atavistic elements embedded within my persona—archaic psychic complexes with unusual real-world effects that I describe (Hughes, 2014, unpublished) as *psychocthonian extrusions into objectivity.* My ingestion of a carefully formulated psychotropic plant admixture (as listed in *Tolheit des Raben*) was the crucial catalyst for the activation of the phenomena. In an effort to carefully replicate the proscribed setting, I located an arrangement of standing stones—a remarkable rock structure known as the "Hand" (a loci of considerable folkloric power) in rural West Virginia. The precise astrological timing was calculated using Solar Fire Gold 8™ software (Astrolabe Inc., Brewster, MA).

The initial ritual invocation, performed under a new moon and as reconstructed from my painstaking comparative poetic/analytic hermeneutics, resulted in a constellation of extraordinary phenomena I am still attempting to classify. The concretization of psychic manifestations (including but not limited to rushing wind and other aberrant atmospheric phenomena, marks on the body, and dramatic alterations of local flora and fauna), and the inflorescence (or "download") of novel temporal/spatial insights accompanied by visual *ursprache* eruptions of glossolalia, pose extreme challenges orthodox naturalistic ontologies. In the dismissals of critics, my experiences were derided as "pseudo-Castaneda drivel" [Myers] and "drug-addled . . . schizophrenic word salad" [Nickell]). Nontheless, and despite the failure of all recording equipment, the phenomena I have documented demand rigorous analysis—not just via the lens of science, but from philosophy, theology, psychology, biology, cosmology, and physics.

The occurrences related in my report argue for the creation of a novel, revolutionary metaphysics in light of their unassailable refutation of scientific reductionism and Materialism. Hence, the academy's rejection, marginalization—and *refusal to even acknowledge* —my extensively documented account was not unanticipated. I am encouraged, however, by the popularity of the manuscript among the so-called "occult underground." Ongoing accounts by lay-scholars and self-described ritualists who have followed my protocol have proven enormously popular; statistics on torrent aggregator websites (Fraser, 2014) show my report to be the most frequently downloaded document under the categories of "occult" and "magic." This global network of independent scholars are doing the real work, unencumbered by the shackles of outdated science and superstition, and their experiences reshaping and refining the *Verfluchte Buch's* encoded rituals are opening up vast new avenues to transdimensional gnosis and communion with extraplanar entelechies.

Acknowledgments: I would like to thank the Miskatonic library special collections staff, Christopher Mullins of Shamanic PlantTech®, and my anonymous contacts in the *Unaussprechlichen Kulten.* And a special note of thanks to those pioneers (you know who you are) who have continued to explore this primordial path of revolutionary revelation.

Hey Robert: You have to read this! At first I thought it was a joke or a Sokal-style prank, but Hughes has a solid track record and has published some very good papers, so I actually think he's sincere. Which is scary! I rejected it (of course!) but I asked for his recent paper because this shit is so fucking nuts. Apparently he's off-the-grid or locked up—I can't track him down, and the university said he'd been arrested a while back—but I got a copy of the paper by snail-mail yesterday, no return address. Scanned copy attached. This puts all the other stuff in the crank file to shame, and it's 47 pages of pure whack-a-doodle! Enjoy. :)

—Augie

Dear Augie,

Wow. That's a keeper. Definitely one for the crank file but so very well-written (and surprisingly compelling)! It almost makes me want to try out his "ritual practices for psychocthonian extrusions into objectivity." LOL.

I'm off until next Thursday on a camping trip. I'm taking the paper along to read to Margi by the campfire. If we find some standing stones, and I don't come back, I blame you!

Best,

Robert

Sent from my iPhone

The Hound of Kn-Yan
- Jeff C. Carter -

May 7, 1901
Lady I.A. Gregory
Coole Park,
Cori,
Co. Galway.

Lady Gregory, *A Chara*,

Enclosed please find a copy of some newly discovered materials to aid you in your work on the legends of Cúchulainn. A local farmer in the Hebrides Islands recently unearthed these documents sealed in a metal cylinder engraved with Pictish symbols and buried in a prehistoric mound.

When translated from the Old Irish, these fragments appear to be an alleged first-hand account of *Compert Chon Culainn*, the birth of Cúchulainn.

The account was inscribed on the last pages of The Book of Invasions. Naturally, the Gaelic League gives no credence to the pagan fantasies contained therein. Some of the sundried events described may be poetic figments, a few are probable, others improbable, yet most seem invented for the delectation of fools.

We pray that you will see past the heretical elements and glean some useful details or context from this manuscript.

Mise le meas mor.

Douglas Hyde, LL.D., Litt.D.

President

Conradh na Gaeilge

The Gaelic League

———

'Twas I that destroyed the hero, Cúchulainn.

I am Anann Mac Ciall, last bondmaid of Sualtaim mac Róich, and this is my confession. May the gods have mercy on my soul.

To give sooth to the words I write, I must first tell you of Tuan, forefather of my clan. 'Twas Tuan that first journeyed across the western sea. 'Twas Tuan that first travelled beneath the mound into *Ildathach*, the multicolored place. 'Twas Tuan that first discovered the hidden land of the *Tuatha Dé*, the supernatural race that men nowadays call Faery folk.

The Tuatha Dé gave Tuan a vision of how they came to our land, long before the first man. They arrived in dark clouds that blackened the sun for three days and three nights. The legends would have you believe that the Sons of the Gael came to this land and drove them out. Forsooth the Tuatha Dé had moved underground ages before to escape the great floods that washed over the earth.

The Tuatha Dé were eager to know of the surface world, and whether 'twas safe to reclaim. Tuan spun wild stories of the Roman's gods and their merciless armies in the hopes of sowing fear. The Tuatha Dé chose then not to rise, for immortals have great patience.

They gave him an enchanted ring bound to their ancient god Tulu, and with it, Tuan lived far beyond his mortal years. He was both hostage and honored guest, and they instructed him in strange feats and forgotten rituals. He was free to explore their blue-lit land, down to the red-lit realm beneath, and the black pit deeper still.

Tuan accompanied a party of explorers down to the center of the earth, and there they found horrors beyond imagining. There were idols of ancient and terrible gods, protected by beings with invincible flesh that flowed like water. The monsters swarmed the Tuatha Dé, giving Tuan a single chance to escape Ildathach.

Generations had passed, but Tuan found his way home to my ancestors and imparted all that he had learned. He gave them the ring of Tulu, and when it left his person, the forestalled years crashed upon him like a wave, and he crumbled into dust.

Each head woman of my clan has seen a hundred harvests, thanks to the enchanted Tulu ring, and we have preserved some measure of knowledge about the Tuatha Dé. The ring protects us from the Unseelie Court, those evil spirits of dreaming Tuatha Dé that wander the world to foretell deaths and sow misrule. It is with this accursed ring that I begat, and ended, Cúchulainn's life.

The story proper is this, which follows now.

One winter, during the reign of King Conchobar of Ulster, my Lady Deichtine grew wide with child. I tended to her as mid-wife, but the gods saw fit not to breathe life into the babe. My Lady's heart was shattered, and she keened in such a way that I was sure she would follow her babe into the next life.

I knew of a way to restore to my Lady that which she had lost. My grandmother had taught me how to summon a changeling, in such ways that the Tuatha Dé might exchange a mortal's child for one of their own.

The legends say that Cúchulainn was born on the famous burial mound of Brú na Bóinne, and it is nearly true. While the Tulu ring is drawn to the hidden gateways of Ildathach, 'twas drawn to Brú na Bóinne not at all. Instead, the ring guided me, my Lady and our tiny burden across the ocean to the western isles, where the ruins that rise from the sea were old long ere the mounds of Ireland were formed.

The ring nearly throttled me as it dragged me to the place where I should lay the babe to rest. A circle of giant stones guarded the entrance to the mound, each graven with terrible serpents and many armed fish from the sea. I prayed to the ancient host that an exchange was possible for our cold and ashen offering.

On the morrow, I found the boy child mewling where I had laid it. The night before the clean dead form had been white as snow in one night fallen. 'Twas now in a pool like Parthian crimson and wrapped in a sack of thick ebon flesh. I had seen dogs born in such wise, and babes veiled in the caul, but in all my years as mid-wife, naught had I seen the like.

I tried to cut the caul away but it rippled and jumped in my hands. When I peered into the wailing babe's face, the oily black skin melted and withdrew into its tiny body. It soon resembled Lady Deichtine's child in most respects. 'Twas only years later that I recalled how the changeling had reflected my face as well.

I gasped when it first opened its eyes. The boy had seven pupils, and upon inspection showed seven toes on each foot and seven fingers on each hand.

Lady Deichtine snatched the crying babe from my arms. I was certain that my Lady would look at the changeling and know the trickery I had wrought, but she wept and pulled the babe to her bosom. She named the child Sétanta.

We made sail for the House of Sualtaim mac Róich in County Louth. By the time we arrived on the Plain of Muirthemne the babe was as fair in form as any I had ever seen.

When we brought Sétanta home, the beasts and cattle ran riot. Sualtaim mac Róich did not see this as an ill omen, so overjoyed was he to behold his heir. We rid the land of its hounds and life was good thereafter.

I was Séntanta's nurse night and day, and as such was the only one to notice anything strange. When he grew irritable or cried, his skin would turn bright red and scalding hot. He could scream for hours, and would not be content until fed large amounts of black pudding. Over the years, I mastered the art of soothing his outbursts with lullabies and quelling his savage temper with the strings of a lute.

Sétanta grew fast into a bold gilla, renowned throughout Ulster for his marvelous feats of strength and skill.

One day Culain the Smith invited the boy to a great feast. I was unable to stop the lad from tarrying on the hurling field and we arrived late, after the feast had begun. Alas, Culain had forgotten his invitation and loosed his giant Spanish wolfhound.

The Smith's baneful dog bayed at the sky and bared its teeth at us. The rapacious hound was taller than us at the shoulder and said to possess the strength of hundreds. Young Sétanta, though he was unarmed, snarled back and charged the beast. I shut my eyes and screamed, certain we would surely perish.

There was a sound of tearing flesh and a blood curdling cry. When I chanced to look, I beheld Sétanta's wild contortions. One eye had bulged wider than the rim of a chalice, and the other had fallen down his cheek. His crimson hair jutted out like thorns, his back swelled like a sail in the wind and his skin twisted around his stretching limbs. A dozen clawed fingers sprouted from each hand as they coiled around the wolfhound's body.

Séntanta unleashed a lion roar and dropped his jawbone to his waist. A great bony spear erupted from his throat and pierced the beast's skull. From the spear burst seven barbs, and every barb sprouted seven more, until they had invaded every vein and sinew of the wolfhound and shredded it to ribbons.

A great clamor arose inside the hall as Culain's guests struggled to unlock the door. A powerful revulsion swept over me at the thing Séntanta had become. He was my charge and I was bound to serve him. More so, he had saved my life. 'Twas a marvelous feat, that an unarmed boy could defend himself from a beast twice his stature. I could not allow the men of Ulster discover him such wise.

I stilled my galloping heart and sang my sweetest lullaby. The childhood song, combined with the satisfaction of hot blood in his gullet, soothed the lad forthwith. The door flew open and Culain the Smith ran out. He doubtless expected to find us torn apart by his hound, and not the other way around.

The guests marveled at Séntanta's manful deed. Culain was grateful that we were unharmed, but lamented the loss of his friend and most able guardian. Séntanta offered to guard the Smith's home until a new pup was reared, and that was how he came to be called Cúchulainn, the hound of Culain.

In the years that followed, Cúchulainn's strength grew fifty fold, as did his manful deeds. In his twelfth year, he became a knight of the Red Branch. In his fifteenth year, he was one of the greatest champions of Ulster. He became the doom of foes and the terror of great hosts. In the grip of battle madness, he slew kith and foe alike, and yet the more bloodthirsty his deeds the more the men of Ulster cheered him.

Poets spun odes to his excellence in horsemanship, in single combat, and in plundering from the neighboring borders. The minstrels sang of how there was naught his equal in size and splendor, shape and power, or strength and feats of valor.

King Cochran gave free reign to the slaughter, until he was well pleased that all beyond his borders dreaded the name Cúchulainn.

I tell you also that Cúchulainn's beauty increased in reflection of every handsome man he met. In such wise, he became unsurpassed in form, shape and build. He was the desire of every woman in Ulster, and tales of his enchanting countenance spread across the seas.

'Twas princess Derbforgaill of Lochlann that brought doom to

Ulster's women. Cúchulainn, Lady Deichtine and I set out to meet the fair Princess. I will not proclaim the length of her golden hair or the glow of her cheeks. I will say only that she was a great beauty, and more the pity for the fate that befell her.

When she arrived in Ulster, thrice fifty women were there to meet her, until all the lasses and ladies of marriageable age had gathered beneath one roof. The darkest rumors say that they killed the princess out of jealousy. When Cúchulainn found her slain, he fell into a rage and shattered the pillar stones to smite them all in revenge. I wish that even so grim a tragedy were the truth.

Cúchulainn was there, but 'twas lust, not jealousy that destroyed the women. The hound of Culain bedded them all. Those that survived the savage congress did not so the fruits of their labors. The painful cries of birth and death filled the night and the Plain of Muirthemne became unto a river of blood.

I will not describe what happened to my Lady, but I swore to the gods that I would never serve as mid-wife again. I knew then that I had brought a monster into the world. Worse still, I saw that Cúchulainn might one day succeed in planting his evil seed and rearing others of his brood.

Sualtaim went to King Conchobar and took the blame for the massacre. Conchobar ordered Sualtaim beheaded, but not for the foolish reason given in the tales. It is said that Saultaim was executed when he spake out of order before the king and his druids. In sooth, his death was a way to appease the grieving families of Ulster and maintain the honor of its greatest champion.

Conchobar arranged a marriage betwixt Cúchulainn and the beautiful Emer of Leinster. Chieftan Forgall the Dexterous, her father, knew the fate of the other women and would not allow it. Before he would consent, he bade Cúchulainn first go through Dun Scaith, the warrior school of the barbarous northern isles, in the hopes that he would die in the attempt.

'Twas in the North that Cúchulainn met Aife, a Pictish warrior woman strong enough to bear his seed. When Cúchulainn returned, Forgall locked Emer away in a tower. Even the legends tell it true how Cúchulainn stormed the fortress, slew twenty four guards, and threw Forgall from the ramparts.

Aife arrived at my door soon after, deep in the pangs of labor. I could not save poor Aife's life, and try as I may, I could not steal it from the babe. The creature was born with seven pupils in each eye and seven fingers on each hand. I fed it poison and burned it with fire, but naught would vanquish the changeling spawn.

At last, I crafted a plot to destroy Cúchulainn once and for all. I named the boy Connla and raised him in secret, never revealing who his father was. Connla grew up quick, possessed of incredible strength like his sire. I sent him to Dun Scaith to learn the arts of combat and strife from Aife's sister.

When Connla was ready, I bade him to challenge Cúchulainn. The champion of Ulster haply greeted the upstart at the border. I watched the battle from afar and prayed that the abominations would each slay the other.

They collided in spectacular combat, and afore long both shed all human aspect. They transformed into galloping masses of shrieking, gnashing flesh. Glaring eyes boiled across their skin and their flesh surged like river rapids in spring. They clashed like dragons, and the heat of their fury and roars of their pain echoed over all the countryside.

The Father hewed his son in twain. The son gnawed and mangled his father to deal great affliction. It seemed as though the monsters had laid waste to one another until Cúchulainn vomited his barbed spear. With it, he impaled Connla. I felt my own heart break as Cúchulainn ripped his son inside out and devoured him.

The men of Ulster witnessed Cúchulainn's transformation. Instead of fleeing in terror, the fools composed quatrains about his invincibility in battle and dubbed him *siabartha*, the distorted one.

Knowing that I could find naught in Ulster to assist me, I travelled beyond its borders. I persuaded Queen Medb in the neighboring province of Connacht to wage war. Fergus mac Róich, the exiled king of Ulster, mustered his troops to our cause. In addition to these hosts, there came legions of goodly Gaels who desired naught but revenge on the scourge called Cúchulainn.

Cúchulainn met our army at a narrow fjord and invoked the rite of single combat. Thus was he able to slay Connacht's champions one at a time, in a grueling battle that lasted for weeks. Bodies were crushed, cleaved and stacked like walls on the field of combat. The rivers filled with blood and grew clogged with severed heads.

This slaughter was part of my plan. The multitudes of knights and retainers, with their chariots, spears and swords were naught but bait. I knew that neither points nor edges of weapons could harm the changeling, and so I endeavored to destroy him with succor.

I waited until Cúchulainn was spent from battle to let fly my final attack. I snuck into Cúchulainn's camp in the dead of night. I was an old crone by then, but Cúchulainn remembered me and the tender nurture I had provided in his youth. I offered him a feast he could not deny, a flank of fresh dog meat. His jaw gaped down to his chest and he swallowed the bloody slab whole, and with it the Tulu metal ring planted inside.

The ring held instant sway over Cúchulainn. It drew him thence from the field of battle to the ill-fated mound of his birth. I had a chariot ready to take us to the ship that would bare us across the western sea.

Cúchulainn said not a word as he splashed across the drowned plains, sprouting fingers and tendrils as he went. He uprooted the trees and dashed the boulders that had collected in front of the rune scarred entrance. I watched in horror and relief as he let slip his mortal guise and flowed through the narrow hole, back to his womb in the earth.

The gathered years crash fast upon me as I write these final words. I wanted to save Ireland from the terror I unleashed on her shores. I wanted to dispel the glamour of Cúchulainn's legend and lay bare his bloody deeds. Now as my flesh withers and my sight grows dim, I realize I have doomed us all.

I have returned to blue-lit Ildathach their greatest spy, battle hardened and learned in the ways of man. How long ere they raise an army of the formless things? How long before the final chapter of this Book of Invasions is penned in mankind's blood?

The Case of Virgin Mary Smith
- L. K. Feuerstein -

August 9, 1928: I heard a strange raving outburst in the parlor of Professor Marshall Eddington, a curiosities and antiquities restoration enthusiast with a great deal of wealth from his expeditions. While I waited, the short, thin woman nearly yanked her auburn hair out in howling fervor addressing the other members of the staff. I had been waiting in a chair bound in the corner of the room near a cup of English Breakfast tea, and it was not until much later that the women realized I had been party to their aggressive gossip.

The initial and nearly incomprehensible tidbits came from a Mrs. Lydia Smith, whose sister had died of unknown causes in a meadow where a unicorn had been rumored slayed days earlier. I would have dismissed the tale as hearsay female frivolity had she not mentioned that her sister barely knew how to read or write, but had written down disturbing memoirs of the one-horned animal before her strange passing. Ms. Smith had temporarily placed her sister Mary's memoirs in the care of Professor Eddington. Although she'd brought them to him to dictate so that she would understand her sister's plight, he convinced her to decline her curiosity. He decided it best after a few passages that to preserve Lydia's delicate mind, he need not torture herself with the violent ravings of Mary. Had she requested the documents back, he had considered burning them for fear of corrupting other minds.

I was only in Westport, Connecticut in connection with a small conference on statues and idols being attended by myself and the professor. However, after walking in on such half-spoken fearful conversation, I could not help plot to see the memoirs of the late Miss Mary Smith. I broached the subject lightly with Marshall over cigars later that evening, at which time his brandy and sleep deprivation led him to leave the memoirs in my care. What I read bred terrifying curiosity and stipulated investigation.

Here is the tale as written from the young virgin from the perspective of a one-horned beast she allegedly aided in slaying:

THE UNICORN'S STORY – A BEGINNING

You think you see them—out of your eye's corner. They may have been, just there, a moment ago, a few moments from now, but never quite, and certainly never now. He called them sages. Years ago my brother went looking for them, yet he refused my offer to help him.

"Stay invisible," he said, "Stay in the forest. Stay alive."

I listen often to the countryside's peasants—the day to day tributes and escorts abounding to fulfill the newfangled rituals of time. They look for signs long past whilst trying to move forward.

A bride in an elegantly overstated tiara waits steadily in the forest for a unicorn—an old myth to beget a blessing from a horned beast who may visit a virgin bride, predicting a fruitful marriage with imminent prosperity.

I cannot tell you anything about prosperity. I do not visit the townspeople or the courtiers, the people we followed here from older lands to find new forests to dwell in and protect. Some people believe we led their cause, bringing the blessing of the alicorn across continents to heal a new and changing empire, but we too have always been searching.

I was never and I am always. I battle my unnatural curiosity of the aberrant and abysmal shadows that have become my forest. I know about my territory in the light, but stray away from the darkness in water, stark winter, and the high hidden rocks protruding only slightly from my meadows surrounding mountain cliffs.

You do not understand the alicorn and you will find the unicorns have no singular origin in earth's history. Some will tell you how to capture us, but our truth resides in the traces of light scattered by the soul's mirror. Some light and some darkness can only be seen out of the corner of your eye. I do not recommend seeking those visions. The true ugliness of evil and beauty of light are often shaded in the same gray area--a sight both frightening and wonderful enough to seal a man's heart to cease.

I have watched many venture toward the novelty, but recently I crossed paths with a peculiar gentleman seeking fortune in the darker parts of the forest. He lived near the edge of the forest in a small estate with his large family, and his ventures led me to find things I cannot unsee. He never glimpsed me against the backdrop of atrocities partaking of his ignorance. He is the only person I have ever touched with my alicorn.

This is the story of my cursed burden through the eyes of a man so darkly affected; he was blind to my presence even as I saved him. These were his thoughts as he recanted the things half-seen in the forest:

THE FATHER'S STORY – UNWINDING

It was my son's life I needed to make sense of. Chip was the youngest male Abbott. He was the strongest leader and never seemed afflicted with an overactive sense of self-importance or cruel abundance of curiosity.

I was taking my sunrise Sunday stroll along the eastern path of the family gardens when I saw massive amounts of blood clumped through the bushes and dotting thick strands along the dirt path. The ground almost eerily produced steam and coagulated with the red masses, creating a ghost-like appearance that palpitated my heart at an exponential rate as my walk increased from a steadied stroll to a panicked run toward the source of the monstrosity laying next to a form occupied by my son's wild eyes.

In one hand, he adamantly clenched what looked like a knife; a solemnly florescent dagger with abnormal green coloration and ornate but opaque stone carvings. I almost cannot bear to remember in the other hand—which bore the half-present body of his baby sister, Margaret—her blood coating the pathways, staining the garden at his feet. The hand bearing the knife was his only clean appendage, the blood coating his person, myself awestruck in the nameless, accursed horror no father should witness.

My eyes fixed on that bloodless blade. It glimmered mysteriously, a warm angry edge gleaming in triumph over a stone. I felt it was meant to cleave against the pure sacrificial water from my innocent daughter, filling nature with unnatural infant's blood. Its loathsome form freezing my body into painted silence, entrapped in a moment where I could not fear death, only affix my eyes to my youngest boy covered in the blood of my newest born daughter.

I thought about the stories about monsters I read to them; wolves in the forest, a young maiden waiting for a flock of sheep to cross a stream, and the small expected tragedies of children in the wilderness. I could not shift my focus. This tragedy bewitched my simple fact heart. I could not discern if the young man of my flesh was truly alive or if he was to commit patricide. Was he a madman and a murderer or an innocent child entrapped in a witch's curse?

I woke up later in the evening, my skin cold to the touch, calling out for my family, but the night was silent, stark, and moistened by the taste of water condensing on bloodied stones. I do not know if my son had seen me there. I do not know if his sister's death weighed upon his soul. I do not know if I had been intended dead, but as I surveyed my small stead, I felt as I had staring into the knife. A dark fascination came upon me. A combination of hatred, relief, admiration, and disgust haunted me, every step taking me closer to my home. As I reached the entrance, I was guided forward, a pale man nearly sleeping and edging toward the top of the tower.

There, I succumbed to a primordial reaching darkness, holding me stiff in the air, plunging me into thoughtlessness. My eyes flew open, the gore of the glistening, bloodless knife tattooing its image into my every sight. I was aware as my home and the rest of my family burned to the ground, but I did not see it. Only the knife was on my eyes as I heard the screams and felt the fire brush everything away. At the end of it all, I was just standing, on the grass, alone.

It was dawn. My murdered daughter, my disturbed son, dispersed somewhere in the wind and ash. My disoriented walk and perusal of the newspaper documented a fire in my home, no expected survivors; yet I walked in the woods. Now I needed answers. I wanted to absolve myself through seeking the answers to questions that may likely be asked later. For now, hiding was my only option.

I shrugged. There was a large scar on my shoulder. I thought a few moments. I could not find accurate or studious contemplation to aide me in explaining the deaths of my family nor my survival. I set off deeper into the forest to avoid interviews. I passed through clean areas, animal habitation, until I did not feel alone anymore.

I stopped to rest midday in a small meadow. The forest fell deathly quiet without a birdsong in earshot. The grass seemed to sparkle in short, indescribable shimmering, like the ocean in a soft breeze. I slept in the meadow until darkness fell upon me.

In sleep, I began to dream.

There was a man walking on stairs of ink black stone that was quartered and halved, creating only what I could imagine the labyrinth of a greater minotaur from the ancient cultures would look like. It was uncomfortably smooth, beautiful, and racing against my efforts for restfulness. I became afraid of the dark.

There was always something in the light, but I did not dream of it. Only the cold stone, with the door or gates at the abysmal creation of the netherworld, could compare to my deepest felt horrors and losses of the day. I may have stayed in the meadow for days or weeks. I had no concern for food or human interaction – I wanted to find the knife my son had used. I kept falling into the catastrophic stone obelisk and steps – staring into the stark, black undertones for the answers to questions I feared asking.

Were all of their bodies in the fire?

The meadow nourished me. The curse of searching leading to knowing the full extent of the horror-some life in which I'd just been cast, left me sleeping there; a long undeserved surprise for the devil just laid in the grass, awaiting execution.

I was once a good man with a decent family, a versatile plot of land, and humble estate that may have become more had my heirs continued. Headlines for a psychotic, murderous rampage and familial extinction might bear my name.

Distracted by horses, in the wind I saw a watery elastic agent, spewing nature with grotesque, oblique, dark strands as large as ponytails. I saw slimy horses' tails in only one part and big black eyes. I saw wings, and a bloody hand resting in the squirming snakelike beard of the creature standing in front of me. I saw the black stone again.

Silent screams of desperation lifted from my lungs and other beings of the forest, a panic fondled by shadows waiting to suck the light from the soul as blood soaked my hands. Fire set to my hair, and my own shrieking began to sound beautiful as I touched a hand dangling there, it rose from the center of hair almost lifted by a dark mud rising into the air. It calmed my asphyxiation as if I was resting by the mouth of the sea.

I saw star-burned stone covered by long legs and pulsating eyes. I grabbed at cold air and fainted. The last thing I saw was a spiral of golden shell, poignant against the burning sky.

I smelled ash, and then truly awoke as myself again. I'd survived

three weeks in the meadow not nearly alone with the shadows and light that will forever occupy my nightmares.

THE UNICORN'S STORY – AN ENDING

We survived the bloodiest day in Westport. He did not know it was a unicorn that saved him in the meadow. He had never heard of the alicorn's magical properties or attempted to capture one of us. He is the only man to have drained my alicorn's magic to be healed. He was the only reason that I have come up to humanity or lent aide. And it was because of that decision on that day that I am here---awaiting my execution.

After saving the father, I rested my head in the lap of a beautiful thirteen year old virgin. I rested a long while as I dreamed of the hideous and unnatural shadows of the past weeks. She was a servant girl, and had enough kindness in her heart to be a princess ten times over.

As some of the poison from the experience drained from me, I saw in her young face the horror of ancient mysteries too incomprehensible to share. Her eyes darted as the man's had, as if staring into that unbloodied yet murderous knife.

And in that realization, we were surrounded by a pen. Without time to remove the curse I'd disposed in her comfort, she was removed from the iron cage.

As I'd slept, the enclosure was built around me, and I am here with this silent, pale child, awaiting my execution for harvest of my body and horn – if only I had listened to my brother.

I could still read parts of her soul—she'd been promised a sweet pet if she sat down in the meadow. She had experienced her first horror and betrayal in one day. Did she know that we unicorns fight against forces older than time? Could she see any beguiling selfish acts, or hear villainous hearts beating in the leaders of her town and her country? Had she seen where we came from? Why we were here? Would I remain an unrecognized inkling in the book of time because I stayed with a grieving father?

Sometimes poison is of the mind and I could only remove so much.

Those details he needed to remember that time had passed would remain, but I took away the evil poisoning of the black rock, and dark madness which man cannot comprehend. My horn was drained, my life will be lost, and now, I will lose my soul for placing such evil within an innocent.

I thought timelessness made me weary, but here, about to be absorbed and finished after an unrest sleep has trapped me into a cycle of simultaneous indescribable moments of the past that is, the now that was, and the future that may be.

This is how most battles are lost: magic is lost to the beauty of the innocent for the sake of an old, grieving fool.

MARY WROTE

The only remaining text read, *"Help me."*

It sent chills down my spine as I inquired with the good professor if I might keep the girl's memoir with my other strange writing, but he refused and asked for its return. I took time to inquire around town of the disappearances and rumors in the story, but I was unable to obtain any empirical backing. Before planning to return to Newport, as a last resort, I ventured into an apothecary, and noticed a bottle on the shelf. The shelf was newly dusted and there was a green bottle clearly labeled 'Unicorn's Alicorn'. I asked the shopkeeper what ailments he would use the contents for.

He told me that the history of unicorns only confirmed they were rare creatures—most cultures had a form of the beast and only two things remained consistent. When I looked him in the eyes, awaiting a reply, he gulped and shrugged his shoulders.

"The unicorn can be attracted by a virgin woman, and the horn possesses magic and healing properties." I nodded in acknowledgement, but the price for the horn was too extravagant for a professor returning home. I went to the local library and was unable to discern the origin of the unicorn mythos, or the credence in Mary Smith's account of the unicorn's story.

Although the sister had relayed that her sister had died, I was uncertain as to whether she had actually passed away, as there had been no obituary or plan for funeral services. I bought three white roses and went to the Smith home to seek out the virgin or pay my condolences to the family.

When I got to the estate on Farmer's Landing, the doors and shutters were all closed. The house creaked in the slight wind and there was no answer to my knocks at the door. I was about to leave the home, when the police chief came to the home upon suspicion of breaking and entering. He stood next to me at the front and then he slowly twisted the door knob. On the walls, floor, and ceiling, there was black ink depicting asymmetrical stone walls, large eyes, tentacles, and dark shadows drawn into corners full of blood in charcoal and ash. The inside of the house looked burned, but the blood was not charred and the drawings were not disturbed.

A line of blood led out the back door toward the field. The young virgin, Miss Mary Smith sat cold and dead in the center of the meadow, clutching a small sac of white, unburned hair with silver streaks. One of her eyes had turned completely to green marble, but I was unable to obtain a copy of a coroner's report or record a statement for my collection of these events.

The mysterious knife described in the father's portion still baffles me and I have continued to try to find it. I also sent notes to a few of my colleagues to watch for additional texts containing information or conjecture on unicorns and their relation to light and shadow. I do not wish any unicorn ill-treatment, but if there are answers among more charitable beasts, the endeavor for more knowledge may prove more fruitful once we understand more about these magical creatures, and their place in recognizing the beings we may not wish to encounter, lurking out of time in the corner of our eyes, or in the appendices of our course books.

The Lost Town

- Nick Nafpliotis -

"Inspector Swinburne, Arkham Police Department!"

Swinburne's announcement was followed by three loud raps on the door before it opened, revealing a small, toothless man who greeted him with an unsettling smile.

"Evening, officer," he said with a nod. "What brings an officer of the Arkham Police all the way down past Dunwich to visit my home at this hour?

"Well, Mr. Planter, in case you haven't noticed, the rest of your town has vanished," Swinburne responded sternly. "You wouldn't happen to know anything about the disappearance of 104 people on August 14, would you?"

"Now that you mention it, things have been mighty quiet over the last month," the old man said while rubbing under his chin. "My wife and I usually keep to ourselves, though, so there wasn't much reason for us to worry about there being no visitors these last few weeks. We don't care much for the uneducated folks who live…or lived, I guess I should say…around here."

"I see," Swinburne replied. "And you didn't find it at all strange that during your trips into Arkham or Kingsport, no one else from Dunwich was ever traveling to or from town along the same road?"

"Well…no," Planter said with a wave of his hand. "You know as well as I do that folks around here are a bit backwards. They were all probably too embarrassed to go into town anyway after the calf skin debacle, anyway."

Swinburne had wondered if Planter would bring that up. On August 10, a woman who worked for the mayor of Dunwich had traveled to Arkham to sell some goods at the market. According to the vendors working that day, she attempted to unload an alarming number of cow hides for a ridiculous price. After being told by every one of them that she could get no more than 1 percent of what she was asking, the woman stormed back to her car and drove away.

The incident had been nothing more than a local source of amusement until a few weeks had passed. That's when a few of the store owners began reporting that their regular customers from Dunwich had not come by for their usual purchases...except for Mr. Planter, who was able to buy more than he ever had before.

Going out to Dunwich was something that no one in the department ever wanted to do, but it was Swinburne's turn to mingle with the 'inbred yokels', so he made the first trip out. To his surprise, however, the small town was almost completely deserted. The streets and shops were empty, making the tiny village feel even more eerie and unnatural than it already did.

The nearby farms were also completely abandoned, absent of both their owners and livestock. The only sign of inhabitance to be found was a herd of sheep grazing in the back yard of Mr. Planter's home.

When Swinburne knocked on the door that afternoon, Mrs. Planter had nervously told him that her husband would be home later that evening. That brought him back to the now desolate town around 8:00 PM in the evening, where he stood in front of the only possible suspect and witness the department had for the missing townsfolk.

"Can you remember the last time that you saw any of your

neighbors?" Swinburne asked while raising an eyebrow.

"You know, come to think of it, I do remember something," Planter replied as a toothless smile stretched across his face. "There was some big hubbub up near Peasants Pond around the date you say everyone went missing. Seemed like almost the whole town was headed out there. I didn't go, of course, on account of me not preferring the company of such backwards folk. But you may want to check there first."

"I would greatly appreciate it if you accompanied me to that location," Swinburne responded. "Your cooperation in this matter would go a long way towards helping ensure that no suspicions are aroused which indicate any wrong doing on your part."

Planter looked as if he was about to protest, but his face softened again into a wide, unnatural looking grin.

"Of course I'll help you," he said with what Swinburne thought was a little too much warmth. "Allow me to get my coat and boots, then can be on our way."

Swinburne was thankful that the short ride out to the pond had been made in complete silence. Something about the old farmer made him uneasy in a way that he could barely comprehend. It wasn't a fear born of being attacked; Swinburne was certain that he could defend himself against a man as tiny and old as Mr. Planter. The chill that went down his spine every time he glanced over at his passenger was something more primal, as if evil itself sat in the car beside him.

When they reached Peasants Pond, a light rain had begun to fall. The two men got out of the car and walked towards the water, their boots sloshing in the wet earth as they reached the edge.

"Do you see anything, officer?" Planter asked as they peered down into the surprisingly deep water below.

Swinburne turned on his flashlight and ran it over the pond's surface. The water was a little muddy, but still clear enough that he could see very far down. Unfortunately, all that his light managed to catch where glimpses of turtles and an occasional fish.

"Perhaps we could catch some dinner before heading back," Planter said with high pitched chuckle.

Swinburne ignored him, moving the flashlight closer to the bank and looking for anything that didn't belong. Just when he was about to give up, a glint of metal in the light caught his eye.

"Look!" Swinburne yelled.

The metal caught by his flashlight was from a bracelet, which itself was attached to woman's hand which was sticking out from a hole in the side of the pond. After moving his flashlight over the area to see if there was anything else, Swinburne turned it off and began heading back towards his vehicle.

"C'mon," he said with a brusque motion in Planter's direction. "I've heard rumors of an opening in the Tanorian Hills that will lead us underground. I'm assuming you know where that is, correct?"

"Well…yes…" Planter replied hesitantly. "But no one ever goes down there for fear of being eaten by The Beast."

"I thought you weren't like all the other 'backwards folk' who used to be your neighbors," Swinburne said with a wry smile.

"I…I guess I could lead you there," Planter stammered back to him. "But why would you want to go down to such a dark place, anyway?"

"Because if there is an underground tunnel," Swinburne replied as he opened the car door, "then it might lead us right up to the edge of this pond…and the rest of the bodies."

Planter led Swinburne to the cave's entrance as promised, but tried to remain inside the car after they stopped.

"Oh no," the detective barked as he marched around to Planter's door and flung it open. "You're coming in with me."

He grabbed the old man by the arm and led him to the cave's entrance. After putting a flashlight in Planter's hand, the two men gingerly stepped inside. Rock and dirt crunched underneath their boots as they swung their narrow beams of light back and forth, watching for any large rocks or puddles that would could cause them to fall over. As they continued inside, a gentle descent could be felt along their path, leading them underground and back towards the south from which they'd traveled.

"We keep heading this way," Swinburne said as he briefly shined a light on his compass. "That should lead us directly to Peasants Pond."

"And what then?" Planter asked with a slight tremble in his voice. "What will you do if you find the rest of the townsfolk?"

Swinburne didn't answer, turning his light so that it was in front of them again. The two men cautiously walked in silence for the next hour, the sound of their footsteps the only noise that accompanied the occasional drip of water onto the rocks that surrounded them. When they got within five hundred meters of Pleasant Pond's location, the sound of the Miskatonic River could be heard rushing by in the distance.

"Up ahead," Swinburne said as his light settled on something wooden and broken. "Do you see that?"

"It looks like...a barrel," Planter replied, his voice filled with fear.

"Well what the hell is a barrel doing down here?" Swinburne asked as they moved closer.

The top of the wooden container looked as if it had been punched through. Jagged shards of oak jutted out from all sides of it, each of them stained with blood that had long since dried upon its surface.

"Let's keep moving," Swinburne said as he swung his flashlight forward again.

The two men walked closer towards the sound of rushing water. As they neared the location of Peasants Pond, the stream went from a hollow, distant noise to one seemed to be very near to them. Sure enough, they soon came upon a small underground river. It appeared to be flowing in from the Miskatonic River, through the Pond, and back out towards the cove that ran up against Salem and Kingsport.

"Now we know how the fish get into the pond," Planter said with a nervous chuckle. "...and why Pleasants Pond is so deep. You'd think those dimwits would have known not to all get so close to a body of water with such depth."

Swinburne heard Planter speaking, but he paid no mind to the old man's words. His attention was focused completely on the underground river running before him, where his light was catching dismembered arms and legs as they slowly drifted by. Before he could properly gather himself to react, a low, mournful howl echoed up from the cavern.

"It's the Beast!" Planter screamed as he dropped his flashlight and ran.

Swinburne spun around, cracking the lens of his light against a sharp rock and putting it out. He cursed and searched the ground for Planter's flashlight, which had also gone out after it fell onto the ground.

"Stupid old man," he muttered while feeling the ground all around him. "Thinks he's better than everyone, but ends up being just as stupid as the rest of that inbred town!"

Swinburne was still futily searching for the flashlight when the low howl came up through the caverns again. He stopped, realizing for the first time just how dark and alien the world around him was without the benefit of light. He was completely blind, unable to see a thing except for a vast expanse of blackness in front of him. The only sounds he heard were that of his own breathing, the running of the underground stream, and the howl, which seemed to be getting closer each time it echoed through the cave.

"Planter!" Swinburne shouted, surprised at the uncharacteristically high pitch of his voice.

He was scared, but of what, he did not know. The howl was now a constant noise with no break or release, invading his ears and crawling into his brain like a worm, determined to mine for his greatest fears. A bead of sweat dropped from Swinburne's forehead and onto his nose as his breaths quickened along with the beating of his heart.

The howling now seemed to be echoing all around him, giving no hint as to its origin or intended direction as it grew louder and louder. Swinburne spun around, desperately seeking some form of a landmark that his ears could use where his now useless eyes were now failing him. To his shock and horror, another sound finally did emerge: Shuffling footsteps from the north, heading with frantic purpose to where he was standing.

"Planter! Is that you?!" Swinburne shouted as the footsteps continued.

When no answer came, he drew his gun, desperately attempting to point in the direction from which the footsteps continued towards him.

"Planter…or whoever you are…don't come any closer! I am an armed officer of the law and I will be forced to fire upon your person if you do not halt and identify yourself immediately!"

The footsteps stopped only to be following by a low, guttural grunt that Swinburne thought sounded like a single word. After the grunt was repeated again, he was able to make it out: "Mayor."

"Are you Mayor Machen of Dunwich?" Swinburne asked as the figure continued to grunt the single word again and again. "If you are Mayor Machen, can you please tell me what happened to the rest of your town?"

In response to Swinburne's question, the grunting stopped briefly before giving way to maniacal laughter.

"Mayor!" the voice screamed between fits of giggles and screams. "Planter said I would be mayor! Planter said I would be mayor!"

The voice continued to repeat the same phrase, each iteration of it sounding less bemused and more enraged. Swinburne tried to speak over it, but the voice never stopped, eventually turning into an inhuman, unintelligible howl.

Without warning, the shuffling started again. This time, it was even faster, kicking up rocks and dirt as it scuttled directly towards where Swinburne stood. He fired his gun once, causing the source of the howling to scream in agony. It then roared and charged again, which resulted in two more shots from Swinburne's revolver. The howling and footsteps stopped as something fell with a violent thud onto the cave floor. As source of the howl hit the ground, a cylindrical object rolled out from underneath it and tapped against Swinburne's boot.

"Flashlight!" he exclaimed while picking it up and turning it on.

As soon as he did, the image of Planter holding a rock over his head caught the corner of his eye. Swinburne pointed his gun at him and shouted.

"Don't shoot!" the old man yelped. "I was simply trying to save you from the Beast!"

Swinburne swung the flashlight back over towards where he'd fired his gun. In front of them laid an emaciated, long haired man. Blood poured out of two bullets wounds in his chest, but he somehow had the strength to raise a trembling finger in Planter's direction.

"Planer...Mayor!" he hissed with a final breath as his finger dropped limply back to the floor.

Both men stood in stunned silence before Swinburne finally

turned and asked "Is this someone with whom you are acquainted?"

"That is…or was…the town shepherd," Planter replied. "Always a bit of a loon…even more than the rest of Dunwich, anyway. You can tell on account of him thinking I'm the mayor."

"From the looks of it, the man was trapped down here and went mad," Swinburne replied. "And I suppose you decided it would be the neighborly thing to do to take care of his sheep after he went missing."

"Yes, well, can't let the poor animals starve to death," Planter replied with a laugh.

Swinburne felt badly about shooting the man, but he'd been given no choice. He decided it would be best to come back the next day with a team and proper lighting equipment to recover the rest of the bodies. There was still something about Planter that made him seem guilty, but Swinburne had no proof or reason to detain him.

After sweeping his flashlight over the ground a few more times, he led the old man by the arm out of the cave and drove him back home. After dropping him off at his door, Swinburne asked Planter to make sure he was available if the Arkham Police Department required his assistance again.

"Of course, officer," the old man replied with a wide, toothless grin. "Anything I can do to help."

The next day, Swinburne filed a report on the shooting and brought a team with him to the cave. Full or partial remains of all 103 missing bodies were found, with the shepherd making it the complete 104.

Forensic analysis on the corpses showed no signs of struggle or forced drowning. It was as if the entire town had all decided to jump into the lake at the same time, plunging down so deep that they couldn't swim back up.

Weeks later, a mass suicide was the only explanation that the department was able to offer until a seemingly unrelated case broke the Dunwich Mystery wide open. A priest from the nearby town of Aylesbury had killed himself in his office after mass that day. An officer called over to Swinburne to say that the priest had written a suicide letter that he may be interested in reading.

After arriving at the church, Swinburne put on his gloves and examined the note, which read:

To Any Who Read This and My Lord and Savior Above,

Please forgive me for the terrible crimes which I have committed. During the last three years, I have had an affair with Audrey Clarendon of Dunwich, who is the wife of George Clarendon.

While the miller was away at his job, I had begun visiting their home in what began as a truly innocent gesture. The church was doing outreach work in Dunwich, which was what lead me to that lovely woman's door. From there, I allowed my sinful nature to take hold over the course of many months, eventually leading to me forsaking my vows as a man of God.

One night, I was nearly caught by the husband in their home. A town farmer by the name of Mr. Planter, who had stopped there for shelter during a storm, was able to help me escape. He promised not to tell my secret, but in return, I had to help him deceive the town into thinking that he'd escaped a death sentence.

Before all this, the farmer had somehow deceived the town into thinking that they could sell their calf skins in Arkham for $3,000 apiece. When this was found to be untrue, those backwards townsfolk sentenced him to death by being shoved into a barrel and dumped into Peasants Pond.

I believed that I would be rescuing a man from death. I thought that in the act of deceit, I would still be saving a soul. Instead, he managed to trick a shepherd into getting into the barrel himself on the promise that it would result in him becoming the mayor of

Dunwich!

I couldn't believe how easily these simple minded people could be tricked, but it was me who was the real fool. In fear of my own transgressions being brought to light, I agreed to tell the townspeople that Mr. Planter was inside the barrel. The shepherd was pushed into the water, never to be seen again.

The guilt from this terrible act was already unbearable, but what happened next broke my heart in soul in ways I did not think were possible. Mr. Planter, who was not satisfied with simply escaping death, told the entire town that he had escaped the barrel and found a flock sheep under Peasants Pond. Not one of those inbred dullards even considered the possibility that he may have just simply stolen the sheep from the shepherd…not even my dear, sweet, Aubrey, who drowned in the pond along with everyone else, diving down to find more sheep.

I wish that all of my guilt was over being such an unrighteous man, but I must confess that my heart breaks for the loss of my forbidden love. It is yet another sign that a man as wicked and evil as me does not deserve to remain upon this earth.

May God have mercy upon my soul,

William Powell

It wasn't hard evidence, but the letter provided enough proof to detain Mr. Planter for questioning. Swinburne hurried over to the still deserted town of Dunwich, warrant in hand, only to find that the Planter residence had been burned to the ground.

As he got out and examined the ruins of the small home, he came upon the carcasses of slaughtered sheep, their wool and skin completely stripped from their bodies. Swinburne called together a team and searched everywhere, but they were unable to find any sign of Mr. Planter or his wife.

The last residents of Dunwich had fled, leaving only a cruel tale of death and deception against the easily fooled behind.

The Witch's Library

– Tracie McBride –

Father's hands shook as he delivered the news.

"Children, you must know how loathe I am to do this, but I have withdrawn you both from school. Your mother and I..."

"She's not our mother." My brother spoke softly, but with a steely undercurrent belying his tender years. His hands clenched into fists at his sides.

It was as if Father had not heard him, His gaze rambling wildly, skimming over the spreading mildew stains on the ceiling, the peeling wallpaper, the broken window covered with sheets of yellowing newsprint, before settling on a point somewhere over my left shoulder. "...your mother and I are too unwell to keep steady employment, so you must both work in our stead. Fortunately, I have secured you positions in my uncle's factory."

Father only had one factory-owning relative, our Great Uncle Gerhard. Gerhard visited us once a year at Christmas, bearing gifts befitting much younger children and hampers of exotic and overly rich foodstuffs that gave us stomach aches. I did not know what goods he produced, only that along with unwanted gifts, he brought the odour of soot, paint and chemicals, inadequately disguised with cologne and cigar smoke. Times had been hard across the city, and we had watched many classmates depart to work in the factories; the ones that returned alive were usually missing digits or eyes or entire limbs, or disfigured by fire or acid.

"You start tomorrow at 6am," Father continued. "It is some distance to the factory, and I don't want you to get lost, so I'll take you there."

"Tell them they have to stay there for the week!" came the strident yet quavering voice of our stepmother, Valda, from the bedroom. I almost pitied her then; when Father first brought her home to meet us, her voice had been the prettiest thing about her, sweet and rich and enticing like an artisan-crafted torte, but whatever "medicines" she and my father had fallen prey to had degraded it. "Tell them they can come home on the weekend, but only if they bring all their wages."

"Ah yes, I almost forgot…Gerhard has a dormitory on site for his young workers. Like Valda says – work hard, be good, and save all your wages, and I will fetch you home later."

Hansel and I exchanged glances. Had it been just Father and us, we could have easily persuaded him to abandon this plan, if indeed he would have formulated it at all without Valda's incessant needling. But to argue further would only put Father under more stress and would ultimately be futile.

"Of course, Father." I tiptoed to kiss him on the cheek. "Whatever you think best."

We dined, if such a word could be applied to our paltry repast, on a watery and flavourless vegetable soup, of which Valda ate the lion's share, and copious cups of black tea. I forbore to eat it, pushing limp vegetables around in the gray broth. Father and Valda shook so much from their affliction that they could barely negotiate their spoons along the path from bowl to mouth. They retired early, and we went to our shared single bed soon after.

"What will we do, Hansel?" I whispered. "They say that once you start work in the factories, the only way out is through maiming or death, and I have no desire to experience either. And what of your scholarship to university? A mind such as yours must not be wasted in such toxic labour." Even at the age of thirteen, Hansel's genius had been pointed out to professors from the finest academy in the city, and he had a standing invitation to enter its halls free of charge once he was of age. I was no dunce myself in academic pursuits, but my intellect paled in comparison to my brother's.

Hansel stroked my hair. "Do not fear, Gretel," he said. I snuggled closer, the better to feel the comforting vibrations of his voice in his chest. "Where there is danger, there is always opportunity. I will find a way to bring us home safely."

Through the thin walls, I imagined I could hear the scratch and hiss of a match being struck alight and the bubble of melting narcotics. Father's and Valda's voices came to us, muted and incoherent, devolving into the animalistic sounds of lovemaking. They provided a curious counterpoint to the noises from the busy thoroughfare one storey below us; various vehicles, powered by steam or alchemy, hooted or chugged or fizzed along the street, and even at that hour, vendors still announced their wares in clamorous tones. We fell asleep in our chaste embrace to this profane lullaby.

———

Father shook us awake before dawn and bustled us out into the street with little discussion. He had shaken off his usual lethargy, taking long, loping strides with which we struggled to keep up, and tugging constantly at the hem of his jacket. I was almost grateful for the pace he set, for it went some way to warding off the cold.

I was unaccustomed to being abroad in the darkness; long, flickering shadows cast by the gas lamps disoriented me, giving the illusion that we were travelling beneath the branches of a chill and menacing forest. And Father took us on a route so circuitous, within the hour I was hopelessly lost. Hansel, however, took a keen interest in his surroundings, and more than once he paused on the pretext of tying his laces or removing a stone from his boots, all the better to more properly observe them. His lips moved almost imperceptibly as he recited a litany of directions to himself, thus committing them to memory.

However my mind's eye had pictured the façade of Great Uncle Gerhard's factory, the reality surpassed it in grotesqueness. It squatted on the outskirts of the city like a gargantuan toad of steel and stone. Chimneys and exhausts jutted haphazardly from the edifice and spewed forth clouds of noxious fumes. Father regarded it for a moment and sighed, a long, drawn-out sound that seemed to originate from the depths of his soul.

"My dear children," he murmured, each hand on one of our shoulders, "if there were any other way…"

Hansel shrugged off his hand and turned to face him. "Never mind, Father," he said with a trace of a sneer, "I'm sure Great Uncle Gerhard will take good care of us." And with that, he strode off, trailing me behind him.

———

The interior of the factory resembled a demonic kindergarten. Scores of thin and filthy children scurried over massive machines and constructions as if it were a playground, darting tiny hands in and out of furiously churning devices or deftly avoiding blasts of scalding steam. If it weren't for the looks of grim concentration on their faces, and the occasional whip-bearing adult lashing the backs of those who tarried at their work, it might have been all a big, risky game. The deafening noise of the machinery and the stench from the melange of chemicals overwhelmed my senses, and I swayed on my feet. Hansel steadied me with a hand under my elbow.

One sad-faced urchin led us to the overseer, a short man of middling years with a sparse beard and cruel eyes. He laughed when Hansel mentioned Great Uncle Gerhard, who was nowhere to be seen.

"If I had a penny for every child who told a similar tale, I wouldn't need to spend my days babysitting you snot-nosed brats," the overseer said. "Let's say you really are the Master's kin. If he cared about you, do you think he would put you to work in this hell hole?" A child a little younger than me scurried by, and the overseer snagged him by the collar of his shirt, causing him to stumble and choke.

"Arndt, take these two wretches to the dyeing vats and show them what to do. Mind that you show them well, or any mistakes they make will come out of your hide as well as theirs."

Arndt looked barely well enough to stand, let alone toil all day in a factory. His skin stretched too tightly over spindly limbs, and was patterned with burn scars in various stages of healing, many of which leaked a thick, yellowish discharge. The overseer released his grip on his collar. The boy did not speak, but jerked his head in a "follow me" gesture and set off with surprising speed through the labyrinth of machinery. It was all I could do to keep my footing and maintain the pace.

Arndt took us to the rear of the factory where a row of enormous vats sat atop furnaces into which several soot-stained children shovelled coal. Arndt clambered up a ladder at the side of the first vat and perched upon a broad wooden plank that ran over the vat's open mouth and extended from one side to the other. He beckoned impatiently for us to follow. We climbed up to join him, taking care not to touch the sides of the vat, which radiated a malevolent heat.

"This 'ere's what we call the 'royal red'," Arndt explained, his sticklike legs dangling over the vat, "'cos royalty is just about the only lot what can afford it. Once the cloth in here is dry and cured, the colour won't ever fade." He pointed down between his feet. Two giant paddles slowly churned the vat's contents. It looked like an immense tub of blood, the occasional fold of cloth brought into view by the paddles like pieces of flesh.

"But it's dead poisonous in this state, and you have to take care it's prepared right, else the first person to wear it will get awful sick. Your job is to watch the paddles, make sure they keep turning and don't jam up. If they do, take these," – he handed us each a long pole, the bottom two-thirds of which was stained crimson – "and move the cloth around a bit. But careful, mind, 'cos you don't want it to tear. That's usually enough to get it moving again. If it ain't, you might have to give the cogs a bit of a clean out." He lay flat on the board and dangled his top half precariously over the edge, pointing at the exposed gears near the top of the thick metal rod to which the paddles were affixed. "You want to be quick while's you does it, 'cos if your fingers are still in there when it starts moving, you'll lose 'em. And the bosses don't want to see that kind of red in the mix." He smirked unkindly. "They must've liked the look of you two or somefink, 'cos this is what you'd call a plum post. Not much to do most of the time 'cept watch the red."

The board on which we sat vibrated gently from the paddles' movement. The odour that arose from the vat was pungent and unnatural, and made my head swim in a not entirely unpleasant way, and the gentle, repetitive swish of the paddles through the liquid was hypnotic. I teetered on the brink of the board, almost welcoming the compulsion to slip into the warm, vermillion waters below…

Arndt's gaze was sharp, his voice sharper, and it snapped me back to awareness with a jolt. "One more thing – whatever happens, do not fall in. Of all the ways to go in this place – and I've seen a few – that's the worst."

An angry shout rose up from the floor. Arndt cast an

apprehensive glance at the foreman below, and without a further word, hastened down the ladder. Hansel kept a careful eye on the man's retreating back.

"We may no longer be attending school, sweet Gretel," Hansel said, "yet there is still the opportunity for a chemistry lesson. Did you notice the generous quantities of chemical substances stored about the factory?" I nodded.

"I recognize the symbols emblazoned on their containers," he continued, "although I wager most of the young workers here do not. Did you also notice that some are carefully stowed on opposite sides of the building? Why do you think that is?"

"I assume it is so there is little chance of them inadvertently coming in contact with each other."

"Well done, dear sister! You shall go to the top of the class. Now, if you will excuse me, I will take this opportunity while none of the supervisors are watching to go make some mischief." He pressed close to me and whispered in my ear. "When I return, do not hesitate – just take my hand and run." No sooner had he delivered his cryptic message than he was down the ladder and slipping amongst the machines.

I kept one eye on the vat beneath my feet as I tried to track Hansel's movements from my elevated vantage point, growing more and more apprehensive as I awaited his return. For the most part, he kept himself well hidden from the overseers, scooting across the factory floor behind their backs and ducking down behind barrels or boxes or bolts of cloth before they could turn. Every now and again he was not quite quick enough; then he would make a great show of lifting a box and moving purposely on an imaginary errand, and the man would turn his bored gaze elsewhere. He traversed the building, side to side and back to front and looping back on himself. To a casual observer his path would appear random and meaningless, but in his journey I sensed complexity and purpose.

The plank on which I sat bucked and shuddered, threatening to tip me into the toxic soup below. The paddles had become fouled with fabric, and strained against their bonds. I thrust the pole into the vat of dye and tried to untangle the snarl. Weighed down with liquid, the cloth was too heavy for me to shift, and I feared that if I put more of my body weight behind the pole, I might overbalance and fall to an untimely and gruesome death.

"Oi! You there! Put your back into it, you lazy slattern!" A supervisor stood at the bottom of the ladder and brandished a whip at me. "Don't make me come up there, or –"

His next words were drowned out by a booming explosion that set the board shaking anew. A great cloud of greenish smoke billowed up from near the factory's centre. Several smaller explosions followed in an almost synchronized fashion, and panicked cries and agonized wails filled the air. I prostrated myself upon the plank and buried my face in my hands.

A gentle tug on my ankle roused me from my terror-induced stupor.

"Gretel! Let's go!" It was Hansel, his voice muffled by a cloth wrapped about his nose and mouth as a makeshift filter. He tossed me a similar length of cloth and gestured to me to fasten it about my face, then gently encouraged me down the ladder. Even if the smoke were not too dense to see through, I was rendered virtually blind, the gases stinging my eyes until they watered uncontrollably. All about, foremen and workers coughed and retched and howled with pain, and the distinct crackle and heat of advancing flames menaced us. But Hansel's sense of direction was unerring as he led us through the devastation, out a service door, onto the street and into sweet, life-giving, fresh air.

———

"It was a horrible accident, Father. We were lucky to escape with our lives. And I fear that there is nothing left of Great Uncle Gerhard's factory." Hansel kept his eyes respectfully downcast, yet he turned his head slightly towards me and tipped a wink that Father could not see. In truth, we had not stayed long enough to see what had befallen the factory, but Hansel had assured me that the chain of chemical reactions he had set in motion would virtually guarantee its destruction.

After his initial surprise, Father was genuinely pleased and relieved to have us home again. Valda, of course, only had thoughts for the pecuniary loss of the earnings we could no longer provide. At first she raged, but soon fell silent, regarding us with acute speculation that was more intimidating than her wrath. I shuffled uncomfortably before her scrutiny, although it was not her attention that concerned me. Once we had escaped the factory and I had found myself whole and safe, my first impulse was to plunge back in to help the poor wretches still trapped inside, or at the very least alert the authorities to come to their assistance. But Hansel would have none of it.

"Were the positions reversed, would any of them have spared a thought for us? I think not," he had said. I had to concede that he was right, yet his callousness was disturbing, and the other children's fates weighed heavily on my conscience.

"Come, dear hearts," Father said, drawing us into an embrace. "We have little to offer for supper, but at least you will have a safe place to lay your heads tonight. Tomorrow we will set about finding you alternative employment."

"Yes," said Valda. "Yes, we shall."

—

It took Valda a day and a half to make good on her promise.

"I have secured you both a position with my former employers," she said. "There are no machines there, no dangerous substances, no inanimate objects that might hack off your limbs or poison your lungs." She spoke in a taunting, sing-songy voice, as if they were petty concerns that only cossetted babies might fear.

"No." Father's tone was flat, his arms folded firmly across his chest. "They will not go to that place." It was a rare show of fortitude on his part, and for a moment I saw him as I had when I was a very young child – as a hero, broad-shouldered and fearless and omnipotent. Hansel and I watched them take the measure of each other; I was equal parts intrigued at the unusual conflict and terrified at imagining the nature of Valda's former profession. After sending us to the horror that was Gerhard's factory, how heinous must this new place be if Father considered it worth defying his beloved Valda to save us from it?

Valda's lip curled. "And why not? It was good enough for you to go there, on more than one occasion. Or have you forgotten how we first met?"

"I have not forgotten," he said softly. "But this is different. They're just children." His voice held a hint of plaintiveness, and I sensed a minute giving of ground.

Valda snorted and waved a hand in dismissal. "Don't be ridiculous. They'll only be doing housekeeping duties - cooking and cleaning and suchlike, and running errands for Madam....at least, to start with. After all, they will not be children forever." The last words landed on Father like barbs; he flinched under their blow. Yet he remained unconsenting.

But our stepmother had one card left to play, and when I saw it fall from her hand, I knew our cause was lost. She slowly closed the gap between Father and herself, her hips swaying beneath her thin shift, then wound her bony body about his like a cat seeking affection. Slipping a hand under his shirt to caress his bare flesh, she stood on tiptoe to whisper in his ear. His mouth fell slack and his eyelids fluttered closed as if he were cast under the influence of a powerful mesmerist; I wondered, not for the first time, if she were not indeed secretly versed in the dark art of witchcraft.

"Very well," he said at last. "But it must only be temporary. As soon as we are able, we will fetch them back."

"Of course, my darling," she cooed. She turned, pressed her back to his belly and drew his arms about her like a cloak. In her triumphant smile we read the awful truth.

They would never bring us home.

—

This time Valda did not allow Father to escort us, but had them send a carriage to fetch us. It was an austerely elegant conveyance, its sleek lines devoid of windows and ornament and painted a glossy black, and was drawn by two equally glossy black horses. I had never seen live horses so close up; only the very wealthy kept them. With the almost metallic sheen of their coats and the plumes of vapour streaming from their flared nostrils, I could almost fancy them as elaborate automatons.

Valda had a hushed conversation with the carriage driver, a man of considerable stature who was dressed as plainly yet impeccably as his charges. He drew a small bundle wrapped in twine and brown paper from the inner folds of his coat and handed it to her.

"That evil bitch," Hansel growled, uncharacteristically obscene. "She's selling us!" He backed away, drawing me with him, but the driver lunged with surprising agility to grab us both by the arms. His massive hands easily encircled our biceps and held us as securely as iron cuffs.

"Oh no you don't, younglings," he said. "You now have a substantial debt to pay." He hoisted us both effortlessly into the carriage and slammed the door shut. The carriage rocked gently as the driver presumably took his seat at the front, and his soft tsk tsk, signalling the horses to walk on, filtered through the padded walls.

The lurch of the carriage rolling forward took me unawares, and I fell to the floor. I was awash with panic, but Hansel merely leaned back against the soft, black velvet cushions and closed his eyes.

"Get some rest, Gretel," he said, "and save your strength for when we stop."

"You have a plan, I assume?" I asked. Eyes still closed, he nodded.

"And my only requirement in this plan is to run when you tell me?"

He opened one eye and gave me an impish grin. I sighed and picked myself up. All my life, Hansel had been my protector and saviour, my wisest counsel and my best friend. I had no reason to believe he would not prevail now. I did as he advised, even going so far as to recline on the seat. Despite my fear, the plush furnishings and the swaying, somnolent movement of the carriage soon sent me into a fitful slumber.

—

I had no idea how much time had elapsed when I awoke. The carriage had stopped, and a lifetime of compliance had me doing my best to rub the grit from my eyes and compose my hair and clothing into that befitting an obedient servant, despite the fact that Hansel and I had no intention of fulfilling our "obligations". We sat in anticipation for what seemed like an age until the door finally opened and we were hauled, blinking and disoriented, into the sunlight.

The driver had us again in his inexorable grip, and Hansel allowed him to propel us forward a few steps before he reached into his pocket with his free hand and cast what appeared to be a handful of scarlet dust into the man's face.

The driver's reaction was immediate; he let us go and clawed at his face with both hands, screaming in an incongruously high pitch.

Hansel burst into a run, and I hitched up my skirts and set off after him. From somewhere close by came angry shouts and stampeding feet; something brushed at my back, a pursuer's grasping hand perhaps, and I yelped. Hansel slowed just enough to allow me to pass him, then threw another handful of dust over his shoulder. The irate yells gave way to cries of pain, then receded altogether as we left our would-be captors behind.

We ran like hunted rabbits, with no consideration for our whereabouts, our only thought to put distance between ourselves and an uncertain danger. We ran until I could run no further and my legs gave out underneath me, pitching me into the gutter where I retched with exhaustion. Hansel threw himself down beside me and huddled close, as much for his own comfort as for mine.

"Where are we?" I asked when I could finally draw adequate breath. Neither landmarks nor street signs looked familiar. The street on which we sat was narrow and ill lit, the cobbled road slippery with moss as if it were seldom used. Hansel looked around with wide-eyed bewilderment.

"I…I don't know," he finally said.

I could not recall another time when he had admitted to an absence of knowledge on any subject; of everything that had befallen us in recent days, this confession was the most frightening.

———

Our headlong flight had worn through the last vestiges of leather on the soles of my boots, making me wince and limp with every step. Hansel's footwear had fared no better. Tired, cold, hungry and lost, we sagged against each other for support. We would have asked a passer-by for directions, but the quarters through which we staggered were oddly deserted. When we stepped out of the carriage, I had thought it no later than noon, yet dusk seemed to descend with unnatural rapidity; the neighbourhood was evidently too stingy for lamps, and darkness descended all too soon.

Then, just when I thought I could go no further, Hansel called out with joy.

"Look! A light!"

A few doors down, a warm glow emanated from a shopfront window. The light illuminated a sign that swayed enticingly from a multi-coloured awning. Painted on the sign in an amateurish yet enthusiastic style was the image of two children, a boy and a girl, with enraptured expressions, sitting side by side and reading from a book large enough to take up both their laps. The children bore an eerily close resemblance to Hansel and me.

It seemed so inviting, and we were so sorely in need of respite, yet as we drew level with the door, I hesitated. Surely the shopkeeper would tolerate us, two penniless ragamuffins, for no longer than a second before throwing us back onto the street…

With a cheery chorus of tinkling bells, the door flew open. A diminutive old woman, her gray hair pulled back into a dishevelled bun, peered up at us. Her face bloomed with creases as she smiled.

"My goodness, children! Whatever are you doing out alone on such a cold night? Come in, come in, you must come in!" She stood back to make way for us, beckoning vigorously. We all but fell through the doorway – and stopped abruptly in wonder.

It was a bookstore. A warm, glorious, light-filled bookstore. The abundant space was rendered intimate and maze-like with a multitude of shelves, all of which were crammed full with books. They overflowed onto the floor in dusty, teetering piles. I inhaled deeply, savouring the musty vanilla aroma.

"Sit, sit," the old woman said, waving a hand at a pair of overstuffed armchairs wedged into a corner. "You two look famished, you poor dears. I'll fetch us some tea and cake." She disappeared into the far reaches of the store.

I threw myself onto a chair as I had been bade; I barely had the energy to open my eyes, let alone explore the shelves, as intriguing as they were. But Hansel could not resist the lure of the books. He moved along one shelf as if in a trance, a forefinger caressing the spines as he mouthed the titles. Halfway along, he stopped and gasped. He stood stock-still and staring for several heartbeats, then with trembling hands lifted one particularly thick and ancient tome from its place and carried it with infinite care to sit beside me.

"Gretel, do you know what this is? It's an original treatise by Johannes Kepler, one of our most influential astronomers. It's exceedingly rare - there are rumoured to be only three copies left in existence." He lowered his voice and leaned closer to me, his eyes glittering with devilment. "They say that his mother was a witch, and that it was she who imparted to him knowledge of the stars." He opened the book and turned the yellow pages with a delicate hand, his mouth falling open in avaricious awe.

Somewhere towards the back of the store, a door slammed, and our hostess's jaunty humming could be heard as she made her way back. Hansel started and shut the book, sending up a cloud of dust, and concealed it beneath his coat. I opened my mouth to protest, but then the old woman was upon us, and the moment was lost. Hansel and I were reduced to trading baleful looks, mine silently exhorting him to return the book, and his warning me to hold my tongue.

"Don't be shy, children – eat up before it goes cold," the woman said as she pottered about pouring tea and buttering thick slices of an aromatic toasted fruit loaf. "You know, I get so few visitors, and my customers seldom care to stop and talk. They only want to make their purchases and rush off. So you do me a kindness by staying to humour a lonely old woman."

My instincts were at war with each other; one impulse told me to take Hansel by the hand and run before his theft was discovered, while another urged me to fill my empty belly with the delectable offerings before me. The latter won out, and I stuffed food and drink into my face as quickly as propriety would allow. Hansel also took the cup and saucer he was offered, and took several polite sips from his tea, but he held one arm pressed awkwardly against his side to keep the purloined book secure, while his gaze kept sliding towards the door.

"I thank you for your generosity, kind lady," he said, "but I fear we must depart. The hour is late, and we must get home – our father will be anxious for our return."

"Your father?" the woman inquired. She stood with her back to us, her posture suddenly tense and alert. "And what of your mother?" An innocent enough question, yet it seemed laden with portent.

"Our...our mother is..." I began. A lie was forming on the tip of my tongue, but the wayward organ became suddenly sluggish.

"Your mother is dead, isn't she?" The old woman turned around, the movement seeming to set the entire room spinning. The cup and saucer slipped from my nerveless fingers to shatter on the floor. Indifferent to my plight, she continued. "Perhaps if she were still alive, she might have taught you better than to steal from defenceless old ladies."

"I don't know what you're talking about," Hansel said brazenly. He tried to stand, but staggered and dropped back into the chair. The book fell from its hiding place, landing with a thump at the old woman's feet. Her lips curled into a mirthless smile.

"A thief and a liar," she said. "And a scholar to boot, judging by your choice of reading material." She nudged the book with her slippered foot. "My my, what an interesting fly I have caught in my web tonight." She studied Hansel for several long seconds, still bearing that unnerving smile, then approached him to take hold of his head, one hand beside each temple, and peer intently into his eyes. I tried to move, but a supernormal lassitude gripped my entire body; judging by Hansel's passivity and his glazed expression, he experienced the same phenomenon.

"Interesting," the old woman said. "Your mind...it is quite unlike any I have ever encountered before. You may be just what I need." She glanced at me with a look of disdain. "As for you – you'll only eat my food and prove yourself a general nuisance." From the folds of her apron she produced a wicked-looking carving knife and advanced on me.

"Wait!" Hansel's brow was beaded with sweat, his eyes wide with strain. "Whatever it is you want from me, if you harm so much as a hair on her head, you'll have none of it."

The witch – for that is what she must surely have been, given her uncanny influence over us – hesitated. "Ah, familial love...what a useless emotion! Mark my words, children, if you survive to escape these walls, you would be best advised to dispense with love entirely, as it will only be used against you."

If you survive... I shuddered in anticipation of the blade cleaving my throat. But the witch sheathed the knife and turned back to Hansel.

"Very well," she said. "I will not slay her – yet – but if you both value your lives, you will do what I say, to the letter."

—

We spent our first night huddled in a dark and dusty closet into which the old woman had dragged us whilst we were still incapacitated. Her name, we learned, was Rosine, and she set us to work immediately upon waking. My tasks, although tiring, were familiar and commonplace; I cooked, scoured pots and dishes, scrubbed floors, and dusted the rows of books that extended much further than the modest store front suggested. With us as her captives, Rosine did not bother with the charade of opening the "store" to the public. In fact, although I explored every nook and cranny, I could find no trace of the store window or of the door through which we had entered. Besides kitchen and closet, there was only one other door in Rosine's library, and that was kept locked.

Hansel's purpose was more obscure. She kept him chained by the ankle to the wall, albeit with a comfortable armchair in which to sit, and I was ordered to keep him well fed and watered with whatever he desired, while I was only permitted the paltry scraps from her plate. Rosine brought him book after book on a wide range of arcane subjects, urging him to read far into the night and fuelling him with stimulating medicaments when exhaustion dragged his eyelids southwards. Her manner towards Hansel veered between extremes; one moment she spoke in gentle, cajoling tones that sickened me with their resemblance to Valda's manipulations. The next she stormed and raged and cursed, promising all manner of gruesome fates for us both if he did not master the texts. Hansel bore it all with equanimity, his only response to bend his head to the books in silence.

Rosine would not let me speak with Hansel, saying that I distracted him from his work while I neglected my own, so we were limited to brief, clandestine exchanges when opportunity arose. But I did not need him to confirm what my vision already told me; Rosine's books had enchanted him more thoroughly than any spell or elixir the witch could conjure. The eagerness with which he received each new tome was unfeigned, and his eyes shone with a fervour that bordered on madness. Many of the books contained obscure, long-forgotten languages, and from time to time I heard him quietly reciting the unfamiliar words in an urgent cadence that set the hairs rising on the back of my neck.

"What does she want of you?" I whispered, and his reply nearly stopped my heart.

"She wants me to summon the gods."

—

Hansel had discovered that the summoning ritual culminated in a human sacrifice, so he claimed a state of unreadiness to keep the witch waiting as long as he could, although I suspected it was as much to continue reading from the library as to prolong our lives. Rosine had been gathering her unholy texts for decades, attempting unsuccessfully to decipher them for just as long, and had searched for many years for the person with just the right paradoxical combination of brilliance and foolhardiness to interpret them for her; one might think that her solitary virtue of patience was well developed. Yet her state of agitation mounted exponentially by the day, until she could stand it no longer.

"The time is now!" she shrieked as she unfastened Hansel's chains. She grabbed us both by the hair, and with a strength surprising in such a frail looking woman, hauled us to the mysterious door, which now stood open at the top of a steep flight of stone steps. We were both too weak to mount much resistance as she lit a torch and pushed us before her. The steps descended into darkness to a seemingly impossible depth, the air growing colder and damper with each tread, and Rosine's flickering brand cast demonic shadows before us. I detected a hint of ocean brine, the stink of rotting seaweed and a spicy, more elusive odour not entirely in keeping with the scents of the sea.

At last we reached the bottom, where we slumped against icy stone walls and breathed great gulps of fetid air. Rosine took her torch to light several others mounted at regular intervals about the chamber in which we found ourselves. The flames revealed a frieze of symbols chiselled into the stone on three sides of the chamber. I did not know their meaning, but recognised some of the symbols from the books Hansel had been studying. On the fourth side, more stone steps went down into an underground lake, large and still and inky black.

Panting for breath with his head hanging low and skin pallid,

Hansel looked close to collapse, yet the sight of the symbols seemed to invigorate him. Rosine twisted my hair in her fist and forced me to my knees. She drew her blade and pressed it against my throat.

"Say the words!" she screamed. "SAY THEM!"

She needn't have forced him; he had already begun, in a soft and low voice that gradually grew in intensity. Back in the library, the language had sounded forced and guttural, but here the words were in their natural element. Echoing off the walls, Hansel's voice was powerful and melodic, yet subtly ominous. It was like listening to the call of giant, fantastical birds coming home to roost. He paced about the chamber like an actor upon a stage, his steps choreographed to music only he could hear.

The water in the lake began to move. It rippled at first from the centre outwards, as if struck by droplets of water from the unseen ceiling. A sound like the heartbeat of some huge creature insinuated itself into Hansel's chants, and as its volume rose, so too did the ripples, turning into waves that leapt higher and higher.

Then the first of the beings emerged.

They came one by one, snaggle-toothed or swarming with tentacles or domed all over with multi-faceted eyes. Some were small and agile, like an unholy hybrid of eel and ferret. Some were leviathans, dripping sediment from the ocean depths, their great domed heads hinting at an immense bulk concealed below the water's surface. And some defied all human perception of dimension and form, their very manifestation threatening to send me plunging irretrievably into insanity. They sang back to Hansel, these god-monsters, and the sound was like the torture of angels.

Rosine released me, dropped the knife, and stepped forward to descend the first few steps into the lake. She stood shin deep in the water, her arms wide in obsecration. The creatures paid her no mind; Hansel was their sole focus, and they swam and crawled and slithered towards him.

"Hansel! You must stop!" I struggled to make myself heard over the cacophony.

He turned to me, the torch light distorting his features. In that moment, he was no longer my brother, but the god-monsters' kin. Then the illusion was gone, and I looked upon the face of a terrified boy.

"I can't!" he cried. "I MUST KNOW!" And he returned to his chant.

The ritual required a sacrifice, he had said. Very well, I thought grimly. They would have their blood – but it would not be ours. I picked up Rosine's abandoned knife and with all my strength, plunged it into her back. She stiffened and half-turned to claw at the spot where the knife entered her flesh, but she was not quite able to reach it. Uncomprehending, she looked up into my face. At the instant the awful understanding reached her consciousness, I pushed her into the lake.

The water churned with the feeding frenzy. I caught a flash of red, a glint of bone, a hank of gray hair whipping through the air, and I turned away. Hansel's face was frozen in a rictus of anguish; whatever I had done, it had not been according to the plan. Terror lent me strength, and I grabbed his hand to drag him up the interminable flight of stairs and into the library. With Rosine's enchantments broken by her death, we found the exit easily.

It led out onto the very street in which our home stood.

———

I wish that I could say that we lived happily ever after, but that is the province of fairy tales. In our absence, our guilt-ridden father had come to his senses and banished Valda. He was overjoyed to welcome us home, but never quite forgave himself for sending us away in the first place, and as a consequence held us both obsessively close until long after we reached adulthood.

Hansel never truly recovered. As we were leaving the library, he tried to take some of the books with him. He lacked the strength to resist when I forced him out empty-handed, and wept as if I were taking him to his death instead of away from it. He spent his first week of freedom in a delirium, and when he finally arose from his sick bed and went out onto the street, he found Rosine's library razed to the ground, its contents nothing but ash. Of the secret stairway and subterranean chamber, there was no trace.

Although I had ample opportunity, I never married. Instead, I became my brother's keeper, guarding him on his frequent visits to the ports where he was wont to stare into the sea and speak gibberish until the fishermen and stevedores threatened him bodily harm. Sometimes I felt the lure of the language myself, even although I did not understand it; it whispered to me in quiet moments of wakefulness and crept into my dreams. Rosine's words too came back to torment me - *you would be best advised to dispense with love entirely, as it will only be used against you.*

The god-monsters will return one day, of that I am sure. And when they do, I fear for humanity. The best I can hope for is that my bones have long been turned to dust before that day comes.

Boots of Curious Leather

– David J. Fielding –

There was something moving out there in the dark.

He had heard it, something that trudged through the undergrowth not twenty yards away, just beyond the stand of tall birch trees.

He froze mid-step, eyes peering into the pre-dawn gloom that was slowly turning the deep black of the forest night to a bleached, mist-laden grey. His hands gripped the musket tight. His palms were slick, his nerves bunched. He guided his thumb slowly up over the hammer and pulled it back, feeling the click when it cocked rather than hearing it. A thin trickle of sweat crept from beneath the rim of his infantry cap, dribbled through his dirty, matted hair and ran down the side of his face, sticking in the thick stubble on his jaw. He mentally cursed the hot and heavy wool of the uniform and stifling weight of the trench coat. He remained rooted to the spot behind the big, gnarled oak, waiting, watching.

Long seconds passed, the time between each stretching on and on, until it seemed that time itself had stopped. The air in his lungs burned, he had sucked in air when he had first heard the sound and had not breathed out since.

Then, just passed the trees ahead, through the growing light and fog, he heard it again, the snap of a twig under a heavy boot.

He threw himself out from behind the tree, his weapon raised and training it from left to right and back again seeking his unseen target, his voice shouting a command.

"Show yourself! Come forth and prove thyself friend or foe!"

He stood, aiming at nothing, sweeping the barrel right and left searching. His arms were trembling, his thighs shaking with nervous energy and anticipation.

How long had it been since he'd slept? Since he'd eaten?

A day and half was it? Hunger and weariness had distorted perception.

An upstart king, dubbed Tatterdemalion by some and the King in Yellow Tatters by others, had journeyed forth from the lands beyond the mountains of the Black Forest and invaded their lands. The reasons for his doing so were never made clear to the infantryman. They had been vague and questionable when he had been drafted into the cause and were, even now, just as mysterious and nebulous these many months later. One man would tell you that dark king and his army had invaded for riches and glory, another that it was a blood-feud between their king and some deadly foe from the East, and still another would say it was because the king was demon possessed and sought to unmake the world through rituals dark and dire.

Whatever the reason, there had been many small battles between this invading army and those who sought to defend their beloved homeland. Until a day before, when the infantryman's unit had joined up with the defending forces of the Duke, and they had laid a trap for the Tattered King. The ambush had been sprung in the fog of the early morn, as the invaders marched over the hill road, and the first few reports of rifles and guns had erupted into a full scale skirmish.

In seconds the air had been filled with the crack of rifles, the boom of cannons and the blood-curdling screams of the wounded and dying. Musket smoke had blanketed the clear morning in a fog-filled, shadowy shroud making it impossible to tell friend from foe. For an untold time the battle raged, first surging in favor of one side, then pushing back toward the other. Finally, the invading King had sounded the retreat and the enemy had fled toward the safety and cover of the Black Forest. The fighting was over.

But the battle weary soldiers would find little respite, as the word to pursue had been given. No quarter! No surrender! And almost as one, the infantryman and hundreds more like him, roars of bloodlust filling the air, had poured into the trees after the fleeing enemy.

In the forest, it was another world entirely.

He'd become separated from the rest of his unit as they struggled through the close brambles and undergrowth. It seemed as though it had been only minutes before. How could they have all disappeared so quickly? They had entered into the spaces between the trees, howling with bloodlust, now there was nothing but silence and the dying echoes of war.

The dark and the fog had been all encompassing and confusing. The air had an odd, eerie quality, distorting sound. Shouts of other men reached him, bounced and echoed, disorienting him. It seemed they were ahead of him, and then behind and then nowhere at all. He had spent the next four hours stumbling through the dark.

He stumbled onward through the dark, and time soon had no meaning. The landscape was foreign, filled with twisted branches and roots, strange smells and sounds.

He had called after them, but his fellow soldiers were nowhere to be seen. Alone, all he could do was to stagger through the trees hunting for the King and the last of his ragtag followers.

Time had lost meaning, and he could not tell one from the other. He had been pushing himself all through the ever-present night, and had grown weary from fighting his way through the tangled undergrowth in the blackness. Stumbling upon a big oak, he hunkered down to wait for dawn, finally falling into a restless, dreamless slumber.

Moments or hours later, something had jolted him awake. A sound. It was then he noticed the subtle change in the light. When he realized the faint lightening of the dark, he had stood slowly, intending to try and find the edge of the forest, to return to the front and find the rest of the unit. That was when he had heard something making its way toward him.

"Show yourself!"

He blinked the sweat out of his eyes, aiming with the rifle, scanning the area where the sound had come from. The roar of his shout rebounded and died deep among the trees. Moments ticked by, when thirty yards across the leaf-strewn forest floor, a tall figure stepped out from behind the thick bole of a massive gnarled tree.

The figure was the tallest – and thinnest – man the soldier had ever seen. He was dressed to fend off the chill and the wet of the fog, in a long shooting coat of dusty olive-green that dragged through the red and brown leaves gathered round the base of the tree. Beneath the coat he wore what appeared to be hunter's garb, thick wool vest and leggings of patchwork leather. The infantryman couldn't spot any insignia or badge that would mark the stranger part of the renegade King's men, but that did not mean anything; the stranger could still prove himself an enemy.

A wide belt at his waist was adorned with a large brass buckle, tarnished with rust. A hunting knife hung from the belt, and was so large, that the soldier at first mistook it for a short sword. In one long-fingered hand the figure held a ball and powder pistol, the barrel pointed down to the ground. The other hand gripped a long carbine and shooting stick, both which rested on his shoulder; the stock and butt were of a dark, polished wood that had a curious pattern of loops and whorls or swirls of golden filigree that told the infantryman that the weapon was one made by an artisan gunsmith.

Atop his head the stranger wore a cavalier's hat of felt, the brim dripping with moisture from the fog. In the shadow under the hat, his gaunt face, with prominent cheek bones and thin hooked nose, was all but obscured by the long black locks that hung limply in greasy strands, well past his shoulders. The lower half of his face was as equally hidden by a thick mustache and beard just as long and as limp as his hair.

"Who are you?" The infantryman spoke in an unsteady voice, his rifle aimed at the stranger.

The stranger said nothing, but regarded him with dark, glittering eyes. There was something about him that caused the young soldier to shiver involuntarily, something about the way he carried himself; there was an air of danger, a hint of death.

The infantryman's finger tightened on the trigger. There was hardly thirty feet between him and the tall figure. At this distance he could not miss.

"Who are you? I will not ask again."

The stranger maneuvered the hand that held the pistol, so that the infantryman could see that he had taken his finger away from the trigger. The gun now dangled from his thumb, useless. His other hand still gripped the long rifle, but it too was of no use resting on his shoulder as it was.

"A simple traveler; lost as you are, in this unnatural wood," the stranger said, in a thick accent. "Who are you that so rudely demands to know of me? What cause do you have to point your weapon at me in such a threatening manner?"

The infantryman was a soldier, but he was also a man, and a man who had been taught that courtesy and respect must been earned. The best way to earn a thing, was to give it in kind, so he lowered his weapon, slowly, in a sign of peace.

"Forgive me my rudeness, traveler. My manners I have quite

forgot these many months of fighting. I am a soldier, of late in battle some distance back there, outside the woods, and who is now lost here among the trees. I mean no offense, but am wary you may be not a friend."

The stranger stared, silent. Those eyes! They were black as pitch and seemed to see right through him. The infantryman shivered.

"Friend am I not, and truth be told – I call no man friend. But neither am I thy foe. You have naught to fear from me."

The infantryman sighed and lowered his weapon completely.

"Then fellow traveler, lost as I am, and who is neither friend nor foe, may I ask if you have some water to share? I have been wandering the whole night and somewhere in this forsaken forest I have lost my canteen."

The stranger stood, not moving, but simply staring back.

"I have coin, I am will to pay for –"

The stranger's eyes narrowed, and for a moment, the infantryman thought the stranger would raise the pistol and put a lead ball between his eyes. Instead, the tall thin man quickly re-gripped his pistol and with a fluid flick of his wrist, stuffed it in between his belt and coat.

"Keep your coin; no man should die of thirst in this accursed place," the grim stranger said.

He set the long gun down against a tree and shrugged a full pack from off his shoulders, withdrawing a wineskin, which he then tossed to the infantryman.

"My thanks," the infantryman said, gulping the sweet red liquid. After the months of marching and fighting, the long night, the fear that had gripped him, nothing that had passed his lips had ever tasted so good.

After a moment, he noticed that the tall stranger had hunkered down across from him, and had pulled out other objects from the pack, among them a roll of vellum from a leather tube. On the vellum the soldier could see markings and lines. A map!

He took a step forward, but stopped short when the stranger's head snapped around and fixed him once more with those dark and dangerous eyes. Curiosity overcame his fear however and he found his voice.

"Is that a map you have there? Does it tell of path out from these dark an oppressive trees?"

The stranger said nothing, but turned back to gaze at the map, fixed his eyes upon it, searching. The infantryman took another long gulp of wine. It was flavorful and cool, deep bodied and with a hint of some flower he could not put a name too. For a moment he forgot the map, his mind turned to the liquid in his mouth. How had it been made and by whom?

"What is your name, soldier?"

The stranger's voice startled him out his thoughts. The light had grown and he could see more and more of his surroundings. He blinked, for the fog had all but disappeared. This wood was passing strange indeed, and the sooner he was quit of it the better.

"I am – my name," the soldier faltered, "is Baird."

The stranger did not look up from the map, or even glance in his direction, but continued to study the paper before him.

"Now it is you who is being rude. When a name is given, it is simple courtesy to give one in return."

The stranger looked up then, slowly. And the soldier saw one hand come to rest on the hilt of the big hunting knife.

"What, may I ask, is your name traveler?" Baird asked, his own hand tightening once more on his own weapon.

The stranger's face betrayed nothing. It was pale as a mummer's mask, still and impassive, as unreadable as stone. His eyes were two points of black flint, filled with a frightening anger.

"Those who know me," the stranger said in his thick accent, "call me Gelbe."

The word was odd and thoroughly foreign to the soldier, though the sound of it tugged at his memory, as though he should know it. Did he know it? How did he know it? Should he know this tall, uncanny man before him? Perhaps it was the weariness or the headiness of the wine, either way; too much thought had set a dull throb in his brain. Best not to think too much. He let the thought go for now; it was just a name after all, if a foreign one. Baird instead forced a smile to curl his lips.

"Well met, Gelbe the tall, wanderer of the wood."

The stranger's eyes held his for a long minute, and then he let the hand drop from the knife hilt, turning his eyes once more to the aged vellum map.

"Well met," Gelbe rumbled in his thick accent. "There is a road, yes. I will not lie, it is some distance from us, if I read this paper true."

"I do not mean to impose, and I would understand if you refused," Baird said. "But as we are both in unfamiliar territory, perhaps we should throw in together, and find a way through this wood as brothers, rather than stumbling about alone. What say you?"

The stranger gazed off into the trees, considering. The silence of the forest around them grew quieter still.

"If you do as I do, move when I move, then I agree." Gelbe's accent rumbled. "But if you turn laggard, or fall and injure yourself, or do anything that to endanger either of us, I will gut you and leave you to your fate. I have come too far to falter in my quest. Do you understand?"

"I do," Baird replied.

"Then," the tall man said, rolling up the vellum and slipping into its leather casing, "I will guide you to this path on the map, after that, we go our separate ways. Agreed?"

"That would be most kind," replied Baird, relieved, and nodded an affirmation.

And then, also with a brief nod of agreement, Gelbe stalked off across the leaf strewn forest floor. And after a moment's hesitation, the young soldier followed.

Soon both men were trudging once more through the undergrowth, Gelbe in front and Baird following behind.

The day had grown steadily brighter and now he could see well through the trees, but in every direction it seemed they were still surrounded and there was no path apparent anywhere. Was the stranger leading him along the right course? Could he trust him? These were the questions on Baird's lips, but they went unuttered. Before he could speak, the stranger asked one of his own.

"You say you are a soldier, yes? And that you belong to those who were fighting outside the wood?"

The infantryman was caught off guard.

"You know of the war?"

The stranger did not slow his pace, but kept walking down a gulley and up again on the other side. Baird followed.

"Aye. I did hear, and have heard, the boom of cannon and the din of men killing and dying. Not even the thick stands of trees could keep that sound from my ears."

The stranger's words conjured up the memory of the battle, and the horror of it as well.

"Yes," he said. "Yes. I fight for the Duke of Maubeuge. We battled against a tyrant who oppresses his people and who seeks to enslave the world; an enemy of God and a fiend who consorts with devils. We have been fighting day and night these last five days, and through strength of arms and with the blessing of the Holy Father, we managed to push the evil monster and his last remnants of his army into these woods."

The tall stranger halted a few steps ahead, and turned back to look at the younger infantryman.

"And you believe this man to be evil? That he seeks to destroy all, to enslave the world?"

Baird stared blankly.

"I had no feeling other than my homeland was threatened. I took up arms to defend her."

The stranger said nothing, no trace of any thought or emotion could the soldier read on that hollow-eyed face.

"A young man like yourself should not so blindly follow. You have a mind of your own, do you not?"

"I did not blindly follow," Baird retorted. "I fought for my country, my king and so that the will of the Chu –"

"Keep your loyalties, your politics and your religion," the stranger interrupted. "I care for none of them. Your war is a vain and pathetic thing, and will be remembered by none. What care I for anything of man, after having seen what I have seen, after knowing what I know?"

The strange traveler's eyes burned into the soldier's for a moment longer, then he turned to continue the trek through the forest.

Baird found himself calling after him.

"You may not choose a side, Gelbe of the wood, but one side or the other will choose you nonetheless."

The tall thin man stopped, and turned his head over his shoulder, his voice floating back to the infantryman.

"Truly?"

"Yes. We all have a duty, to fight, to stand against the dark. You cannot stand idle while evil walks among us."

The traveler turned his face away. And then spun back toward him, a mad grin shone on his face, and his large yellow teeth showed between red lips.

"Evil?" Gelbe's laugh was a harsh and bitter one. "Evil you say? You know nothing of evil."

"I have seen enough!" the infantryman barked. "Women and children slaughtered, bodies rotting in ditches. Elders starving in the streets, diseased and forgotten..."

The tall man's laughter grew in volume and exuberance.

"You call that evil? Tis naught but suffering, caused by pettiness and stupidity, ignorant want and vanity; the callous and indifferent machinations of a few who do not feel compassion, or comprehend what true evil is."

Gelbe's laughter died as suddenly as it had come, but the mad glitter of it still shone in his eyes.

"War is not evil, boy. War is folly. Suffering is not evil, it is a consequence. They are all brought about by man's selfishness and greed, the products of ignorant beings who think they are alone, uncomprehending of that which lies beyond their ken."

And with that, he turned and stalked off once more through the endless growth of trees.

The young man watched him and wondered. What had this mad stranger seen that he thought nothing of death and slaughter, suffering and pain?

They tramped through the trees and undergrowth for the better part of the day, down through ditches and into gullies and back up the other sides; they made their way up steep rises and along the edges of long ravines. They clambered over rocks and boulders slick from the rains and covered in carpets of grey-green moss. The light of the day was dimmed by the thick branches and leaves of the ash and birch and elm and oak, clothed in their fiery cloaks of fall. Above them was a canopy of deep reds and purples and browns, simmering oranges and a riot of yellows, and the same blanketed the forest floor. They waded through low streams, their banks overgrown with wisteria, ferns and wildflowers.

Had the circumstances been different, Baird would have

marveled at what surrounded them, but the stranger's gait, and piercing eyes, and the looming feeling of dread that gnawed at him, all cast a pallor over the beauty around him. Where one would see it as peaceful and serene, Baird saw it as a false and dangerous thing. It was beautiful yes, but it was a snare, a lure that would surely lead him to his death if he did not remain watchful.

After several hours, the sunlight began to fail and Gelbe turned to him, the mad spark in his eyes lessened now, his expression weary.

"Night will be upon us soon. We will make camp, for we have traveled enough for this day."

Some distance from where they were standing, way up on a rise and reaching above the trees, Baird could see a large structure made of stone, fallen into disrepair. It was a like unto a watch tower or castle turret, tall and round with a pointed roof of crumbling slate. Its walls and great wooden doors were covered with vines and festooned with mold and moss.

"Should we not perhaps seek shelter from the chill of the night air in yon –"

Gelbe stepped up to him, a long finger upon his lips and hushing the young soldier into silence.

"Nay. Though tis a passing fair dwelling, aged though it may be, best we not venture too close or seek to enter inside."

The tall stranger's voice was calm and sure, but Baird saw something else in his eyes, a warning, and yes, maybe fear as well.

"It would be best we seek it out when the sun is new born or high in the sky. For by the time we were to reach it, darkness would be all around, and tonight shall be a moonless one. Approaching yon dwelling in the dark would be folly."

"What is it do you think?"

Baird saw a flurry of emotions run across the haggard and lined face of his companion, as though he wanted to say a great many things, but as yet did not want to share them.

"Most likely it is the den of some witch or necromancer. We should stay well out of it until daylight is once more our ally. Let us rest, we are both footsore and in need of refreshment, for we have walked far this day."

The soldier took a last look at the odd tower that stood out on the hill across from them, and then sighed in agreement with the tall woodsman.

"I think truer words were never spoken," Baird replied.

They found a suitable spot, a flat area of ground beside a massive boulder, and set about making clearing it for the purpose of laying out their bedrolls and making a fire. Soon, the warm flames were crackling and Gelbe had put out a pot of stew to boil, using dried meats and herbs he had also kept in his pack.

Baird collapsed onto his rough bed with a groan and ripped the boots off his feet, stretching his toes and rubbing out the soreness.

They passed the time before the meal was ready in silence, each man lost in his own thoughts. Out in the forest, the air was still and quiet, except for the occasional cry of some bird or other. Baird had found it strange that they had neither heard nor seen any sort of forest creature on their trek, but until now had not given it a second thought. Now, knowing that forlorn and forgotten tower was close out there in the dark, he began to believe what Gelbe had suggested, that it was the dwelling of something or someone unnatural. The shape of it had seemed ominous and dire in the blood red light of the dying sun.

The young soldier shivered and turned his thoughts to other things, most notably his aching and weary feet.

Soon, the stew was ready and Gelbe served it in wooden bowls from his pack, with rough made tin spoons. It was the best meal Baird had had in days. Savory and pungent he scooped it into his mouth greedily.

"A curious name, Baird" the tall man said as Baird filled his mouth with another bite. "It means poet does it not? Tell me boy, are you a poet?

Baird chewed, and then swallowed, surprised that the tall stranger knew the meaning of a name in a foreign tongue.

"It does, but I am no poet; I have no skill for it," he said, swallowing. "My mother, gone to the angels seven years past, she named me, I think, that I might escape the family trade. Alas, I was a disappointment to her."

Gelbe chewed thoughtfully, looking at the young man, weighing the answer.

"And what was this family trade, what were you in life, before soldiering?"

The question gave the infantryman pause. The war and the fighting had been going on for some time and what he was before being handed the gun seemed a lifetime ago.

"I was… I am a vinter."

The stranger regarded him with those penetrating eyes and then nodded.

"Ah, a son of Dionysus, the drunkard."

Baird made to protest, but Gelbe held up a hand, a sly grin upon his lips.

"I do but jest with ye. It is a good trade."

"It was something I took pride in," Baird beamed.

"Not the most noble of arts," Gelbe's accented words deflated the infantryman somewhat. "But not one that carries any shame. I will brook no poet or actor, for they are frivolous and given to licentiousness. They sell naught but wind and air, which may at first blow hot, but is soon cool and gone once more, worth no more than the fickle clouds that fill the sky. But an honest tradesman? One who tills the earth or draws from it that which eases the hunger, thirst or toil of his fellow man? A farmer, a baker, a tinsmith or shoemaker?

That man I hold in some esteem, for they are doing honest work."

"I feel it was a worthy trade, and it has some mystery to it as well. My father taught me and his father him, back through my family for seven generations. The making of a good wine is a blend of agriculture and alchemy. It is not just the grape, mind you, that produces a fine wine."

"Is it so?" The stranger looked at him, a bemused look upon his features.

"Oh yes," Baird exclaimed. "For instance, the wine you so graciously shared with me, it has a most unusual scent, the hint of a flower I cannot place. Do you know what it might be?"

Gelbe took the wineskin, lifted it to his nose and inhaled, long and deep.

"You have a keen nose, Baird. That is the aroma of a rare plant in my homeland, the kanak, whose potency is said to bestow virility and vitality."

Baird's eyes widened.

"Though, why they would add it to liquor, which robs some men of the ability, I cannot say."

Gelbe winked at Baird, and then both men shared a hearty laugh.

"You are a puzzlement to me," Baird said and Gelbe gave him a questioning look. "You have an air of dire purpose about you, yet you just now have displayed a talent for mirth and gaiety. Tell me Gelbe the tall, what is your tale? What is that has brought here to this strange wood, to meet a poor bedraggled soldier and to share your food and company with? What were you in life, before war? And what, pray tell, is the meaning of your name?"

The mirth died in Gelbe's eyes, replaced by an angry fire in his black, flint colored eyes. For a moment the infantryman thought he might plunge the big knife that still hung from his belt through his heart, but the stranger looked away, off into the dark spaces between the trees.

Gelbe's voice, when he answered, was rough, guarded

"My name is but a word. Like yours, it does not define who I am. What was I? My father was a leatherworker and I learned that trade, before life offered me…" He hesitated before finishing, "Another road."

The infantryman spooned another mouthful of stew once more, chewing thoughtfully.

"That explains your boots then, strange as they are."

Gelbe grunted, turning his right foot to one side, showing the boots of peculiar leather to the firelight.

"You think them so?"

"Indeed. The color, the texture. What beast's hide were they made from?"

Gelbe ran his long fingers over the surface of the boots, and the gesture seemed almost one of affection, but the expression on his face was one of loathing.

"They are unique, are they not?"

Baird looked at them again.

The grain was strange to his eye, and did not look like leather at all in the dappled light of the campfire. They had a grayish cast, with a yellow-green tinge of verge or new hay. But perhaps that was just a trick of the light. They looked almost the color of a lake trout.

"They are most curious. Pray tell me, what manner of beast produces a hide that tans to such a hue?"

Gelbe's features took on a strange expression, almost one of nostalgia, but also mixed with revulsion or disgust.

"T'was a beast, that much is true," he said in a low tone, "but no beast known to any outside the borders of my homeland. They are our curse, our burden."

"What do you mean?" Baird frowned.

"From the dark days, we have known of them. And have tried,

time and again, to drive them from our lands, to eradicate them. This is why I am here, in this forest, I hunt them here, for now they have infected this country as well."

Gelbe shifted his position, moving the boots out of the firelight, as if to hide them from Baird's eyes. Baird looked up to see him looking directly at him.

"If you continue to follow me, you must understand that I will not waver in this quest. I have sworn to slay them to the very last one. To halt the spread of them, for they are the cause of true Evil in the world."

"I do not understand, they are simple beasts are they not?"

"They are not. They are abominations, a deviant and corrupt race; a culture that worships dark gods and that seeks to unmake the world."

Baird did not comprehend at first, but then he felt his gorge rise.

"You mean to say, that those boots you wear, they are made from the skin of –"

"They are not men. They are something worse."

"Who," Baird stammered, "who are you?"

From somewhere deep in the forest there came the cry of some beast, like none that Baird had ever heard before. It was mournful and bone-chilling, the wail of some wounded thing perhaps. The sound chilled Baird's blood.

Gelbe was on his feet quickly, his pistol in one hand and the rifle in the other and charged to the edge of the firelight. Baird scrambled to reach his own weapon, gained his feet and followed after him.

They moved warily through the thick undergrowth. Baird was just about to whisper a question, to ask if the thing that had made that unearthly sound was indeed the creature Gelbe had been hunting, when the stranger halted, so quickly that Baird almost ran into his back.

"Why have we –" he began, but Gelbe turned on him violently, clamping a hand over his mouth and forcing him back behind one of the bigger trees.

"Still your tongue, lest we be heard!" the tall man hissed.

Baird's eyes were wide with alarm. Gelbe held him fast, the strength of his fingers and arms pinning the young soldier to the tree. Baird felt that if the stranger had wanted to, he could have snapped him in half.

"Through yon copse, close to the hillside there are stairs carved from the living rock. They lead, no doubt, to that black and evil tower. It is, I know deep in my soul, the very dwelling place of those vile and evil things I have been seeking these long years, Baird the vinter."

Baird tried to still the rapid inhale of his breath. The madness in Gelbe's eyes, the closeness of his voice, the heat pouring off his skin, filled him with a dread so powerful he feared his heart would cease to beat.

"Calm yourself, you have seen battle, you know the nearness of death; you are a fighting man, are you not?" Gelbe's bitter tone matched the rankness of his breath. Baird tried to turn his head to the side to keep from gagging. "Be still, and calm your fear, for they are out and about in the dark. It is the time when they show themselves to the world, unafraid in the black and starless night. And if they but catch one whiff of your fear, they will destroy us."

Baird's eyes flicked from right to left, seeing things move in every shadow.

"Stay here and tremble, winemaker, let this not be your last night on this earth. Run, and live."

The tall stranger broke away from him and sprinted for the ancient crumbling stairway and soon disappeared up into the darkness.

From out in the night, the strange cry echoed again, a sound alien and full of horror.

Baird, his hands trembling, gripped his rifle tighter and followed Gelbe up the stairs.

They wound up through the rock, steep and uneven, as though made for one whose legs were abnormal and long. Those steps felt too worn, too smooth to the touch, as if they had been scrubbed and polished by eons of wear and use.

At the top, Baird stumbled out on a flat open courtyard and saw the tower rising evilly above him. Not far ahead, he saw Gelbe standing staring up at it.

Baird approached him and whispered, "Who are you, and what are the things you seek in there?"

Gelbe turned his blazing eyes upon him, and Baird saw the man's tortured madness in them.

"I spoke true when I told you I was a traveler, but that is not all I am. I have kept from you the whole of the truth.

"The battles you have fought, the horror and death you have seen, is because I was the man who crossed into your country with an army of fifty thousand. Not to conquer, not to plunder, not to enslave the world. I do not serve demons, I do not consort with witches, devils or trolls... but out there in the dark, up those stairs and in that ancient and accursed place, dwells the thing I have come to fight.

"I am the man they call the King in Yellow Tatters, Tatterdemalion, the right arm of the Devil. And I have come to destroy that which seeks to destroy us all."

Just then, another of the great beastly wails shattered the night and both men turned to face the tower.

At the base of the tower, time-worn and covered in vines and rot, the great oaken doors to the structure suddenly burst asunder. Pouring out of them came the stuff of nightmare. Great tendrils of some gargantuan beast, coils of spine covered tentacles, roiled and flailed the air, seeking trees and rocks and anything else to crush and destroy. And in the center, an impossibly huge gaping maw, filled with rows of yellowed, sharp teeth.

Baird's mind recoiled, unable to fathom the meaning or scope of what his eyes beheld.

Gelbe fired first his pistol and then the rifle sending metal slugs into the giant limbs that blindly sought the things that caused them pain.

The mad king drew the huge hunting knife from his belt, turned and screamed at Baird.

"You are a soldier, are you not!? See you now the enemy!? See you now the true face of evil? Then fight! Fight! Fight!"

Donkeyskin

~ Brian Kaufman ~

The man smiled, as if at a secret joke, and then answered the question. "Pizzle. Everyone calls him Pizzle."

The poor fellow in question hobbled away, trailing strips of his breeches behind him.

The smiling man closed his eyes and fingered the trimmed patch of hair at the tip of his chin. "The wind outside is terrible, is it not? Yes, you are correct. There is a tale behind the unusual name. And here we are, fellow travelers seeking shelter. The fire is warm, and the ale is strong, not sour. One might expect a tankard in return for a well-told story." His teeth shone in the firelight.

"I am jesting, of course," he said, leaning forward, elbows on the wooden table. "In truth, you are twice-blessed. I will tell you the tale, and I will keep your cup full." He glanced at the innkeeper, who nodded in return. "But the account is intricate, and will require your patience. Sit back. Drink. A storm is coming, but we have a roof over our heads."

He took a sip from his tankard and sat back. He wore the finery of a nobleman, but his cuffs were soiled and his hair tangled. "To tell the tale of Pizzle, I need first to tell of Donkeyskin."

The innkeeper delivered a round of drinks. He was a thick man with a belly like bread pudding. The last vestiges of his hair had been twirled and perched at the top of his head, but when he bent to deliver the ale, the tiny pile spilled forward.

"Yes, everyone thinks they know about Donkeyskin. Children whisper the name to each other. It is all the fashion." He took another sip of ale. "A wise man might say there's a kernel of truth in every fable. I will produce that kernel. Indeed, I will produce the entire ear!" He burst out laughing, and then began:

A fortunate king ruled vast lands and a sturdy castle. He married a beautiful queen who bore him two daughters. And he owned a marvelous donkey. The beast was stronger and smarter than any other animal in the kingdom. And the beast's droppings were laced with gold, which added greatly to the king's wealth.

But the king's reign would not be without heartache. His queen took ill and died. On her deathbed, the queen extracted a promise that he not remarry unless he found a queen as beautiful as she had been.

Time passed—a decade and more. The king realized that the only woman fitting to his promise was his eldest daughter. She was a beautiful girl with dark hair, piercing eyes, faint, lovely freckles, and a sensual mouth. He decided they would marry.

The daughter was distraught. She agreed to the marriage, but with conditions. The king would have to provide a number of stunning gowns, including one that shone as bright as the sun. Another would have to be the color of the sky. A third would have to be the exact color of the moon.

Finally, the daughter required her father to slay the magic donkey, and deliver the skin. This last requirement left the daughter confident that the marriage would never be consummated.

Much to her surprise, the king commissioned the creation of the wardrobe and killed the donkey. He delivered the skin, along with the three dresses, demanding that she keep her end of the bargain.

The daughter agreed, setting a date for the marriage, all the while planning for her escape. Donning the donkey skin as her disguise, she left her father's castle and headed into the forest.

She traveled as far as her resources and stamina would allow. Still wearing the donkey skin, she came to the castle of a minor lord. She knocked on the door of the servant's quarters and begged for work. The cook was a kind old woman who knew that no one would hire such an ugly girl. She gave Donkeyskin a meal and questioned her knowledge of cooking. Donkeyskin's mother had shared long hours in the kitchen, baking for fun, so the girl knew her way around an oven. The cook took pity on the girl and hired her.

Donkeyskin lived in fear of her father, the king. So she stayed in her disguise, and after time, she was forgotten by everyone but the cook, who pitied her.

One day, a prince on a quest stopped at the castle. He was a tall, handsome young man with coal-black hair and eyes like sapphires. The lord extended every courtesy, providing the prince with lodging and meals. The latter was of primary interest to the prince, as he had not eaten since early morning. Supper would not be served until the winter sun set, so the lord's footman delivered the prince to the kitchen for a quick meal to tide him over. Sitting near the cook's hearth, the prince looked up from a bowl of stew and biscuits to notice Donkeyskin.

The girl hunched over a cutting board, brushing folds of animal hide from her face, peering down at her knife and its intended target, a pile of onions. The prince frowned, forgetting the stew for the moment. What was so compelling about the girl? She was ugly to be sure, but something in her shape called to him—not the actual shape that shuffled and scraped behind the wooden table, but rather the suggested shape beneath the folds. She looked up, as if sensing his gaze. Her eyes shone, reflecting firelight. Then she looked away.

The prince smiled. Perhaps the girl had a story.

Later that evening, he went exploring. He'd learned the location of the servant's quarters from the lord's footman. Creeping down stairs and darkened halls, he came to a tiny room behind the kitchen. The wooden door was slightly ajar, just enough to peer inside.

The storyteller paused and smiled. "Convenient, no?" He chuckled. "Therein lies the happy economy of a children's story. No closed doors. And so our hero rushes to his fate, unimpeded by clumsy circumstance."

He emptied his cup and motioned to the innkeeper. Glancing back, he asked, "Another draught? Don't let me drink past you, my friend. My tale has a certain distance to go, and we should arrive together."

He looked around the room, his gaze settling on a young girl tending the fire. "Do you see that lass there? Handsome thing, though her hair is a bit unkempt. And even at this distance, you can see that her eyes are set too close together. Shame." He paused. "Now imagine her more lovely still—her eyes reset, her hair curled about her face like a frame around a picture, her breasts ever-so-slightly larger. A pleasant picture, but not enough to match what the prince found behind the door. Not enough by half."

For she was the most beautiful woman the prince had ever seen. Eyes like onyx in the firelight, a nose upturned at the last moment to give perfection its finishing touch. Dark hair cascaded over her naked shoulders, her breasts, full and ripe, her nipples covered by the very hair he admired but suddenly could not forgive. She pulled free of the donkey skin that had marked her as ugly, discarding her disguise for the night.

He sighed, a reflex that gave him away. She started, crossing her chest with her arms, her lips pressed tight. The prince might have tendered an apology and backed away from the door, but then the story would be over. Instead, he pushed forward, putting a finger to his lips to quiet the girl. "No harm will come to you," he promised, and indeed, he would not have allowed a single hair from her head to be plucked. He was already in love.

The next morning, he requested that the girl bake him a cake. Once again hidden beneath the donkey skin, the girl appeared loathsome and dirty, so the castle's lord could scarcely believe the request. But princes are known to be capricious, and so the cake was baked under the watchful eye of the head cook.

The poor girl did not notice that her ring, a memento from her departed mother, was missing until after the cake was nestled in the bread oven.

That evening, the cake was served, topped with sugars and treats. The prince took a huge piece, and sat staring at the girl as he chewed. Then he bit down on the ring.

"What is this?" he cried, holding the trinket up for all to see. Donkeyskin shuddered with fear. Would the prince beat her?

He stood and, in a voice that rattled the rafters, declared that he would marry the woman whose finger fit the ring. The head cook scurried forward to try, but her little sausage fingers did not fit so well. When Donkeyskin came forward, her slender finger slipped into the ring easily, and the prince was engaged.

His parents, of course, had to be convinced of the wisdom of the union. But when they saw the girl dressed in the fine gowns she'd taken with her when she fled her father's house, they realized that the girl came from nobility, and they agreed to the marriage.

Shortly after the ceremony, the prince and his bride received a message from the girl's father. He'd learned of the marriage and sent congratulations, along with news—he'd finally found someone as beautiful as his deceased wife, and married her. Given the happy circumstances for all parties, the two families formed an alliance, and everyone lived in perpetual joy.

"The end," the storyteller said. He took another drink, and then wiped his mouth with the sleeve of his tunic. He set the tankard down with a thump. The innkeeper jumped at the sound.

"Yes, you know the tale. Probably know it well. Children fall fast asleep to the happy conclusion. But what of the story itself? Is there a lesson to be culled?"

Another draught delivered, he took a huge swallow. His voice became louder, and some of the other guests made their way from the room, perhaps preferring sounds of the storm and the comfort of a warm bed to the storyteller's tale. Within a few minutes, the Great Room of the Inn had cleared, leaving only the Innkeeper, the cook's girl and the sot with the odd walk to hear the rest of the story.

"The moral of Donkeyskin lies in the nature of relations. Daughters marry and leave. Donkeys, on the other hand, are forever." He paused, and then burst out laughing—the sound of a two-handed saw cutting through the trunk of a dead tree.

"A jest, merely a jest," he continued, wiping his eyes with his sleeve. "There is no lesson. A purpose? Perhaps, but a purpose hidden in the folds of the tale." He closed his eyes. "You see, I know the truth behind the prince and Donkeyskin. A hidden truth."

To begin, the prince was not a prince. He was the eldest son of a landed noble, on an errand to pay taxes, secure some needed supplies and see to his father's investments in Boston. You see, the young man was native to the Americas, not the old country.

On his return trip, he took a less-traveled road, through dark woods and narrow glens, over streams and brooklets that gurgled past moss-covered rocks and tumbled over broken ledges into deep pools. At length, he came to somewhat gentler slopes, and a manor house. Presenting himself, he was welcomed as an honored guest.

Impatient for a meal, the traveler sought out the kitchen. There, he encountered a servant girl, who was at once, ugly and fascinating. He resolved to seek her out—a diversion, and nothing more. Later that evening, after paying due attention to his host, the young man went searching. The servant girl's door, so conveniently open in the story you know, was in fact open. Herein lies a lesson: history turns on small details. Why did the girl leave her door cracked? Did she anticipate a visit? Was she so certain of her privacy that she gave the door no thought?

Either way, the traveler was surprised to discover a beautiful girl standing naked in front of a full-length mirror. Though her back faced the young man, her lovely face was visible in the mirror's reflection. The girl wore no animal hide. She was the victim of a horrific condition of the skin that left her covered in scabs and scales.

She did not notice him. Instead, she concentrated on peeling the layers of desiccated flesh that marked her as ugly from the raw, pink flesh beneath, stripping the leathery folds as if shucking an ear of corn. A pile of discarded pieces lay at her feet.

When she noticed him, her face betrayed her thoughts. First, the pure, open-mouthed despair of having been found out. Then her face acquired a tight-lipped sort of resolve, shoulders thrown back, gaze cast down, silently waiting for the derision that was sure to follow.

But the girl had a pretty face.

For the next three days, the noble traveler and the girl stole every private moment together. Being a poor servant, she would have no dowry, but when the girl revealed her true lineage, the last obstacle to their union dropped away. After the third day, the traveler announced his intentions. He would marry the girl and take her with him.

His father was against the marriage. The girl's affliction was not temporary. The hideous skin that covered her grew like a fungus, and had to be pruned. Freshly plucked, she skinned over like a peeled carrot within days.

And, the girl was estranged from her wealthy father.

But Donkeyskin still had some belongings (others having been given to the lord who'd sheltered her and provided her with a servant's position), including a beautiful full-length mirror, which found a new home in the bedroom of the noble traveler's parents.

Thus convinced of the girl's virtues, the traveler's father agreed to the union.

On the night of the wedding, Donkeyskin tore at her carapace so that the marriage could be consummated, even though she'd recently plucked herself raw. Bloody patches being slightly preferable to dead tissue, the deflowering commenced. And that should have ended the true story of Donkeyskin, for since the time of the Bard, the wedding bed is where good stories end.

But not this one.

As the storyteller paused, the wind howled outside, rattling the inn's shutters. Inside, the fire had begun to dwindle, but when the innkeeper approached it with a fresh log, the storyteller waved him off and then pointed to empty tankards. The storyteller's mood had changed. His voice dropped low, matching the moan of the storm. Rain battered the roof, seeming to further dampen his spirits. His gaze darted from room corner to room corner, peering into the shadows with what appeared to be dread. A single crack of thunder caused him to jump, nearly spilling his drink. "Nearly a tragedy," he joked, but his voice carried no humor.

The poor drunk in the corner, Pizzle, had fallen asleep, his head cocked back, mouth open. Only the innkeeper stood watch. The cook's girl had gone to bed.

"You might well ask, how do I know the true story of Donkeyskin?" He leaned forward, his voice dropping, as if in conspiracy. His left eye twitched as he spoke. "The young traveler who married Donkeyskin was my older brother." He sat back, and glanced away. His lip trembled slightly, giving some small air of credibility to his claim.

"It seems the girl left her father for the very reason told in the children's story. He was a vile man, without Christian virtue. He wanted her as his bride. Even so, my father sent me to inform him of the impending nuptials. I gathered what directions I could from

Donkeyskin—yes, that's what I called her, though she was to be my sister-in-law—and I set out to deliver my message.

I'd been warned that the road to her father's manor was rough business, cut through primal wilderness. Along the way, I found nothing but ruin. Old stone chimneys, shattered wood and broken brick littered the poor patches of earth where homes had once stood. The trees were stunted—poor, twisted things with tortured trunks and slick gray leaves that blotted out the sun. The undergrowth ruled the road, choking it with weeds. As the day passed, the road narrowed, and I heard the rustle and slither of the underbrush.

I had begun to despair finding my destination when the road came to an abrupt end in a copse of trees. Had I taken a wrong turn? With sunset approaching, I began to search for a safe place to spend the night. I dismounted and tied my horse to a tree branch, careful to knot the bridle, for the horse was uneasy and might have bolted.

I walked through the copse, hoping for a resumption of the road. Instead, I found the manor where Donkeyskin's father lived. There was no mistaking the two-story house, the old stone well and the low, flat barn, situated in a perfect triangle as she had described prior to my leaving.

The sun was setting, so at first, I doubted my eyes. The triangle that marked the manor's grounds was circumscribed by a perfect circle of gray, which did not appear to be grass. As I approached, my steps slowed. The ground gave way like sand. The poor scrub underfoot thinned and then disappeared altogether, leaving a surface that was more ash than earth.

I could detect no sign of life. The front door to the manor stood open, but my gaze could not penetrate the darkness within. I stopped by the well. A stench from below turned my stomach. Once, when I was no more than ten years old, my father's cook spilled hot oil, burning her legs horribly. The burns festered, and she died of the infection. Though my father was against any such kindness, my mother sent me to the cook's bed with some wine for the pain. The old woman's legs smelled like that well.

Huge trees ringed the house, more gnarled and hideous than any I'd yet seen. The only other vegetation in sight was a patch of something foul, more gray than green, pasted to the north wall of the manor house. My gaze drifted to the second floor of the crumbling building. There, peering through a small window, I saw a face.

I stood for a long time, staring at the countenance, and I'm certain it stared back. Thin, pale, framed with dark, unruly hair. Yet, the face was so still, so motionless, that I began to doubt my eyes.

Already unnerved, I heard a cry issue from the barn.

I am not a religious man. I have my own kingdom—taverns and brothels—and I happily leave the rest of creation to God. But that demon's howl might have sent me straight to seminary, so fierce was the sound, bubbling up from the bowels of hell. And I stood helpless as the sun dropped down—

Gone. The sun had set as I stood there, yet I could see. The trees behind the house seemed to glow. Even the ground beneath my feet had a soft, sickening sheen that lit the center of the triangle. You might call me foolish, and blame the reflection of the moon for the light, but the moon was hidden in the clouds that night. I tell you, the manor and its surroundings glowed.

I am not a timid man. Nothing of this world surprises or frightens me. Yet I trembled, that evening, standing in the circle of ash, for the scene was unnatural. A blight had taken hold of the manor and its grounds. The stench of the well permeated everything.

The unholy shriek came from the barn again, this time with urgency. I took a single step back, but the ground gave way beneath my feet, and I tumbled back flat, my hands splayed out into the repugnant soil. I stared at the barn door, waiting for the beast inside to emerge. When nothing happened, I forced myself up, first by grasping the walls of the well. The cold, vile texture of the masonry was like bone. What horrors nested unseen in the well's depths? And who would dare drink from that festering hole? I let go and stood without further assistance, my eyes never leaving the barn door.

Then came a third howl, more frightening than any other that had preceded it. As I watched, struck dumb with horror, the door swung open. The creature that emerged was a mass of fluttering tissues and pus, lit from below by the glowing ash. Larger than any man by a factor of two, the thing raised its head and bellowed again, all anguish and pain. As it tossed its tortured head, bits of skin shook free and dropped to the ground. And then I recognized the beast for what it was.

The prize donkey from the story, alive but not well, suffering from the very skin disease that afflicted my brother's fiancé.

The thing took a single step toward me. I screamed then, and I kept screaming as I ran from the manor house. My poor horse was gone—frightened, no doubt, by the hellish braying of the donkey. I found the steed miles down the road. I believe that animal was as glad to see me as I was to see it.

The storyteller sat back, a silhouette in the cold, darkened room. The fire had burned down to embers—soft, glowing points like eyes in the dark. The wind continued to roar outside, spraying rain against shuttered windows. When he spoke again, his voice trembled.

"Yes, I promised to tell you about the name." He pointed at the sleeping drunk. "That is my older brother. He doesn't look like much now, but he was a fine one, a long decade ago. But after his marriage, we noticed a change. He took to drink. He ignored his wife, which seemed to cause her great sorrow. He stopped sleeping and acquired a haunted look, as if his wife were a succubus, draining him bit by bit. His face became thin and drawn, his eyes sunken and sullen." The storyteller's voice had become cold as the empty room.

"Then one night," he continued, "he sat drinking in this very inn. All of a sudden, he began to scream and cry. As often as he drank, I thought him to be suffering from bottle ache. Then he pitched onto the floor, right there—"

The storyteller paused to point at a spot just five feet from the table. "That's when we saw the lump in his pantaloons. The way he was screaming, as if he'd been bitten? We thought it was a rat. Others held him down while I slit the clothing open with a knife, ready to stab the vermin that had attacked my poor drunken brother. But it wasn't a rat. The lump was his manhood, rotted off, and dropped down the leg of his clothing."

"And that," the storyteller said, "is why they call him Pizzle."

The innkeeper stood against the back wall, staring down at the floor. A gust rattled the windows, and the embers in the fireplace seemed to shiver and then wink out. In the darkness, any atrocity seemed possible.

"And that is how I came into my fortune, for my father would not leave an inheritance to a son who was no longer a man. And that is also why I mistreat my fortune. I can never own it. I can only spend it." He took one last draw from the tankard and set it aside.

Outside, the wind rose to a shriek.

"The girl disappeared. I think sometimes that my father did away with her himself, though he was loath to touch her, having seen the consequences of a night in her bed." He sat back. Only his outline was visible now. "And so I make visible the purpose behind the children's story of Donkeyskin. It's a fairy's tale, meant to hide the truth from a world that teeters on the edge of madness. Insane fathers and diseased daughters. Glowing ash. Demon donkeys? A well cut straight down to hell? Listen to the storm! Things wait in the darkness! We need stories to recast the truth, lest we go mad."

The innkeeper was gone. The room had gone black.

"One last word, friend, before you shiver your way to your bed."

Pizzle moaned somewhere in the dark.

"A few months ago, a traveler sat in your very seat, telling me the news of the county. That is how I learned the true end of my story. Seems that a nobleman, fallen on hard times but still possessing land and some small resources, married his daughter. You see, the father had two daughters—one much younger than the first. And when the younger girl was old enough, the father wedded her. Not in a church, of course. A local magistrate performed the ceremony. The man claimed the girl was a distant cousin, but people knew about her, shut away in the upper story of the house, and gossip travels."

"So you see," he finished, "at least the father lived happily ever after."

The Batrachian Prince

~ Robert M. Price ~

In my previous life (and that is no mere figure of speech), I was a graduate student in Biology at the Miskatonic University in Arkham, Massachusetts. The place has a certain notoriety for unconventional courses of study, but that was of no interest to me. The school had a strong Marine Biology program, founded decades ago, at least partly because of the historic connection of Arkham with the maritime trade. My own lifelong fascination with the sea and its myriad of life forms, so utterly alien to our own familiar mammals, inclined me to the subject, and I was fortunate to live close to an institution where I might pursue it in real depth. My parents died, I am told, in my infancy, and I was reared by somewhat distant but loving relatives, and my financial situation was secure. I suppose I cannot say I loved my mother and father, never having known them, but I have always felt genuine gratitude for their kind provision.

I possessed no real friends, not outside of class anyway, but my studies consumed almost all of my time, so I felt no lack. The one exception was more than a friend. Gloria Wentworth, my fiancée, was the young and pretty faculty secretary, and I encountered her frequently in passing. Before long we enjoyed lunch together most days. Then I found it was not so very hard to pull myself away from my labs and my books to see a movie with her or just to spend a quiet, romantic evening in either of our campus apartments. We quickly became very close, something which frankly surprised me, given my cerebral, almost cold-blooded, preoccupations.

It was thus with reluctance that I bade goodbye to Gloria for what I assured her would be a research trip of only a couple of weeks. She understood the necessity of it and told me, with loving eyes, that she would be counting the days.

My research had taken an unanticipated direction once I stumbled across some scholarly debate over a theory concerning coastal groups of primates somewhere in primal Africa who thrived on fish scooped up from the waves. The existence of such creatures could be safely surmised from fossil evidence. Where the controversy began was over speculation that these proto-humans, some said apes, gradually adapted to the life of marine mammals, exactly in the fashion of manatees, seals, even dolphins and whales. Supporters of the theory appealed to legends and rumored sightings of mermaids. As usual, such suggestions tended to lend the theory less plausibility rather than more, tempting the skeptics to consign the theory to the same rubbish bin as the legends invoked to defend it. Guilt by association.

Something occurred to me as soon as I read of this scholarly tempest in a teapot; instantly my mind flitted to the near-local rumors of strange half-human forms once found in the swollen rivers of Vermont and, closer to home, the "urban" legends of Innsmouth where xenophobic alarm at the intermarriage of town fishermen with Polynesian women gave rise to hysterical claims of miscegenation with aquatic bipeds. On the face of it, of course, it was absurd. Yet there was somehow enough to make me curious. Perhaps had I lived farther away from the Essex County seaport, I might have dismissed the whole matter. As it was, I couldn't resist the temptation – suppose there *had* been some sort of genetic funny business? No one denied that many Innsmouth denizens had a

pretty strange look about them. Photographs showed recurrent facial and anatomical anomalies that could not be readily accounted for by inbreeding or intermarriage. It wouldn't hurt to get a firsthand look. So I made my plans, for all the good it did me. As you will see, I was utterly unprepared for what, and whom, I would find.

I took a train and a couple of startlingly decrepit busses to Innsmouth. I regretted my decision to make the trip as soon as I got a glimpse of the town from the filthy bus window. It was surprising that the place was still inhabited given the total dilapidation of it. I had of course read about the submarine attack on the wharfs. I knew of the internment camps, something unthinkable today but quite acceptable back in the 1920s. After all, only two decades later, Japanese Americans were herded into the same confinement. But, compared to present-day Innsmouth, an internment camp would have been an improvement. Many rows of once-charming Victorian and Colonial structures lay in ruins, their fronts standing tenuously like neglected stage sets on a studio lot. Streets were pocked with puddle-filled craters and blocked with scattered bricks and boards, to say nothing of the heaps of moldering garbage. Children wandered between cardboard huts and rusting trailer homes that were placed randomly wherever space permitted, some right in the middle of the streets, some lying across the abandoned foundations of long-demolished houses.

The bus could drive only so far into this wasteland, and so I hoisted my suitcase and clothing zip bag and watched my step as I bemoaned the sight of the bus rattling into reverse and leaving me to take my chances. Why didn't I just get back on board and return home? Maybe I thought of Kafka's advice that one ought to press on even once one realizes it is the wrong path. He would have been proud of me.

I found an old hotel shuttered and locked. It had once been called The Gilman House. The sign bearing that name still hung over the lintel, while a later, smaller board had not replaced it but had been merely nailed onto it. It read The Harbor Inn, though I seem to recall it was misspelled. In the street lay a third signboard. The rainwater had diluted the crudely painted letters to the point of illegibility. I kept walking and looking for shelter. I thought I might find some help at a church building. The first I saw turned out to have been repurposed as some sort of Masonic Lodge, the Esoteric Order of Dagon, a name redolent of the boyish play-secrecy with which stolid citizens amused themselves in the late nineteenth century. But it, too, was closed down.

I had better luck (as I then considered it) at another clapboard sanctuary with the improbable name of Saint Toad's. I remembered Minnesota's St. Cloud, a variant on "Saint Claude," and wondered where this odd name came from. Possibly some garbled form of "Saint Thaddeus"? But I thought no more of it once a fumbling at the latch answered my knock.

All within was shrouded by shadows, though the declining sunlight managed for a moment to illumine a stained glass window at the far end of the entrance hall. I think it depicted Noah's flood, but it looked as if some great shapes were surfacing beside the pitching ark. Then the light was gone. As my eyes adjusted to the gloom, I realized the reason for the lack of lamplight in the place: my host was blind or very nearly so, his bulging orbs thickly filmed with cataracts. His lips were thick and flaccid and gave an element of theatrical comedy to his speech. He was clad in black with a white collar, a generically clerical garb. His manner somehow straddled a line between avuncular paternalism and uneasy suspicion.

I told him my purpose (in the most general terms) and my circumstances. The stooped man, not bothering to feign eye-contact, listened attentively, beckoned me to take a seat. Suddenly it dawned upon me that the interior of this building formed the starkest of contrasts with the calamitous ruins of the town outside. Here, even amid the deepening shadows, it was evident that the Victorian furnishings were well cared for, and what I could see of the room was dry, warm, and tidy.

He was a man of few words, but he was quick enough to address my question, my request for lodging. I had not invited myself, but the clergyman, who styled himself Father Merman (a name that struck me as somehow humorous), kindly invited me to stay the night, and longer if it suited me, in a spare room in the rectory. I gratefully accepted and followed his shuffling gait down a dimly lit hall. I was cordial with the wrinkled old man, but I felt strangely reluctant to inquire as to his denominational affiliation. But it mattered little, I told myself, as he was manifestly practicing the true religion of charity to strangers.

As I unpacked my necessities and settled in, stretching out on the fresh bed, I began to review my situation and to lay plans for the morrow. My research was necessarily ill defined, but I began to try to delineate my goals in light of the puzzling contrasts I had witnessed this day. There was plainly a segment of Innsmouth society, what remained of it, that retained social and economic privilege. I thought of the medieval priests who reigned like aristocrats over their dirt-poor flocks—until the latter had finally had enough and rose up against them. Was Innsmouth possibly teetering on such a fault line? I could not imagine the street urchins and vacant-eyed scarecrows I had passed in the street rejoicing in the comforts of their clergy. It was pretty clear that little or none of the resources at the disposal of the priesthood was making its way to the indigent of Innsmouth. Of course, I was an outsider and had no real right to judge. Perhaps I would learn more tomorrow. It was none of my business, but I did want to avoid causing any offense that might hinder my inquiries.

I was tired both physically and emotionally. Ready for sleep, I looked for my cell phone to tell my Gloria of my safe arrival. And I saw that I had forgotten it. Perhaps I could borrow the church office phone the next morning.

I awoke to the shining of the dawn, then washed and dressed. I left my room and found my way to the parlor, where I was in for quite a surprise. There, in the light of day, a semicircle of chairs held the well-dressed bottoms of what appeared to be the aristocracy of Innsmouth. I would have taken them for wealthy merchants, bankers, and other community leaders, as presumably they must have been, but for the manifest fact that the town I saw could not possibly harbor banks, stores, or functioning community institutions. It appeared to be on the losing side of a devastating war. And then I thought again of the Federal assault on the town decades before.

These men, and they were all men, were quite odd looking. One did not notice this at first because all of them *belonged*. They were birds of a feather. Or perhaps fish of a… fin? Frogs of a… well, why belabor it? Their limply hanging suits belonged to earlier decades. All were bald or balding, like the reverse of those clubs where all the members agree to grow beards. They had, really, a family resemblance. Perhaps I had been premature in dismissing inbreeding as the origin of the infamous "Innsmouth look." Their similarity was impossible to ignore, but it was the elephant in the room. One dared not mention it.

On the other hand, this might be the perfect entry point for my study of the Innsmouth population and its genetic peculiarities. I would try to bring up the matter as discreetly as possible as soon as an opportunity might arise. But now, in this peculiar moment, what could these town elders want with me? Were outsiders so unwanted that an unwelcome wagon would turn out in force?

The clergyman rose. "Mr… I believe you said your name was, ah, Ephraim Stanley? Yes, well. Mr. Stanley, we have some idea why you're here. It's, ah, we know some people at Miskatonic. After what you told me last night, I checked with them…"

Here I held up my hand. "Excuse me, but that reminds me!

When we're done here, I wonder if I might use your telephone…"

The man seemed puzzled. "Er, we don't have telephone service here. It's rather primitive, I'm afraid." Now it was my turn to be puzzled. A different man, staring without real focus, spoke up as the priest sat down in deference.

"We hear you are well studied in ja… ja… *genetics*. Is that right?"

Who could they have been talking with? And overnight?

"Well, my field is more general than that, though I do know a bit about genetics, but I'm afraid my focus is on aquatic and marine animals. I confess, I am interested in knowing about your unique… heritage here in Innsmouth. I hope that is not offensive to you…"

A third man spoke up, his voice struggling and gurgling in a sickening way. He spoke as if unaccustomed to speaking, though not unfamiliar with the language. Not exactly a foreigner, but a stranger in some more profound sense.

"No, no, Mr. Stanley! We are quite pleased. Your arrival here is fortuitous. We would much appreciate your help."

"I, I'm not a licensed physician…"

"But you are a man of science, no? I believe we can offer you a unique opportunity to plumb the depths. Of your interest."

Needless to say, I was immediately and thoroughly intrigued. And I told them so. I knew I was stumbling through a door to the unknown, but was that not ever the case with pioneering science?

In the days that followed, they promised, an amazing new world would be opened to me. The secrecy, even the paranoia, of Innsmouth was well known. What could account for this astonishing reversal? Here I was, a virtual unknown to the Innsmouth elders, and they took me into their utmost confidence. I quickly learned that there was ample reason for this exceptional treatment. Though they pledged to initiate me into wonders undreamt of by the common run of mankind, I must swear never to reveal any of it afterward. I readily assented, even though it meant a significant sacrifice. I was to be vouchsafed a momentous scientific revelation that would otherwise afford me professional notoriety. But it was better to gain knowledge that I must keep to myself than to remain ignorant.

After a round of strangely damp and flaccid handshakes, looking into unblinking and almost expressionless faces, I sat down to breakfast over heaping platters of kippers (I think) and some sort of batter-dipped crustaceans. There was nothing offensive or distasteful about this fare, but it did seem a slightly odd menu. There was neither coffee nor milk. No fruit juice, either. Just pitchers of water, water with a faint tang. The rubbery-faced gentlemen seemed about as animated as they could get, for their business was urgent. Let me summarize.

It seemed that the clannish inhabitants of this shunned and isolated fishing village were indeed a unique population, hybrids or mutants. Just looking at them made that clear. And this is why the subsequent disclosures were not as shocking as one might have expected. The facts were undeniably tangible before me, so that, once forthcoming, their explanation struck me as less of a mystery than a resolution of one. Thus can even wonders unimaginable be rendered almost anticlimactic. And that is a good thing.

The old men held a firm belief that sounded to me like any one of a hundred origin myths one might find repeated around the campfires of primitive tribes. It was surprising to hear it from the lips of these modern men, however strange in manner and appearance. They held as scientific fact that, only a few generations ago, their forbears had interbred with roughly human intruders from the ocean depths off Polynesia whose kindred then followed the mariners home and commenced wholesale intermingling. Of course, I recognized these tales, which I mentioned earlier. I had regarded them as the derogatory slurs of fearful outsiders, and it surprised me to hear the same thing from the objects of that mockery. And yet something extremely unusual certainly lurked in the genetic past of

Innsmouth. And then there were those hypothetical sea-apes—who were starting to seem less hypothetical all the time.

The Innsmouthers believed themselves directly descended from ichthyic or amphibian creatures, with whom, however, their human forbears should never have been reproductively compatible. There was yet more to it, for which they did not yet think me ready, but the basic problem was that the unnatural intercourse between the two species, while viable and fruitful for several generations, had gradually run dry. Innsmouth females (they did not use the word "women") could no longer bear young. In fact, the original interbreeding "experiment" had been necessitated because the original, unmixed "Deep Ones" had mysteriously lost the ability to procreate. Some unknown factor (I guessed pollution of the oceans from the surface world) had rendered the females of the species barren en masse. Thus the fish-men sought out the women of Innsmouth in a desperate bid to perpetuate their threatened species. What else had they to gain?

In short, they hoped I might find some way to reinvigorate the Innsmouth genome. And to this end they promised to put all their resources at my disposal. Silently I mused: what resources could they be talking about, given the primitive destitution of the town?

The group arose as one and beckoned me to follow. We entered the nave of the unlit church, then paced up the carpeted steps to the chancel. Behind the altar table was concealed a trap door. I thought momentarily of the panel door that opened to the attic in my family's home. We used to store the boxed-up Christmas ornaments up there. I wondered what secrets awaited us down the stone steps now revealed.

My strange new friends and I descended by the wavering light of a greenish flame far below us. I could not tell how old the architecture was. Parts of the walls bore chipped rows of glyphs, others featuring bas relief murals swarming with eerily life-like aquatic creatures, though none that I recognized from any conventional zoology or mythology. We plodded on in hushed silence.

I suppose I half-expected eventually to come upon some cobwebbed alchemist's den. The sight that greeted my light-startled eyes was instead a modern scientific facility complete with glittering instrument banks and shiny steel lab tables and gurneys. At once I knew where the wealth of Innsmouth had been directed. I gaped for a few moments, then took tentative steps around the vast chamber, examining the equipment. Finally I turned to the waiting committee.

"I don't understand, gentlemen. If you have such science, you must have scientists. Where are they? And why on earth do you need me?"

The priest stepped forth from the rest. "We *had* scientists. But their experiments killed them. They must have picked up some contagion they didn't mean to create. We don't know. None survive to explain what happened—if they even knew themselves."

"That's a challenge, that's for sure. I'm really flying blind here, but I'll do what I can. First, though… I get the impression you were *expecting* me. Am I crazy, or what?"

The men looked at each other; then one spoke. "You are not entirely unknown to us, Mr. Stanley. We have, er, kept up with you…"

I could tell I would not be getting much more of an explanation, at least not for the present. One more try. "Listen, I really need to contact my fiancée. It looks like I'll be away longer than I thought. Are you sure you don't have a telephone I can use? Just this once?"

"Mr. Stanley, we'll, ah, look into it."

In view of the technology surrounding us, it was ludicrous to pretend these people were too rural and remote to keep up with the modern world. I shrugged. I probably should have suspected danger here, but I guess I am one of those naïve scientists. And I was genuinely eager to embark on the project at hand.

I decided that Gloria would not be worried yet. I would see what I could do in a few days.

The next few days were an adventure in crypto-biology, if not exo-biology. My hosts understood that I needed to have as much information as possible concerning the evolutionary development of their people. I was in for a shock when they paraded before me a series of individuals representing each major stage of their people's metamorphosis. It was like one of those textbook evolutionary charts depicting the slow march of pre-humans on their way to Neanderthal and Cro-Magnon. Only these embodied the milestones in the very long life of each Innsmouther. The sight of the advanced specimens was naturally startling to me, but I was not afraid as a layman might have been. What a thrill it was for me as a biologist to see in living flesh not only the hunched and bulge-eyed type I had met and conversed with, but also the upright cousins of the shark and the Dimetrodon. I thought of various 1950s monster films. You know which is stranger between truth and fiction.

But the greatest surprise of all was that even this was not the end goal of the evolution of the Deep Ones. Eventually the creatures would swell and bloat, quite slowly, till they lost all definition and became what they called "shoggoths." The succession of radically different forms was analogous to the larva-pupa-adult sequence of insects, but it was strange to observe it in higher life forms, especially since these beings actually did pass from mammal, not merely to water-dwellers, but to amphibians, to fish, and then to amoeboid, albeit gigantic, creatures. My neck became stiff from constantly shaking my head in amazement.

Another peculiarity lay in the mechanism of the mutation. The elders told me wild tales of the old days when the sea-denizens mated with the Innsmouth women. It sounded like the rape of the Sabine women, an atrocity, but these oldsters recounted the events as if they were nothing unusual or untoward. It was chilling. But as I listened carefully, it began to dawn on me that sexual union was not the only factor in the mutation process. According to town memory, it was not only the offspring of the original unions who mutated, but, given time, even those first mothers. I began to wonder if there was another means of contagion, perhaps a gene-altering virus. Or maybe something like pheromone transfer might have something to do with it. This was a hopeful possibility in that, if the well of sexual fecundity could not be refilled, there might be an alternate route to our goal.

I did not yet realize that I was already engaged in a productive experiment along these lines.

Absorbed in my work, I am ashamed to confess that the need to communicate with Gloria receded to the back burner. I kept thinking I would somehow do something about it, but the vagueness of the proposition, how I was to gain access to a telephone, made it easy to put it off. As weeks went by, I dreamed of her more and more. I felt more and more guilty for making her worry, as I knew she must.

But a new development vastly complicated the situation. At first I fancied it was only my imagination, but before long I had to admit to myself that *I was manifesting the Innsmouth look*. My eyes, my lips, my hair, my coloration. And there was a creeping sense of emotional detachment. I shunned the realization for as long as I could, but at length I could not deny the facts. And with this understanding came another: I must not, I could not, return to my life as I knew it, especially not to Gloria.

But this matter was soon to be taken out of my hands--when Gloria arrived in Innsmouth, looking for me. Somehow I had not foreseen this. My reaction when one of my hosts told me the news was a strange mixture of relief and panic. I longed for her but dreaded to reveal myself. As I wrapped up what I was doing and shed my lab coat, my blank-eyed patron informed me in flat tones that Gloria had appeared *fully two weeks ago*. They had provided comfortable accommodations, at least by Innsmouth standards, and promised to let her see me but kept putting her off with excuses that must have been pretty creative. Presumably, they did not want me distracted or tempted to abandon the research to return to my fiancée. But then it struck home with a feeling of absolute certainty that their motive was to give me more time to *change*. When she beheld what I had become, what I was *becoming*, surely she would conclude that the man she loved was gone forever. And she would be right.

Gloria was seated, waiting patiently, in the front pew of the church, so that I saw her as soon as I came up through the trap door from the catacombs below. I had hoped to remain in the shadows while I did my best to explain and apologize, but that was now quite impossible. She saw the whole, ugly truth in a single glance and rose, running to embrace me. I wished to crush her precious frame against me, but I know she felt my reluctance. I did not know what to say.

"Oh Ephraim! They warned me what to expect, but I don't care as long as it's you! And it is! The crucial things shine through no matter what a person looks like! I'm just so glad to see you and to hold you!"

My protruding eyes began to shed salty tears. I croaked out something like, "But look at me! I'm not really even *human* anymore! Gloria, I can't ask you to…"

She pulled back enough to look at me unflinchingly. "Ephraim, do you think I'd abandon you if you'd gotten in a car accident or something? And don't you realize our appearance would change pretty totally as we grew old together, I mean, even if this never happened? Sure, it'll take a bit of getting used to, but I think I'm already over the most of it. The only thing I won't be able to accept is if you can't accept your*self*. Can you?"

Instead of waiting for me to say something, she kissed me. I suppose that single act should have convinced me she was right, but I just couldn't accept her protestations of love. I just could not imagine cursing her with my grotesque presence. Nor could I even picture how we could make a life for ourselves in the world. I could never dare show myself in public. Nor could I consider asking Gloria to live with me in a hell hole like ruined Innsmouth. I said as much, my sorrowful words punctuated by her sobs. It was a terrible parting. But at least I felt I had now made a clean and necessary break from a past to which I could never return. I had my work to pursue—among my own kind.

Months passed as I pursued my studies. If I was to make any progress, I had no choice but to conduct experiments on "human" subjects. Perhaps this would have gone easier on my conscience while I could still view the Innsmouth dwellers as alien to me. But, like it or not, I had perforce come to identify with them more and more as I came more closely to resemble them. Still, they were willing enough, seeing whatever risks might be entailed as being for their race's greater good. I tried hormonal adjustments, artificial insemination, even manipulation and implantation of genetic materials from other deep sea species. For a while I thought great promise lay in exploiting the super-malleable tissue of the shoggoths, but this proved too unstable. After all, shoggoths were not born as shoggoths and did not reproduce except, rarely, by fission. They were an advanced, and yet decadent, version of life forms whose reproductive systems lasted no longer than their previous anthropomorphic mode.

Once I had reached this point in my research, the Innsmouth elders decided to share two rather important pieces of information with me. First, the viability of their society had long been predicated upon a proportionate balance between the largely humanoid, surface-dwelling people of Innsmouth (and, it now seemed, nearby Kingsport), the full-on Deep Ones who had retired to the off-shore trench popularly known as Devil Reef, and the shoggoths. This balance had been wholly disrupted with the sterility of the race. Even among the deep water versions things were awry as more of their number transformed into the amorphous shoggoths.

Apparently this bizarre evolutionary development, I mean, that into shoggoths, had a certain survival value, as might be expected. The ancient civilization of the Deep Ones had historically been divided into warring clans, competing for the resources of the sea floor, even though one might have thought there was plenty to go around. Though the man-like Deep Ones were able warriors, the juggernaut shoggoths functioned as a kind of artillery, protoplasmic tanks as it were. The Deep Ones proper guided the shoggoths via a kind of telepathy, a skill anciently evolved to allow communication between deep-underwater creatures.

The present plight of Innsmouth became clearer to me when I learned that these sub-sea wars had never really ceased. So devastating had they become that the Deep Ones were now at the point of extinction. There were so few left, here in Innsmouth, over in Kingsport, and a few other small settlements, that they feared their years as a species were numbered. Yes, I knew these beings had once had designs on the surface world, but that danger was long past. If their population were to become resurgent, might they not renew their plans for invasion? One could not take this for granted, and as a scientist, I felt it my duty to try to preserve a sorely endangered species.

The other bit of news concerned me personally. I had wondered how and why the elders of the town had known about me and apparently kept watch over me. Who was I to them? It was not like I had a professional reputation to attract their attention. I was still only a student. Granted, they had been confident in my expertise, but even this presupposed some prior interest in me: how else would they know? Now I found out. I have said that I knew nothing of my parents, who died in my very early childhood. But it seems they did not die. They had first moved to Arkham from *Innsmouth* and dared remain there only so long as their physical aspect did not attract remark. When it did, they had to return to Innsmouth. They wanted me to grow up in the more prosperous Arkham because of the many opportunities, particularly educational ones, especially compared with the dismal state of decaying Innsmouth. Thus they placed me with a family who told me they were my relatives. It was through them that certain interests in Innsmouth followed my progress. Where were my true parents now? I wasn't sure I wanted to know.

Why reveal all this to me now? I suppose in order to impress upon me that their plight was fully my own. But I was not convinced of that. You see, to my complete astonishment, careful daily self-examination showed me that *I was gradually returning to normal*. I was mystified but obviously delighted. I didn't know how my "employers" would react to this development. But I was not worried, for my own reversal caused me to recognize what ought to have been obvious. The key to reversing the collective fortunes of Innsmouth lay in the same sort of reverse metamorphosis. And I thought I knew how it might be accomplished!

I had, as I have said, already studied the shapeless giants called shoggoths in great detail. I dismissed it as a dead end, but now I realized that a very different approach might do the trick. The shoggoths were practically infinite in their ability to change form depending on the task at hand. Otherwise their military utility would be close to nil. What if they could mimic their earlier form as Deep Ones? Suppose they could simulate their earlier state right down to their original organs? If this were possible, there was no reason to think they would possess the reproductive defect that threatened their race. The quivering behemoths were very nearly mindless. What I would have to do would be to enlist some of the most human Innsmouthers to employ the telepathic links that had always enabled them to direct the shoggoths.

I would have to provide a crash course to my recruits so that they might grasp and form a mental picture of the Deep One genome, the corrected version, for I had managed to find the glitch. I just hadn't yet known how to fix it. But if the pristine genetic pattern might be placed in the consciousness, such as it was, of several of the shoggoths, they should be able to hold the restored form of their healthy ancestors long enough to reproduce. It should work. At any rate, it was the best I could do.

We began the experiments, and it was an amazing experience to observe the reduction and redefinition of the quaking masses into humanoid form. Surely I had beheld marvels never before seen by surface-world mortals! And I may add that there was no longer even the faintest temptation to share my secrets with anyone else. I knew full well that no one could be expected to believe in either my story or my sanity, not without evidence.

My own transformation might have counted as sufficient proof, but by this time I had completely reverted to full humanity, a thing, I was told, without precedent among the Innsmouthers. As our attempts to re-fertilize the Deep One females seemed to be proving successful, the elders took my reversion as a sign that I must be allowed to return to the outer world, and I did so with their extravagant thanks as they pressed upon me many rich presents including various bits of jewelry cast in some silver-gold metal unknown to me and encrusted with strange-hued gems. To tell the truth, I had suspected I should never be permitted to leave, knowing rather too much, but once I had begun to show the Innsmouth look, the point became moot, as I did not fancy trying to resume a normal life in such a state. But now everything was different. What had caused my return to my normal condition? Perhaps surprisingly, none of my researches offered any clue. The only thing I knew was that I had noticed the change beginning shortly after Gloria's visit, after her kiss. But, as a man of science, I knew better than to confuse correlation with causation. Well, what matter? All I cared about was that a very surprising happy ending seemed to be at hand.

Of course, as soon as I disembarked at the Arkham train station, I headed for Miskatonic and to Gloria's office. Another occupied her desk chair.

"Well, Mr. Stanley! We've all been wondering when we'd see you again! Welcome back! I know Gloria will be delighted to see you."

"Not half as delighted as I will be to see *her*! Is she home, do you think? I hope she's not ill?"

The woman frowned at this. "I'm afraid she is. I haven't heard what exactly is wrong with her, but she calls occasionally, in fact, asking if anyone's heard from you. She doesn't sound too bad, maybe a little hoarse. But she's convalescing from something. I'm sure she'd appreciate a visit."

As I hurried toward Gloria's campus apartment, I reflected how she had always been severely afflicted with allergies, and it was now about the season for it. I would rejoice to do whatever I could to care for her. I hoped my sudden return might itself turn out to be a nostrum. It was with such eager anticipation that I knocked on her door. Her welcome voice, muffled through the thick wood, sounded from within.

"It's open. Come in."

By this time it was late afternoon, and I saw that no lamps were lit. The apartment was characteristically tidy but looked somehow like it had not been "lived in" for some days. I continued to the bedroom. I went on in. No lights here either, no surprise, given her illness. I stepped toward the window and pulled the curtain aside, allowing the radiance of the street lamp to reveal my face. I hoped it would be a welcome sight.

"Ephraim! Is it really you? Can it be?" Her voice faltered in stunned disbelief. But I did not discern the expected note of joy.

Perhaps she had not forgiven me for rejecting her so many weeks ago. If so, I would make things right. I was sure her love for me survived, even as mine had through all those days in Innsmouth.

"You see, my love, things are back to normal! It's a miracle!"

"Miracle, yes. Normal? Well, see for yourself, Ephraim." And with that she clicked on the bedside lamp. My eyes widened as hers bulged. Blood drained from my face as I beheld the reticulated leather that covered her own.

The Orthometrists of Vhoorl

~ Pete Rawlik ~

What is done is done. How much is my fault, the result of things I did, I cannot say. It is possible that the course of events was inevitable and that no matter what I had done the outcome was set. I do not believe in destiny, and yet I know for a fact that god-like things infest the universe and take pleasure in manipulating the lives of lesser life-forms. I know this, for I was one of their victims. Once I was a man, a writer, a dreamer, and perhaps in my own way, a mystic. Once I was Randolph Carter of Arkham, and now thanks to the whim of an entity of immense cosmic power, I had been cast through time and space to live as a stranger in a strange world.

Yaddith is a harsh place, civilized in a way, but still bleak, and as time passed I grew progressively weary of my so-called life amongst its people. I longed to return to home, but from my studies I knew that Arkham, Earth and even the Twentieth Century were not only thousands of light years away, but also eons into the future. I had come to dread this time and place that was not my own. Even my body was alien to me, and sharing it with its original resident Zkauba, a respected mystic in his own right, made my occupation of that semi-insectoid form a burden, with little joy, and less hope.

Thankfully, Zkauba's personality had retreated into a kind of catatonia, a response to his solving the Riddle of Thaqquallah, and learning the truth about the Nug Soth, the Dholes, and the Divinity that had spawned them both. I still had access to his memories, his skills and his encyclopedic knowledge of sorcery, enchantment and necromancy, and with them I had become a traitor to those around me. Where Zkauba had been a Wizard, I had become a Warlock, an oath-breaker in the old tongue, the Warlock of Yaddith.

And I swore I would find a way home.

No matter what the cost.

The science of the Nug Soth was so advanced that it would look like magic to the men of Earth. Using it, I was able to begin my quest for a way to return to my former life. The Nug Soth were desperate for ways to fight the Dholes, and although I knew their battle to be futile, I joined their quest in order to further my own ends. Using a light envelope I journeyed to Shonhi, Mthura, Kath, and innumerable worlds throughout the twenty-eight galaxies that we could reach. Using the Silver Key and certain signs known to those of Yaddith I was even able to move forward and backward through time, at least to a limited extent. The Silver Key being a product of Hyperborean manufacture was attuned only to humans. Being trapped within Zkauba's body and interlaced as our minds were, the power of the Key was limited, and any movement through the temporal dimension was unsustainable. For this reason and a host of others, not the least of which was the retinue of Tindalosian Hounds that seemed to follow me, I eventually ceased using the Key to move through time.

Not long after, as the Nug Soth mark time, I found myself roaming through the stars of the Twentieth-Eighth Nebula moving from one inhabited world to another, when rumors reached me of an incredible artifact. The peoples of the world of Vhoorl had, through the combined forces of their science and artistry, travelled to the heart of the cosmos, the very nucleus of the universe and there captured a shard of the thing that dwelt there. It was a blasphemous and cacophonous thing of chaos and madness. It was an ancient aberration that had once stalked the stars, but had, through the passing of eons, finally retired from wandering and taken up residence near the very center of the twenty-eight galaxies. The installation of the thing had attracted lesser beings to its orbit and by the time the artists and engineers of Vhoorl arrived in their ships of sculpted order, there was a veritable court attending their daemon-king. There was gravity to the thing and with that came an atmosphere with which the sycophantic attendants could pipe and call upon thin alien flutes. It was to this place, to the very nucleus of the known universe, that the Vhoorl ship came and dipped its nets of light and force into the swirling mass of the thing that howled and roared in cosmic anguish. They stole just a tiny bit of the creature, a minuscule droplet, a shard so small it could not even have been said to exist, a fleeting, ephemeral thing, a tear and little more than that. In a prison of light and magnetic fields the amorphous thing resolved itself into a multifaceted gem of exquisite brilliance, a shining trapezohedron that they named after that which they had stolen it from, the Seed of Azathoth.

The Vhoorl'kth and the Vhoorl'hst, for those that inhabited the planet were not of one species but rather two, having evolved from a common ancestor were pliant, boneless things reminiscent of polypus anemones from the abyssal plains of terrestrial oceans. Of the two, it was the Vhoorl'kth who had evolved furthest from their common ancestor, for they had achieved a greater level of cephalization, with a head, six eyes and a bundle of facial tentacles, but they still maintained a pair of great frond-like gills that spread out from their backs like the wings of some primitive dragon. In contrast, the Vhoorl'hst had clung to their trilateral symmetry and manipulated their artisanal creations with three ochre tentacles that were set about a ravenous mouth full of rasping, chitinous teeth. Both species had devoted themselves to orthometry, the practice of properly constructing verse, but they had pursued very different paths. The Vhoorl'hst had devoted itself to art, to poetry, to prose and the theater, and in some ways seemed obsessed with their own history and long dead dynasties. In contrast, the Vhoorl'kth were masters of the word-sciences and used them to create tools and ships and constructs all to aid their understanding of the physical universe and how it functioned. However, unlike the Vhoorl'hst the Vhoorl'kth lacked any sense of humility or self-understanding. They were in some ways soulless reflections of their semi-brothers.

And those pursuits made both of these great races arrogant, and in their arrogance they were dangerous. Both races had a dream, a kind of queer racial goal, they both wanted to become more than what they were. They wanted to go beyond their absolutes or as they put it, their Hlu, and their uncertainties or as they put it, their Tru. They wanted to become something more, the distillation of their true nature, their Lon.

The debate about what to do with the seed had lasted for weeks. The discussion was open to the public, and participation from the gallery of attendees was encouraged. Indeed those of Vhoorl had sent messengers to many of their nearest neighbors, including colonies of the Mi-Go, X'han, and t'Sathqq. Most strange was the presence of a small cluster of Rathk, an enigmatic race that had once established a small empire of worlds but then had suddenly become reclusive, to the point of xenophobia. Yet despite that they had shunned contact for more than five generations they had sent delegates, five of them in fact. They stood regal and aloof, towering over the others, their green, willowy bodies draped in diaphanous fabrics that concealed their six limbs, leaving only their faces full of tusks and compound eyes exposed.

Only one species had failed to respond to the call. The Q'Hrell, the starfish headed carnivores had been invited, but the small outpost that they had established on a moon in a nearby system had refused the first overture with a kind of panic. Days later when more experienced envoys made a subsequent visit, the Q'Hrell were gone, their small colony abandoned. A search of local space found them; they were adrift on the solar winds, sailing at just below the speed of light, dreaming, waiting for the stars to be right once more.

The debate proceeded without them. It delved into the science of what the seed was, and much was said of its potential for warping space-time. There was an analysis that suggested that the seed was a kind of exotic matter, it exhibited a kind of conscious energy, not sentience but a potentiality for sentience that itself was dense enough to cause a dimple in the very fabric of the universe. Even contained in a metamemic bottle, sealed off from any contact with the gravitic and magnetic forces of the cosmos, its presence could still be felt in the membranes that layered the universe. It was this property that the scientists and philosophical-artists of the Vhoorl were most intrigued by, and further exploration was what they suggested.

The Vhoorl'kth proposed exposing the entire population of Vhoorl to the seed, transforming both races in unimaginable ways. In contrast, the Vhoorl'hst proposed exposing just one individual, and then seeing what happened. If the results were favorable, then the numbers of individuals could be expanded. The problem that the Vhoorl'kth argued was that exposure of just a single individual might not be enough to allow the Vhoorl consciousness to have an impact on the seed. They reasoned that because the seed was already composed of conscious energy, a single mind might not be enough to overwhelm the existing structure. A greater number of minds might be needed, only the collective consciousness of an entire species might be enough to establish control over the energy bound within the seed, or so the Vhoorl'kth reasoned.

As this debate raged on, I found myself drawn into the fray, and while the position taken up by Vedic Ghat supporting the exposure of the entire population was well reasoned, the risks were high. Likewise, the caution expressed by the poet Scilda, seemed to me simply too cautious. That the two positions were so diametrically opposed seemed to me ludicrous, and a compromise seemed in order. Indeed, I was not the only one to have this thought and around me the other members of the gallery rose to express the idea. Sadly those words seemed to fall on deaf ears as both Ghat and Scilda unreasonably rejected any such possibility.

It was apparent to me that in this situation the direct approach was not going to work. They were like children, refusing to listen to even the most rational of ideas. My mind, my human mind hidden within Zkauba's insectile body, raced. I had an idea, a germ of a thought and as I sat listening to the debate, my thoughts gelled into a coherent plan, a strategy. If they were acting like children, then perhaps they should be treated like children. When the opportunity came, I rose and waited to be recognized. I did not wait long, for even here on Vhoorl ,the knowledge and wisdom of the Nug Soth were well known.

When I finally spoke, I tried to strike a balance between the serious and the sublime.

"Esteemed colleagues, gracious hosts, I thank you for your hospitality and the opportunity to speak. This debate, this discussion reminds me of a story, a legend from a long forgotten culture, a story that I feel has a lesson relative to the issue. If you will indulge me, just for a few moments, I think my tale can be somewhat illuminating to the situation at hand."

There was a murmur that passed through the gallery, a wave of discussions that spiraled into the ears and out of the mouths of those in authority. They took a moment to let the opinions and desires of their peers slosh back and forth within their consciousness. Then with no more or no less fanfare than had marked any of the previous proceedings, I was given an almost imperceptible signal to begin, and so I did.

Once, many years ago, so long ago that few remember the true time or place that these events took place, there lived a beautiful juvenile of the female gender of a two gendered species who went by the name of Amber Setae, or in short, Amber. She was, at least for her species, considered a relatively attractive thing, though rather small and frail, and truth be told, a somewhat ignorant and arrogant child. Her parents had in a way, spoiled her, and in doing so made it seem to her that the world, and perhaps the entire universe, existed only to fulfill her every whim and desire. As a result of her view of the world, a world of privilege and protection, Amber had no sense of fear, or responsibility, or reticence.

It was Amber's lack of such concepts, for she was completely devoid of any sense of self-preservation, that led her to wander from the path on which her parents had set her, and instead made her way through fungal rings, boughs of old trees, and fields of flowering plants. She reveled in the beauty of the natural world; she played with avians and watched insects dance from flower to flower. Her frolic took her deeper and deeper into the wild, and further and further from the road, until, at last, and inevitably young Amber was utterly and completely lost.

In being lost she wandered further, and her wanderings took her further from the path she should have been on, and deeper into the forest. Somewhere along the way the woods turned from welcoming to dark and foreboding, which only became worse as the planet's rotation caused the light from the primary star to fade, leaving only the glow from a small moon and an arc of stars, to allow her to sense her surroundings. In the gloom of the night, young Amber stumbled onto a well-worn game trail, one that led to a small cottage, a rural dwelling of primitive construction. It was not a place she was familiar with, but it offered comfort and security, and those were things she desperately wanted.

Entering the cottage, she immediately caught the scent of prepared food. She called out, but no one answered. The home appeared to her, abandoned by its inhabitants, at least temporarily, and she followed the enticing odor from the entry way down the corridor and to the dining hall. There, set out on a great table, she found three bowls of food. Being hungry Amber sat down in front of the largest bowl and tasted it, but it was too spicy. Undeterred, Amber slid down the table and tried the contents of the mid-sized bowl, but it was too sweet. Finally, with no other options left to her, Amber sat down in front of the smallest bowl and found the contents a little sweet and somewhat spicy, and overall, just to her taste. Indeed, it was just right.

Afterwards, Amber wished to warm herself and so made her way to the hearth room. There was a small fire and Amber sat down in the closest chair, but found that spot to be too warm. Moving to a smaller chair, one furthest away, but to her disappointment, the location was too cold. Finally, with no other options, she sat down in the smallest chair, which was situated between the other two and found that position to her liking, neither too hot nor too cold. Indeed, it was just right.

As little Amber sat in that chair, she grew drowsy, and eventually nodded off, falling out of the chair. As she struggled to get back on her feet, she grabbed on to the chair and, unfortunately, once more lost her balance. While she was able to catch herself, her weight broke the back of the chair and tore the stuffing.

Not feeling the least bit apologetic or remorseful, Amber made her way down the halls and, after a little exploring, found a large room with three beds. The largest bed was most attractive, but as she tried to lie down in it, Amber found the mattress too hard for her back. The lesser bed was prettier than the largest bed, but as she climbed into it, she discovered that it was simply too soft, and she sank into it so deeply that she felt like she was drowning. It was the third bed, the smallest of the three that Amber finally settled into and found to her liking. As she fell asleep, Amber thought to herself that this bed was just right.

It was not long after Amber fell asleep that the owners of the cottage returned. The Faetch bore a superficial resemblance to the species to which Amber belonged; they were, after all, distantly related, but the differences were enough to drive the Faetch into hiding. They were so rare that Amber had only heard about them in stories. Indeed, in a generation or two, the Faetch would be extinct, and then forgotten, passed into legend; but in this age, they were still things to be feared, at least by juveniles lost in the forest.

As soon as the Faetch came into their home, they knew something was amiss. The paternal Faetch looked at his bowl and said, "Somebody has been eating my food!"

The maternal Faetch looked at her bowl and said, "Somebody has been eating my food!"

Then the juvenile Faetch looked at its bowl and said. "Somebody has been eating my food, and they ate it all up!"

Now the Faetch were rightfully upset about this, and began a search of their abode. They started in the hearth room and there, found more evidence of their intruder. The paternal Faetch stood over his chair and took a deep breath through his proboscis. He could smell Amber; tell that she wasn't one of the family. "Somebody has been sitting in my chair!"

The maternal Faetch, whose sense of smell was more sensitive than her mate's, could smell Amber too, but also knew that whoever had invaded their home, was not of the Faetch. "Somebody has been sitting in my chair, and they don't belong here."

Then the young Faetch whose sense of smell was not yet developed, and could not sense much, said, "Somebody has been sitting in my chair, and they broke it all up!"

Following their noses, the Faetch made their way to the bedroom where, once more, the paternal Faetch looked and said, "Somebody has been sleeping in my bed!"

The maternal Faetch agreed with him and announced, "Somebody has been sleeping in my bed!"

And then the young Faetch roared, "Somebody has been sleeping in my bed, and they're still in it!"

With the sudden commotion, young Amber awoke with a start and began screaming. The Faetch screamed back, and their voices caused little Amber to flee from the house in terror. She ran through the woods, driven mad by the sound of the Faetch screaming. She ran and ran and ran until her legs gave out and her chest burned and her heart was near to burst. They found her, her parents and the villagers who had been searching for her. They found her, and in time they healed her bruises and her cuts and scrapes, but her mind, poor Amber's mind was never the same, and she would never go in the woods again.

When I finished my tale, I took my seat and listened to the crowd mumble. I heard comments of approval and an acknowledgement of my wisdom. I was pleased with myself, and when Ghat and Scilda rose and adjourned the conference for the day, acknowledging that I had given them much to think about. I was more than pleased with myself, and reveling in my accomplishment, almost did not notice the most junior member of the Rathk delegation staring at me with those cold, compound eyes. His look was disturbing, unsettling even, and I made a move to confront him; but his fellows suddenly whisked him away, and I lost him in the crowd. I forgot the incident and let my self-satisfaction overwhelm me.

I was a fool, and I should have known better. As I sat in my quarters of my light ship, the minds of the inhabitants of Vhoorl turned and churned and thought in odd and alien ways. I sat there, a man hiding in an alien body, pretending, assuming that I knew what I was doing. I dined on some local delicacies and a vintage of alien wine that was particularly enjoyable. It was not until I was disturbed by the presence of someone at my entry that I was roused from my smug attitude. Even still, I answered the call in a casual and even somewhat jovial manner. That state of elation was destroyed by what happened next.

I will confess that the presence of a member of the Rathk standing in my entryway was unexpected. Further still, that it was the junior member of the delegation, the one who had stared at me so intently, was admittedly a surprise. That his finery was disheveled, even torn in places, and stained with bodily fluids from a small wound, aroused in me suspicions that dashed my mood. Yet all of this was nothing compared to the words that uttered forth from his tusked and rasping mouth, words that were, despite the inappropriateness of his anatomy, clearly spoken in the English language. "My name is Charles Meyer! I'm from Earth. Please, you must help me!" Then, as if he was a character in one of my own modest tales of terror, he collapsed in a heap at my feet.

I knew nothing of his physiology or anatomy and so had little idea of what I could do for him. I made him comfortable, bound the wound, and waited. It took an hour or so for the thing that called itself Charles Meyer to revive, and when he did, it was with a start. One moment he was laying unconscious, and the next he was stumbling across the floor, his arm flailing about, and his legs looking as if they would buckle at any moment. I spoke calmly to the obviously agitated creature, but to no avail, he would not respond to anything I said, and seemed to grow more frantic by the second. Finally at my wit's end, I twisted my mouth and throat with a supreme effort, and blurted out the name he had called himself. "Charles Meyer!"

The great, giant insectoid ceased his struggles abruptly, and stared at me with those multi-faceted eyes. He turned his head in a strange bestial way and looked me up and down. "Yes," he said with a voice as equally strange as mine, "I am Charles Meyer, of Earth. You were the one who spoke at the forum today. You told the story of Goldilocks and the Three Bears. Who are you?"

I sat myself down and my guest followed my lead. "My name is, or at least was, Randolph Carter. I, too, come from Earth."

In an instant, the Rathk was back on his feet. "Randolph Carter! Surely not Randolph Carter the fantasist? He would be long dead by now."

"My name is indeed Randolph Carter, and I have taken pen to paper and produced a few modest tales. As for being dead, I regret that the reports of my status are more complicated than simple death. I am a victim of a cosmic joke, cast back through time and across space to dwell in an alien body, on an alien world, and to never see the green and rolling hills of my home ever again." I paused, for I realized I had grown melancholy in my speech. "But who are you Mr. Meyer, tell me how you come to be here?"

Over the next few hours, I learned the tale of Mr. Charles Meyer, of Toledo, Ohio, in the last quarter of the Twentieth Century, and in the Twenty-First Century a graduate of that city's university. Meyer described himself as a master in a field of technology I did not understand. In the future, he described how men had given control of much of the world, and the civilizations that covered it, to a kind of machine proto-intelligence, one that existed not only in circuits of copper and steel, but also in the sub-aether virtual world that men had built up to ease their lives and entertain themselves. When he spoke of these things, my suspicions were raised, but when he spoke of the cat he had recently adopted, and his concerns over its care, I knew that he was a kindred spirit. He spoke the truth, even though I grew despondent as I learned of how war had so filled the world, and that whole cities had been wiped out of existence in seconds by weapons I could not even imagine my species possessing. Even the map had changed. The British Empire had never recovered from the Great War, and as its grip on China and India relaxed, these great cultures had risen up to fill the void. Likewise, Imperial Russia had fallen and been replaced by a collective of the people that had itself, eventually succumbed to corruption and internal strife. Africa was still dark, South America still mysterious, and the polar wastes still mostly unexplored. I ached to find out about home, about Arkham, Massachusetts, about New England, and the country she was part of. He told me of the trials and tribulations that had beset my beloved homeland, of race wars and women's rights, of the rise and fall of a president, of a landing on the moon, and the men who walked there. He told me that men had sent machines to Mars. His voice wavered when he spoke of men who used religion and superstition to prey on the young and the old alike. He told me all this, and from it I drew a single, undeniable conclusion.

The Republic still stands.

The exact manner in which Charles Meyer's mind had been extracted from his body, and cast through time and across space to dwell in the body of a Rathk, was unclear. What he did know was that the Rathk were no longer what they seemed. Just as Meyer's mind had been displaced, so had thousands upon thousands of those belonging to the Imperial Rathk. A strange invasion had occurred, and overnight the ruling members had been supplanted. Even so, it had taken time for the invaders to consolidate their power, though this was helped by recalling forces, and abandoning vast stellar holdings. In the end, it took only a few years for the invaders to completely infiltrate and parasitize the Rathk society to meet their own needs. After that, there was no need for pretense and the invaders revealed themselves for what they were, a species that had long ago abandoned the physical in favor of the mental, a race so powerful, so great, that they could travel through time and space simply by amplifying their own disembodied minds. A race that called themselves by the name of the world they had last occupied before abandoning their bodies. They were the Great Race, a race of historians, of archivists, of researchers, of students and of masters. They were the Yith, and no race could stand against them. Still, they were not fools, and while they were confident in their superiority, they used their powers to not only explore the universe of the present and the past, but also of the future. These expeditions in time had led them to believe that one day they would have to migrate again, for they would face an enemy that they did not and could not understand. That migration, the date of which Meyer did not know, would take the Yith to Earth, a world the disembodied minds found strangely attractive. Whether the Yith would occupy men, the coned and tentacled things that came before them, or the giant coleopterans that came after, was also a mystery. Presumably, that was the whole motive behind the transfer of Meyer's mind with one of the Great Race, to allow their agent to explore the world of men and determine when and where to strike.

As Meyer spoke, a thought crept up on me. It wormed its way into my head, wrapped claws around my mind and shouted at my prosaic human psyche. The Yith could help me, if I could persuade them. They could use their power to move minds through time and send me home to Earth. I would have to displace another poor soul and, proving who I was to friends and family, proving that I wasn't simply a madman impersonating Randolph Carter, would be difficult, but it could be done. Surely my friends, surely Manton and de Marginy would recognize me no matter what face I wore. Yet as these nefarious thoughts permeated my brain, I made an observation that brought me crashing back to how horrific such an act would be. Charles Meyer hated the Yith. He hated what they had done to him, hated how they had ripped him from friends and family and his life, and hated what certainly must have been a trauma to those who cared about him. His hate on this matter was almost palpable, and in seeing this, I realized I could have no party to doing the same to another. The Yith may have had the ability to send me back to where I belonged, but the price was simply too high.

Then, without any warning at all, my communications array chimed on and began transmitting a horrific and terrifying sound. The claxon of the city, put in place to warn residents and visitors of potential natural disasters had been triggered, and an order to evacuate had been issued. Meyer and I looked at each other and wordlessly agreed that we were more interested in learning what was happening than fleeing for our lives. We emerged into the teeming metropolis and were immediately enveloped by the chaos of a populace in panic. From a distance we could see that the science gallery was embellished by a glow of black light, a glow that was slowly expanding, and enveloping the area around it.

My first instinct was to flee but, encouraged by Meyer, we drove forward instead, battering through the crowds. All around us representatives of other worlds were evacuating, while the Vhoorl'kth and the Vhoorl'hst seemed to be unable to do anything but panic and scream. There was reason to panic. The black hemisphere was more than just a light; it was spewing out tentacles of energy and enveloping the natives, drawing them into itself like an octopus or spider. It was a slow process, methodical and thorough, and nothing the Vhoorl did seemed to be able to stop it.

Above the noise, I heard a voice yelling my name. It was Scilda, the proctor from the Vhoorl'hst, she was running toward me and behind her, a great arm of black energy was bearing down on her. "Help me Zkauba, please help me!" she pleaded.

I had left my weapons inside my ship, but that did not mean I was defenseless. I sprinted forward, grabbed the trisymmetrical artist, and spun her behind myself and Meyer. My hands, all four of them, traced sigils and signs in the air and drew energy out of the very fabric of space. I molded it, shaped that energy into familiar patterns, weaved it into a shield and placed it between myself and the inky, dark rope that was grabbing for my sudden charge. It hit my armor hard and drove me back on my heels. I pushed back and the attacker suddenly recoiled and then turned away, searching for easier prey.

With the respite, Meyer and I helped Scilda to stand, and then, together, we began to make our way back to my light ship. Yet as we approached the entryway, Scilda suddenly pulled away from us and looked at me in scorn. "Ghat opened the containment field. He heard your story and he understood what you were trying to say."

I shook my head. "What I was trying to say? That story is about being cautious when encountering new things, and not being malicious with things that don't belong to you!" I was suddenly screaming; the noise of the siren and the people of Vhoorl screaming had become overwhelming. Meyer fell to the ground trying to cover his ears.

There came over Scilda's form an attitude, a position, a stance that seemed to imply that I had said something wrong, something that she rejected. "Was that your intent?" Her three tentacles were trembling. "We didn't see it that way."

"No we did not." The voice booming the air was unearthly, echoing like thunder in the sky. There was a horrific quality to it, as if it was not one person speaking but thousands. Yet even though it had such an alien quality, I recognized the source and the floating figure that accompanied it. The Vedic Ghat was surrounded by the black energy, and in his hand he held the crystalline Seed of Azathoth. "We must thank you Zkauba of the Nug Soth," but as he said those words his head twisted in an odd way. "But you aren't Zkauba, at least not entirely. How interesting. I can see inside your mind, Randolph Carter, and inside that of Charles Meyer. Earth seems like such a lovely place; I must be sure to visit it someday."

"Ghat, what have you done?!"

He roared back at me like an angry god. "I did what you suggested, Randolph Carter, or at least what your story suggested. Oh yes, I know what you think your little story was about, but I saw the truth. Your little parable about Amber and the Faetch may have seemed to you a simple tale to educate children about the dangers of straying off the path and not stealing, but I could see the truer meaning."

"Which is?" I stammered.

"The universe is a dangerous place. To be small and powerless in it is a precarious position. If we are to survive, we must stop being so small; we mustn't be Amber, we must be something else, otherwise we too shall find ourselves mad and too afraid to go out into the forest. The Vhoorl'kth and the Vhoorl'hst will not be children any more, we shall be a force in this universe, a force to be respected and feared."

"You're mad!" countered Scilda.

She meant to say more, but Ghat wouldn't allow it. "We aren't mad, Scilda we will become more! We will no longer be Vhoorl'kth and Vhoorl'hst. We will move beyond Hlu, and beyond Tru." Ghat waved his hand and great tendrils of black energy smashed through my shields as if they weren't even there. "We shall be Vhoorl'Lon!" Then the tentacles swallowed up Scilda and she was gone, as if she had never existed.

I braced myself, prepared for the tendrils to move on myself and Meyer. I cast what protective cantrips I could, knowing they were likely useless. Thankfully, the great spouts of power at Ghat's command didn't attack, but rather withdrew.

"Leave us, Randolph Carter and Charles Meyer." Ghat moaned in a thousand hollow voices. "Take your ship and leave, before it is too late. Before our transformation proceeds to the point at which we no longer care that you aren't of the Vhoorl."

I took a step back in retreat, and as I did, helped Meyer rise to his feet. Before I could usher him back, my fellow man spoke his mind, screaming at the horrific thing that Ghat had become.

"You monster," he cursed. "You aren't a man any more; you are a thing, a nightmare, the living embodiment of all that is wrong in this universe. I may hate the Yith, despise what they have done to me, but you – what you've done here is inhuman."

Ghat turned and a bolt of inky darkness shot across the space between us. It hit Meyer faster than either of us could react. He stood there for a moment, but only a moment, and then his body fell to the ground, still and lifeless. His head was gone. Whatever Ghat had become, he had casually reached out and plucked Meyer's head off of his body like a ripe tomato. Ghat had eaten Meyer's head with no more than a casual thought.

The monster smiled, wickedly. "I was never human to begin with Charles Meyer, why does it surprise you that I behave in an inhuman manner? Are my motives so foreign to you, so alien, so unfathomable? Are you so bewildered by us? Perhaps by being one of us, by being absorbed into our collective consciousness, you will one day understand." And then he laughed, and the city shook as he bellowed.

I ran. I ran past the screaming, dissolving hordes of the Vhoorl. I ran to my ship, and as the very fabric of the planet began to shudder and fail and then collapse, I sped into space. I was not alone.

Around me, a fleet of ships sped away from Vhoorl. There were Whamphyri, Xiclotl, X'han, t'Sathqq, L'gy'hx, Yekub, and even the weird saucers that the Mi-Go used to transport their young. And of course there were a few ships of the Vhoorl, desperate refugees trying to flee the destruction of their home. As we sped away, the planet of Vhoorl, once a verdant green world of vast oceans, was dissolving, being swallowed up by the inky blackness that spread out of the Seed of Azathoth. It was like watching a balloon deflate on a cosmic scale, a balloon with cosmic tendrils that reached out and very carefully picked out those ships carrying Vhoorl and drew them back into itself.

In mere moments, nothing of the Vhoorl'kth or the Vhoorl'hst remained; perhaps on far away planets there remained a few researchers and poets and diplomats who had escaped, but as I watched I felt a great loss for the destruction of two great species, and their home. Nothing was left of them or their art or their science, save that strange black mass that occupied the place where once the planet Vhoorl had been. We hung there in space, we survivors in our ships some; in shock, some in awe, all of us in silence, save for a weird interstellar hum. They say that in space, no one can hear you, that there isn't enough of an atmosphere to carry sound. They are wrong. If you make a sound loud enough, you don't need an atmosphere, the sub-aether itself will carry that sound, and you can sense it with your very soul, like when you feel vibrations in your teeth.

I didn't have any teeth, but I still had a soul, and I could hear the universe screaming. We all could.

From the darkness a shape took form. It was in a way, beautiful; a thing of light and harmony, massive, larger than any life form had a right to be. It was a fusion of the 'kth and the 'hst but it was also neither. There was something primal about it, perhaps even celestial. In shape, it was not unlike a squid or octopus, though it was not limited to eight or even ten tentacles, but instead had innumerable such manipulators and tendrils. It was no longer black, but instead was a kind of green streaked with yellow. It pulsated, and over the hours that we sat there watching it, seemed to consolidate itself into something that the cosmos itself had never seen before. I think that was why the universe was screaming, because this thing that had come into being, no matter how beautiful it was, hurt it. The very fabric of existence was wounded by its presence, and in that perhaps, we should have known that this new thing was a cosmic abomination. Perhaps it was akin to the thing from which they had stolen the seed from, that floating nuclear chaos, perhaps a kind of child or even cousin to that unfathomable madness that was known as Azathoth.

For a moment that stretched into infinity, the thing seem to coalesce into a corporeal entity; one that with a single thought, replaced the screaming of the universe with that of its own name, a sound that echoed through my very soul, and chilled me to the core. That name, that sound was "VHOORL'LON!"

Then, as if the use of its name was anathema to its very existence, the great monstrosity that had named itself Vhoorl'Lon shuddered and filled the aether with a new sound, one that made the screaming of the universe pale in comparison. The cacophony drove me from my feet and I held my head, screaming in agony, rocking back and forth on the floor of my ship. Even there, writhing on the floor, I could see in my mind what was happening.

For some reason, the thing that was Vhoorl'Lon was unstable. Its existence was at odds with itself and it was taking measures to rectify the situation. Vhoorl'Lon was tearing itself apart. Like some sort of galactic amoeba, the mass that was once the Vhoorl began to divide. Where once a mass the size of a planet had been, there were now two moon-sized formations with great streamers of matter gushing between them. Founts of plasma flowed between these two gargantuan entities. Arcs of energy, enough to power a thousand worlds forever lit up the void.

Most of the observers retreated as the local chaos intensified. But where the ships that moved under their own power could flee, those who took advantage of the latent forces of the cosmos weren't so lucky. A brace of Mi-Go became caught in a random vortex of dark matter, swallowed up by one of the two things that were coalescing in the endless night of space. These things that the Vhoorl had spawned were less than what they had been. The god-thing that they had been was gone, and in its place were two titans.

Not that it mattered; the universe still screamed at their presence.

They were no longer the glowing thing of harmony. They were still gods, but they were monsters as well. One was not unlike the Vhoorl'kth in that it had a bulbous head with a crown of tentacles atop of a pulpy body, with two great wing-like gills spreading out from its back. Likewise, the second was reminiscent of the Vhoorl'hst in that it was possessed of three, great yellow tentacles around a central hub of eyes and mouths. They screamed at each other and lesser ships fell, collapsed at the sound of their rage. I thought at first they would attack one another; their enmity was obvious, but instead they turned and departed from each other's presence. One stalked off between the stars, using its wings and powerful leg-like tentacles to walk away as if space was simply another surface to walk across. The other seemed to crawl away, sliding through space, pulling itself across the emptiness with those three tentacles, almost spiraling forward.

As they departed, the pain subsided and I rose to my feet and looked out at what now was leaving to explore the cosmos. What were these things that I had had a part in bringing to life? Were they forces of good or evil, or did those concepts even apply? Did they even have names?

And with that simple questioning thought, the two titans both turned and casually screamed, not at each other, but at me and all the other observers who remained. What the others did, I cannot say, for I did not wait to see. I fled. I fled through space as fast as I could and did not cease until I stopped screaming. It took me days to recover from what I saw and heard, and from what I understood it to mean. Days for me to come to terms with what I had done, and what abominations I had unleashed upon the universe.

Even now, I seek an explanation, a reasoning, and a sense of absolution for what I have done. That what happened, was going to happen, no matter what. I have come to believe that my presence was some sort of cosmic joke perpetrated on me, and the entire universe, by a cosmic trickster who cast me back into time in the first place. I wondered what had happened to Charles Meyer. Did his consciousness still exist? Was he part of one of those things or the other, or perhaps both? Perhaps this was why I was sent back. Perhaps the cosmic intelligence that had punished me so was trying to teach me something, about life, about the universe, about everything. Perhaps someday I might understand and then I could finally rest.

But those things, those two creatures that now roamed the cosmos, they would be out there forever, for eternity, and I and every delver in the darkness, every explorer of the eldritch, every seeker of the unknown, would know their names: Names that would echo through time and space and generate immeasurable horrors, two halves of something so perfect that the universe itself rejected its existence. Two things that had a mutual enmity of the likes this reality had never seen before, and had chosen names to reflect what they once were, and what they sought to be. The names they had chosen and that had reverberated through the empty void of space, would do so for unfathomable depths of time. May the universe find a way to forgive me for what I have unleashed within it. Those names were Kth'Hlu and Hst'Tru, or as men would know them in eons yet unseen, Cthulhu and Hastur!

The Hundred Years' Sleep

– Mary SanGiovanni –

As it so often is with the things that impact your life the most, I knew nothing about the Sleepers and their cults of followers, nor would I have cared. Spirituality, let alone religion, had never been priorities in my house growing up. An only son in a small Irish-American family subsisting on averted gazes and unspoken words, I was born Catholic but my family never brought me to church, nor was any sense of the spiritual instilled in me during everyday life. My mom was a worrier and a list-maker, my father a construction worker and a drinker, and they tackled these jobs with the whole of their hearts and souls. To them, that left no time for gods or ghosts in the day, and nothing but exhaustion and uninspired sleep to pass the night. At nineteen, I already had mounting debts, so I had little time to sleep at all, and less to dream.

That's another thing – the Sleepers spoke to people in dreams. In fact, that's how they found Natalia.

Natalia – my sole reason for wanting to keep this dirty, twisted, illogical world going, simply because she was in it, and she made my little piece of it brighter. Now that I sleep, I see her in the vines, her soundlessly screaming mouth pulling her face out of shape. Those are my bad dreams. In my worse dreams, we are together and happy, and we never close our eyes, not even to blink.

Many things fascinated me about Natalia back then, not the least of which was that she was the only actual princess I had ever met. Her family was directly descended from royalty and she was, in fact, in direct line of rule, though neither the poverty of her small Eastern European country nor its governmental unrest lent her family financial or political security. Quite the opposite, in fact – it was closely whispered that Natalia was sent with caretakers (her "aunts") to seek political asylum in America.

While in her homeland, her being a princess meant certain death, here in the wild woods of upstate New York, it meant nothing much, really – a conversation-starter at parties, and an awkward one at that. She would never talk about it if she could help it. She wanted to forget. No glass slippers or golden balls here.

The first time I saw her, she was napping on a friend's couch, and she took my breath away. I wanted to kiss her, crazy as it sounds. She looked so peaceful, so soft, almost glowing in the slant of afternoon sun streaming in from a window across from her. It was a crazy compulsion, wanting to kiss a strange and sleeping girl like that, and I stifled the urge. But if you've ever met someone like that, someone whose presence sort of stupefies you and somehow changes the hues of the world with every moment you are near her, you probably understand what it felt like to first encounter Natalia.

I loved her. Her beauty was inarguable but severe and aloof, as if ice and not muscle defined the angles and contours beneath her skin. I loved her accent, and the way that when she was amused, the corner of her mouth would turn up just a little while she looked at you with dark eyes from beneath thick, dark lashes. I loved the smell of her skin and her short black hair, scents like blackberries and heady brilliant-hued flowers.

She loved me, she said, because I was smart and quiet, and kind of cute in that clueless sort of way. I'm not sure what she meant by that, but I was glad to give her any reason at all to love me back.

—

At the end of the Hundred Years' Sleep, it is said that there will be deep and impenetrable night swallowing the stars. There will be a cacophony of screams. There will be fire that will raze the cities of men and shreds of flesh carried by rivers of blood. There will be blazing symbols of power. And there will be the return of the Sleepers. More people believe in this than Scientology. More copies of the Doctrine of the Sleepers are sold on Amazon than any of the occult texts, which have gained, through misdirection and movie inaccuracies, and kind of pop culture fame.

All across the world, there are groups of people who believe this, who devote their lives to making this happen. These people keep to the shadows, the night places, the off-the-grid and out-of-the-way places where their secret meetings and arcane rites herd fear and ugliness through the world. In these places, blood soaks carpets so that it sponges up wet around their footfalls. In these places, the dead lie still but find no peace. In these places, doors and windows look out on vistas of terrifying magnitude and alien strangeness, and the rabid laughter of inhuman voices drives the unstable to madness.

It was here, in these places all over the world, where it was discovered that the Hundred Years' Sleep was reaching its end, and the rarest, most sacred, and powerful opportunity was at hand. The era of the Ancient Ones, the elder gods of myth, was to begin, and deaths would make it happen.

It was Natalia that told me about the Hundred Years' Sleep and the Sleepers themselves. We had gotten very close, inspecting and experiencing and sharing the world and each other as if no one else existed. It felt good when she confided her secrets in me, when she fantasized about a future with me in it. I'd never had that kind of closeness before, certainly not with my parents, never with my limited circle of friends, and never with girls. It made me feel like more than just an echo of a person. I liked that. Hell, I thrived on it.

A few days before the sirens, she gave me a book from her library to read. She had hundreds. That's where I first read about the Hundred Years' Sleep, in a book on the occult called Unaussprechliche Kulten. One of the original German editions which she helped me translate, bound in leather with iron clasps, it told of a cult ritual that would bring about an end to everything human. It was fascinating, even thrilling to me, the way campfire stories and urban legends are thrilling. But it was just a story.

Actually, when I think about it, it was much earlier when I first read about it, in an old book of Grimm's fairy tales – an English translation of the German, that time. A princess pricked her finger on the spindle of a spinning wheel and fell asleep. It wasn't until a prince came along a century later and, moved by her beauty, kissed the sleeping princess and woke her up. Also just a story.

When I asked her why she was giving me fairy tales to read, Natalia told me about her dreams – about ancient and impossibly slanted buildings forming huge cities, of creatures only visible in glowing outlines of irregular shapes. She told me about the messages of death and change and resurrection they whispered to her-- those things I just spoke of, or at least parts of those things. She claimed she didn't know enough English to verbalize it all in a way I would understand. I think she just didn't have the words in her heart, in her soul, to get past the horror.

They weren't just dreams, see. Not to her. It was crucial to understanding Natalia to accept that she saw patterns in the universe, and those patterns, deliberate as they were, contained signs and messages. I thought it was all just a part of her eastern European folklore, a charming quirk of her foreign upbringing, but I'd never dare dismiss it. When the sirens began, I can almost say I expected it. At least, I didn't doubt Natalia's belief in what those sirens were signaling.

See, Natalia had a way of believing something so strongly, so perfectly, that you found yourself believing it, too.

——

When the first of the sirens went off, Natalia and I were asleep. We often fell asleep, just holding each other, in the silent and tucked away places of our hometown: my basement rec room, her library sofa, the abandoned cemetery's office or tranquility gardens, the side street behind Krausers, and a dozen or so places in the nearby woods where we would watch stars between the speckled canopy of leaves and branches. This time, we were camped out in one of those wooded clearings, having nodded off on the hood of my car where we had been reclining against the windshield, talking about outer space. It seems funny to me now that we had been talking about life from other worlds just hours before we saw it. She had even been telling me about the Sleepers.

"My people believe the Sleepers, they come from another planet in another dimension," she said. "There are many mens who think it wise to offer them...what is the word? Appeasements? Twice a year they do this – May and October. To keep the Sleepers from waking."

"Oh yeah? What kind of things do they do?"

Natalia's face darkened. "I do not know. They do not tell me this thing. But...they fail this last May. It is why I am here."

I glanced at her to see if she was being serious. The look in her eye told me she was.

"Really? I thought you were here on political asylum."

"I am."

"Oh," I replied, not quite understanding. "I guess I always assumed there were factions looking to take over the country, maybe hurt you or your family, and they sent you away to avoid, like, terrorists or radicals or something." I held my breath, listening for her feelings in her ensuing silence. Was she upset that I had brought it up? It was the one thing we never talked about, not in any kind of detail.

Finally she smiled, but it was a tiny thing, twisted by bitterness. "In a sense, that is true. There are radicals in my country, but they are more...religious than political. Sleeper cults, determined that now is the time to bring their gods back to earth. They require...different kind of appeasement. Sacrifice, that is the word. A farmer, a priest, a sage, a whole list of people they need to kill to awaken the sleepers. Then they need to kill a princess to keep the Sleepers awake for good. And when they kill me, the end of everything will begin."

"Baby, I'm sorry. I had no idea. These people sound crazy."

"My parents are strongly opposed to the ideals and agendas of these cults. They sent me to live with.... "

"With your aunts," I finished quietly.

"No," she finally said, although the hesitancy still clung to her words. "They are...I don't know the word. Mages? Very learned. Very knowledgeable in occult, and knowing spells and sigils and incantations to protect me from the cults. They are part of my father's counsel. I am safest with them than anybody. Except maybe you." She smiled at me and I felt an overwhelming surge of love for her. I wanted to keep her safe, and would spend the rest of my life, if that's what it took, protecting her. I told her so.

"That is noble, and a reason why I love you. I think you'd brave even the Sleepers and their legion of unholy things to protect me."

"You really believe the Sleepers exist, don't you?" I asked gently.

"I used to think I just couldn't afford to discount the possibility," she said, and turned her head to look me in the eye. "But they've spoken to me, in dreams, like I told you. Things are different since. The smell of the air, the taste of food and water, the skittishness of the animals. Even the trees shudder in a strange way. I believe, yes. I feel it in every part of me. Which means the cults have been successful in killing many good people and will come for me soon. If I die and the Sleepers awaken, we will become memories, Declan. Mere stories. We will become the fairy tales."

I pulled her closer, but didn't answer. I didn't know what I believed, if anything at all. I supposed that scientifically, there had to be life on other planets, even sentient life, and probably on millions or even billions of them. I could even entertain the possibility that there might be other dimensions containing other universes and possibly billions of planets with yet even stranger alien life. But that any of it could be here, on this single little rock floating on one little part of one arm of a single galaxy among countless others in a nearly infinite universe? The odds seemed against us in that regard, and frankly, I was glad for it. This world, and all the life on it that so often seemed incomprehensible to me, was enough to contend with.

I didn't get the chance to express any of that to her, though. By the time I found some inadequate words to try, she was already asleep on my chest, breathing softly. And I remember thinking that everything I needed in this world, this universe or any other, was right here with me, right then.

Then I must have drifted off, too, because I had one of Natalia's nightmares about the Sleepers. She would have said, I guess, that they were finally speaking to me, as well, and maybe trying to use me to get to her, but I can't say for sure. It certainly seemed like a dream, although it was incredibly vivid. In it, the history of the Hundred Years' Sleep played out in graphic detail.

I saw a great battle from back when the earth was just jungle. I saw what I knew to be the Ancient Ones from the starless edge of a different universe. I'm not sure any description would do them justice, but there were masses of shining blue-black flesh peppered with eyes and mouths and tentacles, there were mile-long, miasmic swaths of black cloud in the sky and acidic ichors that burned paths through the new life on the ground.

I also saw those other-dimensional formless things who would come to be the Sleepers, just as Natalia had described them, iridescent and irregular outlines. These shapes were also colossal in scale, so much so that the invisible swipes of their appendages felled trees.

I saw meteorites rain fire and tumultuous waves of ocean water tossed into the sky. I saw flashes of light in colors I'm pretty sure we don't have names for, and they lit up the night sky of the dream. There was what I could only guess might have been blood, sprayed across foliage and sand and rock, and there were utterances I assumed might be prayers and battle cries, but in the end, the Sleepers were nearly wiped out.

The Ancient Ones cursed their remaining enemies with a restless death. It was powerful magic, so powerful that the curse could not be completely lifted even by the most skillful wielders of ancient and cosmic arts. However, it could be lessened, and so the priests of that old and alien race transmuted death to sleep, a sleep that would last eons, until all could be set right. Every 10,000 years, there would come a single century in which the stars would be positioned just so and the land and sea of this world fertile and brimming with life energy, and at the end of this century, the Sleepers would have a chance to awaken and reclaim their domain, feeding off the life energy of the lesser creatures who were, I guess, just simply in the way. I saw the Sleepers' perception of what Natalia had called appeasements. These were sigils carved in rocks by the sea and in the walls of deep canyons and at the entrances to caves, followed by a series of ritualistic practices I didn't fully understand. And I saw the Sleeper cults' sacrifices. I will never be able to unsee the atrocities of that part of the dream.

I had just been forced to witness the evisceration of an elderly woman when it occurred to me that I could hear her screaming even in my ears. It took a moment, but I realized it was a real sound from outside my head – an air raid siren, the kind of canopy of wailing that filled all the air around and above you. It reminded me of old war movies, or those storm warnings towns in the Midwest used to send people scrabbling to their storm cellars. I'd spent my whole life in upstate New York and had never actually heard one in our town before. It took another moment for me to sit up, aware all at once that the sound meant some enormous and immediate danger.

Natalia was already awake and standing by the passenger door of my car. Her head was cocked and her eyes were fixed on the sky, and she looked as if she were listening for something beneath the siren.

"Babe?"

She shook her head and looked at me. "We need to go. They're here. The other mages couldn't stop it...."

I hopped off the hood of the car, keys already dangling in my shaking hand. "Where?"

"To my aunts."

—

We saw many terrible things on the way into town. There was the dented school bus, flipped completely over on its roof. That was pretty bad. Blood was smeared against the side, and a single tiny pale arm hung limply from one of the broken windows. There was the police car half in a ditch created by caved in pavement on Main Street, and the bloated police officer flung over the hood. A severed tentacle the color of dead skin was wrapped around his neck, and its suckers were still weakly working to draw out the last drops of blood from the officer's jugular. We saw downed trees splintered like toothpicks, houses caved in, gouges in the street. It reminded me a little of those old Godzilla movies I used to watch as a kid. It really did look like something huge had come crashing through, kicking cars aside and stomping through buildings.

We saw a lot of dead people. Other than my grandfather's and my great aunt's funerals, I had never seen real dead people before. And these dead weren't washed, drained, manicured, combed, and made up for public viewing. They were bloody, rotting, torn apart or twisted into unnatural angles. Their faces had grown stiff in expressions of shocked horror and pain. Some were curled up in fetal positions, haloed in pools of blood and muck. Others had broken arms thrown up in useless defense probably seconds before something crushed them into the pavement. There were hands, arms, legs, even a head amidst the rubble of the residential homes. There was broken glass. And there were fires, just like it said in that book that Natalia had given me.

Just like she had told me about the arrival of the Sleepers.

The most terrifying of all, of course, where the vines. They were black and jointed like splintered twigs but incredibly strong, given the way they seemed to bore through wood, glass, metal, flesh and bone alike. They were coated with a kind of shiny, slimy substance that smelled vaguely of acetone and gasoline, a cloying smell that turned my stomach sour. And the vines were everywhere – along the curbs into the storm drains, wrapped around the wheel wells of cars, along the sides of buildings snaking in and out of windows and doors, around telephone poles, speared through trees and even the sides of brick and stone buildings. I have found out since that day that they are drawn to sudden movement and heat, and resistant to axes, weed killers, and fire. They waver when attacked, becoming something less substantial, and it's only then that maybe, maybe, you stand a chance of escaping their grasp. But they're fast. They move fast and they choke and puncture and kill fast. It's not often that I've seen a victim of theirs move faster.

I'm not sure why I thought Natalia's house would look any better than the others we had seen. Maybe it was because of the desperate hope in her eyes and the nervous way she soft-chewed her nails as we made our way across town. I saw tears in her eyes, but she wouldn't let them spill onto her cheeks. It made my heart ache for her. I wanted to say something, wanted to block out the world again with her, now more than ever, but one horror after another took the wind out of any words I tried to say. So maybe it was as much for me as for her that I pictured her house untouched, her aunts okay. I guess I needed to believe we were working toward something, toward someone who could fix it all, or at least stop it from getting worse.

But her street, her whole neighborhood was torn open and torn down. Raw wounds in the street exposed sewage and gas lines, telephone wires from downed poles sparked and writhed in the street. We couldn't drive the whole way, but instead, had to skirt around the mess to make it to her front lawn.

Her front door was caved in. We could smell the blood even from the front porch.

Even now, I get a lump in my throat thinking about Natalia finding her aunts, all three of them stabbed all over, with throats slashed and symbols carved into their foreheads. No gods or monsters had done that. She didn't cry, but every time I picture that look on her face, it breaks my heart over and over again.

I made Natalia stay close behind as I went from room to room with a knife from her kitchen. I wanted to get her away from the terrible sight of those bodies' cloudy eyes, the way the linoleum floors crackled under our feet from the sticky, drying blood. But I also wanted to make sure that whoever had done those things was gone now. We found no other trace of the cultists.

As I stood there in the upstairs hall, panting and clutching that kitchen knife, Natalia dragged me, silent and serious, to the library. She showed me a safe hidden behind a fake section of the bookshelves. It had not been discovered by the cultists, and for that, she seemed relieved. She spun the tumbler lock back and forth so fast I couldn't quite catch the combination, then flung open the door and pulled out the contents.

"Here," she said, thrusting two thin, very old books into my hands. The covers looked sort of leathery, but that wasn't exactly right. I had the inexplicable but sure notion that they were made of some kind of skin, but not from any living thing I had ever seen. There was no title or author name stamped on either book, nor were there title pages.

"What are these?" I looked at her, confused.

"Knowledge. Information. My aunts' most prized grimoires."

I turned the yellowed pages in the first book with care, afraid they'd crumble to dust between my fingers. "I...I can't read this. I don't understand what – " but then I did. I honestly don't know how, but suddenly the lines and squiggles made sense to me. When I looked up, Natalia was gesticulating with her hands, her eyes closed, her lips moving in quick, silent words. When she opened her eyes, she said to me, "I can feel them coming, Dec. If they find me – "

"They won't," I told her.

"If they do," she insisted, "then what is in those books is the only thing that can protect you. I cannot teach you what's in those books; there is no time. But I did the same incantation to help you understand them that my aunts did for me. Do you? Do you understand that language?"

I nodded.

"Good," she said, and sighed. "It should last for about a week and a half, two weeks. Study them in that time. Learn the things you need to protect yourself and others. There are ways to send the Sleepers back to the great Dreaming Cities. Maybe some day...."

"Natalia," I began. It was all so overwhelming, and I wanted to ask her about what she was implying beneath her words, the way she seemed to be suggesting I would be doing this alone. I wanted to reassure her again that I would always protect her, keep her safe. I wanted to tell her again that I loved her, because I knew deep down that she believed her time was running out, and that I would be facing this alone, without her. And Natalia had a way of believing something so strongly, so perfectly, that you found yourself believing it, too.

I was going to say all these things, but as she was speaking, she slumped against one of the open windows and put her hand down on the sill. She hadn't noticed the needle-like tip of the vine that had snaked its way up the side of the house and over the broken glass. I hadn't noticed it either until I saw all the color drain from her face, and a look of sick and knowing horror distort her features as she looked down at her hand. The tip of the vine had pricked her finger, while several other tendrils had begun to wrap around her wrist. I ran to the window and began stabbing and slashing at the vine. In the yard below, I saw hooded figures gathered beneath the window, looking up at us, but I couldn't worry about them just then. The vine was snaking its way up her arm now, and my knife was glancing off it. I dropped the knife and dug my fingers in, trying to yank it off her. She whimpered, trying to pull herself free, but it wrapped tighter. Her skin was growing waxy and red, and just before the vine tore off her arm, she finally began to scream.

In that scream, all the fear and pain of her sixteen years of running and hiding and dreaming welled up and out of her. Her face, her beautiful face, was splattered with blood, her mouth pulled open in a scream that was losing steam, losing sound. I saw her love for me in her eyes. I saw her good-bye in her eyes. And yet again, I couldn't find the damn words to give her anything. I held onto her, fighting the vine that wrapped around her throat, digging my ragged little finger nails and even my teeth into that slimy, stinking, bitter vine stalk. The burn scar on my jaw is a testament to the failure of that move, but damn if I didn't try everything I could to save her.

The vine that lifted me off my feet and smacked me across the room broke my collarbone. It's healed since, but still aches when it rains. I had the wind knocked out of me, though, and by the time I was able to scrabble to my feet and make it back to the windowsill, she was yanked out the window. For one endless moment of abject horror, I could only watch the robed figures bent over her sprawled and bleeding form. They waited until the escape of her last breath, then turned and left. They left her there, this precious prize they had searched sixteen years to find, left her in a sleep from which she would never wake up.

I knew I had to leave her there, too, but I couldn't quite bring myself to do it. I sat by her body for hours, holding her, talking to her, watching the body I had admired so often change into something that was no longer Natalia. I brought her back inside at dusk and laid her on her bed. I kissed her forehead, her lips, then took the books she had given me and left.

———

It's been eleven years since that day. According to the books Natalia gave me – books I spent a week and a half furiously studying and making notes in English in – the window for casting the ancient endless sleep spell will open tonight, and I'll have eleven days. The endless sleep, which dreamers managed to learn in secret from the masters themselves, is the only way to put the Sleepers back under for good. Eleven days, and a group of about 600 survivors across the world waiting for my go sign.

I never had anyone but Natalia count on me for anything until now. I hope it works.

I couldn't protect Natalia, couldn't keep her safe, but I think she always knew that. She loved me anyway. I think what she did know was that without her, I would throw every fiber of my being into protecting those I could with the tools she gave me, because she wanted it. Because everything she touched became a brighter little piece of an otherwise ugly, twisted world, and what I had learned from those books, what I had spent over a decade teaching others, could maybe bring that brightness back.

If I could give her any reason to love me, to be proud of me, I would. I owe it to her.

I've written all this down in this ratty old notebook, because of all the times I couldn't think of what to say – to Natalia, to my parents, to the well-meaning acolytes and survivors we've helped who have asked me about my scars and my story. I put down in words what I want to remember if I survive long enough to go senile, and that I want others to know if the events of the next eleven days prove a failure. I am where I am because I loved a princess. I was never a true hero, at least not like those in the fairy tales, but made me fight to be a better person.

For her, I will destroy the Sleepers, now the Sleepless, or die trying.

There is no time for sleep now – The others are waiting for my sign.

Good night, dreamers....

The Wonderful Musician

~ William Meikle ~

Rickman could never quite manage to reproduce the music he heard in his head.

It had been in there as long as he could remember—even when the nursery rhymes and the pop music of his pre-teen years had long since faded into a monotonous background drone, still the music was there. It was alive and vibrant, singing to him from all the dark places in his mind, there as he worked, there as he played—there as he slept, haunting his dreams. Over the years he'd tried almost everything to get it out—guitar at twelve, piano at fourteen, an interesting experiment with drums and drugs in his early twenties, and violin throughout his thirties.

None of them, although each diverting in its own way, had made any difference to his peace of mind. The music had stayed in his head, refusing to take a life of its own, preferring to hijack Rickman at the most inopportune moments with snatches of wistful rhythms and soaring choruses full of longing. The frustration Rickman felt at not being able to share this inner beauty was almost too much for a man to bear.

But now he had hope—technology had just caught up enough that he might finally have a chance at bringing his inner music out into the real world. It had taken every penny he had, and the resulting hardware filled most of his already cramped attic apartment—but it was a small price to pay. He would call it "Soundscapes of the City", and it would make him his fortune, of that Rickman was certain.

How can it fail?

All it had taken to get him on track was a demonstration of a machine from Dreamsoft Productions, and the latest sampling software from MythOS. A mixing deck and a holographic array did the rest. Music and images could be created from the subtle difference in electrical impulses in his brain while he dreamed, and then merged with any sound—or indeed any part of the electromagnetic spectrum—that he desired. Rickman's visions of bringing his magnum opus to the world were now that much closer to reality.

For the past forty nights he'd sampled and tweaked, taking the raw sounds that streamed into his loft apartment from the city outside and merging them with his dream compositions to form a holographic construct of sound and light and ionized gas in an ever-moving plasma bubble. It now hung like a giant ameba in the array in the center of his room—an ameba that sang and danced to his ever more insistent tune.

It had been a long, hard journey to this point.

During those first few days everything was sharp and jagged, harsh mechanical discordance that, while it had a certain musical quality, was not what he needed… not if he was going to take the world by storm. The plasma had roiled and torn, refusing to take a permanent shape, and Rickman despaired of what the city was telling him. Everything was ugly, mean-spirited. The music of the city spoke only of despair and apathy, and his dreams didn't make a dent when he overlaid them.

Then he had his epiphany.

Aptly, it came to him in a dream more vivid than any he had

ever had previously, as if the mere act of accessing the dream machine had unlocked something within him, allowing the full vision to emerge.

It starts with thin whistling, like a simple peasant's flute played at a far distance. At first all is black. The flute stops, and the first star flares in the darkness. And with it comes the first chord, a deep A-minor that sets the darkness spinning. The blackness resolves itself into spinning masses of gas that coalesce and thicken, bubbling and foaming before resolving into great black eggs, oiled and glistening, calving, over and over, reaching critical mass and exploding into a symphony that fills the void with color and song. Stars wheel overhead in a great dance, the music of the spheres cavorting in his head.

Rickman jumped from his bed and checked the sampling box—it had recorded nearly thirty minutes of material, streamed directly from his brain as he slept.

I have it. I finally have it.

He hooked the sampling box to the mixer and holographic array and started to play with the resulting sounds. He had hoped for immediate results, but he was to be disappointed again. At first it was still all too mechanical, with none of the grandeur and sweep of his dreams. Then he remembered the stars. He went out onto his balcony and realigned his antennae pointing it, not down toward the city, but up, to the sky and the dome of stars above.

He got results almost immediately. The plasma roiled, rolled, and formed a sphere, a ball of shining silver held in the holographic array, hovering at head height, quivering like quicksilver.

At first it just hung there in space, giving out a deep bass hum that rattled his teeth and set all the glassware in the apartment ringing. Things changed quickly when he double, then triple tracked the sounds from his dreams, adding depth and resonance to them with each new layer of aural complexity. Shapes formed in the plasma, concretions that slid and slithered, rainbow light shimmering over their surface like oil on water.

They sang as they danced.

Rickman soon found that by moving the antennae to point at different areas of the sky he was able to get the plasma to merge or to multiply; each collision or split gave off a new chord, the plasma taking on solid forms in a seemingly infinite variety of shapes. As they swam, his creations sang in orchestrated overtures to the dark beauty of the night. But it still wasn't right—the song still wasn't what he heard in his head, and nothing else would do but to keep trying until it was perfect.

He turned a knob to see if applying some distortion to his dream samples might do the trick. The array continued to whine and throb is a strangely musical beat, but the plasma burst with a soft *pop*, spilling like viscous liquid to the bottom of the box, coalescing and congealing.

By the time Rickman walked over to investigate, something lay curled at the bottom of the array.

At first he could not quite believe what he was seeing. This was no plasma—this was a creature—alive and breathing. The thing that had Rickman most worried was that he recognized it—a thing from childhood nightmares. It used to hide in the downstairs closet of the first house he remembered—a beast that had the body of a man but the head of some grotesque misshapen rodent. Its fur was patchy—mange and age had left it showing pale sallow skin in places where it should have fur, with weeping sores running the length of its body. Long yellow teeth hung over a short lower jaw—the left incisor was cracked and broken near the tip, giving the face a lopsided expression that was very far from being comical. Worst of all, a long pink tail rose and fell, swished once then thumped in time with the musical vibration and hum that ran through the array. Red eyes blinked, opened and looked straight at Rickman.

Rickman stepped back, half-expecting an attack, but the thing seemed more interested in the music. It pawed at the air in an obscene parody of an orchestra's conductor, then stood, unsteady on back legs that looked more suited to crouching. To Rickman's astonishment it began to dance, its diseased body swaying softly, almost seductively. Then it surprised Rickman again. It sang along with the beat, nonsense words in a guttural tone that sounded almost like a chant. To Rickman's ears the whole thing was as harsh and dissonant as the city sounds outside the window.

That isn't right at all.

Rickman retreated to the mixing desk and turned a knob. The rhythm speeded up. The rodent-thing danced faster, legs pumping, an almost frantic jig. It sang, putting everything it had into it, as fervent as any tenor, screeching and wailing as if in pain. The whole room shook and vibrated and Rickman felt as if the top of his head might come off with the pressure. He dialed the distortion knob all the way back to the off position and finally, with another soft *pop* the mutant rodent vanished, its form being subsumed back into a swirling glowing mass as the plasma reformed in the dead center of the array. The ball of shimmering quicksilver hung there, quivering, as if daring him to try something else.

Rickman, while dismayed that his experiment had taken such a strange turn, was not too disappointed.

I'm onto something here. I'm really onto something.

He played with his dials and knobs, testing the boundaries of the plasma with multi-tracking, distortion, feedback and echo effects. He found that at the top range of power, with echo full on, the plasma was forced into an egg-like configuration, no longer silver but black and roiling, the surface covered in an oily sheen that cast a rainbow aurora around the room. With only the minutest twitch of the knobs things could be born from the egg—things that would dance—things that would sing, just for him.

After his disappointment with the rodent-thing, he was only

slightly happier with his second creation. As before, the field boundary popped when he turned a knob just slightly too far.

This time the floor of the array was coated in several inches of gray slime that was already hardening and fusing into a solid, glass-like mass. There were things embedded in it—blood and hair and bones and eyes, all jumbled like a manic jigsaw, fused and running into one another as if assembled by a demented sculptor. It was only when he spotted the chipped and yellowed incisor that he realized what he was seeing.

He had no idea what to do next, but fortunately the decision was taken from him. Something rose up out of the glassy mass, slowly at first, then punching its way through the surface with a tinkle of broken glass that was clearly audible even above the vibration and hum. When Rickman looked closer, he saw it was a bone, hollow and holed in several places along its length—a bone that immediately started up a piping whistle, high and reedy, like a gull soaring and swooping though the room, keeping time with the thrum and beat from the array. The sound was not unpleasant—almost harmonious in fact, so Rickman decided to let things play on for a spell to see where they led.

More bones forced their way up through the slime, sending their high whistling voices to join the first, a flock of flautists that blended and merged until it was like an orchestrated choir, singing in time with Rickman's dream compositions.

But it's still not right.

Without hesitation he turned the echo knob sharply to the off position. Once again the plasma reformed into the shining quicksilver globe in the center of the array. The chamber fell silent. By small, almost miniscule stages, Rickman began to turn the knob again, taking care not to go too far, determined to prevent the plasma from popping this time.

He was rewarded for his patience.

A new black egg formed and quivered, an oily rainbow aura dancing over it. Ever so slowly it became two, a shimmering sheen running over their sleek black surface. They hummed to themselves, a high singing that was taken up and amplified by an answering whine from the enclosing array. As two eggs became four, the whole room rocked from side to side in rhythm as a drumbeat kicked in to force the tempo.

Better.

The dance had begun.

Four eggs became eight.

The air above Rickman filled with singing, filled with the rhythm of the dance.

His whole body shook, vibrating in time. His head swam, and it seemed as if walls of the room melted and ran. The scene receded into a great distance until it was little more than a pinpoint in a blanket of darkness, and he was alone, in a cathedral of emptiness where nothing existed save the dark and the pounding chant.

And then there was light.

He saw stars—vast swathes of gold and blue and silver, all dancing in great purple and red clouds that spun webs of grandeur across unending vistas. Shapes moved in and among the nebulae; dark, wispy shadows casting a pallor over whole galaxies at a time, shadows that capered and whirled as the dance grew ever more frenetic. He was buffeted, as if by a strong, surging tide, but as the beat grew ever stronger he cared little. He gave himself to it, lost in the dance, lost in the stars.

He did not know how long he wandered in that space between. He forgot himself, forgot everything but the dancing in the vastness where only rhythm mattered. He may even have been there yet had the hologram's boundary not collapsed with a shriek.

This time he had to hurry to dismiss the thing that the collapsing field left behind. It was the size of a grown man, but looked more like a hideous shrimp. The body was segmented and chitinous like that of a crustacean, but this was no marine creature—it had membranous wings, currently tucked tightly against its back, giving it a hunched appearance. There were no arms or hands to speak of, although Rickman counted four pairs of limbs. The pair the thing used as legs was more stout and thicker than the rest, each being tipped with three horny claws extended to balance its weight at the front, while a segmented tail completed the tripod behind it. The other appendages looked more flexible and nimble. It turned slightly and Rickman got a good look at its face. Instead of features, there was only a mound of ridged flesh, pale and greasy, like a mushroom towards the end of its cycle. A multitude of thin snake-like appendages wafted around its head, turning as one and looking straight at Rickman. They started to thrash—at first he thought it too was dancing in time to the beat of the music, but the walls of his array began to quake and the thing inside thrashed harder. Its wings unfolded, and the huge tail beat at the confinement of the boundary field. Rickman's plasma container wailed and screamed louder than any amplified feedback whine at the assault.

This isn't right at all.

He was forced to switch the machinery off completely, and even then the thing seemed reluctant to go, fighting and thrashing as it was torn into mere scraps of plasma that wafted gently in the air before finally winking out with another soft *pop*.

Rickman stood at the mixing desk, fingers gripping the edge of the box so tightly that his knuckles were white and his palms felt bruised and battered when he willed himself to let go and relax.

The music in his head took longer to fade than the pain in his hands. Once he had recovered his breath, the main thing that Rickman remembered was not the hideous prawn-like thing in the box, but the dance, and the time he had spent lost in the rhythm of the spheres. He wanted that again. He wanted it badly.

I'm close now.

He switched his machine back on. The holographic field sparked and buzzed and the array began to throb and vibrate. The plasma formed almost immediately and started to sing and dance even before Rickman turned the echo knob slowly clockwise.

A tear formed in reality, a black oily droplet appearing to hang in the air, a perfect black egg, already singing.

The walls of the room throbbed like a heartbeat. The black egg pulsed in time. The singing got louder, like a chorus of angels, far away, singing into a wind.

Rickman turned the knob a millimeter to the right.

The egg calved, and calved again.

Four eggs hung in a tight group, pulsing in time with the throbbing music that was getting steadily louder and more insistent as a distant drumbeat kicked in, hard and heavy. Colors danced and flowed across the sheer black surfaces; blues and greens and shimmering silvers on the eggs.

In the blink of an eye there were eight.

Rickman started to sway and hum along with the beat, singing under his breath, getting lost in the moment.

It's working.

Sixteen now, all perfect, all dancing.

The vibration grew louder still.

Thirty-two now, and they had started to fill the array with dancing aurora of rainbow shimmering lights that pulsed and capered in time with the music.

It's really working.

Sixty-four, each a pearl of black light.

The colors filled the room, spilled out over the floor, crept around Rickman's feet, danced in his eyes, in his head, all though his body. He gave himself to it, willingly. The room filled with stars, and he danced among them.

A hundred and twenty eight eggs in the chamber now, and already calving into two hundred and fifty-six.

Rickman danced.

Rickman sang.

The eggs sang with him.

There were too many of them to count now. They spilled out of the array, filled the space in the room, their song raising higher, the beat and thrum of the music filling his head, the dancing rainbow colors filling his eyes with blue and green and gold and wonderment.

Rickman was at peace. He danced in empty spaces filled with oily, glistening eggs. They calved and spawned yet more eggs, then even more, until he swam in a swirling sea of eggs and colors and songs and dancing.

Lost—so lost that he did not even noticed when he was joined in the dance.

First came the rodent things, tails thumping, paws slapping, their voices raised high in a chant that called their gods to them. High and free, a whistling rose up, soaring as a myriad bone flutes came in on the beat and joined them. Membranous wings fluttered somewhere high above. Eggs calved, releasing even more of their number into the dance, and calved again, and again.

Rickman's room could no longer contain them.

They spilled out into the city.

Rickman went with them.

When Light Returned to Karakossa

~ Thomas Lynch & Joseph S. Pulver ~

Born among the Bottomliners of waterless Dun Beach, while shutter and shatter barked under the Wormwood Stars, Xiao Gǔ, or Little Falcon, grew into something man-sized. At seventeen, before another round of yawns could wholly silence his *might-get-out-of-this*, he collected all the parts of his famished and pretty fed-up and weary, and looked at the beyond. Shoulders set to push at forward, he wandered from his tin-and-twine shack below the purpling sky. Walked or stumbled, dipped his oar in riverwide or sailed seas coastal, he moved, sun or suburbs, from light and spring to unmanageable blast of deepest night and back again. Climb or under fence, around the tilts of THAT and by shapes commissioned in carnivorous dreams, year slid into year as he lined-up miles of done and done.

In the Land of Seven Slow Rivers, Xiao Gǔ spent the morning of his 33rd birthday in the Temple of To-morrow's Fire. The clouds in the skycanvas above were nightfall-gray and full of the thunders of the Laughing Furies.

The following night he found a room and a meal of course bread and uncommonly-spiced noodles in the House of a Thousand Injuries. Brewing around him in the smoke and shadows of the tavern room, dark whispers and glances darted. Ill at ease he went to bed in a common room he had to share with five hard and unpolished men. Flipping and flopping with heated notions of murderers lighting his thoughts, he dipped in and out of sleep as they snored and grunted.

Before the sun could splash light into the sky the next morning he rose, and smelling murder, knowing it to be en route, dressed quickly. Cat-stepping between five sinister characters while they were still fingering trouble in their dreams, he exited a window and fled, following the venturesome of southerly winds.

Moonscapes and no traffic, he moved. He rode the roads on his jade turtle with a golden shell, Màn Lùjìng, meaning Slow Path, whom he won in a game of mahjong with a very drunken trickster, to see what he could learn of the great, wide world. Over mountain and valley and along rivers reflecting the desires of the stars he travelled. He watched. Stumbled. He saw. Dealt with many hungers. He learned what there was to learn when it was offered, and with it tucked away, perhaps for future use, he traveled on.

For many days the land he traveled became tainted. Greens and new leaves stretching toward the waning light were touched by autumnal forces out of season. Gray mosses covered areas of bare rocks and boulders. Fungi the color of rust clawed in cracks and upon boughs. The lead-colored sky and its vulture-shadows pressed down, bring stinging winds, and periods of chilled rain. The wind changed and became blustery and chill, making Xiao Gǔ's phoenix-kite buck, dip, and strain against the cord he had tethered to the back of his saddle.

Every inch forward was dulled, no sound or flash or beast or fowl stirred around him.

This land was an ocean of dying.

As a new day dawned with cloud-shaded gray-light pawing at the ground, he went through a stunted hollow of dread that disordered the heart, and coming out of it took a fork that lead around a bend crowned on each side with massive boulders. Before him stood a great lone hill in the dry wilderness. Xiao Gǔ gasped, the ghostly-land of shrubs and roots had been punished by decay, and dying grass and rocky soil rose to a distant peak where a shorn Cassia-tree stood. All the nearby hills and fields were green and bursting with fruit since it was the height of summer, but this desolate hill… all its breath and tranquility had been stripped from it.

"Has this desolate place offended the gods?" He had seen barren and found his intent crowned in rain, had strained to move his restlessness in the face of necessitates or greed, or when the river's flow would not dent, but this tomb of dismal was a crime, it sapped all vigor.

In the horrible silence, Xiao Gǔ was surprised to see a shepherd standing on the hill when there were so many better places to feed a flock, so to discover the perplexing why, he turned Màn Lùjìng off the road and up the hill to where the shepherd stood. Two more surprises awaited him. First, the shepherd was a beautiful young woman dressed in heavily-soiled, tattered rags, and second, her grief was a plague, graying hand, eye, and expression. Taken aback, Xiao Gǔ asked what misery and bothers clung to her.

"Oh, Sir," the woman moaned. "Fortune has forsaken me, and I am in need and ashamed. Since you are kind enough to ask I will tell you all. I am Cassilda, the youngest daughter of the King Who Once Wore Golden Silks across the Sea of Hali. I was married to the second-son of the Water Dragon King of Ponah Pei, Pàng Chen. Yet my husband ill-treated and disowned me. I complained to my father-in-law, but he loved his son blindly and did nothing. And when I grew insistent father and son became angry, and I was cast out and banished to this dismal curse of dead branches and silent dread. This is my prison… my tomb."

"To tend this flock, on this barren hill when such rich fields stand so near?"

"These are the rain-sheep, the thunder-rams, and they must stay on the Hill of Sorrows where once the golden Cassia-tree knew no fever or scalding, until they are sent to slog through the mundane world of dust, removing the mortar between the fortunes of men and replacing it with ill luck when men fall into the Winter Sleep. This gives rise to despair and the destruction of dreams, and I am cursed by some foulsome spell to tend them.

"I am given no rest in my task . . . And no companion."

On its way to darken some poor soul's dreams one of her flock brushed against her. She shrunk from its touch.

"One by one, my flock must leave me and not return... and when the last has left this hill I will wither completely and my bones will be taken below to further stain this Palace of Ill." When she had spoken, the pale child burst into tears and lost all control. She fell to her knees and her shoulders shook with futility.

Her anguish dizzied him. To endure he had sometimes been a thief of small things, mostly nourishment, but he could see no offense that should sentence her to this hell. "There must be some way I can aid you? Surely one so fair need not be dissected by melancholy and for-ever be chained to this gray damnation?"

"Thank you for your kindness, but I am for-ever bound here."

He looked at her gloom and torment, and his anger a magnet seeking future, stepped forward. "I will not hear there is no remedy for your woe. Honor and simple kindness demand we find a path that will lead to liberty. All human sensitivities stand opposed to your plight. There must be something I can do to help you? Would that I had wings and could fly away with you." And there it was. "Come, and I will take you away from here. There is ample room on Màn Lùjìng's saddle for another."

"Alas good Sir, it cannot be. I am compelled to stay here by the will of my great and terrible father-in-law, the Water Dragon King."

More tears hammered her and her clothes constricted, as the pain of the woven-web of death bound her to the greywound of grieve she kneeled on. Her breath became shallow for a time. "The Sea of Hali is far from here; yet if you travel in that direction and go far enough, you may come it on your journey. I should like to give you a letter to bring to my father, but I do not know whether you would take it."

"I will be glad to deliver the letter to your father. Yet the Sea of Hali is long and broad, and how am I to find your father's kingdom? Is there a map? Can you speak of markers?"

"I am no guide. Of thorny paths and how many days and nights one would need to navigate to reach my father's palace, I cannot say." Her arm rose and she pointed. "On the southern shore of the sea stands another Cassia-tree, a twin to this one, which people call the Winter Tree. When you get there you must loosen your girdle and strike the gong which hangs from the branches of the tree three times in succession. Then the guardian who you must follow will appear. When you see my father, tell him in what need you found me, and that I long greatly for his help."

Then she fetched out a letter from her breast and, placed it in a beautiful, but cracked porcelain teapot decorated with plum blossoms, and gave it to Xiao Gǔ. She bowed to him, looked toward the east and sighed, and, unexpectedly, tears came from the eyes of Xiao Gǔ as well. He took the letter and the pot and gently placed it in his saddle bag on the broad golden shell of his jade turtle, Màn Lùjìng.

The traveler turned and bowed to Cassilda, promising to return with aid from the Amber King in distant Carcosa. Clouds parted, a songbird settled on the Cassia-tree, and Cassilda smiled. With that, Xiao Gǔ took his leave, setting out now with a purpose.

Many evils tried to sway good Xiao Gǔ from his quest. He rode along the River of the Cunning Voices one day and he passed a small island in the river inhabited by beautiful women who tried to coax him with the honey-throated songs, but to Xiao Gǔ, their music sounded like the hissing of serpents, and he traveled on. Many miles further on, an Ill-Dream Tree wished to play a game with Xiao Gǔ, offering prizes of majestic riches, but the tree had the most bothersome odor, and Xiao Gǔ was fast to leave the troubles it promised. Rising dust and more dust blooming around him, he crossed the Desert Sea of Sleeping Dragons, and the sun beat down making Màn Lùjìng's progress a wound of sluggishness. In the middle of the sand-swept landscape, he passed a small company of people in considerable terracotta pots lifting shells over themselves as if bathing, yet there was not a drop of water in the pots or the shells. One empty vessel sat at the edge of their community and they offered him a chance to reside and thrive in their oasis, but he thought better of it and with a polite NO traveled on. Even-minded, he was not one for bounce & hopHOP, no, dash, ripe with bump & jostle, he'd always stood against the temptations of FAST, but today, under the animal-sun, he wished he'd bought a rabbit for a stead.

At the far edge of the desert, he happened across a small village with an open market offering herbs, flowers, and spices and silks. Talking birds in delicate cages and sea creatures carved from wood said to be imported from the eastern jungles were for sale. All the peddlers called to him telling him how high quality their produce was, but after careful examination, Xiao Gǔ saw that every single offering on display showed signs of wilting and rot, and the birds looked sickly, so he traveled on.

Stars rose, but they offered his desire no warmth. The sun appeared, only to bite and finally bleed to death in the arms of the horizon. Without maps he put nights and miles and forests and grasslands behind him. He saw shores, he saw mountains—climbed or went around as response, rain churned, he went that way… and toward. There were colors and splinters, but ugly, or phenomena to be disregarded, nothing changed.

Between a vast expanse of dry grass and noon he noticed his food supply was low. As his stomach urged him to eat, he quickly urged his stead onward. They came to a valley filled with peach trees, but every single peach had already had a bite taken out of it. Poor Xiao Gǔ found himself in a land of plenty but he could not eat. One night, while keeping warm by his campfire in the Valley of Sess Qua, he heard vile hopfrogs croaking in the dark with the tongues of demons. Long ago at another campfire, he'd heard the legends of their feeding habits—"Young, male flesh… to tear and taste."—and quickly fetched and mounded much wood onto the blaze, wishing it higher and higher, to keep the dreadful creatures of many a tavern-tale away.

But the terrible croaking grew louder, became a great chorus, a *dark spell*, and he felt faint, thinned, and passed into a deep deathlike slumber. He slept for three days, and finally his turtle, sensing Xiao Gǔ was in the grasp of some deathly enchantment, reached down and snapped him up in its beak and carried him away from the Valley of Sleeping Death.

Xiao Gǔ rode all day. His belly grumbled and began to look for a place to bed down for the night. Ahead he saw a crossroads and thought to camp there. Simmering a salted fish, some roots and herbs in a small pot, he looked up and read the fingerpost he was camped under.

LONG IS THE WAY

slow this way

THIS WAY PLEASE

COMFORTS ½ DAY

UP

doors and ladders to suit your eagerness

INFORMATION

He shook his head after reading each finger. "I have spent time with slow and long. To-morrow we try information, my friend."

Màn Lùjìng, munching on a leafy bush, made no reply.

In the morning they rode and rode. Noontide arrived and twilight as well.

Nothing brought more nothing.

And the cloak of Mother Night unfolded around him.

About him, the stony terrain grew more mountainous, and Xiao Gǔ was unsure of the way. Happily, he saw the abode of poor folk by the side of the road, so he made his way to it. There was a figure out front working busily, so Xiao Gǔ watched. As he did, he saw that it was a young man and he was sweeping the courtyard in front of the broken shack, trying to use some form of magic to move his broom.

"Greetings, Young Sir!" called Xiao Gǔ. "How are you managing that wonderful trick?"

"Why, by magic, of course," answered the man. "I am Xuétú Wūshī, apprenticed to the Exalted Wizard, Zang Chu Hsu, who dances on the Battlefield of End-Night, fighting the Flames of Naught and Dread. It is he that lives in this humble abode."

Xiao Gǔ thought it odd that a great wizard would live in such poverty.

"But why are you sweeping the courtyard when it is only sand?"

"I am doing my master's bidding."

Xiao Gǔ saw the wisdom in this and nodded. "I find I am also in need of guidance, and any food you might spare" Xiao Gǔ continued. "I am trying to reach the Sea of Hali, and know I am close, but I do not know which way to turn."

Xuétú Wūshī smiled and pointed to a tall mountain. "Turn south at Dà Yāncōng and follow the old road down to the sea, and you will have arrived at your destination." Xuétú Wūshī stepped inside and returned with an oddly-shaped fruit and a small roll. "This is all we can spare."

"Many thanks," said Xiao Gǔ. "I wish you luck with your tasks." He waved and he traveled on.

From this point onward, Xiao Gǔ noticed that the land seemed to be drained of color and signs of life. Dry, pale, gray. Everything was worn or cracked or crumbling. Weighted down by what he saw, and feeling he was thinning, he traveled on . . .

They moved slowly.

Swarms of dead black moths littered the ground. There were no creatures here, except the black deathbirds arcing above. The whole of the land was gray. Leering stars looked down. The lonely frequencies of dead things warbled in slow low tones . . .

"Everywhere... such *grayness*."

"Màn Lùjìng, my slow friend, what swollen evil in its joy unleashes an assault such as this to condemn what was once radiant and beautiful?"

Four days of a lifetime later, Xiao Gǔ found himself, finally riding along the seashore, in search of the Winter Tree, the twin Cassia-tree from the hill that he'd left so many leagues behind. There, clinging to the rocks and being buffeted by waves, the tree stood. Xiao Gǔ rode over and struck a tiny gong that hung from the boughs three times with his girdle.

Then he waited.

Twitched where he sat.

Stood.

Walked around the tree in circles. Searched the distance, yelled hellos, toed and tossed pebbles to past time, looked to the sky for portents . . . waited and walked. And waited.

Night came. Morning and afternoon followed. He turned toward the stony beach and looked out over the cloudwaves. The clock assaulted Cassilda; he must deliver her plea and convince her father to come to her aid.

There was warmth in his heart as he thought of her. He wanted to look into her eyes and see them discover the rewards of pleasure. He wanted to see her smile.

"Those lips…" His knitting heart to heart.

Ready to dash, he paced.

Waited.

As he waited, gazing out over the sea, two men walked passed him on the beach. They stopped on the other side of the tree, and turned and looked at Xiao Gǔ, and he at them. They turned away, whispering animatedly to one other, and turned back again. One of them sat on a large stone, and struggled to take off one of his boots. Once he got it off, he shook it, again and again, as if to shake a pebble out of the boot with the sizable hole in the sole, but saw nothing fall out. Closing one eye and telescoping the other, he looked inside. "Nothing… to be done," the man muttered to himself. There was a to and fro of exchanged glances between the two men followed by a wink replied to by a smile. The one in the bleak hat pointed. His companion stood, shook the dust from his holey greatcoat and looked back at Xiao Gǔ. No nod, no shrug, they, offering no word, moved on.

Xiao Gǔ glared and kicked a small rock at the tree.

"I will not be turned."

Night came and he began to worry.

He paced. He sat and stared.

He thought to strike the gong again.

The Weaving Maiden Moon rose and dropped her light upon him.

"Have I not performed my task properly?" he asked her, truly hoping for a reply.

Xiao Gǔ looked for portents in the sky. Looked over the cloudwaves for a sign he had been heard.

Nothing.

And nothing.

Despair rising within him he said, "I have made a promise and would not break it. A lady is in dire circumstances and needs assistance.'

"Won't someone help me to help her?"

Again his thoughts turned to her eyes… and her pale lips, as dawn broke over the horizon.

Out of the cloudwaves appeared the Sentry That Sees Behind Every Mask, standing tall and strong, clad in armor and wearing the mask of a fox. In his mighty hand, he held a great, curved broadsword which flashed in the early morning light. "Who are you, and why do you summon me? Are you not a mortal? How is it you have known to ring the Gong of the Winter Tree?"

Xiao Gǔ bowed before such a commanding presence, and when he rose, he said, "My name is Xiao Gǔ and come at the request of Cassilda, bearing a message for her father the Amber King."

The sentry gasped in shock. "You have seen Cassilda? How does she fare?"

"Not well good sir. She has been cursed to tend the rain-sheep by her hateful husband and father-in-law, and cannot leave the barren hillside where they have imprisoned her. Her plight is dire. I have a letter written by her hand to give to her father."

"Come," said the sentry. "We must be quick to the king's court. There you must tell him of what you have seen, that we may free his royal daughter." The sentry turned, and faced the water. He reached into his belt pouch, and pulled forth three iridescent, deep black feathers and threw them toward the heavens. The air was suddenly filled with great, black birds, cawing to the sky. They ascended into the air rapidly and made circles. Then they flew and whirled in a funnel toward the water. They dropped closer and closer to the water, until they joined, forming a feathered, black walkway across the Sea of Hali, allowing Xiao Gǔ and Màn Lùjìng to follow the sentry across the water. The three travelers stepped out and walked across the Bridge of Crows over the cloudwaves to the Kingdom on the Other Side.

A cold wind blew against their every step, making the going difficult. Still, they trudged forward, pressing against the chill air, until finally the other side could be seen. The thin light was dying and twilight surrounding them as they reached the far shore.

"What is *this* place?" Xiao Gǔ asked. *This is a place of no delight… shadows in shadows cast a winterspell of ruin here.*

"This is Carcosa," the sentry said. "Welcome to the dominion of the King in Yellow."

The armored man led him up a hill toward a massive structure surrounded with 1,000 columns made of cracked and pale yellow stone. Surfaces here were bent, strained, despair had unspooled here. Between each of the two columns stood a great doorway of the heaviest wood, rivers of unkind had splashed against them, and to keep the ink of misery from snuffing what light remained in the city, the doors had been closed to the world. Faced with difficult, Xiao Gǔ examined the Great Dragon Castle, and saw that it was marked and ravished by disrepair, and that all the gates and windows-high were shuttered against him. There were no locks or handles. The sentry turned to him in front of one of the gates, and said, "To open each gate you must combine saliva with a drop of your blood and inscribe your name on it in your best calligraphy. If you have picked the right door, it will open and grant you entry into the king's court. If you have not yet gained access by sunrise, I shall be forced to slay you."

Xiao Gǔ tried many doors, but none opened to him. He stopped, and stood back to consider his predicament while the sentry merely stood and waited. He looked into the East, and saw the sky begin to pale, and realized he had little time. He looked back to the gates, studying each in turn, until finally he found one that was different. On this one, near the center of the great oak door, was a tiny, worn carving of a Cassia tree.

"Surely this is the one," Xiao Gǔ said. So he spat into his hand, and pricked his finger again, stirring his brush in the mixture, and wrote his name at the base of the carving of the tree. There was a resounding click, as if from a giant lock, then, on the wind came the sound of a gong, and the door swung open.

The sentry turned and bowed to Xiao Gǔ, and bade him follow. They walked many dim halls where the floors were caked with the dust of many years. Long dead and dry flowers leaned in vases. The walls were shaped by failure, any capacity or meaning they once had leeched out by a language of nothingness and woe. And all the statues in the halls were cracked, broken… many were headless. Faded paintings of courtly grace and threadbare tapestries hung everywhere.

Eventually, they reached the hall of the Great Black Doors, where the sentry informed him that he was allowed only two steps at a time. Each time he wished to move further, he had to request it, and be granted permission to continue on. It was a laborious process, but Xiao Gǔ did as he was bidden, and they reached the far end of the hall where they came to two great black doors. Upon each of them were pale yellow symbols, which seemed to shimmer and waver, causing Xiao Gǔ to clutch his belly in sudden dizziness.

Xiao Gǔ entered the great hall, and made obeisance to the figure on the throne. The Yellow King sat, slouching to one side, his pale, ragged raiment hanging from his skeletal figure. His bony hand held a pale mask to his face, and his breath came from behind it, sounding ragged and labored.

"Who is this who comes before me?" rasped the king.

"It is I, Xiao Gǔ, your majesty," cried the traveler, not raising his eyes. "A simple traveler who brings news of your daughter Cassilda, who tends the rain-sheep on a barren hillside, cursed to do so for all eternity by her husband, the son of the Water Dragon King of Ponah Pei."

Suddenly the ground shook, and there came a distant roar on the wind. Xiao Gǔ was terrified and perplexed, whereas the sentry and the king merely appeared saddened by the great noise and thunderous rumbling. The king saw his reaction and said, "That is my brother, the mighty black dragon Nyarlheiloong. The Water Dragon King imprisoned him long ago, and made off with my daughter so she could marry his son, and he could claim dominion."

"How is he imprisoned, may I ask?" Xiao Gǔ queried.

"A great seal has been laid over the entrance to his underworld citadel below this very palace. The entrance is guarded by the Seven Daughters of the Wolf: one has the head of a bird, one the head of a cricket, one the head of a carp, one the head of a viper, one the head of a goat, one the head of a boar, one the head of an eel. Beyond that, the great seal itself is held in place by six magical bolts that cannot be broken."

Xiao Gǔ had an idea. "Cannot be broken, you say? But can they be loosened?"

The king slumped and covered his mask again. "I am the sole cause of these woes and troubles," he cried. "I failed to defend my daughter and my kingdom, and now we all suffer in this dim, dispirited land."

"All may not be lost," Xiao Gǔ said. "Please. Let me see this entrance and examine this seal. I may be able to be of aid."

With the permission of the king, the sentry brought him down the mountainside and to the cave entrance. There, guarding the entrance were the seven monsters and covering the opening was a great seal three times as tall as a man, and shaped to have six wholly-equal sides.

"How do we dispatch these monsters?" the sentry asked.

"I must ask the aid of my friend, for Màn Lùjìng is not only my steed, but a minstrel of the highest order." He crouched down and whispered to Màn Lùjìng, who nodded and strode down the path toward the monsters.

As soon as the turtle reached them, the Seven Daughters of the

Wolf made to attack, but Màn Lùjìng fixed its ruby-pupiled pearl gaze upon them, and began to sing, and sang of the beginning of the world, of the gods of the mountains and the dragons of the rivers, and finally of the rise of man. The monsters were awestruck by the beautiful voice, and momentarily lulled.

"Each is chained to its post, yes?" Xiao Gǔ asked. The sentry nodded, so Xiao Gǔ walked up to each and from a pouch on his belt took several vials, looking at each vial to determine which one to use on the monster he faced. Then he blew a different color dust into the face of each beast saying "Unday ah-na nay." The beasts stiffened into statues after Xiao Gǔ was finished.

"What is that?" the sentry asked when Xiao Gǔ returned.

"Kufra Dust. When I was very young and had not been on the road very long, I once shared my meager pot with a fellow traveler who named himself, Black John the Conqueror. He was a strange old man—the 7th son of a 7th son, a healer and an ancient wizard from a land he said was a vast swamp on the other side of the world.'

"To thank me for my kindness he reached in his heavy carpet-bag of *gris-gris*, as he called his spells, and told me, if I ever needed extra hands to bind evil's bent until I could slip away, this 'Will sure cure yer ills, boy.'

"Black John explained how to use it, but I've never felt I had the need."

At each corner of the seal behind the monster statues was a great metal bolt. Xiao Gǔ went over to Màn Lùjìng, his turtle, and lifted the topmost part of the saddle. There, hidden underneath was a small compartment, and he took out an oddly-shaped small jug. "This is magical oil that I acquired in my travels," he said. "It is known to loosen the most stubborn of locks."

With the beastly guardians hardened, Xiao Gǔ went to each of the bolts and applied the oil. With ease he gave each one a twist, and they started to come loose! Nyarlheiloong, brother to the king, and brother to Uagio Tsotho, Shupnikkurat, Kas-Ogthqa, and Assaatur, felt his bonds loosening, and he started thrashing on the other side of the prison door. The earth trembled beneath their feet. Xiao Gǔ hastily climbed down and ran to one side with the sentry, and the great dragon burst forth, blasting the great seal into a thousand and a thousand pieces. Before them, a massive form, dark as glowing midnight, took to the free air. Several smaller forms, slayers by the look of their malformed teeth and claws, followed. As a single voice, they roared a mighty roar that shattered the sky, and flew through the passageways into the king's palace.

With little grace, but much speed, Xiao Gǔ and the sentry pursued until they gained the throne room. There, the king was relaying Xiao Gǔ's story to his brother. The dragon turned as Xiao Gǔ entered. Hissing smoke and puffing clouds, Nyarlheiloong, He Who Dreams of Light, but Dwells in Darkness, raised a massive clawed fist, from which still hung a chain and broken shackles from his imprisonment, and spoke. "I owe you my life, young mortal. You have freed me, and given me the chance to right many wrongs this night; my tigers and I will fly out and set things back to the design they were formed to fit." Xiao Gǔ then saw these retainers of the black dragon. They were five tigers, and each tiger had four fire-bearded heads and wide mouths full of saber-fangs. They were named Venom, Anger, Wrath, Vengeance, and Ghostbringer.

"The abasements I have suffered shall be put right. By the Light of zO and the Truth of the Teevs, and the mighty fires under the pot of ZuZu, I will return." Promising joyous fortunes upon his return, the great black dragon and his tigers flew into the sky, crying out with ear-splitting roars as they marched through the heavens to have their revenge for their overlong isolation.

Before dawn, the warriors, showing no mark of torn or weary, returned. They crashed down into the grand hall, and a victorious grin split the face of Nyarlheiloong. The four-headed tigers roared triumphantly, and in a gleeful dance, the great black dragon stamped his mighty feet. Holding a rolled tapestry, Ghost stepped from their midst and gently unrolled it. Unfurled, it revealed Cassilda returned to the songs of earth.

"Wild, I went hunting to vanquish the hideous cowards, and upon finding them, unfolded my quicksilver claws. I offered the King of Death two beating hearts as a gift and he accepted them. As reward, honor returns and the flame that gives sweet to soul and skin and wakes color is forged anew."

Untainted. Back. Free from the backhand of villainy. Cassi remembered spring and what could be spun from hope, her fingers trembled with possibilities. Her eyes were damp with joy's tears. A princess, standing in a pool of blessed, golden sun that bathed the palace in majesty once again. Cassilda's robes, no longer ragged, were woven of the finest rainbow-colored silks. With love and respect she looked at her father. The Amber King stood straight, and his sickly cast left him and he filled his lungs anew in the full majesty of the King in Yellow.

"Princess Cassilda I welcome you back to your father's palace," Xiao Gǔ said.

"Again, I am called Cassi, now that light has returned to this land… and we have you to thank for this. We could never have done this without your help!"

"But daughter," cried the king as he stepped down off his dais and held her once again. "Tell us what happened. Was my brother terrible and rough with the Water Dragon King? Was there much destruction?"

Cassi tried to hide her mirth. "Oh, there was much destruction, My Lord Father. When my most illustrious uncle landed, and the paltry army my husband led fled in the face of the righteous anger of Nyarlheiloong. My husband, Pàng Chen was given a vicious but justified end. My uncle and his retainers bared their teeth and stretched out their claws. One furious tiger with fangs like magic knives bit off the hand that withheld bread, another bit off the other hand which withheld fairness, a third bit off a foot that stomped on dreams, the fourth one bit off the other foot that marched over hope, and finally the fifth opened Pàng Chen's bowels. Nyarlheiloong, surrounded by purple flames, called my loathsome husband a scoundrel, a prince of evil, a liar, and an ogre of greed. The Great Black Dragon then opened his fearsome jaws and ate Pàng Chen's head and heart, snatching the quicksilver of life-breath."

"'There will be no more FAT pleasures for this criminal! I, by right of fairness and judgment, deny him the fountain of life,' roared Nyarlheiloong, as his tigers descended upon the lifeless remains of Fat Chen and devoured all, leaving not a trace, not even a drop of blood."

The princess smiled sweetly and continued, "The Great Black Dragon's worthy warriors then surrounded my father-in-law to keep him from fleeing. Cowering in the face of superior numbers and a greater class of fighter, the Water Dragon King begged for clemency. It was not granted. Uncle grabbed my mean-spirited father-in-law by the neck and cast him out to sea, where he was pursued by Uncle and his warriors, and imprisoned beneath the waves of the Southern Sea of Peace where he can do naught but gnash his teeth and dream in agony and eternal, undying solitude."

A cheer rose through the court, and everyone cried the name of Xiao Gǔ, the hero. Feasts were prepared in his honor and his name was sung all through Karakossa. For three days and three nights, he was honored and feted.

As the end of the third day came, Xiao Gǔ feared it was time to go. He packed his saddle bags, and mounted Màn Lùjìng. As he did so, the princess stood there, blushing, bowed to him and said, "We will probably never see each other again!" Tears choked her voice.

The King of Golden Karakossa stepped forward and said, "My

daughter owes you a great debt of gratitude, and we have not had an opportunity to make it up to you. Now you are going away and we see you go with a heavy heart!"

Xiao Gǔ bowed. "My Lord, it was an honor to serve you and your family."

"My family was done much wrong by my daughter's former husband and father-in-law, and she is now without a husband. I should like to find another husband for her. Do you know of anyone willing to take the hand of my daughter?"

Xiao Gǔ bowed again. "My Lord I would be honored to take your daughter's hand if you would excuse my temerity. I have come to respect and love your daughter, and would much prefer to stay by her side."

The king smiled, and turned to his daughter Cassi. "Would you have this man?"

"Would I have the man who traveled half the world for me, freed my family, and in so doing freed me from misery and captivity? Yes, Father, *yes*... I would have this man." She smiled at Xiao Gǔ.

The phoenix-kite broke away from Màn Lùjìng, flying out over the Sea of Hali and burst into golden and crimson fireworks, bathing the wedding party in rapturous light. At that moment, jade and gold turned to flesh and Princess Camilla stood draped in green and gold raiment, where the turtle once was. The Sentry That Sees Behind Every Mask then stepped forward, and removed his fox-mask. Thale, brother to Cassi and Camilla stood in their presence. Cheers and rejoicing arose as the children of the King were returned to Karakossa.

Xiao Gǔ dropped to his knees and pressed his head to the ground in front of Camilla. "Oh great princess," he cried. "Despise me not for treating you as my steed, for I knew not of your illustrious heritage! Forgive me, I beg you!"

Camilla smiled and took Cassi's hand, bidding Xiao Gŭ rise. "Dear brother-in-law, none of this was an accident. It took many years, but you did all that was necessary, and learned all you could so that you could free my sister from her bondage, and my uncle from his imprisonment. How could I not be happy to have helped you along the way? It is I who should be thanking you."

Tears of joy filled the majestic Golden Hall of the Golden King and joyous songs were sung. Xiao Gŭ and Cassi held hands, and bent to whisper phrases of endearment to each other, while about them another grand feast and celebration was held. That night when the Weaving Maiden Moon rose, she smiled and caressed all with soft light.

Xiao Gŭ awoke as though from a deep sleep, and next to him was the lovely Cassi. They were lying on the great hill, now covered with lush grasses, and crowned with a Cassia-tree in full bloom, dropping yellow petals onto the two lovers. From that time on both were very fond of each other.

Light grew over Karakossa and returned to the world, cold winds turned into warm zephyrs, and in front of every home the Flower-Elves made the long-dead lotus flowers bloom. Inside the comfort of every abode the soothing fragrance of Golden Cassi-leaf tea perfumed contented hearts.

The Sovereign of Fear

~ Richard Gavin ~

Joseph Curwen was a boy of singular mien. His conduct unfailingly pleased his elders, for unlike other children, boys in particular, Joseph was couth enough to speak only when spoken to, to keep his body still without appearing aphasiac, to accept with thanks whatever food or drink his elders set before him, and to forever convey the impression that he was enjoying himself.

His father, an Englishman, was so gifted in the art of conversation that scarcely a day went by where the elder Curwen would not receive an invitation for supper or a spot of tea with one of his neighbours in Salem-Village, many of whom were of nobler strata than the widowed farmer and his boy. Still, despite this slight disparity in social standing, Joseph would scrub himself clean after his round of chores and then accompany his father to hovels and posh houses alike.

One particular grey afternoon included afternoon tea in one of the finer homes. Gertrude Corey, wife of one of Salem Village's most successful importer of spices, was their hostess. While Joseph was acquainted with Mrs. Corey, as he was with all those villagers with whom he shared the pews of the town church each Sunday, this was her inaugural invitation to the Curwens.

They huddled about the tortoise shell table in the drawing room as two servants executed the preparatory rituals for teatime. Slender side tables were set next to each of the three wingback chairs, cups and saucers of china the colour and sheen of wet bone were positioned, a trolley holding polished tea ware was wheeled in. Having supped in extravagant households before, young Joseph was markedly unimpressed by such pageantry. He was prepared to do nothing more for the next hour or so than sit stoically, sip tea (though only after his hostess had begun to drink hers), and steep himself in the fancies of his own interior world.

This was Joseph's great secret; an eternal curiosity and an innate ability to satisfy said curiosity with whatever explanation his imagination could conjure, and the more outlandish the conclusion, the greater his amusement. What his elders mistook for attention to etiquette was in truth a prodigious lack of interest in the apparent, the mundane. It was as if Joseph's mind was a pulsating toad that used any and all aspects of his immediate surroundings as lily pads, leaping-off points from which his reveries would vault to the summits of entertainment and absurdity.

He happened to be engaged in just such a mental exercise, concluding that the tortoise shell table was undeniably a rare breed of headless turtle that walked on carved wooden legs and sustained itself on slab cake served by its wealthy keepers, when destiny intervened and introduced to Joseph's world irrefutable evidence of the Strange.

While fussing with an apt scientific name for his new species of tortoise, Joseph watched as one of the servants swiftly concealed his focal point with a circular doily of fine white lace.

It was a handsome thing, a very handsome thing indeed. Its centre was an out-fanning spiral of what looked to Joseph to be wolf's teeth, laid out as adroitly as the God-forged ridges in horn coral. From this keen spread were figures, lean and lucent and nimble. Like revellers rapt in ceremonial dance, they formed a wider circle. Beyond this circle blazed a ring of pale fire.

Joseph likely would have equated this doily with a holy mandala, had he but known what a holy mandala was, so profound was its impact on him. For this highly feminine piece of decor managed to enlighten Joseph to a hitherto unknown aspect of his soul. Namely that the cause of his dumb aloofness and dependence on his own reveries was simply that, up until that moment, the physical world had never revealed anything that not only equalled but actually surpassed his own fanciful dreams. Like a white lace agate, the patterns held faint promises. Something grand was woven into that complex pattern, Joseph could feel it. It excited him, and frightened him also, for he knew that whatever dwelt within or behind that lace veil was not merely a product of his imagination, it was something beyond him.

After lamenting the village's inability to secure a suitable minister for its fledgling church and forecasting both the seafaring weather and the harvest prospects for the coming year, discussion began to wane between the two adults. Joseph heard his father grunt "Well, my good woman"; a telltale sign that their visit was drawing to a close. Quickly Joseph gulped down his now cold tea, heavy with milk, and set the drained cup upon its saucer.

His father rose to leave while Mrs. Corey spieled off false promises of a future meeting. Joseph's gaze remained fixed on the doily, whose ivory rim now seemed to spinning beneath the silver decanter, faster and faster. Would it vanish, he wondered? Heartsickness and panic coursed through his slight body. A black hopelessness that no child should ever know began to claim him as his father announced that they must return to their farm now. Was he never to see the white lace world again? Would its truth forever be denied him?

"May I have this?" Joseph blurted with a suddenness that startled both his father and their hostess. Mrs. Corey turned her puffy face to the boy, who was standing with his finger rudely indicating the doily beneath the tea ware.

He did not have to look at his father; Joseph could feel the fiery glare of disapproval scorching him.

"The doily, my child?" asked Mrs. Corey.

"Forgive him," Mr. Curwen interjected, "it seems he has been possessed by the spirit of impropriety, Mrs. Corey. Please accept my apologies."

The old woman raised a soft-looking hand, one completely unscarred by labour. "Nonsense." She went to the table and requested that Joseph lift the silver decanter for her. He did so. She peeled the doily from the tortoise shell table and held it before him like a flag of submission.

"Well _thank_ the good woman, child!" his father cried.

"Thank you, good woman," Joseph echoed. He noticed neither his inappropriate phrasing nor the hostess' chortling that followed it, so enraptured was he with the manmade web that was tented upon his bloodless fingers.

There was much tension wringing between father and son during their homeward walk through the groves of Salem Village, but Joseph was either oblivious or immune to such negative energy.

"I have a good mind to burn that napkin in the hearth and give you the switch!" the father grumbled as they entered their humble house.

"I will take the switch but please, father, do not destroy _this_!"

It was, Mr. Curwen privately acknowledged, a momentous occasion; the first instance of his boy expressing a clearly distinct opinion. The recognition of this hallmark tempered the father's anger by lacing it with a humbling sadness. Their path through life had diverged and with each subsequent day the gap between their forking fates would widen until both sire and sired would appear as indistinct specks in the periphery of the other. So it had been for Mr. Curwen and his father, and his father before him, and likewise unto Adam and Cain.

"What is it about that little rag that you fancy so?"

"It made me promises," Joseph replied.

"_Promises_?" retorted the father. "Come now, boy! What fool's stuffing is this?"

"It has promised to teach me."

"_Teach_ you? What, pray?"

"It has promised to teach me what Fear is."

"Really, boy! You know well and true what fear is! Must I once more tell you the story of how you became lost in the forest when you were five?"

"I wasn't frightened in the forest, father. Never have I been frightened in the forest."

With that, Mr. Curwen's memory was clarified. The child was correct: when the search party had located him wandering through the woods in the gloaming, the boy had been emotionless. There were no tears, no cries, no moment of elation upon realizing that he was being rescued. Joseph had been collected, like an experienced wayfarer enjoying a fresh stretch of foreign terrain.

"I think it is high time you were in bed, child."

Joseph did as he was told. He lay awake, and once he was relatively assured that his father had retired for the night Joseph satisfied the urge that had been chewing at the edge of his mind all evening.

He lit the paraffin lamp at his bedside, fine-tuning the knob until only the merest amber glimmer was cast. With care, Joseph draped the lace doily over the lamp's chimney of contoured glass. The flat-wick, now partially smothered, began to fume more persistently, diffusing strange runnels of heat up to and along the chamber's low ceiling. Joseph watched these colourless streaks weep and weave through the shadow-double of the doily's intricate pattern. They pressed forward, and seemed to carry some of the darkness with them, like soil upon the back of the ravening coffin~worm. Their trail appealed to Joseph's eye, and he allowed his gaze to trail after them, which made him feel like their straggling inexperienced kin.

The doily's lightless double appeared infinitely larger than the lace mat itself, which made Joseph ponder the curious nature of the great and the small.

Viewed in the distant corner of his chamber, the once minute figures were now rangy, their arms frozen in a gesture of heralding. The tedious weave had become a dais draped with curious flowers, each a different shade of black.

It was through these heralding figures and onto this offer-laden dais that the Sovereign of Fear appeared to the child Curwen.

Nameless, mute, this sovereign dignitary was known to Joseph as such through a mysterious process that worked underneath the act, the word, the thought. Unnervingly tall, unsettlingly thin, the Sovereign of Fear was dressed in raiments that were equally splendid and horrid. A simple sheet of the dreamer's bed had been appropriated to form a monkish robe whose hood was cave-deep, cave-dark. Staring out from beneath this hood --- eyeless but observing --- was not a face but a ghastly hand with flesh the colour of fresh portico. Upon its bent fingers were rings of copper and lead, each of which bore a single letter from the grammar that is known to waking man only by the shriek of one flung back from the underworld of Nightmare. A pair of lustrous objects appeared to hang freely within the gape of the Sovereign's flowing sleeves: the first, a flask aglow with a serpentine light of many colours; the second, a flower whose labial folds would be known the Joseph Curwen in later days.

The Sovereign of Fear then wordlessly assured the child that a third bestowment would be made in due course.

If this was fear, Joseph wondered why the emotion was spoken of so unfavourably by so many. Here was wonder and otherness.

Would you know yet more?

Joseph, hearing the question with the ears of his heart, nodded enthusiastically.

My Gift is One: the knowledge that there is nothing to fear. This Gift is thrice-given, but the third is the final seal...

The boy raised his arms.

The hand within the hood wriggled its fingers into a fresh gesture. A soft ruffling sound stirred somewhere to Joseph's right.

Meshes of shadow quickly dissolved into an aura of light so blazing that Joseph had to shut his eyes against it. A moment later he felt the lace veil slipping onto his face like a tight mask, one that blinded him, snatched his breath.

Joseph struggled, shrieked, but both were futile. Only after the Sovereign of Fear had deigned to release him was Joseph once more able to breath, to scream, to stand.

He found himself in a nocturnal wood. The moonlight was wan, sickly. Though there was no chill to the air, Joseph was unable to stop shuddering.

From the glen, the Sovereign of Fear stepped forward. *My first gift is to awaken you, should you wish to know the secret nature of fear...*

Joseph nodded.

The secret is...you have nothing to fear...

And with that, a pale mist surged from the black folds of the Sovereign's robe. It slid quickly and crossed the gap between eidolon and child. Joseph found himself touched by the fog; a benediction that utterly transformed his surroundings.

Where there had been a mere cluster of trees and wild grass, something vast and ominous now stood. Each massive old growth tree seemed to suggest a presence far older. The stars above glared like numberless eyes, scrutinizing Joseph's every twitch and tremor.

The mild breeze now bristled with a chorus of inhuman voices, each so eager to share, to instruct. Toad and owl conveyed a new and awful sentience from their respective hiding places. Joseph somehow knew that these and all other fauna of the night were now only too eager to share their secret languages with him.

All was alive, all moved independently and serenely, not in the spaces Joseph knew, but between them.

Never forget... the Sovereign assured him. *You have nothing to fear...*

His bravery, or perhaps simply his naivety, was plucked. Joseph felt his shudders fading. He took a cautious step forward, his first true step on the Way Nocturnal. The child was enraptured to find that the denizens of this Way were only too pleased to invite him to their company.

And so it was from that night forward. Though the Sovereign of Fear did not appear again for another five years, Joseph Curwen began to withdraw from the world of men and became increasingly ghoulish, increasingly Other.

His initiations fueled an unnatural independence that Joseph's father and many of his peers could not help but notice. That he was becoming something different was obvious to all in Salem-Village. What troubled their heads was that no one, not even the village's latest minister, would articulate just what it was they feared young Curwen was becoming.

Shortly after his fifteenth birthday Joseph encountered the Sovereign of Fear for the second time.

I have come to bestow my second gift, should you choose to accept...

Joseph's mind was boiling with questions, with secrets he'd been longing to share, but the Sovereign showed no interest in such trivialities. Finally Joseph whispered that he accepted the second gift.

The gift was an instruction for the boy to leave the new world.

He was to travel to a remote corner of Europe, to the rarest of all academies of true learning: the Scholomance. There Curwen would be instructed by the living Devil who would teach the language of birds and the deepest pleasures of the flesh.

Joseph once more accepted.

The Sovereign handed him the flower with its labial folds. Before he dissipated, the Sovereign reminded that Joseph had nothing to fear.

And so at age fifteen Joseph Curwen found his way (with unnatural ease) to the mountain lake south of the Hungarian city of Nagyszeben. He carried the lace doily in his pocket, and each day at eventide Joseph would find new coins had materialized there, along with clearly demarcated maps to show him the way.

Upon reaching Nagyszegben Joseph swam across the tiny lake, to the remote island that sat untouched by anything but dark waters. Upon this island, a half-ruined building, within which Joseph found the Devil and his concubines, each of whom were dizzyingly wise and painfully beautiful. For many years Joseph Curwen remained cloistered in the satanic academy's walls of primal stone. He learned and yearned, lusted and fed.

In 1692, his thirtieth year, Joseph's education was deemed complete. Enraptured with the world, for he had gleaned its manifold secrets, Curwen returned to his beloved Salem in search of new experiences in the new world. There he met kindred spirits such as Edward Hutchinson, with whom he exchanged a variety of secrets.

In the summer of that year rumours abounded that Curwen, Hutchinson and other "wytches" received "the Marke" from a darksome figure who appeared in the woods near Hutchinson's abode.

But lesser known accounts (namely, the final entries in the

celebrant's own Booke of Shadows) suggest that the Sabbath in the woods had a different character for Joseph Curwen.

After receiving "the Marke", Joseph encountered the Sovereign of Fear, whereupon the third and final teaching was bestowed.

Once more the hooded avatar reminded Curwen that he had nothing to fear.

Then, peeling back his sleep-sheet raiment, the Sovereign unveiled his final bestowment.

His exposed torso was a freshly-dug grave. Eager worms burrowed through the upset soil that was piled around the edges of the pit. The grave itself was a vacancy, a void bereft of all the pleasures Joseph had known in his life. What waited for him with the infinite patience of the inevitable was pure absence, dissolution, vacancy.

This was nothing. And it terrified Joseph Curwen to his very core.

He ran shrieking from the woods that night, constantly glancing back over his shoulder to confirm that the grave was gliding after him. It slid across the night air, slowly and gracefully. It filled Joseph's ears with the sounds of coffin lids being nailed snugly shut, of clumped earth raining down upon a stifling box. Of the realization that death would not make him nothing, rather it would make him aware of nothing. He would spend eternity in that vacancy, aware of its dark nothingness, its futility, its utter lack of taste, of agonies, of pleasures. He would not even have the faculty to cry out against this torment. Joseph knew that he would be a passive witness to his own oblivion.

Arriving back at his home that night, Joseph Curwen swore an oath to himself: he would not go gently into that vast night. A single lifetime was not enough to yoke the pleasures of flesh and terra firma, to suss out the pleasures that lay beyond the realm of the senses.

And so his life became one of obsessive study. He penetrated the secrets of alchemy, of necromancy, and became a frequenter of charnel grounds, the sight of whose graves with their wind-smoothed, anonymous markers instilled in him a terrifying reminder of precisely what he was running from. Death, specifically the ability to triumph over it, became his reason for being. He had disposed of the lace doily after a recurring nightmare saw him being lowered into his grave with the enlarged doily serving as his pauper's shroud.

It is said that Joseph Curwen never recovered from the Sovereign's final bestowment, and that the chasing grave pursues Joseph without rest. From body to body leapt the soul of Joseph Curwen, each incarnation fueled by two desires: to partake in the pleasures of the Earth, and to learn those chymical secrets that might stave off the stalking pit that wants nothing more than to envelope its guest in the ironic final teaching: we have nothing to fear. For nothingness is what stalks Joseph Curwen to this day.

The Boy Who Cried Bigfoot
- Desmond Reddick -

Jumping off the bridge into the river was the quickest way to learn to swim in Samuel George's neighborhood. He knew to kick swiftly and wiggle his hips and shoulders to reach the bottom. His mother had never been able to afford swimming lessons, but after nine seasons of practice he was as good as anyone else he knew.

The water was cold and got colder the closer he got to the bottom, but he'd been in the water for a long time and was well adapted to the temperature. He came here almost every day as long as the temperature was tolerable from early March to late October. The elbow in the river had a remarkably deep basin that kept the beachfront tract almost static.

Today, the water flowed slowly, making the basin completely still. It was the perfect time to catch crayfish. And since his friends had decided to go to school today, he had them all to himself. His eyes caught movement from a patch of long freshwater grass, so he turned his body and aimed at the area.

Samuel reached through the grass with his right hand and grabbed the tail of the rust-colored crustacean. He brought the butterfly net in his left hand around in front of him and cocked his wrist to open the net. He dipped the crayfish into the threshold of the butterfly net and pulled up to send it to the bottom with seven other crayfish, but not before the tiny creature swung around and nicked his finger with its pincers.

Samuel flinched. He couldn't count how many times he'd been pinched today, but this cut deeper than the others. Spinning around, he twisted the net to cut off the entrance for any enterprising crayfish with escape on their minds. He kicked off the soft river bed to ascend quickly to the surface.

He sucked in lungfuls of air and swam over to a shallower area closer to a large rock protruding above the water's surface. He pulled himself up, sat on it and dumped the contents of the butterfly net into the already teeming ice cream bucket full of crayfish.

As he sucked the blood from his finger, Samuel looked into the bucket and watched as the swirling mass of crayfish climbed over each other in a frantic attempt to escape. He laughed a little at their helplessness, but he quickly tightened his face into a squint as they continued to try and climb the wall of the ice cream bucket.

It was a hypnotic and cyclical process. One would stand on the back of his fellow prisoner, get himself completely vertical up the wall of the bucket and fall over to the side, only to have the one he was standing on do the same. He had to admit that it was commendable that they never gave up. The activity continued, randomly, and yet patterned all at the same time as he watched, rapt.

A branch snapped, pulling Samuel's attention away from the bucket of crayfish. It came from his left. He looked across the river at the sun drenched river bank below the Catholic cemetery. He would often see people there placing flowers for loved ones, but not today. He turned back and looked further up the bank, into the shaded cedars dipping out over the water.

The sun made it difficult to see anything that far away in the shade. Samuel squinted, focusing on a patch of green. Something black moved behind the leaves. The tree shook as whatever it was left the riverbank.

Fearing a bear, Samuel put the lid on the ice cream bucket and stomped through the water back to the beach. He slipped his wet, bare feet into his sneakers and walked quickly home.

"I brought dinner," Samuel said walking through the front door and dropping the ice cream bucket full of water and crayfish. A few tiny splashes of murky water popped through the holes perforated in the bucket's lid and landed on the kitchen counter.

"No," Samuel's mother said walking up to the bucket, "you brought me work."

She peeled off the lid and looked down into the bucket.

"For God's sake, Samuel. There must be fifty of them!"

"Forty-two."

She sighed heavily.

"Dinner's in the oven. It'll be ready in twenty minutes. Enough time for you to dump these fellas back in the river and come back."

"Mom," Samuel pleaded.

"No." She turned back to the sink where she was peeling carrots. "When you're back we can talk about school."

Samuel stiffened as he turned to carry the bucket back to the river.

The sun began to set, bathing the world in a pervasive pink. He walked quickly because his mother's tone meant he should be back in time for dinner. Jogging down the gravel embankment that doubled for a parking lot when families came to spend the day, he stopped halfway. Instead of walking down to the river's edge, he cut in and scaled the rock face.

Samuel stepped carefully along a small ridge that took him out over the middle of the river, roughly twenty feet above the water. The rock was warm, having faced the sun for much of the day. He took the lid off of the bucket and dumped the crayfish into the river. He was right above where he found most of them, and they were tough enough to survive the drop. He leaned back against the rock and looked out at the world around him for a moment.

He saw the mountains completely surrounding him. The valley had been his people's home since before recorded time, but he didn't care about any of that. All he knew was that you had to drive over one of two mountain passes in order to leave this shit-hole. The remnants from the mill dumped into the river downstream, made the place stink in the summer when the water level receded and things started to cook in the sun. But Samuel supposed that anything could be beautiful if you really didn't look that hard at it.

Samuel made to leave by slowly turning back around, but he was struck for a moment by a feeling he couldn't give voice to. It felt, perhaps, that he was being watched. He swung his head back around to where he'd looked only minutes earlier, the dark shaded patch of leaves. From his vantage point, he could see behind it much better.

This time, he could see that it was definitely a black hairy creature of some kind. It was not a bear, because it looked like it was standing on two legs. Peeking out from behind the trunk of a small maple tree, he could see one luminous yellow eye.

———

"I saw a bigfoot," Samuel said through a mouthful of lasagna.

"Sure, you did," his mother said, finally sitting down across the small table from him. "There's no such thing, Samuel. You know that."

"Grand-dad told us all about the bigfoot he saw on Haida Gwaii."

"Your Grand-dad said a lot of things. Not all of them were true." She took a bite of lasagna before continuing. "Your Grand-dad used to say you were a lot like him. I got a phone call today to prove it."

Samuel raised his eyes to look at his mother. She looked down at her plate and took another small bite of lasagna. He looked back down.

"I got a call from Abby...someone today," she said.

Abby? Oh!

"Miss Gordon. She's my counsellor." Samuel liked Miss Gordon enough, but she had that whole 'save the world one kid at a time' vibe that he found annoying. She was pretty though.

"She said you've been at school one day this week, and that you've been lying about why you've been gone."

"Well – "

"Said that you said you were communing with Spirit Bear as part of a cultural retreat."

Samuel remained silent.

"You're not just lying; you're making yourself look stupid. You're going to school tomorrow. Period."

———

Samuel remembered when he would dread being called to the principal's office. That was a few years ago. Now it was a welcome change from being in class.

His days of caring about school were long gone.

"Have a seat, Mr. George."

Mr. Waite was *every* high school principal, or at least that's what Samuel and his friends said. Tall enough to be imposing, but thin enough to be considered weak, Waite was a distant administrator, preferring to have his cult of counsellors and vice principals do the day-to-day management of the school. Being called in to his office was a show of dire circumstances. Last resort kind of stuff.

His office was small and mostly barren. A couple of certificates and diplomas in dark wooden frames and a matching, thin bookshelf with old, leather-bound books were the only things in it other than his desk, fancy black chair and two less fancy guest chairs.

Miss Gordon sat smiling at Samuel from one of them. Samuel

took his time sitting in the other. Mr. Waite gestured toward the chair the entire time, unmoving.

Samuel looked from Gordon to Waite. Gordon was pretty with shoulder-length brown hair and bright green eyes. She oozed genuine niceness. Waite was painfully average-looking with a sweat-covered bald head and eyes so dark they almost entirely lacked color. As different as they were, Samuel still saw two white people trying to imprison him.

"Miss Gordon tells me your days of attendance are far outweighed by your truancy. When you do decide to grace us with your presence – today, for example – you're almost an hour tardy."

Samuel tried not to smirk at the word 'tardy.'

"You're a promising student, Mr. George. Last semester you were on Miss Gordon's list of students who would need help seeking post-secondary funding. Now, it not only looks like you won't graduate next year, but I'm grasping at straws for reasons not to expel you. What have you been doing these past few months?"

"I've been on a series of vision quests," Samuel began.

Abby Gordon audibly sighed and turned away.

"Raven led me astray. He tricked me and drew me down a long path. I should have known better."

"Mr. George...Samuel, I have been an educator in this district for twenty-seven years. I have been at the forefront of First Nations education policy in this district, in this province. I taught your mother. Don't presume to fool me, confuse me, or play on some cultural shame I might have so that I won't call you out on your bullshit. Think about what your elders might say about you using cultural based lies in order to validate skipping school. Smarten up and go back to class."

———

After dinner, Samuel quietly did the dishes and left them to dry in a rack on the counter. He said good night to his mother, who sat on the couch watching the news, and went to his room. The shame of being called out today and the fear that Miss Gordon would be visiting his mother was part of the desire to go to his room. The other part was spending an entire day at school, bored and annoyed. He was exhausted.

Samuel got undressed down to his boxer briefs and climbed under the single sheet on his bed. The night was unseasonably warm and muggy, but sleep came easily.

He slept soundly until the sound of sweeping woke him. Opening one eye, he zeroed in on the red digital display of the alarm clock that he never set the alarm on and read 2:17. Samuel closed his eye and rubbed the side of his face into his pillow, consigning himself to sleep once again. But the moment he closed his eyes, the sweeping began again.

Samuel sat up, and struggled to open his eyes while he listened for the noise. It sounded like it came from outside. He rose quietly from his bed and walked slowly to the window. It was open wide enough for him to poke half of his head through. Looking down the wall at the back of his house he saw it.

It was the black thing he thought was a bigfoot, he was sure of it. It was maybe as tall as him, but oddly proportioned. It did not look like a sasquatch from where he stood. Whatever it was, it was about as wide as a man, with a much wider and stockier head. There were shapes protruding from the top of its head that Samuel could not make out in the dark. Nor could he see below the thing's waist, as the tree line cut off the moonlight at that point. But the thing lumbered oddly, as it dragged its shoulder against the side of Samuel's house. The shoulder-dragging emitted the sweeping sound until the thing got to the end of the house, turned and walked off into the darkness of the forest.

Sleep didn't come so easily after that.

———

"You're Cynthia George's boy, aren't you?"

Samuel was stirred from thought. He'd reluctantly begun attending school regularly and coming home to work on assignments he had missed. He supposed he wanted to graduate to make school a thing of the past, but that was secondary to his desire to drop out completely. It weighed on him for the past week; it didn't help that he couldn't stop thinking about the black thing he saw outside his bedroom window. It was clear to him that whatever it was, it knew where he lived.

It was Dale that asked the question. Normally, he found Dale painfully annoying, but today it was a welcome distraction from the polar monotonies and terrors of his life.

"Yes, Dale."

Dale was a drunk. He was a family friend his mother preferred Samuel stay away from in his drunken state, which usually meant all the time. Samuel assumed it was because he reminded her of his father.

Dale was skinny, looked much older than his thirty-odd years, and wavered when he stood. A faded black Harley Davidson T-shirt and a very dark blue pair of cheap jeans rounded out his particular fashion sense.

"Marnie said your mom told her you saw a bigfoot."

Samuel panicked, not out of memory of the black thing, but out of the lack of interest in discussing bigfoot sightings with a man he'd known since he was a baby, but who was always so drunk he didn't remember him. Samuel pitied him.

"Nawww..." Samuel said. "I was just messing around."

Dale blinked, twisted up his mouth and stared at Samuel.

"Oh, 'cause you wouldn't be the first around here. Used to be an old white man lived up the hill. Know the place?"

Samuel nodded. He'd seen the place. It wasn't any more than a foundation today.

"People used to say he made friends with strange creatures. Fish men, bigfoot, other things they ain't got a name for. Used to meet them at night on the other side of the hill."

"Cool," Samuel said. "I got to get home. See you."

Samuel began walking.

"Don't go out there at night," Dale called after him.

Samuel knew a bullshitter when he saw one. It takes one to know one, after all. He couldn't shake, however, that there was some truth to it.

He'd grown up hearing the legend. A weird old white guy who built his home on their traditional land. No one minded because no one went out there. Stories of surgeries, weird creatures and disappearances kept them away. He had always chalked it up to a boogie man story.

———

"Can we get him in some courses that would be easier for him to finish next year?" Samuel's mother tried not to sound desperate.

Samuel sat beside her, head down, lightly scratching the kitchen table with the nail of his index finger.

"I put him in Creative Writing this semester because it's one of his strengths, but he's only attended nine times." Abby never liked telling parents that their child was not likely to graduate on time. It felt like she did it a lot, but she always tried to keep things hopeful.

"Yeah," his mother said looking at Samuel again, "he's good at making up stories."

"Well," Abby said, "I think with some very hard work, Samuel can make it happen next year. It is up to him though. We have a deal?"

Samuel looked up and nodded with one corner of his mouth

turned up in mimicry of a smile.

Abby smiled genuinely and excused herself. She picked up her copies of the graduation plan she laid out for Samuel and his mother and collected them in a manila folder.

"Thank you, Cynthia," Abby said as she made her way to the front door, short heels clicking on the thin linoleum floor. The rain, which began spitting after school ended, had picked up considerably since she showed up. The sound of it oppressively beat on the roof and walls of the small, poorly-insulated house. She also wanted to get home before it was too dark. Living out of town ensured that she was able to leave her work at work, which became more important when she began dealing with more sensitive cases. In her first six months on the job, she had reported three instances of sexual abuse, taken part in a half dozen drug and alcohol interventions and overseen countless referrals to an ever-increasing load of mental health diagnoses. Cases that made Samuel George look like an Honors student.

Abby made a concerted effort not to let the less severe cases slip through the cracks, though. Which is why she often did home visits after school. Actually going into the community did wonders for her outsider status as a white counsellor of First Nations students.

Unfortunately, it also meant that she often did not get home until eight o'clock at night. She wouldn't be that late tonight, but it was still dark early and raining heavily, not uncommon in a valley on the west coast of Vancouver Island.

She walked to her car with the manila folder over her head. She turned on the squeaky windshield wipers and pumped up the defog, turning the temperature more definitively to hot. For the thirty foot walk to her car, she was surprised at how wet she got.

Abby backed her Chevy Cavalier slowly onto the street. The reservation was an illogical web of streets all laid out and paved at different times and in various states of disrepair. She took the drive slowly. The area was poorly lit, and the wipers did little to clear her view.

Her car crested the small hill putting her at the centre of the web of streets. She continued forward from memory as the rain and dark made the area look almost completely different from when she arrived. The car dropped from the pavement to the gravel of the downhill road. As her rear tires did the same, the car slid to the right.

Abby gasped sharply and slammed on the brakes, the car sliding a little more. She laughed out loud when she stopped sliding. She took her right hand off the wheel, put it to her chest to feel the pounding of her heart. She stuck her tongue out and exhaled, laughing once again. Even though it *did* feel like the gravel road had been tilted more than it was earlier. Taking her foot off of the brake, the car began to inch forward.

As she accelerated, something smashed into the front of her car over the front driver's side wheel well. Abby screamed, stepped on the gas and tried to turn the wheel to the left, but it was too late. The Chevy was knocked almost sideways before the tires gripped the gravel beneath them.

It was far too dark to see, but Abby knew that she had driven off of the road. The air bag deployed when the front of the car smashed down on the steep embankment. Abby's face crashed into the airbag, and her head snapped back against the headrest. She was thrown in all directions as the car tumbled and rolled sideways down into the roiling river below.

If she was conscious, she would have felt the cold water pouring through the broken windows of her car.

Samuel was stirred from sleep by another noise outside his house. He felt a stinging in his forehead, like he'd only just closed his eyes before waking up again. He rolled over and looked at his alarm clock: 10:48 PM.

"Shit," Samuel said. *I did just close my eyes!*

He blinked several times and focused on the sound. It was another sound of something being dragged along the outside wall of the house. He wasn't sure what it was, but it was loud enough to be heard over the rain beating down on the roof.

Moving toward the window, he arced to the left to try and see. The window was closed, so he didn't want to risk opening it. From his angle, he saw movement, but it was unclear. Dark on dark. And it felt as though he was not seeing the whole image.

Samuel pulled the window up from its resting place. He did it almost silently except for some minor squeaking when it got to the top of the frame. Sticking his head out, he saw the shape of the black thing from before, only something was different. There was something on its back. It took a moment for Samuel's eyes to get used to the dark, but he could see the black thing did indeed have something slumped over its shoulder. He knew this because the thing scraping against the wall of his house was a woman's leg with a short, pointed heel on her shoe.

It took a moment to process, but who else would the black thing parade by his window than his counsellor? Samuel slipped on track pants and a hoodie before bounding from the window. He hit the grass behind his house in bare feet, tiptoed behind the black thing before diverting to grab a pair of gumboots off of his front porch. He stuck his wet feet into the gumboots and looked up to see the black thing disappear behind the tree line up the hill. Samuel picked up the pace, following the path the black thing had taken, and headed up to the old white man's house.

He continued up the hill, hearing only the gravel crunching under his boots and his own breathing. The higher up he got, the trees began to thin out. More moonlight was able to punch though the heavily clouded sky, lighting the ground before him.

When Samuel reached the clearing at the top of the hill, he turned. On the ground were the cracked foundations of the old white man's house. The old concrete had not crumbled from age. It looked as if it had been smashed. Large chunks taken out of it littered the empty bottom of the pit that used to be a basement. Even in the dark, Samuel could see that the chunks of concrete were larger than his head and that the holes left in the foundation looked like clean breaks. He wondered what could have made that damage; he wondered where everything else that remained of the house went.

Remembering the place Dale spoke of, Samuel took a guess and took a slight angle down the other side of the hill. He knew it led to a tree-covered, slow-moving shady area of the river. Samuel had been by it before while floating on an inner tube. It always felt creepy there.

Though his eyes had adjusted to his surroundings in minimal moonlight, this side of the hill was darker. He had long lost track of the black thing, but he had some idea where a cave was. It could barely be seen from the river, so he imagined it was not too far down the hill.

He heard the sound before he saw the cave opening. It was a low moan that turned into an incessant buzz. Disorienting. So much so that Samuel, in trying to follow the sound, walked right by the cave. He only stopped when he saw moonlight reflecting off of the river in front of him. Having gone too far, he turned around and looked up the hill. A faint glow could be seen emanating from exactly where Samuel knew the cave to be. And yet he spent minutes walking right by it.

Leaning forward and using his hands and feet to climb the steep hill, Samuel perched on the lip of the cave's opening. The cave was odd shaped. It opened very wide right from the mouth. It was twice the width of his house and dipped very low immediately. While the width was impressive, the depth and height were almost impossible.

Samuel imagined the cave went all the way back to the area under the foundations he'd seen at the top of the hill, and the cave's height seemed to climb as the hill rose. It essentially worked out to be the size of a small auditorium, which accounted for the sound.

The buzzing moan was far more prominent from the open mouth of the cave. Samuel was dizzied. The bizarre noise pulsed inside his forehead. He blinked and tried to take in everything he was seeing.

There were torches lining the walls of the cave, flickering and sending shadows jutting up to the centre where a woman lay on a raised stone slab. It was Miss Gordon. She wasn't moving. All around her were people in long, hooded cloaks. The black hoods hung low over the faces of the attendees. There were twelve of them that Samuel could see, not including the black thing that stood with its back to him.

From his vantage point, Samuel could see that the black thing was a thick beast. Its body was almost rectangular from ass to the top of its head. It was covered in a thick black fur, the individual bristles shimmering by firelight. It was built like a man from the waist up. Below its waist, two thick bovine legs stretched to the ground with cloven hooves spread upon the rocky floor. Two yellowed horns curled out of the top of the beast's head, sharp and gnarled.

Twelve men in cloaks and a goat-man. It took a long time to process for Samuel. The moaning continued to fill his head with confusion. His forehead throbbed.

One of the hooded men...people...things approached Miss Gordon and towered over her. The other hooded ones moved closer into a tight circular formation. Samuel fought the urge to gasp when the man closest to Abby removed a knife from his cloak and held it above her.

Miss Gordon began to stir. Her eyebrows rose before her eyelids did. When she opened her eyes, she screamed as two other hooded figures pulled open her blouse just below her neck, exposing her from throat to bra. Her eyes went wide and her mouth opened again to scream, but no noise came. No noise except for the buzzing moan of the cave and the wet thud of the blade punching a hole between Abby Gordon's ribs.

Samuel opened his mouth and almost screamed before sticking his knuckles in between his jaws. Miss Gordon, as much of a pain in the ass that she was, was always worried about him and seemed to actually like him. Now her body was jerking on a stone slab with a dagger in her chest. The hooded man who had stabbed her yanked upward on the hilt of the dagger, a grating noise echoing through the cave as the sharp double-edged blade scratched bone on its way out of her rapidly undulating chest. Blood seeped from the wounds in her chest and back, slowly spreading to hit the outside edge of the slab and flow to the ground, as her movements slowed and then ceased.

The cave began to shake as the moan was drowned out in favor of the buzzing. Shadows danced on the wall as the hooded figures surrounding Samuel's dead high school counsellor raised their arms in religious fervor. Samuel didn't know where the shadows were coming from, though it looked like someone was waving their thin fingers close to the light source.

There was clarity in Samuel's confusion. An awareness of the situation flooded over his panicked mind, but something in him – perhaps it was his logic, or maybe it was his brain refusing to allow everything he knew of reality be corrupted. He did not know what was happening, but he was terrified. So terrified that he began to scream uncontrollably. He was seeing something, but he blinked in such rapid succession that what unfolded in front of him was some sort of macabre flip-book. He wasn't sure if it was that he couldn't comprehend it or if he couldn't truly see what was happening and his mind was making something up to fill in the visual void.

He did know that, regardless of the volume of the buzzing, his scream had attracted the attention of the cave's living inhabitants. The Black Goat turned to Samuel, displaying its full, massive face to him for the first time, and bleated in what sounded like three terrible octaves before sprinting up the hill toward Samuel.

Samuel was confused and terrified, but he knew that if he were to run uphill, he would be caught in short order. Instead, he stood and backed out of the cave until he could feel the rain the upper lip of the cave had been protecting him from. He turned, took three huge loping steps down the hill and leapt into the river.

The water was a shocking cold. The heavy rain added to its torrent, so it was all Samuel could do to remain above water. He kicked and waved his arms to try and gain some control of his body. His left ankle slammed into a rock on the riverbed, but he didn't stop trying to swim. He reached stride moments later and moved through the river by floating on top of the water. He couldn't see anything, so he kept above water and hoped that he didn't hit any of the huge rocks that jutted out of the river.

Samuel had no plan for stopping. He knew that he would empty out off the small falls eventually. It would hurt, and he would be very far from home, but that didn't seem to bother him at the moment. Even if he could stop at the beach and get home, some of the hooded ones would probably be waiting for him there. He decided to ride the river until the falls dumped him into calmer waters.

The river snaked to the right, and Samuel got turned around. He was floating sideways very rapidly. His back slammed into a large rock taking all of his wind out of him and shooting sharp pain through his entire torso. He didn't see it coming. Opening his mouth to gasp for air, he swallowed river water. Lots of it.

Samuel flailed and sank in the rushing water. His eyes opened wide but saw only blackness. Chilling pain dominated his last thoughts before consigning himself to death. That is, until he snagged something with his hand.

Samuel was being pulled from the river before he realized what was happening. He blinked hard to get the water out of his eyes, rubbed them with the palm of his hands and squinted before he could make anything out in the darkness.

The rain soaked his mother's hair, pasting it to her face. She looked concerned.

"Mom! There was a goat..and Miss Gordon..."

"Shhhhh..." his mother offered. "You almost drowned, but Dale saved you."

Samuel could see Dale standing behind his crouching mother. He didn't look too concerned.

"But..."

"It's okay, baby. You're okay. Momma's got you. No need to make stories anymore. It's all over."

Samuel furrowed his brow in confusion before unconsciousness took him.

—

It was the cold that woke him. The cold or the pain. Samuel was certain he felt both. A remarkable warmth, though, pressed down on his body. His back cold as ice. His ankle throbbed in agony. He tried to roll onto his side, but found that his hands were pulled up over his head. He opened his eyes and his vision was bathed in a warm orange blur. He blinked his eyes to clarity to see Dale staring down at him from his left side.

"Dale?"

"I told you not to come here, Samuel," he said. He was stone cold sober. Samuel couldn't remember when he'd last seen that.

Others stood around Samuel, farther back than Dale. To his right he saw his mother, and beside her, Mr. Waite. There were a few others from the community and a couple other white people Samuel didn't recognize.

"What? Why?" When he tried to sit up, he realized his hands were bound together above his head with heavy rope. He pulled and kicked with his legs, despite the pain in his left ankle, but his feet too were bound. He twisted on the stone slab in a vain effort to free himself.

"Calm down, Samuel," his mother said, placing her palm on his forehead. "It will be all over soon."

"What? Like it was for Miss Gordon? What the fuck, mom? What are you doing here?"

"You should never have come here, Samuel," Mr. Waite said. He'd always looked unremarkable, but with the hood over his head and the flickering torchlight on his face, he looked positively skeletal.

"So I'm told..." Samuel said under his breath while straining with his wrists. The pain faded from his mind as he focused on getting away. It wasn't working.

"We don't want to do this, Samuel," Dale said.

"I tried to tell them it would be okay," his mother said. "That the stories you tell would make it so no one would believe you no matter what you said. They believed me, too – "

"Until," Mr. Waite interrupted, "I brought up that you ruined our sacrifice."

"What?"

Mr. Waite came around to stand behind Samuel's head. Samuel could see the Black Goat standing and watching him, heaving huge breaths. Two sickly yellow eyes peered out from under its heavy brows.

"That's what we do here, Samuel. We appease our god in hopes that she will look upon us favorably. We still need to do that, Samuel. You understand." It was a statement, not a question.

"That's your god?" Samuel asked, unable to take his eyes off of the Black Goat.

"No," Dale said. "He is the emissary."

The Black Goat exhaled quickly out its thick snout, blowing steam into the air before it. It did it two more times, and Dale nodded at Mr. Waite.

"It may not feel like it right now, Samuel, but this is an honor," Waite said, raising the dagger up into the air.

The hooded ones began to moan, and the Black Goat joined them. The noise built and caused an irritation in Samuel's ears until it shook his vision. He tried to keep his eyes open as much as he could. The last thing he heard, other than the moan, was his mother.

"I'm proud of you, Samuel."

Waite brought the dagger crashing down into Samuel's chest. Samuel gasped sharply as he saw the black tendrils dancing into the sky from the spot behind the slab, behind Waite. They weren't shadows that he saw earlier, after all. The tendrils shuddered like snakes slithering and the room shook, the moaning noise taking a far deeper tone

Screams of the hooded ones joined the cacophony. Orgiastic tears of reverie rolled down their faces. Samuel expired to the sound of ecstasy all around him.

Sticks and Stones, Skin and Bones
~ Morgan Griffith ~

A red-winged blackbird halted its song abruptly, listening to whispered movement in the brush. Trailing an elusive deer, Boone Skelly and his younger brother Luke tread lightly through stands of birch and black willow. Two squirrels dangled from Boone's belt. They slapped his leg as he stopped to part a curtain of Spanish moss with his rifle.

Luke hefted his metal detector onto his shoulder.

"Sure it ran this way?"

"Shut up."

"Never been this far north, is all. You?"

Boone grunted an indecipherable reply that Luke took as a no.

The copse of trees in Wilder's Creek had thickened dramatically as they ventured north. A dirt trail turned into a breathtaking tunnel entirely encased by foliage, and then the path had disappeared altogether. Boone didn't falter. He was an infamous tracker. Brief flashes of the buck spurred him on.

Luke scanned for predators with a lump in his throat as his older brother cleared a path. This area was remote and wild. If any man had ever ventured this way, the woods would have devoured his trail long ago.

Boone muttered something under his breath. His straw-colored hair and square shoulders were framed in a hacked archway of green. Luke pushed forward to see. Beneath the dome of entwined trees was a clearing. On the left a ruined church lay like a decomposing giant, stones and cross toppled and askew in lush beardgrass. To the right stood the markers of a dozen graves. Weather and time had taken their toll. Three wooden crosses had completely fallen over and were nearly lost from view in the weeds. Weary, stone slabs jutted at odd angles as if their owners had tossed with fitful dreams.

Shadows lay heavy behind the church. Luke thought he could make out a backdrop of rocky hillside with a possible cave entrance. His eyes were better than Boone's, but there was not enough light to be sure. What he could see was a form lying near the edge of church rubble. Still as death, the fawn markings and hooves were unmistakable.

They checked the perimeter and approached with caution. Without question this was the deer they had been tracking. Boone's eyes narrowed as he clenched his teeth. This buck had been a four-point beauty. It lay dead at their feet with strange wounds at the base of its throat. Something had feasted on its blood. Both its eyes had been removed.

"What the Hell did that?"

One sick son of a bitch.

Boone kept the thought to himself. He had pulled out his knife to take meat, but on examining the strange wounds again he thought better of it, keeping his rifle in the crook of his arm.

Luke knew it angered Boone to waste the tracking time. Firing up his metal detector he let his brother keep watch as he began searching the church grounds.

"Be quick about it."

Boone frowned as the metal detector waved over wild grass and foundation stones green with lichen. It was a bone of contention. His little brother---the dark-haired, blue-eyed boy most girls in Twiggs County fell for, who never learned to track or hunt properly, was of all the men the one to find a lost child. The mayor's daughter, no less. She had fallen behind on a school camping trip and become disoriented. A search party went out, but it was Luke who found her. The reward had been substantial. He spent most of the money bailing out their drunkard father's debts. With what remained he chose a single luxury item from a catalog. A god damned metal detector.

High-pitched beeping caught both brothers off guard. Luke narrowed down the heart of the detection and pulled out his own knife to dig. Moist, black earth parted easily. Bloated grubs wriggled away. With ringing stabs the knife found a metal box.

Thready roots and dirt flew as Luke ripped it free. Encrusted, several swipes with his shirtsleeve were required to reveal its surface. The box was unmarked, made of a hardwood he didn't recognize, likely some rare species of maple or walnut. A gold clasp securing its contents gave way to his blade with a puff of sour-smelling air. Brow furrowed, Luke hesitated, glancing up at his brother. A nod passed between them and he lifted the lid.

Stench of a decomposing corpse flew out and was gone as quick as the escape of a trapped bird. Rotten burlap swaddled something. It bore markings in black ink that reminded Luke of the odd signs his grandfather had slashed on his bedroom wall in the asylum.

"Maybe we shouldn't..."

"Get on with it."

Lifting away the burlap revealed a book. It looked older than dirt but was sturdy, bound in thick, black leather. An inlaid stamp of gold with a beckoning skeleton adorned its cover. On the spine, also in gold, were letters that Luke presumed to be the book title and author. He read them aloud slowly.

"Nespus de Mare Grimorie, by Dragoi Nicolescu."

Boone cut to the chase.

"Can we get money for it?"

Luke stood up, wrapping the book back in its burlap.

"We? I found this, Boone. You never would have known it was here."

Boone's jaw tightened. "You never would have been here without me."

"Fine. We'll split it. We can take it to Earle Claiborne's stall at the Fair next week. He'll know its worth, or be able to find out."

As Luke bent to pick up his metal detector, a hunting knife flashed. The blade caught him in the back. His eyes looked skyward as he sank to the ground. Blood rushed from the wound without sound.

Extra digging widened the hole. Boone worked quickly, pushing the metal detector in alongside his brother. There seemed less dirt to cover than came out originally, so he drug over loose stones and mortar from the church. It was close enough to have rolled there, he reasoned.

With the book back inside its box he tucked it under his arm, hefted his rifle and made his way home.

As swaying foliage closed over his departure, subtle movement stirred in the cave behind the church. A vaguely human shape stepped forth from shadows. It was a shockingly thin silhouette, black and faceless, crowned with inward facing horns. Folded behind it were slick, bat-like wings and a long, barbed tail. A bright gleam that might have been eyes blinked twice as it surveyed the clearing and disappeared again into the dark recess of cavern.

The following week Boone made an appearance at the Fair. Rumors were swirling about his little brother. Luke had been popular enough to spark several versions to explain his disappearance. Some said he had bolted to attend college in Mount Vernon; some said he had run off with a girl, or met with foul play because of one. A few theorized that a bobcat or bear got him while treasure hunting with his metal detector. No postcard had come and no body had been found. Playing the grieving brother was wearing thin. All Boone wanted was to sell the cursed book, take the money and hop the bus for a bigger town.

Earle Claiborne inspected the cryptic burlap through gold spectacles perched on the end of his nose. He raked a hand through his unruly, white hair and scanned the fairgrounds with shaken nerves.

"Where did you get this, Boone? The Skelly family has never brought me anything like this before. Your brother found a couple of rare comics in town, but nothing, nothing like this."

"What does it matter, old man? I was hunting south of Wilder's Creek. Found the box in an abandoned house. Now I'll ask again, what's it worth?"

Using burlap as a buffer the retired professor checked the book's interior, sliding the mouthpiece of his carved pipe into its pages. The dark circles beneath Boone's eyes had not gone unnoticed. Experience had taught Claiborne not to trifle with antiquities.

"Afraid of it?"

There was a glint of madness in Boone's steely gaze. He had never been a kind man, but something shadowed him, some unseen, unwholesome spirit that had not been there before.

"As should you be. There were thought to be only two of these in the known world, Boone. I don't really want to know how you came by it. And valuable, you ask? Evil doesn't begin to describe it. Nespus de Mare Grimorie means Unspeakable Grimorie. It's Romanian. A textbook of dark, forbidden magic. Instructions on how to raise the dead and invoke demons. Worse than that, spells to call forth The Great Old Ones from their slumber. The book itself has power. There are some who would pay obscene amounts for it."

"Buy it from me."

Claiborne covered the book again and shut it away in its box, dropping his pipe in a trashcan by the stall.

"No. Even if I had that kind of money I would have no part of this book. I will put you in contact with someone. That at least will take it away from Twiggs County. But I fear something terrible has been awakened."

Boone turned to leave but an idea stayed him.

"Who are The Great Old Ones? Could I make more money by raising them?"

The color drained out of Claiborne's face.

"My God. No. Boone, as insane as it may sound, even you don't want to summon gods from beyond the stars. I can't begin to impress upon you the dire consequences. It would mean the end of our world."

"So you say."

The old professor leaned forward across his table, spilling college pamphlets to the ground.

"I don't know what you did to your brother, Boone Skelly, but karma will have its due. Tentacled demons be damned. Best watch your back."

"Call me what you please, old man. Words will never hurt me."

As Boone disappeared into the crowd Earle Claiborne collapsed in writhing fits. Green foam bubbled from his lips. Fair attendants rushed to his aid, but the professor had drowned in a mysterious, dark fluid that smelled of brine.

One week later Boone was $500,000 richer. He had no idea the professor had died without making inquiries. All that mattered was the appearance of a man at his door with a briefcase full of money. The fellow had been tall, with a pale, brutish face and arms as big as trees. There had been no conversation, just a simple exchange. Once he had been relieved of the book the world seemed smaller. Boone experienced a pang of loss. He had never felt this for any of his family. Without the book he felt weak and vulnerable.

He bought a house the next town over and lived in high style, but miles and money couldn't vanquish the nightmares. Luke haunted him. A crowd of people from his hometown whose eyes had been gouged out chased after him with torches and signs that said Murderer. There were other dreams too, far more nasty and disturbing. Dreams of probing tentacles and cyclopean eyes; of diaphanous columns overgrown with flowering sargassum, and a night sky lit eerily by a dozen moons where winged creatures feasted on souls.

More often than not Boone called out a name in his sleep. He didn't remember at first, but woke with the residue of gibberish running through his brain. It was elusive as a deer he once knew. He paid exorbitant fees to psychiatrists and sleep analysts. A hypnotist swore that he had been cured. Eventually he bought a tape recorder to capture his ramblings.

While all this was happening a young man was out walking with his dog in Twiggs County, throwing a stick for him to fetch. The spaniel broke away and was out of sight for a long while. His owner followed, hearing whining and the thrash of digging. The noises led him to a clearing deep in the woods. The tops of grave markers could barely be made out in snarled weeds, and beside the crumbling remnants of a church he found his dog. The spaniel's white legs and muzzle were covered with black earth. Something was sticking up out of the ground.

Beneath crisp starlight the thing seemed luminescent. The young man crouched down for closer examination. It came away in his fingers---a small bone he thought most likely from a woods animal or stray pet. Its shimmer was extraordinary. He pocketed the find, and being a guitar maker took it home for ornamentation in a project.

When the instrument was finished its rich wood shone with a

luster unlike anything the young man had ever crafted before. Eyes were drawn to its first fret, the polished bone carefully fitted across fingerboard. The young man fancied that it gave his guitar spirit. He sold the piece to an agent representing an anonymous buyer, who was well known in the rock industry. That first day it was lifted from its case, the guitar held power over the musician. He became obsessed, driven to write a song that he could not explain.

The story it told was that of two brothers chasing a deer through the woods. It spoke of jealousy and betrayal, and a secret treasure that spread madness. The song was completed in one sitting. The musician, a platinum selling artist and multi-millionaire with his own private recording studio, chose to lock himself in the bathroom of his small guest house. Using his smartphone he recorded a grainy video of his initial performance of the song with his new guitar. Once finished he posted it to social media sites and put a gun in his mouth.

Viral in record time. What crime scene specialists couldn't determine was how a handful of random images that flashed with strobe-like quickness had been edited into the performance. The first was a lightning-effect image of two men standing in a wooded area. A sinister church loomed behind them in abandoned disrepair. The second image was that of an outdated metal detector. After that was a knife gripped tensely overhead. Second to last, during final verse, flashed a shot of one man filling in the other's grave. The handle of the detector could still be seen poking through soft dirt. Right before the song ended, with acoustic strings still vibrating their final notes in the cramped bathroom, a closing image filled the screen in slightly longer duration before fading to black. Walls were splattered with bright blood. The rock star was motionless, slumped backward. The gun had fallen to his right, landing in the bathtub. The prophecy was completed by indecipherable words slashed at odd angles in blood on the walls and ceiling. How all of it got there in a simple selfie video posted two minutes after being recorded was an impossible mystery.

Police immediately removed the posts, but once on the Internet, the damage was done. The number of estimated viewers was staggering. There was no way of telling how many had recorded the video file, stashing it away for posterity or to sell to local news agencies. Some of those viewers knew the Skelly brothers.

Detectives hopped the gate when there was no response from the intercom at Boone Skelly's home. The front door stood wide open. A thin, weaving trail of blood drops led to the kitchen, where a housekeeper's body had been peeled of its skin. Marks at the base of her neck were like nothing any of them had ever seen before.

The lead detective called out, signaling his men to search the house.

"Come out, Boone. Let's you and I have a conversation about what happened."

A deep voice startled them from the top of the stairs.

"What's done is done. I'm sworn to the God of a Thousand Forms."

High above them at the apex of a steampunk, metal staircase, stood a naked man that had once been Boone Skelly. His skin was the color of something long dead and submerged, bloated and wrinkled and disturbingly soft. His throat bore the same strange mark of feeding police had observed on the housekeeper. His eyes were still intact, but shone with the fever of madness. Nightmares swam in his pupils.

A hailstorm of bullets ripped him apart as easily as a rotten jack-o-lantern. Pulpy mess rained down. Bits of flesh and brain matter were supernaturally driven like remote controlled cars to form wet letters on the tile entryway.

NYARLATHOTEP

After the cops filed out, some carted away for the collection of possible human remains from their clothing and hair, CSI and the coroner's unit took turns in the house. The same bizarre sigils found in the dead musician's bathroom were rampant in Boone's home. Some of the rooms were clean, without a single piece of furniture. Others, especially those in the sunken first floor, looked as though a commune of hoarders and mad scientists had joined forces. A Hazmat team was called in to dispose of frightening things not disclosed to the sea of reporters camping at the gate.

Darkness fell. Officers were stationed on guard duty once all evidence had been collected and admittance restricted with yellow tape. Stubborn paparazzi remained, hoping for a glimpse of insanity that would finance fame and retirement.

Gaunt creatures with membranous wings hovered in the shadows of Boone's kitchen. When one of the cops stepped aside for a smoke they swarmed him, bringing the offering to their master. In a disturbing caricature of human form, Nyarlathotep appeared, grinning with silver shark's teeth. Beetles scurried in his long locks of unwashed hair. His guise had been somewhat more refined when he had offered the briefcase of money to Boone. He had since found a suitable scholar for the ancient tome of Nicolescu. Nodding with a smile, he changed his guise once more to that of an ancient pharaoh.

With the subtle resonances of freshly devoured soul pulsing through him, the Crawling Chaos, messenger of The Outer Gods and servant of Azathoth known as Nyarlathotep, flicked on the remote to Boone's big-screen television. Already the major news channels were beginning to air special reports on widespread power outages and nightmarish beasts of slime crawling out of the sea. Inexplicable crop circles and pulsing pods from the night sky would soon follow.

House of the Sleeping Beauties

~ Jason Andrew ~

Dawn's light shone through the lace curtains of the open bay windows onto the canopy bed. Birds chirped outside tempting her to rise from the comfortable mattress with their musical serenade. Aisling awoke with a frightening start as her head and stomach tried to trick her into believing that she was falling a great distance like a cartoon villainess.

It felt appropriate as she had always personally identified with the wicked stepmothers in the stories. She adored their beautiful ruby lips and style. Aisling decided that she'd much rather be the villainess doomed to tragedy than a victim once she started working at the House of Sleeping Beauties. Why had flowing black cloaks ever gone out of fashion?

Sometimes right before a gig, when her stomach rebelled from the stress and there were a hundred places that she would rather be, Aisling fantasied about pushing her House Mother out the window. Last year in European History, she learned that there was an entire word devoted exclusively to describing a murder via pushing them out a window: defenestration. It had become her favorite word, even if she struggled to find occasions to use it properly.

It seemed such a random, pointless way to die, romanticized in Technicolor cartoons as the honorable way to kill evil step-mothers.

Heroines can't get their hands dirty, she mused.

Aisling always resisted any malicious urges and simply smiled sweetly until the House Mother appeared to lead her to the bed chambers and then slowly drank the Cantarella-laced tea. Aisling disliked the thought of surrendering control, but she trusted in the House Mothers to keep the business running at a profit for everyone involved. This was a good gig for a college student. What other job would allow her to work only one night a month and still provide her with the cash to afford her own apartment?

She stuck out her tongue trying to moisten the inside of her mouth. Cantarella brought forth a temporary coma that Shakespeare dubbed the *still-waking sleep of death*. It dried her mouth and swelled her tongue. What was the warning issued to Juliet towards the end of play? *I hear some noise, Lady, come from that nest of death, contagion, and unnatural sleep.*

Aisling lay naked upon the bed, perfectly center, with her hands folded just above her stomach and her head raised slightly by a silk pillow. Her arms ached so she rubbed them gingerly trying to force the blood through her veins to remove the numbing sensation. It couldn't be helped. Charmings paid well to be able to pose, position, and utilize the Beauties as desired within the limits of the agreed upon contract.

It was a simple job. There were no dreams or memories just listless sleep. When she opened her eyes, the gig was over and then she immediately started checking her body for clues about what might have happened during the nap. This time her nails were manicured French style, painted with white tips on a field of pink. Aisling craned her neck to verify that her toes had been similarly marked and then sighed with relief. There was only one Charming that devoted such time and effort to her nails. He was a gentle asexual man that the Beauties secretly gave the les petits noms d'amour of the Doll-Maker from his habit of dressing them like

Gibson Girl dolls.

The Beauties whispered to each other and jealously shared information. The House Mother never told the Beauties the identity of the Charming they were serving at any time. It was strictly against protocol in this delicate socioeconomic system. Knowledge was power and the Charmings paid the House a great deal to protect their privacy while they fed their secret cravings. The Beauties relied upon the House to watch over them while they slept, via the hidden camera, and protect them when they couldn't protect themselves. The House served as the middleman, catering to both groups.

Cantarella always made it difficult at best to wake. She allowed her body to breathe enjoying the slow sensation of her limbs feeling refreshed from the numbness of the deep sleep.

Aisling always felt restless after a gig as though the night's sleep hadn't counted. She glanced around the room to discover dozens of white dresses and spools of pink ribbon littered the Persian carpet. Clearly, the Doll-Maker had been quite busy last night. She wished him well wherever he might go after such nights.

The House Mother entered silently through the secret side-door, carrying a silver tray of tea, milk, and butter filled croissants. She wore red stain robes embroidered with Chinese dragons. Aisling glanced over at the window wistfully and then remember she had yet to be paid for the gig.

"I trust that you slept well, Beauty."

She resisted the urge to scowl, knowing that this moment was part of the ritual. Aisling often wondered if the Charmings watched this part to ensure that their privacy had been maintained. "Yes, House Mother. I slept so deeply that I remember nothing but warm and happy dreams."

"Good." The House Mother set the tray upon the nightstand and poured two cups of tea. Aisling accepted her cup gratefully and smelled it with pleasure. She waited, as was custom, for the House

Mother the other Beauties referred to as Dragon Lady to take her cup. They drank together. The tea was bitter, but it helped cleanse the remaining toxins in her veins. "Thank you for your service to the House. I have an offering for you, but I was forgetful and left it in my office."

The House Mother never forgot anything involving money. "Shall I wait here, then?" Aisling asked.

The Dragon Lady shook her head and smiled secretively. "Please take your time as usually preparing for the day. I shall return with your tribute and a bonus."

Aisling cast her eyes downward. "Have I caused offense?"

It was like trying to read an emotion from a statue. "Not at all. I'd like to discuss your next assignment with you before you leave."

Her heart-rate quickened fearfully. She rarely discussed an assignment ahead of time with the House Mother. Was there another reason? Some sort of compliment from a Charming? Aisling waited until the House Mother left and then rushed to the luxuriously decorated bathroom to check her pale, petite ballerina's body carefully for any cuts or bruises in the 360 degree mirror. She understood logically that all Charmings had to undergo expensive medical screening by the House to be vetted as a Charming, but the creeping fear always roiled violently in her stomach just after a nap.

Aisling found the reflection of her oval face with a delightful set of dimples and smiled. Bright blue eyes blinked back at her without any bags under them. Her strawberry blond hair had been brushed and then braided perfectly by the Doll-Maker. Relieved, she showered quickly and slid into her Sunday's best pink sweatsuit that proclaimed her bottom *Juicy*.

Sipping a steaming cup of tea, the Dragon Lady waited for her on the bed. Someone had already cleaned the room and removed the white dresses that had littered the floor. It was as though the previous night had never happened.

There was a plain white envelope resting on the nightstand. Aisling smiled gratefully and then slid it into her front pocket. She didn't bother to open it, but noted that it was considerably thicker than normal. The House of Beauties clearly wanted something different from her. "Tell me about the nap. Why is it so special?"

"Our client list is quite exclusive. Those we welcome into our houses are amongst the elite in terms of wealth and power." The Dragon Lady did not hide the sheer greed upon her face. "You have been selected for a nap for an extremely powerful and wealthy Charming that requires a special level of privacy."

"I don't understand."

"The Charming is unknown to us. His intermediary is a man of extreme political power and wealth in his own right. He visited you himself several months ago." The Dragon Lady sighed and then took another sip. "Would you care for a drink?"

"I think I might need it."

The Dragon Lady poured a second cup of tea and continued. "The Charming has made an offer to engage your services next month. It is very generous."

The eccentric rich could be crazy with their money, but they always expected more in return. "How generous?"

"You would be paid two hundred thousand for the night."

That was enough for her to retire until she finished school without any student loans. She wasn't entirely certain how much the House was paid for their services, but it had to be at least equal to her share. "What does the Charming expect for such generosity?"

"I am told by the intermediary that the Charming is quite concerned about his privacy with good reason. The House is not to have any information about this Charming in any fashion. The intermediary shall monitor your sleep in lieu of our people."

Aisling gasped. "I'd be sleeping completely blind."

"I have had a good business relationship with the intermediary for almost twenty years," the Dragon Lady countered. "He has assured me that the Charming is quite reasonable and respectful of limits. The potential for scandal is simply too great to risk."

"What about his medical records? How can we be certain that he's clean?"

"I have been assured with a personal bond of one million dollars that the Charming is in perfect health," the Dragon Lady answered quietly. "The intermediary has assured me that you shall not have any reason to be unhappy with the assignment and that he would personally pay for any unforeseen circumstances that might arise."

Aisling scowled. *If it felt too good to be true, it usually was.* "Thank you for the offer, but I'm sure one of the other Beauties will take this nap."

"The Charming specified that this deal was solely for you." The kind façade of the House Mother had completely faded from the Dragon Lady's face. "This job will be for a single night and could greatly benefit the House of Beauties in the future. I'd be very disappointed if you simply rejected the offer."

Disappointed in this context was just a discrete way of saying angry. Aisling shivered. She had seen the Dragon Lady angry, and it was clear that if she simply said no that she'd have to find employment elsewhere. "I'll do it for five hundred thousand with half in advance."

The Dragon Lady simply nodded without giving the matter a second thought. "Agreed. I will have a cashier's check delivered to your apartment this evening. As usual, the company will mark this down as a bonus in our business division and pay the taxes to avoid legal issues."

"Simple as that?" Aisling asked. "Don't you need to verify that the Charming will pay?"

The Dragon Lady drank her tea never turning her eyes away from Aisling. "I am aware of the limits available in this mediation.

The Charming has reserved the night of the 16th. Two Saturdays from now. I know that we usually try to keep at least a month between jobs, but I think we can afford to be a little more relaxed."

Aisling checked her calendar on her phone. That was roughly a week before per period. "That should be fine." She felt dizzy. Who could afford such a thing? What had she gotten herself into? "I need some air. Is there anything else?"

"Please remember that discretion is our shield as always."

———

A solemn courier in a black suit with a red tie arrived at the apartment later that night as promised. He opened his silver briefcase and presented to Aisling a certified cashier's check for two hundred and fifty thousand dollars. The courier tipped his hat and then quietly departed without ever having said a word.

Who was this Charming to cause such fear? Who could afford to spend such money on a single night? She lived in Ithaca near the University. The House of Beauties was hidden near Lake Beebe on a small vineyard. Important Charmings commuted by helicopter from the Big Apple and all of the large cities in the area.

She tried googling the date of the gig, but found nothing interesting except that it was the night of the full moon during a strange alignment with the cyclical passing of Peltier's comet. If her Charming were interested in the stars, then surely he would have better things to do that night. The United Nations planned a series of G8 summits the week after. Did one of the leaders need a vacation beforehand? *Wouldn't it be strange if it were the President*, she thought with a bit of exhilaration.

Aisling called the Beauties she felt closest to and was confident would keep her inquiries discrete. There was much speculation, but little actual insight. She went to her classes, wrote her term papers, and slowly ticked off the days to her next and hopefully last nap.

When she arrived at the House of Beauties, the Dragon Lady took her to the bathhouse that had been prepared for her arrival. The facilities had been transformed and decorated to a bright festival celebrating the two-faced god Janus. A comfortable altar had been assembled from a legion of silk pillows at the edge of the steaming baths. "Is this safe? Sleeping near the water?"

"I have been given certain assurances that lead me to believe your safety is vital to them," the Dragon Lady promised. She smiled like a proper House Mother and presented her with strange gossamer robes that did little to hide the curves of her body. "A death would bring scandal, after all."

Aisling drank the offered Canterella and laid down peacefully upon the pillow altar and closed her eyes.

—

A hot and humid wind swept through the winding back allies of the strange city, billowing her gossamer robes about her legs. Aisling felt the wall. It was a finely polished rock. She once went to the Ape Caves near Mount St. Helens, and the dead lava tunnels had this exact feel to it. What was the word the professor had used? Basalt. *Where was she that had such walls?*

She stepped out into the cobblestone street amongst the strangely garbed strangers with thick beards and questioning eyes and glanced down at the shimmering infinite sea. Grim galleys with black sails and impossibly heavy oars littered the harbor. "Where am I?"

The strange language the people spoke felt harsh somehow and alien to her sensitive ears. Veiled woman with bright green eyes pushed past her with indifference. The people of this dark city moved with great alacrity, carrying large trays covered with lush delicacies as though they were preparing for a vast celebration. "Can anyone understand me?"

The only answer was a soft meow. She searched the alley until her found a ragged, lost kitten that looked as helpless as she felt. She picked it up and cradled it in her arms. "There, there, no one will hurt you."

"No man or women will hurt a cat of Ulthar, not even in Dylath-Leen, where the moon beasts rule." It was then that she noticed the twin girls of blond hair and eyes of blue. They laughed in unison. "Cats are the keeper of secrets and the moon is their patron."

"Who are you?"

The twins took turns finishing each other's sentences. "A dream of the future in that last free city in the realm. They celebrate all that ever was and a life that will never be again."

"Free from what?"

"Free from the city that sleeps where that which is dead can never die. It grows in our dreams and then wakes in your world. There isn't time. Take this."

The twins gave her a silver key. "The Canterella makes it almost impossible for us to reach you. Only the magic of creation allowed us to break through the Wall of Sleep. Dream of us and we can help you before Father finds you."

"Wait! How can I take the silver key to the real world?"

"All worlds are real."

She awoke to tears streaming down her face. Aisling blinked twice trying to remember what the twins had warned her about. She coughed, choking on the snot and bile caught in her throat. Aisling opened her hand, hidden under the pillow to discover a silver key. Had she been dreaming? *That was supposed to be impossible!*

Aisling turned her head to the side to catch her breath. Her belly lay flat upon the pillows and her ass was positioned upwards towards the ceiling. Her body ached everywhere and there was little doubt what nocturnal activities the Charming elected to explore. She wiped away her matted, wet hair from her eyes and sighed thankful for the free intrauterine device that the House provided to all of their Beauties.

She started to stir when the House Mother entered with the usual tray of tea. There was an unfamiliar uncertainly in the Dragon Lady's usual graceful steps. "I trust that you slept well, Beauty."

Aisling noticed the lines of bruising on her arms as though she had been held down by something strong and vicious. Her hands were shaking. "Yes, House Mother. I slept so deeply that I remember nothing," she replied weakly

"Good." The House Mother set the tray upon the nightstand and poured two cups of tea. Aisling took her bitter cup and quickly drank it without waiting as custom for the House Mother. "Thank you for your service to the House. I have an offering for you. Tribute for your services."

Aisling practically snatched the envelope out of her hand, but quickly caught her composure and nodded politely at the House Mother. "Thank you for the kind tribute."

"Please take as long as you need. Enjoy the benefits of the House of Beauties and let us know when you are ready to work."

Aisling waited until the Dragon Lady left and then ran to the bathroom. The 360 degree mirror revealed a number of bruises and cuts along her legs and thighs. There was a jagged bite mark squarely on the curve of her ass that already turned a dark purple. Her inner thighs felt raw and beaten. Some of the customers wanted sex; few of them were this brutal. She had the option of using the House Doctors, but really all she wanted to do was run home and soak in the tub.

She slipped on her sweats, grabbed her bag, made certain that the key was safe her pocket and ran home.

———

The bruises healed very slowly, but her body never felt the same again. She realized something was wrong when her next period was a trickle of black blood. Aisling had gained a few pounds over the month, but had explained it away as stress from quitting her job and dealing with her new found fortune.

She took her last final and then changed her plans. There were eyes constantly watching her and she needed time to think and to plan for the future. Aisling called her father and begged for a favor. The family had long ago lived out near the coast in Providence near a small village named Innsmouth and still owned a cabin. It was little more than a shack, but it was comfortable, with a wonderful stone fireplace to keep her warm, and a view over the chilling Atlantic waters.

Aisling waited until the last day of winter break to buy a pregnancy test. It shouldn't have been possible, but she knew the truth in her bones. Somehow the twins were the dream of her unborn children.

She slept each night with the silver key under her pillow and the twins took her to new and wondrous places. They ventured to the frozen fields of the north and danced with the satyrs known as the Men of Leng. In the town of Ulthar, they watched as the mysterious cats wearing black boots brewed sensual spirits and told stories of the moon and far away worlds. They explored the grey stones with unusual glyphs and signs in the devastated ruins of Sarnath on the shores of a black lake. The twins refused to answer any questions about their father.

When her belly was full and round, the dreams started to fade. It became more difficult to dream of them or the other world. She paced the cabin late into the night in a listless attempt to tire herself just enough to sleep, even a little, until there was a knock at the door. Aisling sniffed the air and somehow knew that it was the Charming that had fathered her children.

She opened the door to greet a hauntingly familiar, handsome face with large bright eyes and a dimple in his chin. Somehow she knew instinctually that this appearance was somehow a mask to hide his real face. "Do you know who I am, Sleeping Beauty?"

"Charming. The one that got me pregnant."

"We lost track of you when you left Ithaca, but I smelled your pheromones upon the scent of the sea." Charming smiled as though he fully expected her to fall into his arms. Her stomach turned as she realized she wanted to. "Instincts brought you here to the waters of my home."

"What's happening? How did I get pregnant? Who are you?"

"A Prince of a city that sleeps beneath the waves born of a line blood from the very stars." Charming pointed through the large bay windows to the distant, cold stars. "Our ancestors wait for us in the land of dreams to bring them across. We bred with the humans to allow our blood to thin enough to access their dreamlands. First, we conquered their dreams and then later their world. Our daughters will be Queens of the New World that is coming when R'lyeh rises from the dark waters of the world. Thanks to our children's siren call, the star-spawn stirs once more, ready to come home."

"Don't I have a choice in all of this?" Aisling horrified.

"We needed you. Your blood is that what remains of Father Dagon and Mother Hydra and the cult of Innsmouth. The humans thought they wiped all of you from the world, but you survived." Charming smiled and Aisling felt her resistance fade. "I would make you my wife and unite the royal linages. I am not a gentle man, but I love well, especially one that will bear the children of tomorrow that shall rule on the land and under the sea."

"What will happen to the people of the world?"

"Some will be allowed to live as slaves," Charming answered magnanimously. "Certainly, any human you wish to be spared, shall be. The rest shall be cleansed in a spectacular decimation as the Old Ones rise from the water and take their rightful place on this world."

She looked at the window that overlooked the sea and the rocks below. Prince Charming followed her to the balcony without asking. Aisling knew that at this moment she could use her favorite word in action and this strange man that had violated her would die on the rocks below.

Charming seemed to be kind man in his own way and children needed a father as well as a mother. "I'm cold. I have a cloak in the bedroom. Will you fetch it for me?"

"For Sleeping Beauty? Anything!"

The Piper In Yellow

- Brett Talley -

A very long time ago, before the rise of the kings of Aon and the empire of Yorn, a traveler from a distant land came to the country of Edunia. Amongst the broken stone and rotting timbers of that once great kingdom, he stumbled upon a hermit who lived in a hovel of thatch and oak.

"Come," the hermit said to the stranger. "Sit by the fire and warm thyself, for the night is long and it is not often that I receive visitors."

The traveler did as he was bade. The old man brought food and water, and round the fire they sat as the sun sank and the moon rose and a shadow covered the countryside.

"I was lucky to come upon you," said the traveler, "for yours is the only dwelling I have seen for some while, since I entered the vale. There was a village a ways back, a town in the old time. The homes and farms had rotted away, and all that remained of the town-proper were heaps of shattered rock and an ancient church on an overgrown town square."

In the dancing firelight, the old man's eyes shone.

"That would be old Bethlehem," he said. "The people of that town were devout, and the village prosperous. Before he came."

"He?"

The hermit rose and walked to a cupboard, removed two tankards, and filled them from a cask on the table.

"All storytelling is a thirsty business," he said as he handed one to the stranger. "But some telling is more thirsty than others. Come," he said, "sit by the fire. And let us talk of things about which no man should speak…"

——

These lands are steeped in time and in mystery. It hangs over them like a heavy shroud, like a fog that never lifts. The domed hills and shadowed vales feel older than they should.

Life flees from here, and most men avoid it. It is not a mindful decision they make, no cold calculus is involved. It is much deeper than that. It comes from something forgotten. From *somewhere* forgotten.

But whatever the cause, they avoid old Bethlehem. The travelers and merchants do not know why they no longer turn down the road through the glen. Why instead they take the long way round through Fingoyle. They do not choose. They simply do, and their memories escape them. That you would dare to do what they cannot is an enigma unto itself, and what it says of you, only you may know.

But it was not always so.

There was a time when the valley was prosperous, when the game was good and plentiful, the sun shone bright and the crops came up tall and straight. The goods flowed freely down the Brachen Road. The merchants travelled from far kingdoms and all prospered.

It was Bethlam that prospered most. It had many names you see. Beth'lem. Little Bethlehem. New Bethlehem. Lil'ham. But whatever it was called, its future—straddling the trade road through the vale— seemed assured. So when the plague came, it struck like a judgment from a vengeful God.

It started with the Goodspeed child, a family that lived just beyond the borders of the town. She returned from the forest one night with a cough. Nothing all that unusual for the young. But by the next morning her face had become pallid, and her limbs shook from the cold even as her body burned from fever.

But it was what she saw in her pain-racked nights and febrile waking dreams that sent a chill of fear through the families of the village and drove her poor father mad. She spoke of mountains that walked, of darkness that crawled, and creatures that surround us all, floating unseen and sleeping just beyond the vision of man.

But it was when she spoke of *him* that they feared the most.

"He is coming," she said, that last night before mercy extinguished her flame. The poor child's body went rigid, her eyes focused on some world far beyond our ken. "The watcher at the threshold, the rider on the plain. The sword and the flame. The pestilence and the plague. None will be spared, not from the yellow man." Her eyes fell on her father. "And you, daddy. You will go first. You will prepare the way."

I cannot say what it was that the accursed father Goodspeed saw in the languid gaze of his only child, but it is said that as he stared into the depths of her soul, his body began to quake, and in one moment of sanity-breaking fear, he leapt to his feet with a shriek and ran from the room. They found his body hanged from a tree by the brook, dead by his own hand, horror still etched upon his face.

That is how it began, with the death of the father, the daughter close on his heels. It did not end there.

Kate Bridges was next, and then Patrick Longlin, and then Stuart Mars. Each one lived just a little closer to Beth'lem than the one before. The pestilence was on the march, and like the great plague that consumed Egypt of old, it cared not for the grown and the aged. The children were its victims, though it made no accounting for first-born, and no blood of the lamb could stave off its fury. When it reached the town-proper, it spread like a field set to the flame.

When the first town child fell ill, the people prayed. By the time they all had—every son or daughter of Beth'lem below the age of 14—the people cried out for anyone, be he god or devil, to save them.

And something heard them, be he god or devil.

He came from the east, the yellow man. Whether because of the robe he wore or his sallow skin, that's what they called him. He was tall of stature, four and a half cubits if he was a span.

He arrived by the Brachen Road. No beast bore him, and had any of the townspeople noticed the flocks of birds winging south at mid-summer, they might have wondered what drove them to take flight.

No watchman met him at the town gate, and he entered without question or hassle. He walked through empty, silent streets, heavy with the stench of pestilence, and a rare smile curved the edges of the stranger's lips. He followed the High Street to the town square and the church that even now holds sway over it. It was there that the townspeople had gathered, beseeching their god to save them from the plague that threatened to take their children.

It was not god that answered them.

Father Johansen was in the middle of prayer—one of many that had gone up that day, buoyed by fear and desperation—when it happened, when the stranger arrived.

"Please sir," said Father Johansen, always a nervous man but in that moment particularly undone, "this is a house of God."

"God? Does your God answer you now? How long have you prayed?" asked the stranger. "And still your children suffer."

At these words, a murmur swept through the assembly. Who was this man? How could he know that? Might he have the answer to save them?

"That is blasphemy, sir," said the preacher, but there was no conviction in his voice, and by inches he had moved away from the podium.

"I think not. Blasphemy is to speak lies. I speak the truth." The stranger took a step down the aisle, and then another. The feeling in the congregation was as that of a man, standing on a hillside before a storm, the electricity pulsating around him. "I have come from far away, beyond the lake of Hali and the jeweled cities of Carcosa. I have come here, to you, in your time of need." He raised his arm and extended one finger of a boney, blackened hand that stretched forth beyond the sleeve of his cloak. "You worship a broken god, a god that failed. He does not hear your cries. He does not answer them."

There were those in the church that day who, in brasher moments past, filled with drink and with vigor, would have sworn that no man would so curse our Lord without soon meeting Him. And yet even they sat in silence as the stranger spoke, their fear overawing their religious devotion.

"You cower here. You cry out for salvation. Salvation has arrived. You pray for a deliverer. He stands before you. You ask for a sign. He who has eyes, let him see."

The stranger raised his hand. A shadow fell upon the tabernacle of the Lord. Day became night, and the stream of light from the great stained glass windows ceased. The air grew cold and dense, and tendrils of mist wrapped around the legs of the assembled villagers like cats' tails, and every man and woman it touched felt a little bit of life fade away. There was a deep groan, like the shrieking of wood on a ship in the midst of a storm. Then the shadow lifted as quickly as it had fallen, and the light returned.

"This and much more I will show you, if you so choose."

"Can you save our children?" came a cry from the front. "Can you save my baby?"

"Perhaps. If you are willing to pay."

"So it's money you want," cried another, one who still doubted.

For the first time in their midst, the stranger smiled.

"Oh no, not gold. Not silver. Not jewels or trinkets. Something much more precious. But sacrifice? Yes, sacrifice will be required. A price must be paid. The price of power. And the power you seek is great indeed. So too is the cost."

The stranger sighed, deep and long.

"Now I tire of this place." He turned and almost staggered to the entrance, and it seemed to those who still could bear to look upon him—for many could not, nor could they say why not—that the figure no longer seemed so large, so stately. In fact, he seemed to diminish.

He cast one last glance back at them and said, "Choose, but choose now. I will await your answer at sundown beneath the dead oak that keeps watch over the river bend. Send three men. No more, no less. Sundown."

The doors to the church swung open at his touch, and slammed shut behind him as if carried by a strong wind. The people of the town were left to shiver in the pews, astonished at what they had seen and fearful at what would surely come after.

———

As the sun descended, three men were chosen. The Lord Mayor, the Sheriff, and one man who bore no title but was trusted by all, a woodsman who lived in the forests beyond the town proper. All of them had children. All of them had something to lose.

They found the stranger at the bend of the river, on the spot where he had said he would meet them, beneath the branches of the ancient oak. Whatever stature he had lost upon departing the church had returned to him now, and in the growing shadows of a waning day, he was even more fearsome than they remembered.

"And so you came. Are you prepared to pay?"

"Whatever the price," said the Lord Mayor. "For while we are by no means rich, we have enough. And what we have is yours."

"Ah, you listen, but you do not hear. A price must be paid, but it cannot be paid in gold and silver."

The sheriff stepped forward. "Then what then? My Jeannie is dying and we have not the time for trifles or false hopes."

The stranger grinned, though it felt more like a sneer. "Then to the point, shall we? All for one. The many for the few. All life, for one life."

The Lord Mayor looked to the Sheriff and saw only confusion. It was only the man of the forest who understood.

"Oh my God," the woodsman murmured. "He means to have a sacrifice."

The Sheriff drew his sword. "You are as filled with lies as you are evil."

"Put down your weapon," the stranger said, and as he did he waved his hand before him. To the sheriff, the weight of the sword became as if he were holding a cart-full of stone. It dropped from his hand, the point driving deep into the ground.

"I have not lied to you. I told you the price was steep, but one well worth paying."

"You want us to kill a child?" The Lord Mayor whimpered. "But why?"

"The plague will not pass on its own. It will lay in the grave all that it touches. To stop it will require a great power. And as power comes only through sacrifice, great power comes only through the greatest of loss."

"We won't do it," said the woodcutter. "I don't believe you can heal them, whatever imposture and parlor tricks you may possess." He gestured at the sword of the Sheriff, still driven into the ground, the other man having no desire to touch it again. "And besides, no one would pay that price."

The stranger stepped forward and stretched out his hand to touch the shoulder of the woodsman. The other man did not flinch. He would show that he was not afraid. But when the stranger touched his arm, he did know fear. The touch was not cold, precisely. Instead, the woodsmen felt empty, as if he had been gutted, everything inside of him ripped away.

"You have a son, do you not? A boy named James? From this moment he is healed. When you go home and see that what I say is true, let that be the answer to your doubt. But it is only temporary. The illness will return to him, unless you do as I say."

"I can't," and the tears began to flow down the granite face of that man, "even for James. I can't trade his life for the life of another."

The stranger lifted his hand from the woodsman's shoulder to touch his cheek, almost caressing him with his cold, bone-thin finger. "Simple creature. You pay that price every day. How many in your trade lay down their lives to build the houses and shops that make up your town? How many have been hanged from this very tree to keep others safe? How many soldiers die at your king's command, for his glory or his treasure or his land?"

"But how can we choose?" said the Lord Mayor. "How can we even begin to pick one of our own?"

The stranger never looked at him, keeping his eyes instead upon the woodsman. "You are a devout man."

"We are all devout men, my lord," interrupted the Lord Mayor. The stranger ignored him.

"Do you remember the story of Jonah and the great fish?"

"Of course," answered the woodsman.

"And when the storm beset the ship in which he hid from your god, how did his companions determine who was to blame?"

"They cast lots."

"Yes, and when the lots fell upon Jonah, they threw him into the sea?"

"They did."

"And did the storm abate?"

"It did."

"Then that is your answer." The sun had fallen, the moon taking its place. Even the wind had died away, and but for their voices, silence held sway. "Go home," said the stranger, "check on your son. See that I speak the truth. Then make your choice."

———

The woodsman returned to his home to find his wife in tears. Their only son had been made whole; it could only be called miraculous. The boy's fever had broken just after sunset.

———

They gathered in the old church to cast the lots. I can see that you are surprised that they would so decide. Ah my friend, fear and wonder are powerful drugs, and the townspeople had both in abundance. Fear that their children would die. Wonder that the son of the woodsman had been cured. There was only one who objected, only one who spoke reason in the face of madness.

The woodsman went to the church that evening to plead with his friends and neighbors not to choose a path that could not be unwalked. But the stranger had done more than cure the woodsman's son; he'd robbed him of the faith the people once had in him.

"You have already received the stranger's blessing," said one. "Your child lives, while ours stand on death's doorstep. Why would you deny us what you enjoy?"

The woodsman's pleas for them to hear reason were rebuffed, and soon words turned to shouts, arguments to threats.

The Sheriff stepped forward, his hand on the hilt of his sword. "You've said your piece, woodsman. Now get out."

"He stays," said a voice from the back, and that cold command chilled the blood of all present. The stranger stepped from the daylight beyond into the church. "For the pact must bind you all."

"I won't be a part of it," said the woodsman. "I won't be bound to this."

The stranger chuckled and to all who heard, it sounded like a growl.

"Do you think you have a choice? What in this life led you to that conclusion? You are no island. You are bound to the decisions of the whole. You wish to disagree? The blood of untold women and children slaughtered for the crimes of their cities or their kings mocks your innocence. Stay, or go. It makes no matter. You will be bound."

The woodsman fell silent, and the stranger turned to the congregation.

"Have you made your choice?"

"We have," answered the Lord Mayor.

"And what have you decided?"

"We will do as you ask. Cure our children, and the life of one will be in your hands."

The stranger held his arms high above his head. "So it has been spoken, so you are now bound." Down his hands swung, meeting in one great crash.

Every man and woman in the assembly fell backwards as if buffeted by a mighty wind. Many cried out in pain. The woodsman clutched his hand, the agony as if he had grabbed a glowing brand. When he looked down at his palm, he knew why. His skin sizzled, and already, the red, seared flesh had begun to rise—and it formed an image. A ring, with a single point at the bottom of the circle. At its center, three spheres melded together, as if one globe but with three lobes. It was a sigil, one that the woodcutter doubted many had ever seen before. He knew not what it meant, only that it was of a dark and deadly purpose, and that all who gathered that day bore it. The smell of burning flesh hung heavy in the air.

"A spoken oath, sealed in flesh and fire. One you dare not break."

The stranger reached inside his cloak and removed a leather satchel. He threw it at the feet of the Lord Mayor.

"Now your god decides. Inside are circles of marble, one for every family in this town. All are white, save one. He who draws the black sphere, from him shall the sacrifice come."

The stranger turned and made his way to the door of the church. "Where are you going?" cried the Lord Mayor.

"The rest is for you to do," he said without turning. "I go to prepare myself. Tonight I cure your children. Tomorrow I collect my price."

Into the dying light the stranger disappeared.

The lots were cast. It was the son of the Lord Mayor that was chosen.

——

That night, the people of Old'ham huddled behind closed doors, clutching their sick children close, praying that the oath they had taken would yield fruit.

It began sometime after midnight. A single sound shattered the perfect stillness of that evening. Some said they heard a child's cry. Others, the shriek of a bird. Still more, the moan of the dying. And others, the wail of an injured beast.

But whatever they heard at first, all agreed about what followed —the sound of piping.

Discordant, yet melodic. Soothing, yet daemonic. A single flute, the music of which did not bring joy. Rather, it seemed to bore into the minds of those who heard it, to steal their happiness and replace it with pain, taking some of their very sanity with it.

And yet as the sound passed, so too did the suffering. In its place came joy, for as the pipe played, the children were healed, one by one. By the time the last note died away, the town had been restored.

The people poured into the streets. They sang, and they danced, and they drank wine. Many things were done beneath the moon that I will not speak of here. But the sun rose, as it must on every night. And when it did, it rose on a day of reckoning.

The stranger came forth. He walked down streets that still echoed with the revelry of the night before. He met no one on his way to the church to collect his prize. He strode up the steps and pushed open the doors.

It was deserted, or at least, that's how it appeared. In an instant, a half-dozen men surrounded him, their swords drawn. The Lord Mayor stepped from behind a pillar, his countenance that of man who has played another for a fool. But to the Lord Mayor's annoyance, the fool still did not seem to comprehend that he had been played.

"Did you bring the boy?" the stranger asked.

The men chuckled, secure behind the points of their blades.

"Why no, my friend," said the Lord Mayor. "No, I think a new deal is in order. You get to keep your life, and all debts are paid."

"So you mean to break the bargain, then?"

The Lord Mayor took a step forward, drawing his own sword. "Did you not hear me? Your payment is your life. Oh, you had the others fooled, with your trickery and your black magic. But we know how to deal with witches in this town, especially the ones that poison the well and then claim to have the cure. You turn and you go, and if we ever hear of the like of you in these parts again, I will personally ride out and have your head."

The stranger took a step back and into the morning sun. "By your own word, then."

There was a flash of light and smoke, and when the swordsmen opened their eyes again, the stranger was gone.

What came that night became the stuff of legend.

Darkness fell hard and fast, and there were few who thought that it did not come several hours before its appointed time. The moon, a full half the evening before, never rose that night. Ebon night held sway, and silence joined it, the kind that breaks men's minds. But what followed made those who heard it wish that the maddening silence had never been shattered.

It was the sound of piping. But not one pipe. Nay, it was thousands. Drums had joined it. Deep, throbbing drums that pounded into the mind and chased away all thought. A dry wind began to blow, to whip through the streets and rap upon the doors. A chorus of screams was added to the cacophony. Those howls of pain were no illusion, however; they were very much of this earth.

Hell had come to Old'ham, the Devil seeking his due.

In his home in the forests, the woodsman heard all. His family huddled in fear, but he took up his sword. They begged him not to go, but when the woodsman looked to the mark upon his hand, he knew that he had a duty to stop whatever the townspeople had so foolishly started. He rushed into the darkness to the fate that awaited him.

By the time he reached the church, the roar of satanic song and the pitiful cries of the dying and those who wished they were dead had become an almost solid wall of sound. But when he turned the corner and ran into the High Street, it was then that his sanity almost slipped.

A great beast filled the city street. Or at least, that is how he perceived it. One moment, it was a monster, unlike anything he had ever seen before, with whip-like arms that buzzed and slapped against the earth in great thunderous strikes. Then it was a column of smoke and fire that roared and burned and spat out noxious fumes. Then it was a dragon, a great black dragon with the arms and wings of a bat. Then it was a swirling vortex of wind and dust that ripped apart all in its path. But whatever form it took, the piping never ceased, nor did the beating of the drums.

As he watched, the form, whatever form it was at the moment, continued its slow march towards him. A door would swing open or a wall would be torn down, the inhabitants therein vomited out into the streets screaming and gibbering and clawing at the ground. Before him they were sliced in half by a crashing, caber-like arm; snapped up by the jaws of an enormous maw, ripped apart by a whirlwind, or turned to ash by toxic vapors. The end was always the same; they all died. All of them—men, women, and children.

The woodsman dropped his sword. He stepped forward. "You want a sacrifice!" he screamed. "Take me."

The swirling chaos before him halted. Then it seemed to part, and out stepped the stranger. His amber cloak billowed like smoke, and in his hand he held a small flute.

"Woodsman, you would offer yourself as a sacrifice?"

The woodsman hesitated but for a moment. He closed his eyes and uttered a prayer to God—both the one that he worshiped, and those to whom his ancestors bowed before beyond the veil.

"Yes," he said. "I am ready."

There was a rumble that shook the earth. It came from the stranger. He was laughing. "Do you not see?" he said, sweeping his arm behind him as if to encompass the entire town. "Do you still not understand? What is the sacrifice of one, when I can have hundreds? You offer yourself now. But these, they offered themselves before. They swore the oath that you rejected. A blood bond, to make full the debt they owed if it were not paid—with interest accrued."

"But I am bound as well," the woodsman said, almost begging. "Take me instead."

"What does your life mean to me? I have lived a thousand of your lifetimes. Do you think I care for you, or this accursed place? Their blood gives me power, and one day, when it runs like rivers, when the power is enough, then I will use it to change the very course of the stars in the sky. And when they are right, all will bow before their true masters."

The woodsman looked down to the sword that still lay in the dust. The stranger began to laugh again.

"You are a fool. But I must say, bravery such as this I have rarely seen from your kind. Go back to your family. Tell them you love them. And then send them away, your wife and your child. This I give to you, but you must give me something in return. I will come for you. When I finish here."

Then he turned and stepped back into the storm.

The woodsman ran home. He hugged his wife and child tight, and then he told them to run, to flee to the next town and then the one beyond that and not to stop until they reached a place where no one had ever heard of Old Bethlehem. They did not protest. They knew that death was on their doorstep. They knew that this was their only chance. I hope that wherever they fled, they lived out their lives in peace and joy.

The stranger came to the house of the woodsman. The roof did not fly away. The wall did not collapse. Instead, there was merely a knock on the door.

The woodsman opened it.

The stranger stood before him.

"To you," he said, "I grant my pardon, be it on one condition. Here you will stay, and you will spread to all those who pass by my story. You will tell them what came to be in this town, so that all may fear the name of Nyarlathotep, the Piper in Yellow!"

———

You see, my friend, I am the man who spoke with death that day, all those centuries ago. And this mark upon my hand is the sigil of my mission—and my curse.

You seem confused? Oh you've never heard of the story of the piper? Well, I suppose the details change in the retelling, and there are many who stray within these borders and then go on to their homes or to far horizons who no doubt soften the edges, for the sake perhaps of their own sanity.

And of course, there's the name of the town itself. For I told you that, whatever its fathers may have wished, Bethlehem never really stuck. So it bears many names, in tales and in song. But there is one that is most prominent. One that seems to fit Lil'ham more than most. A strange thing really, for it is not only a corruption but an inversion.

Most people have never heard of Bethlehem or New Bedlam or Lil'ham.

No, in the story that gets retold the most, the story that most people have heard, the town went by another name—

Hamelin.

In the Details

– Silvia Moreno-Garcia –

They get details wrong in the telling.

The kiss does not transform him. The scales do not wash off from his body, the smell of brine clings to his clothes. The teeth remain, pointed and sharp, like the maw of a dangerous tropical fish or a shark. Tiny little teeth, white, serrated, in his smiling mouth.

Other bits are correct: My father did sell me to a monster to pay off a debt. It was quite natural, he had already sold my sisters to others; told them to put roses in their hair and some rouge, to lift their skirts when a gentleman paid the coin.

I was the youngest, so he saved me for last. He had me mend shirts and take in the washing. Hard work. No time for games or merriment. I called him "Sir" because that was the proper way a daughter spoke to her father. I spoke to his shoes, to the ground, not to him, my voice a whisper in the hovel we called a house. Sometimes he'd take my chin in his hands and tilt it up and he'd say "What a pretty mouth you have, so very pretty, like a rosebud." Or he'd say "What pretty hair, so thick and long." Or "Hush, my pretty."

My pretty, he called me. My beauty. My girl.

My. That's what I was. His pretty, pretty girl. 'Til the day when he came back home, pleased with himself and he said now I'd be someone else's pretty pretty one.

He said "Here now, beautiful, it's your turn. I've found a gentleman who would appreciate your company."

I said " No, sir, please no."

He slapped me, but not so hard I would bruise.

I went into the old quarters of the city, to a house of weathered stone and iron and coloured window panes. A house surrounded by a tall wall of stone, thick with ivy. A house of high ceilings and great chandeliers. And in the middle of this house – not a castle, they also get that wrong – sat a beast of slim, long limbs. Sat in the shadows, in the damp.

The beast my father pledged me to is the colour of moonlight, with skin that is almost translucent in some places. Pale thing from abyssal depths. When he sits still he could pass for a statue of the purest ivory. An ivory carving of an impossibility.

He showers me with gold. Gold chains, bracelets, rings. Some of them bear strange, geometrical designs of marine creatures. Carvings of people that look like fish and frogs that look like people. I run my fingers upon them and wonder where they came from and I ask him, and he answers, and he speaks in his soft, silvery voice.

Jewels spill through my fingers. The jewels of old wreckages lost at sea, rubies like blood, smoky black pearls and playful amethysts. The crown that belonged to a Spanish princess and went to rest upon a bed of algae now adorns my head.

When I was a child I read cheap little books of adventures. I played pretend. Played at pirates. I longed to find a ship and sail off towards coral reefs and azure waters, but it was not to be. In the beast's home I dress myself like a pirate queen, gold coins strewn upon the floor and a jeweled dagger at my waist.

I stopped playing when mother died, when I was six, but I can play in the beast's den. Play pretend that I am a pirate captain and sometimes a maiden and sometimes a slick sea serpent.

I went back home one summer, foolish nostalgia clouding my thoughts. My father's eyes were cold when he saw me, my sister's face listless.

They disliked my finery. The little ring upon my third finger, the silver mirror and matching brush in my bag, the cut of my dresses and the sound of my voice, the words I used.

"I do not like the way you look at me, little girl," he said. "The way you hold your head up."

"Why shouldn't I? Hold my head up, look you in the eye?" I asked.

My father said I'd grown proud and vain; I did not know my place.

He slapped me twice for good measure. Left bruises this time, which bloomed like roses upon my cheeks.

He said I would not be going back unless the gentleman paid more. He had been cheated. He'd gotten a rotten bargain.

I said "I must return."

He said "Shut your mouth."

He took the little ring resting on my third finger and the silver mirror. He sold them, sent a letter to the beast in the stone house and he wrote "If you want her you must pay."

I said "It's a beast that lives in the house of stone, behind the wall of ivy."

"'Tis just a cripple, a deformed child that should have died in the womb," he said.

I said nothing. He knew little of the world and my learning had surpassed his. I went to my room and sat upon the bed, listening to the patter of the summer rain against the window. I'd feared him once, but I'd been a child then. A child who wanted to play at pirates and sail the high seas. I'd learnt there be monsters, but not at the edges of maps.

Near midnight I heard a scream. Only one. Then only weak

murmurings.

I stood up and walked out of the room, past the overturned furniture and the carpet stained in crimson. Towards the pale beast, hunched upon a man. It was no pretty pretty sight, the creature wrapped around him like an albino eel, wrapped so tight, eating, devouring him bit by bit. And the man a pulpy bit of flesh without features. The beast has chewed his nose and lips, and was now savaging his hands, eating each finger like a bonbon.

"Hush, my pretty," I told my father, stroking his hair, which was matted in blood. "Hush now."

Then I touched the beast's shoulder and pulled him from the man. The rain had turned into a drizzle which washed away the blood and together we walked back to the old house of stone with its walls of ivy.

The kiss does not transform him. The scales do not wash off from his body, the smell of brine clings to his clothes. The teeth remain, pointed and sharp, like the maw of a dangerous tropical fish or a shark. Tiny little teeth, white, serrated, in his smiling mouth.

They get details wrong in the telling.

Of course they do.

Black Goat of the Hundred Acre Woods

~ James Pratt ~

The Little Yellow Bear paused and sniffed the cool night air. Up until now, the trail wound through quiet meadows and gently sloping hills where visibility was high and the likelihood of an ambush low. But he was approaching the edge of the Wood, where strange things had taken up residence since the night of that terrible storm. That was the night everything changed. He would have to be careful at this point. Though the sun wasn't down yet and they didn't seem to like the daylight so much, he had no reason to believe he wasn't being watched.

It seemed strange to feel such agitation in a place where he'd spent so many happy years. Every day had seemed like an adventure where anything was possible. There had been some close calls, but things were always sorted out by supper time. Sometimes a lesson was learned, sometimes it wasn't; it didn't matter. Each night he went to bed content, his tummy happily digesting a king's ransom in honey as he sleepily anticipated whatever pleasant diversions the next day might bring.

Then the storm came and everything changed. How was it possible that, in the space of mere days, the only life he'd ever known had been relegated to that far off kingdom of Long Ago, becoming something dimly remembered during those brief and scattered pauses in the strangeness of his new reality?

The sun hung low and the sky was already starting to take on the angry red hue of twilight. The zoogs would be coming out soon. The Little Yellow Bear wondered if they were already about. He could practically feel the weight of staring eyes that glittered like gemstones gazing hungrily at him from out of the leafy shadows. No proper eyes for a furry creature, they belonged on insects. No, that wasn't right. They belonged on something from another world. There was nothing recognizable in them. He shuddered to think of what those eyes had seen.

The Little Yellow Bear contemplated bedding down where he stood. Granted, he was out in the open, but at least he had a good view of his surroundings. Traveling through the Wood at night was a far riskier proposition. It was *their* place now. Besides, it had taken him hours to pull the sled this far and his burden wasn't getting any lighter. He resisted the urge to look back for fear his heart would break at the sight of what lay beneath the tattered blanket serving as a shroud. The Clever Rabbit was gone. So was the Wise Owl. With the possible exception of the Curious Tiger, they were all gone. Now only the Little Yellow Bear remained. Who could have imagined it would end like this?

The Little Yellow Bear tightened his grip on the makeshift spear he'd cobbled together from a carving knife, the walking stick for which the Clever Rabbit certainly had no more use, and a bit of twine. Small and crude, it worked well enough. It had certainly given that shantak something to think about. A smile flickered across the Little Yellow Bear's face but vanished just as quick. With a little help, he'd managed to take care of the shantak. By then, the Clever Rabbit was already dead and the Gentle Pig was soon to follow.

The Little Yellow Bear decided the meadow was his best bet. He began gathering kindling and stones for a campfire. Tonight's meal would consist of the remaining leftovers from the picnic, the last picnic they'd ever have together. His tummy began to rumble as he lit a match and dropped it into the kindling. The Little Yellow Bear would have killed for some honey. Literally.

Hours later, the Little Yellow Bear laid down his book, a strange tale of a strange journey and all that remained of the Wise Owl's once grand library, and gazed into the fire. Sleep was out of the question. He wasn't sure how close the zoogs were willing to come to the fire, and he didn't feel like taking any chances.

Savage little creatures, those zoogs. Almost cute, the first time you see them. Then they look at you with those terrible, glittering eyes and a grin slowly creeps across their face, showing you what a piranha would look like if it could smile.

What a strange turn of events it had been, the Little Yellow Bear mused. And to think it had started on the day after the Fair-Haired Boy's going away party.

The Fair-Haired Boy was their friend from beyond the Hundred Acre Wood, where the Forest grew thick and gave way to the unknown. Inquisitive and generous, he had shared many of their adventures and his youthful insights had even saved the day more than once. They were all quite fond of the Fair-Haired Boy; even the Clever Rabbit, who could be cross with his own shadow. And so, after learning he must leave them soon, they spent the morning preparing a surprise farewell picnic in the shade of a small stand of pine trees. The Clever Rabbit, who bragged about many things and was actually quite good at a few, had fixed a fine meal and prepared a three-tiered carrot cake covered in a delicious vanilla frosting. The Little Yellow Bear, the Gentle Pig, and the Curious Tiger hung streamers and a large, hand-painted banner between the pine trees. The Wise Old Owl oversaw the whole thing, giving orders and dispensing advice whether it was asked for or not. Even the Melancholy Donkey's admonitions seemed half-hearted; like the rest, he awaited the Fair-Haired Boy's arrival with some anticipation.

Hours passed. As the sun crawled across the sky, the shadows lengthened until they were appropriated by the deeper darkness of the approaching night. As the moon rose, it was silently acknowledged among the friends that the Fair-Haired Boy wasn't coming. One by one, the guests bid their adieus and, agreeing to return the next day for clean-up, departed. The Little Yellow Bear and the Gentle Pig were the last to go. After seeing his timid friend safely home, the Little Yellow Bear walked back to the picnic site for one last glance. He wanted to be sure the Fair-Haired Boy hadn't shown up at the absolute last minute. Lit by the moon's pale glow, the deserted picnic presented a ghostly sight.

The Little Yellow Bear had always been fond of the moon. It was like an old friend whose visits were clockwork, yet whose appearance still seemed a pleasant surprise. He looked up into the night sky, rubbed his eyes, and looked again. The moon seemed… bigger. For as long as he could remember, it had been content to simply look down and smile as it hung in the sky. Now it seemed to *loom*, its familiar smile twisted into a lecherous grin. A shadow crawled across its surface, perhaps cast by something drifting through the vast, lonely spaces between earth and sky. If the Little Yellow Bear didn't know better, he would have sworn it was a ship, a ragged-sailed schooner adrift on an ocean of night.

That night, a terrible storm descended on the forest. It tore through the Wood like a rampaging beast, uprooting trees and howling its fury at the leering moon. Incomprehensible save in its malignancy, the storm raged like a living thing. Each lightning bolt was a snarl of defiance, each gust of wind a cry of impotent fury.

The Little Yellow Bear huddled beneath the covers. He could only imagine what the Gentle Pig was going through. It had already been late when he walked him home. He chastised himself for not inviting his friend to sleep over. A tiny little thing, the Gentle Pig could have comfortably stretched out on his couch. But hindsight was 20/20, except, of course, in the Melancholy Donkey's case. His hindsight was 20/40.

The next morning, the friends gathered to assess the damage. Blown to who knew where, no sign of the picnic remained. The stand of pine trees which had overseen so many picnics lay broken and scattered. Old and steady as the seasons, the storm's fury had reduced them to kindling. Trees or not, it seemed strange to imagine life without them.

The Little Yellow Bear was walking toward the edge of the clearing when he noticed a dark blur against the green curtain of the forest. A Black Goat was on the far side of the clearing, standing just outside the tree line and watching them intently. It stood on all fours, like a proper goat, but the tight focus of its gaze implied an intellectual intensity beyond the mild curiosity of a dumb beast. The Little Yellow Bear shivered. He had always found the eyes of goats to be equal parts fascinating and unnerving.

The Little Yellow Bear turned toward the Gentle Pig. "Do you see that?"

The Gentle Pig scanned the tree line. "See what?"

The Little Yellow Bear started to point but, when he looked back, the Black Goat was gone.

"Nothing," he said. "Never mind."

"Well, at least we won't have to clean up the picnic," the Curious Tiger offered. He always tried to see the positive in things.

"There's more to this storm than meets the eye," the Wise Owl observed. Everybody nodded in agreement, though no one knew what he meant.

"What does he mean?" the Gentle Pig whispered to the Little Yellow Bear.

The Little Yellow Bear patted his friend on the shoulder. "Don't worry. No one ever knows what the Wise Owl's talking about, sometimes not even him. We'll all find out together."

And they did. Hours later, the Curious Tiger came bounding into the clearing in front of the Wise Owl's house where the friends had gathered for afternoon tea.

"I've found something! I've found something!" Someone whose trousers had spontaneously burst into flames wouldn't have moved with more vigor, but the Curious Tiger's excitement was hardly contagious. His friends had long grown accustomed to his antics. To him, every leaf was a curiosity, every shadow a spy, every dawn the start of a new adventure.

The Wise Owl's gray-blue feathers ruffled and spread out like a fan, making him seem one-and-a-half times his true size. "Get hold of yourself, you silly cat! What are you going on about?"

"I was on my way to visit the Melancholy Donkey down by the bog when I came across...I came across..." He was breathless and therefore speechless, truly a momentous occasion.

"Yes?" the Clever Rabbit prompted. "What did you come across?"

"A bridge is something you cross," the Little Yellow Bear volunteered.

"Was it a bridge?" the Gentle Pig asked. "Is that what you came across?"

"Technically, you would use the bridge to cross something else," the Wise Owl said. "For example, a river, a stream-"

"A trapdoor!" the Curious Tiger exclaimed. "It was just sitting there on the edge of the bog!"

"Well, I hardly see how a trapdoor could sit," harrumphed the Clever Rabbit. "It hasn't got a proper bottom."

"I'm sure he means lying," the Little Yellow Bear offered. Sometimes, he wished the Clever Rabbit wouldn't take everything quite so literally.

The Curious Tiger looked at him indignantly. "I'm not lying!"

"That's not what I meant," the Little Yellow Bear protested.

The Wise Owl held up a wing. "Enough. Let us see this alleged trapdoor."

An hour-and-a-half later, which was how long it took the Clever Rabbit to prepare a picnic basket for them to enjoy on the way, they set off for the soggy, perpetually overcast bog where the Melancholy Donkey made his home. The Little Yellow Bear sometimes wondered if it was where the donkey resided that made him melancholy, or if, somehow, it was the donkey that made the land drab and inhospitable by virtue of his mere presence. It was a well-established fact that the Melancholy Donkey had the dubious ability to *sadify* everyone and everything around him. Six of one, a half-dozen of the other, he supposed.

"Does it seem like we've been walking an awfully long time?" the Clever Rabbit asked.

Heads nodded in agreement. What should have taken no more than an hour was stretching into two, as if the distance to the bog had doubled or even tripled, since the Curious Tiger had shown up with news of the phantom trapdoor.

Mentally composing a song about the seventy greater virtues of honey, the Little Yellow Bear was happily humming away when he felt a tug at his sleeve.

"Do you hear that?" the Gentle Pig asked.

The Little Yellow Bear listened for a moment then shook his head. "I don't hear anything."

The Gentle Pig nodded. "Right. No insects, no birds calling. Nothing."

"Ah," said the Little Yellow Bear. Setting the song aside, he paid close attention to the Wood the rest of the way.

The trapdoor was exactly where the Curious Tiger said it would be. The Melancholy Donkey was there as well.

"I don't suppose you came all this way just to visit me?" the Melancholy Donkey asked. Despite the heavy heaping of sarcasm, a sliver of hope that they had in fact come to visit him slipped through.

"Of course!" said the Little Yellow Bear. "But we thought that while we were in the neighborhood–"

"Right." The Melancholy Donkey wandered off, but not very far.

The Clever Rabbit tapped the trapdoor with his walking stick, as if to verify it was real. "So this is it? Curious, indeed."

The thing was ancient, that much was obvious. It *oozed* history. The trapdoor consisted of eight wide planks, each thick as a man's fist, made from a wood that apparently grew stronger with age. The planks were held together by thick iron bands, brown with rust which all but obliterated the curlicue letters or symbols that had been etched into them long ago. It could be opened by a large iron ring bolted to the middle planks. On one end, two large hinges held the thing firmly bolted to the massive stone frame on which the trapdoor sat

The Clever Rabbit looked at the Wise Owl. "What do you make of this, then?" he asked, a hint of challenge in his voice.

After a moment, the Wise Owl registered the silence, glanced around, and realized he was the epicenter of a ring of expectant stares. He sighed and cleared his throat. "Well, empirical evidence would seem to indicate it's…a trapdoor."

The Little Yellow Bear and the Gentle Pig exchanged glances.

"Brought here by the storm, perhaps?" the Gentle Pig asked.

The Wise Owl shook his regal head. "A reasonable theory, but one that falls apart under scrutiny. Note how the earth around it is smooth and undisturbed, though the thing itself is half-submerged in the soil. The frame was sunk into the ground by time and/or design, not a sudden, savage impact. This would imply the trapdoor has rested on this spot for ages." It was the shortest and most concise answer the Wise Owl had given in a very long time.

"Then why didn't we notice it before?" the Curious Tiger asked.

Again, everyone looked at the Wise Owl.

"Don't look at me!" he cried, his feathers puffed in exasperation. "I'm not the one who lives in this gloomy place."

All eyes shifted to the Melancholy Donkey.

"What?" he asked defensively.

"Maybe we're both right," the Gentle Pig said thoughtfully, but so softly that only the Little Yellow Bear heard him.

"What we have here is a mystery," the Curious Tiger declared, "and there's only one solution for mysteries! Who's with me?"

The friends looked at each other, looked at the trapdoor, looked anywhere but at the Curious Tiger.

"Don't be ridiculous," the Clever Rabbit finally said. "You have no idea where it leads. For all we know, there's nothing but dirt on the other side."

There wasn't. Working together and using the Clever Rabbit's walking stick as a lever, the friends managed to pull the trapdoor open, revealing a deep, dark shaft in which a cold, damp mist lazily swirled. Stone steps started at the lip of the shaft, steeply descending into darkness.

The Curious Tiger began bouncing in place. "I-"

"I propose," the Wise Owl interrupted, "an expedition through the trapdoor. We are obligated to investigate this phenomenon in the name of scientific exploration. Nay, we are compelled, for fate itself has called upon us-," (the Gentle Pig poked the Little Yellow Bear who struggled not to grin) "-to act as pioneers. It is our duty as thinking creatures to expand the furthest boundaries of knowledge when the opportunity presents itself. For all we know, we stand at the very threshold of an entire new reality. Dare we step across?" He glared at the circle of faces, daring them not to be impressed.

"Hmm," said the Clever Rabbit.

The Curious Tiger grinned. "We don't step. We leap!"

"Capital," said the Wise Owl. "Who's with us? Who else wishes their name to be recorded in the annals of history?"

No one spoke. The Little Yellow Bear felt the Curious Tiger's expectant gaze tugging at him, and so he focused on the Gentle Pig with all his might. His small friend looked up and slowly shook his head.

The Wise Owl shrugged. "Well, then. More glory for us. No time like the present." He regarded the shaft for a moment. "On further consideration, I think only a bit of preliminary scouting is warranted. A true expedition will require more planning."

The Little Yellow Bear thought he detected an uncharacteristic hint of concern on the Curious Tiger's face, followed by a barely audible sigh of relief in response to the Wise Owl's reassessment of the situation. "In that case, we'll wait for you here."

"Excellent. We shouldn't be gone more than a half-hour, an hour at the most. Come along, friend tiger."

As he started down the steps, the Curious Tiger looked at the Little Yellow Bear who looked away once more. Then they were gone, gobbled up by the molasses-thick darkness.

A half-hour became an hour, which then became two. The sun crawled toward the horizon, a relentless gauge of the dwindling daylight. That, combined with the strangeness of the day and thoughts of the long walk home, was steadily transforming the general mood from anxiousness to apprehension.

"How long should we wait?" the Clever Rabbit finally asked.

The Little Yellow Bear sighed. "Just a little longer."

The Gentle Pig tentatively approached the hole and looked in. "I...I think I see something." The rest peered over the edge. Sure enough, a pale smudge moved in the darkness, slowly growing larger as it crept closer and closer to the daylight. "Wh-what is it?"

"Is it a ghost?" the Melancholy Donkey asked.

"Do you really think it's a ghost?" the Clever Rabbit asked, sounding as if he wasn't sure himself.

A minute later, a white shape stumbled out of the hole and into the waning daylight, took a few awkward steps, and collapsed at their feet. A few moments passed before anyone realized it was the Wise Owl, his feathers miraculously changed from pinecone brown to bone white.

The Clever Rabbit, who had known him the longest, dropped to his knees and propped up his old friend, cradling him in his arms. "What happened down there? What did you see?"

The Little Yellow Bear crouched beside them. "Where's the Curious Tiger?"

The Wise Owl said nothing nor even acknowledged their existence. He simply stared up at the sky.

"Should we go after him?" the Melancholy Donkey asked.

The Clever Rabbit shuddered. "I don't think I can go down there. I…I can't." He met the Little Yellow Bear's gaze. "Don't look at me like that! He's my friend, too."

The Little Yellow Bear paused and took a deep breath. "The Curious Tiger can look after himself. He's had more experience with adventuring than the rest of us put together. We'll come back later when we're better prepared. Right now, we need to get Owl home. Let's get him on his feet."

The Melancholy Donkey nudged the Little Yellow Bear. "Put him on my back. I'll carry him." He shrugged. "I just don't want to stay out here tonight, not by myself."

"At least things can't get any stranger," the Little Yellow Bear said.

The Gentle Pig winced. There was no better way of asking for trouble.

Night caught them deep in the Wood, the dim heart of the forest where the trees grew thickest and the sun never shined. The Wise Owl's house lay on the eastern edge. At the Gentle Pig's request, the Clever Rabbit had fashioned a makeshift torch from a bit of wood and a strip of cloth from the picnic blanket. The fire's wavering light cast ragged shadows that danced like clumsy marionettes.

Just as the Little Yellow Bear was about to ask if anyone else had noticed the conspicuous absence of night sounds, the Clever Rabbit paused. Whiskers twitching, his ears swiveled back and forth. "Did you hear that?"

The rest of the group came to an abrupt halt. "I didn't hear anything," the Melancholy Donkey said. Now his ears stood at attention, too.

The Gentle Pig pointed to the base of a nearby oak, illuminated by a sliver of moonlight that had managed to squeeze through the thick canopy high above. "Look."

Half in shadow, something small and hairy sat trembling.

"Um, hello," said the Little Yellow Bear. The Clever Rabbit drew closer with the torch, revealing a long, sleek shape. Its head was tucked beneath its forelimbs. The digits on its paws were long and jointed, like fingers. It even had opposable thumbs.

"Here, take this and step back," said the Clever Rabbit, as he handed the torch to the Little Yellow Bear. "I don't think it likes the light." He bent over the huddled, still trembling shape. "There, there, little fellow, it's quite all right," he said in a soothing voice. "We're all friends here."

Head still down, the shape turned toward them. One concealing paw slid away, then the other, revealing an unexpectedly flat face, vaguely man-like but covered by a thin coat of brown fur. No longer trembling, it raised its head and slowly opened its eyes. The sight of them elicited a gasp from the Gentle Pig. The thing's eyes burned with a light of their own, like enchanted jewels illuminated by a mystic glow. It raised its left paw as if in greeting, slowly uncurling its fingers to reveal hooked claws. Then the corners of its mouth pulled back in an impossibly wide grin, displaying a mouthful of teeth as long and thin as needles.

The Gentle Pig took a step back. "I think-"

Hissing like a frightened cat, the thing launched itself at the Clever Rabbit. It slammed into him and they both toppled to the ground. The others stared dumbstruck as their friend grappled with the strange creature. Locking its arms around the Clever Rabbit, the thing sank its fangs into his neck. The Clever Rabbit screamed as the thing gnawed at his neck while simultaneously raking his belly with its hind claws, partially disemboweling him.

The Gentle Pig shoved the Little Yellow Bear. "Do something!"

The Little Yellow Bear stepped forward and brought the makeshift torch down on the thing's skull, knocking it off the Clever Rabbit and singeing its fur. More stunned than hurt, the snarling creature rose up. A pair of hooves struck it from behind with enough force to send it hurtling into a nearby tree, which it hit with a sickening crunch. Now both stunned and hurt, the thin stubbornly rose to its feet.

While his friends occupied the creature, the Gentle Pig reached into the Clever Rabbit's discarded picnic basket and withdrew a thin, gleaming object. He looked up in time to see the thing slam into a tree, only to rise up again. Black blood flowed from its nose and mouth, but its expression remained savage and fierce. The Gentle Pig took a step toward the creature then paused. Looking down at the object he held, he saw the Clever Rabbit's prone form reflected in its shiny surface. He squealed and charged the creature, which turned just in time to receive the Clever Rabbit's carving knife in its chest.

A moment later, two of the friends stood panting over the thing.

"Is it dead?" the Melancholy Donkey asked.

The Little Yellow Bear nodded. "I think so."

"So is he," said the Gentle Pig.

They turned and saw the Gentle Pig crouched over the Clever Rabbit. He looked at the Little Yellow Bear, his eyes glistening a little bit. "He wasn't such a bad fellow, was he?"

"No." The Little Yellow Bear slowly shook his head. "He wasn't a bad fellow at all." He reached down and gently closed the Clever Rabbit's eyes.

The Gentle Pig stood up. "Now what do we do?"

"Lovecraft," the Wise Owl moaned.

The Melancholy Donkey leaned in close. "What did you say?"

"Lovecraft," the Wise Owl repeated.

The Little Yellow Bear nodded in the direction they were originally headed. "Let's keep going to the Wise Owl's place. Maybe there's something there that can help us, or at least tell us what's going on."

"What about…" The Gentle Pig didn't have to finish. Everyone knew what he was referring to.

Glancing at their friend's body, the Little Yellow Bear quickly looked away. "We have to leave him here. We need to get moving and we don't know if any more of those things are out there. We'll come back for him when we can." He met the Gentle Pig's stare. "I'm sorry. He…"

The Gentle Pig nodded. "He was your friend, too."

They started again for the Wise Owl's house. As he walked by the still form, the Melancholy Donkey paused long enough to nuzzle the Gentle Rabbit's whiskered face.

The rest of the trip was nerve-wracking, but uneventful. After reaching the Wise Owl's tree-house, the Melancholy Donkey and the Gentle Pig saw to the Wise Owl while the Little Yellow Bear built a roaring fire and made sure that the doors and shutters were secured.

After making the Wise Owl as comfortable as possible, the Gentle Pig went to look for his best friend. He found him in the library. "What are you looking for?"

The Little Yellow Bear scratched his head. "What was it Owl said?"

The Gentle Pig thought for a moment. "Lovecraft, I think."

They glanced at the countless volumes lining the walls of the Wise Owl's expansive library. Somehow it seemed even larger than the last time they'd visited. The word 'vast' even came to mind.

"Of course, they aren't in alphabetical order," the Little Yellow Bear observed.

"Where do you suppose Owl got all these books?"

The Little Yellow Bear considered that for a moment then shrugged. "I don't know. I never really thought about it."

The Melancholy Donkey soon joined them, and they spent the next hour scouring shelf after shelf of books.

"Found it," the Gentle Pig said.

The three gathered round and stared at the book he held. It wasn't ancient, but certainly old. Bound in a rough green cloth, the book's cover was blank. Bold letters on its spine announced *THE DREAM-QUEST OF UNKNOWN KADATH by H.P. Lovecraft.*

"Do you think this is it?" the Melancholy Donkey asked.

The Little Yellow Bear opened the book. "Only one way to find out."

The work of an author with an astounding imagination, but a style only a few degrees removed from pastiche, *The Dream-Quest of Unknown Kadath* was the story of Randolph Carter, a man who escapes the boredom of his mundane existence through his dreams. After discovering the gate to the Dreamlands, a fantastic realm as real as Earth but accessible only through dreams, he embarks on a quest to find the gods of that land who dwell in the mysterious and forbidden land of Kadath. Descending the Seven Hundred Steps of Deeper Slumber, Carter emerges in a place called the Enchanted Wood where he encounters the zoogs...small, vicious creatures with a taste for human flesh. Deep in the Enchanted Wood, Carter discovered a massive trapdoor which leads to the Underworld, a dark realm inhabited by an endless variety of horrors, each more bizarre than the last. Worst of all were the-

"But it's just a story," the Melancholy Donkey interrupted.

The Little Yellow Bear nodded slowly. "Of course it is."

"What does it mean?" the Gentle Pig asked.

"The Fair-Haired Boy," the Little Yellow Bear said after a moment, "once told me something I promised never to repeat. He said that in the Outside beyond the Forest, he once came across a book. The book caught his eye because of the characters on the cover...a bear, a pig, a tiger, a donkey, a rabbit, and an owl. He began to read the book and discovered all his friends were in it, having the very same adventures that we've had over the years."

"What does it mean?" the Gentle Pig repeated.

The Melancholy Donkey glanced at the dark corners of the room. "It would explain a lot."

"I think," the Little Yellow Bear said after a moment, "it means that there's no such thing as 'just a story'."

They stood in silence for a few moments, contemplating the Little Yellow Bear's words.

"Suppose it's not just a coincidence," the Melancholy Donkey said. "So now those things, those...zoogs are in our story?"

The Little Yellow Bear shrugged. "Maybe we're in theirs."

The Gentle Pig scratched his chin. "Maybe...maybe it's a brand new story altogether. I wonder..." His voice trailed off.

"What do you wonder?" the Little Yellow Bear prompted.

The Gentle Pig's face darkened, then became a smile. "I wonder if we're going to be able to get a good sleep tonight."

The Melancholy Donkey snorted. "I'm sure going to try."

"Good," the Little Yellow Bear said. "You're going to need it. We're going to check on the Fair-Haired Boy tomorrow."

The next morning, the Little Yellow Bear found a knapsack and filled it with some food and a few odds and ends. Among them were a compass, a map of the forest with a signature in the lower left hand corner implying the map was the Wise Owl's own work, and some matches. After a bit of rummaging, he came across a ball of twine and a hatchet, which he used to make a crude spear with the Clever Rabbit's walking stick and a carving knife. After that, he went to look for his friends and found them talking quietly so they wouldn't disturb the Wise Owl whose condition hadn't changed.

"I'd like you to stay here and keep an eye on things," he said to the Melancholy Donkey.

"But…" The Melancholy Donkey sighed. "Oh, okay."

The Little Yellow Bear looked at the Gentle Pig. "Well then, off we go."

At the edge of the clearing, they turned and looked back. The Melancholy Donkey was watching them from the terrace.

The Little Yellow Bear waved. "See you soon."

He received a small nod in reply, which was a major expression of emotion for his friend.

As they departed, the Little Yellow Bear and the Gentle Pig kept looking back every few minutes until the Wise Owl's house was swallowed up by the forest.

"Do you think they'll be alright?" the Gentle Pig asked.

The Little Yellow Bear nodded. "They'll be fine," he said, trying to sound as sincere as possible.

They had never been to the Fair-Haired Boy's house before. It was too close to the Outside for comfort. They didn't even know what the Outside actually was. The forest wasn't just their home; it was the totality of their existence. It was hard to imagine anything beyond the forest, anything…outside.

They walked for hours, sometimes talking but mostly in silence. When they did speak, it was of trivialities. Out of the Wood and beneath the warm glow of the sun, it was almost possible to pretend the previous day had been a nightmare. Their mood began to lighten, and a few jokes were even exchanged. Then a mundane rabbit darted into view and vanished just as quick, taking with it what little good cheer they had managed to regain.

The Little Yellow Bear checked the compass he had taken from the Wise Owl's house. A lifetime ago, the Fair-Haired Boy had proudly showed them a compass he'd received on his birthday, telling them his house lay exactly halfway between North and East. It was the closest thing to directions they had.

Night found them in a meadow that stretched across a wide valley where they decided to make camp. After a light supper, they bedded down and took turns assigning names to unfamiliar constellations as they drifted off to sleep. Only later did it occur to the Little Yellow Bear that even the stars seemed different than before.

During the night, a shadow detached itself from the inky blackness beyond the ring of firelight and crept toward the camp. Though man-shaped, its eyes blazed with reflected light and it sniffed the air like a beast. Had the Little Yellow Bear or the Gentle Pig been awake, they would have glimpsed a hunched figure, gangly as a scarecrow, with a strange mixture of human and canine features.

Perhaps the strange figure wasn't partial to bear or pig meat. Perhaps it was simply curious. Whatever the case, it was content to quietly rummage through the Little Yellow Bear's knapsack before fading back into the night empty-handed.

Morning came. Rising with the sun, the friends packed up camp and were quickly on their way.

"I had a strange dream last night," the Gentle Pig said.

"That something came into the camp and was watching us sleep?"

"No," he replied, shaking his head. "I dreamed we were playing hide-and-seek in the Wood. Everybody was there, even the Fair-Haired boy. He seemed a little sad, though."

"Hmm. Maybe you were dreaming of one last game before he had to leave for good."

"Maybe. All in all, it was a nice dream."

The rest of the trip was uneventful. Nothing sprung out of the tall grass, nor came down from the trees or across the hills to harass them. Spirits rising, they were in reasonably good moods when they reached their destination.

The Little Yellow Bear knew they had come to the end of their journey when he saw the house. It was exactly what he'd pictured based on the Fair-Haired Boy's description. Before them stood a quaint cottage; wide and cozy, it seemed like a mansion in their eyes. For a child, it would have been the perfect place to pause between adventures and rest one's weary head. Except…

Except that the house looked quite old and decrepit. It appeared to have stood abandoned for decades, untouched by any hand except the hand of time.

No one answered their knock. The Little Yellow Bear wiped dirt from a window and peered in. The walls were bare, and dust lay thick as a carpet on the floor. There was nothing to imply that the cottage had ever enjoyed a single occupant.

The Gentle Pig shivered. "What does it mean?"

The sun had vanished behind brooding clouds spread thick across a dull gray sky. A heavy fog had crept up on them, hungrily gobbling up the world as it went. Past ten feet away, the cottage would have been nothing more than a pale smudge.

"I don't know," the Little Yellow Bear replied, shaking his head. "Let's see what's out back."

Rounding the corner, they stopped and stared in silence.

"How did we miss that?" the Gentle Pig finally asked.

The cottage sat at the foot of a stony mountain whose peaks were obscured by a thick mist. Carved into the rough face of the mountain was a series of stone steps. Like the mountain peaks, the upper steps vanished in the mist.

"How many steps do you suppose there are?" the Gentle Pig

asked.

"Seven hundred would be my guess." The Little Yellow Bear wanted to smile but knew that if he smiled, he might laugh and if he laughed, he might not be able to stop.

The Gentle Pig eyed the steps apprehensively. "What do we do now?"

The Little Yellow Bear thought for a moment. "I don't know about you, but I think I've had enough adventuring for a while. I just want to go home."

The Gentle Pig released the breath he had been holding. "Agreed."

"Should we stay the night here? Perhaps look for a way into the cottage?"

The Gentle Pig looked at the cottage and shivered. "I'd rather not. I...I don't like it here. It doesn't feel real. You know what it feels like? Like we've stepped into a painting. It's a very convincing painting, almost good enough to fool one into believing it's the real thing, but a painting nonetheless."

"Hmm." The Little Yellow Bear scratched his chin. "For some reason, the word 'unraveling' keeps popping into my head. Anyway, I concur. Let's see how far we can get before sundown."

They only talked for a little while before falling into a semi-comfortable silence. Neither was used to so much exertion. However, most of the toll was mental. It wasn't like the friends hadn't already seen some amazing sights in their time, or had adventures almost as exciting as those in the storybooks. The Little Yellow Bear knew for a fact that dragons were real, as were brownies and bunyips and boggarts, though he knew them by other names. But nothing could have prepared them for this. It was as if the world they knew was a tapestry, slowly unraveling in preparation to become something new.

It was hard to tell what sort of progress they were making. The fog at the cottage was following them home, muffling light and sound as it closed in on them. The landscape was soon reduced to a thick gray soup, rendering distance a meaningless concept. There was no longer any real distinction between earth and sky, no distant horizon to demarcate where a given point stopped and another began. They could only judge the sun's progress and the passing of time by the relative shades of the murkiness that had swallowed the world.

"Well," the Little Yellow Bear said, "this is as good a place as any, I suppose. Let's get a fire going, shall we?"

The Gentle Pig nodded. "That would be nice."

Less than an hour later they were enjoying a warm supper before a roaring fire, both courtesy of food and matches found at the Wise Owl's place. Neither had spoken in a while. Rather than being uncomfortable, the silence was like a haven from the chaos of the previous days. No matter what the words, speaking would break the spell and invite the chaos back in. The Little Yellow Bear cringed when the Gentle Pig finally spoke.

"I…I have this feeling. I don't know how to describe it. It's like a…a sense of…"

The Little Yellow Bear sighed. "Finality?"

He considered that for a moment. "Hmm. Maybe that's what it is, finality. What do you suppose that means?"

The Little Yellow Bear shrugged. "I don't know. Everything comes to an end eventually. Maybe…maybe it means whatever has been going on is finally winding down."

"Maybe. Good night, Bear."

"Good night, Pig."

Within minutes, the Gentle Pig was asleep. The Little Yellow Bear soon followed.

Tap, tap, tap.

The Little Yellow Bear moaned. "What is it, P-"

A furry, long-fingered hand clamped over his mouth. His eyes flew open and he found himself face to snout with a saucer-eyed dream-thing, a haunter of nightmares made flesh and blood. The Little Yellow Bear had once seen a dog from a distance and that was what the thing put him in mind of, more or less. The dog he had seen had been four-legged and mundane. Crouching on two legs, this thing had the arms and torso of a man. Smelling of earth and moss, it pressed a thin, hook-clawed finger to its snout. The Little Yellow Bear recognized the gesture and what it implied. Something nasty was nearby.

The thing pointed to the far side of the fire where the Gentle Pig lay. Something was over there, a large, sinuous shape whose diamond-pattern scales glittered in the moonlight. The smacking and tearing sounds of a predator hungrily feeding could be heard as the shape bit and tore into something just out of view.

The dog-faced thing removed its hand from the Little Yellow Bear's mouth and faded back into the darkness. Creeping out of his bedroll, the Little Yellow Bear started to follow before remembering the Gentle Pig. He began crawling toward his makeshift spear instead. Weapon in hand, he slowly circled the fire, giving him a better view of the serpent-thing. Resembling the sort of creature that might be seen on an ancient mariner's sea-map, it had a sinewy, reptilian body with an earless, bullet-shaped head at the end of a serpentine neck. Folded tight against its body was a pair of membranous, thick-veined wings. Teeth and claws slick with gore, it was too absorbed in its meal to notice the small, quiet form creeping up on it.

The Little Yellow Bear already had a fair idea of what the serpent-thing was eating, but actually seeing it was another matter. He simply watched for a moment, a casual bystander without any role to play in the scene unfolding a few feet away. The world became hazy and indistinct, a dream version of itself, the blurring of perception just before unconsciousness or sleep.

Pausing in its ghastly meal, the thing's head slowly swiveled until it faced the Little Yellow Bear. Its liquid-metal cluster of arachnid orbs locked onto the Little Yellow Bear's button-eyes.

The Little Yellow Bear blinked and the world exploded back into focus. The serpent-thing lunged; its long neck snapped whip-like at the Little Yellow Bear who dove aside and came up on one knee, spear at the ready. The thing's bullet-shaped head swayed back and forth, tracking the Little Yellow Bear as he climbed to his feet. Keeping the point of his spear between them, he began to circle the thing. The Little Yellow Bear had almost made a complete circuit around the creature when it struck again.

Coming in low, it bit deep into the Little Yellow Bear's left thigh and latched on. The Little Yellow Bear screamed and stabbed at the thing's head; strong as chainmail, its thick scales turned the spear point aside. Ignoring the spear, it continued to chomp down; its jaws ground together like a bone-crushing vice.

Up until that point, the worst pain the Little Yellow Bear had ever experienced was a dozen or so near-simultaneous bee stings during an ill-fated honey gathering expedition. Comparing it to being poked with a thousand red-hot needles, he couldn't have imagined anything worse.

This was worse. Wave after wave of pain washed over him, threatening to drown him in a tide of relentless agony. Using the spear as a club, the Little Yellow Bear beat at the thing but might as well have been hitting it with a peacock feather. Head buzzing like a crowded beehive, the world was melting before his eyes. The Little Yellow Bear collapsed, the spear tumbling from his fingers. A moment passed before he realized that the thing had let go.

The Little Yellow Bear opened his eyes. Through a red haze, he saw the winged serpent rear up, hissing at something across the fire. On the other side crouched the dog-faced thing; it held a good-sized rock in either hand. The man-dog threw one of the rocks, which the serpent-creature easily dodged. While the creature was distracted, the Little Yellow Bear retrieved his spear and jabbed the thing in the rump. The blow did no real damage but diverted the thing's attention long enough for man-dog to connect with the other rock, striking it on the left side of its head. Enraged, it snapped wildly at the air before returning its attention to the Little Yellow Bear. The thing reared up and the Little Yellow Bear tumbled backwards, raising his spear as the creature struck. Mouth wide and fangs dripping in anticipation, the thing's head shot forward only to impale itself on the modest spear that had once been a walking stick and a carving knife. The creature's jaws clamped down, driving the point of the spear through its gullet and out the back of its neck. Jerking backwards as if stung, it shook its head violently and clawed at its snout in a vain attempt to dislodge the spear.

The nightmare-thing collapsed, twisting and squirming like an immense worm impaled on a fisherman's hook as it shredded its own snout. Snarling like a real dog, the dog-faced creature charged on all fours, leapt through the air, and landed on the thing's back. It bit into the serpent-creature's neck and tried to latch on but the creature dislodged it with a shrug. Tumbling across the ground, the man-dog was back on its feet in an instant. Twice more it charged and twice more was rebuffed.

Bleeding profusely from mostly self-inflicted wounds, the creature's thrashing slowly subsided. It finally emitted a hacking, gurgling sound and lay still. Approaching it cautiously, the man-dog held a large rock. The thing seemed to sense the impending danger and began to stir; unable to rise, it lay back down. It didn't even look up when the dog-faced creature raised the rock high above its head and brought it down with tremendous force, then did so again and again. The thing's skull burst open after the forth blow, disgorging something that looked like cottage cheese.

Oblivious to his own wounds, the Little Yellow Bear sat and

stared. It wasn't like before, when he had felt a sense of detachment as he watched the serpent-thing feed on his friend. Now part of the scene, he was simply too numb and exhausted to do anything about it.

The Gentle Pig moaned.

No, the Little Yellow Bear thought.

Nothing could have lived through that. The Gentle Pig was practically in two pieces. Then he moaned again and the Little Yellow Bear was at his side.

"Please," the Gentle Pig whispered. "Please."

He's going to ask me to kill him, the Little Yellow Bear thought. *Not that. Anything but that.*

"Not here," he said. "Not here. I want…I want to…go home."

The Little Yellow Bear nodded. He understood. "I'd never leave you out here."

"I know." The Gentle Pig took a deep breath. When he exhaled, his throat made a wet, raspy sound. "You…I…"

"Pig?"

The Gentle Pig's eyes drifted to the left, rolled back, and closed. The Little Yellow Bear sat in silence. A few minutes passed before he realized the man-dog was watching him, its furry head cocked to one side. The Little Yellow Bear motioned toward his backpack. The creature fetched the backpack then sat nearby as he washed the wound on his leg with water from the canteen. Afterward, he wrapped the wound with bandages made from strips of cloth shredded from the Gentle Pig's bedroll.

One more chore and it would be time to go home. The man-dog circled and sniffed the serpent-thing's carcass, occasionally pausing to urinate on it while the Little Yellow Bear set about building a crude sled. It took him a few hours to figure out the simplest and most effective way of using the limited materials at hand but, once he was finished, he ended up with something actually quite decent.

All that remained was to load the sled which he did as gently as possible. Afterward, he covered the sled's contents with the Gentle Pig's blanket.

The dog-faced creature watched him struggle with the sled for a half-minute before intervening. The Little Yellow Bear wasn't sure how much it understood, but it certainly seemed to understand what was needed. Leaning on the spear, the Little Yellow Bear set off with the man-dog and the sled close behind. He looked back only once, when they topped a hill which would soon obscure the clearing from sight. He half expected a bittersweet storybook scene with the ghost of his friend standing on the spot where he died, perhaps waving and wearing the hint of a smile on his lips, but only the serpent-thing's twin rows of alien eyes looked back.

The journey back was surprisingly uneventful. That night they broke for camp during which they managed to communicate with gestures and images traced in the dirt. The man-dog indicated that the zoogs, the species of glittery-eyed creature the Little Yellow Bear and his friends had encountered earlier, were the mortal enemy of its own kind. After witnessing the thing's death, the dog-faced creature felt it owed the friends a debt of gratitude. Sadly, the Gentle Pig was already dead by the time it caught up with them.

They reached the Wise Owl's house early the next day, where it was obvious something had smashed its way in through the windows. The dog-faced creature shied away from the house so the Little Yellow Bear entered alone. The interior was ransacked. Owl lay on the floor, feathers slightly ruffled but otherwise untouched. A quick check verified that he wasn't breathing. Of the Melancholy Donkey, there was no sign.

In a way, the Wise Owl's death was a blessing. It would have broken his heart to see his beloved library, accumulated slowly and painstakingly over the course of a lifetime, reduced to dog-eared shreds. The sight of the library, a place the Little Yellow Bear had been as fond of as its owner, was the straw that broke the donkey's back. The tears came in a torrent, but vanished just as quickly. Time waited for no bear, and night was creeping up on them. He would come back later and see to the Wise Owl. For now, it was time to move on.

The Little Yellow Bear managed to scrounge up a few supplies for the rest of the trip. He thought of spending the night at the Wise Owl's place, but immediately changed his mind. It wasn't really Wise Owl's place anymore. It was just a place. Like his friends and the life he had once known, Wise Owl's place now existed only in his memories.

For years, his safe, predictable existence had seemed eternal, as dependable and changeless as the path of the sun and the cycles of the moon. There was something to be said for the conventional, for monotony and routine. For all the claims he had once made at longing for adventure, maybe he had known all along that pretend adventures were preferable to the real thing.

As the Little Yellow Bear was leaving, he noticed the corner of a book peeking out from under the shredded remains of Owl's couch. It was the copy of *The Dream-Quest of Unknown Kadath* that he had started reading after they brought the Wise Owl home. The Little Yellow Bear slipped the book into his backpack, took one last look at the corpse of his former life, and left.

The dog-faced creature had slipped away. Apparently, whatever obligation had compelled it to partner up with him had been satisfied. The Little Yellow Bear had almost reached a point that was beyond despair, but still had enough energy left for a bit of melancholy. He was used to companionship and didn't relish the premise of walking home alone, much less the lonely life to come. Sighing, he hoisted the sled-straps and began to walk.

And now we're back to where we started, with the Little Yellow Bear camped out at the edge of the Wood, his only companion a small, motionless shape beneath a makeshift shroud. With one eye, he watched for zoogs, with the other he finished reading The Dream-Quest of Unknown Kadath. At one point in the story, the main character encountered something called a shantak, a savage, bird-like creature with the head of a horse. Even though the description didn't quite match, he suspected he and the man-dog had faced such a creature the night before.

Hours passed and nothing emerged from the Wood. By the time the Little Yellow Bear fell asleep, the moon was well past its zenith. During the few hours he slept, he had a strange and disturbing dream. The Little Yellow Bear found himself in a narrow high-ceilinged hall, with walls of roughly-chiseled stone. Lacking doors and windows, he intuitively knew it was an abode of ghosts. Torches sitting in sconces evenly spaced throughout the hall provided a feeble light, casting restless shadows. All his friends were there save the Curious Tiger, sitting still as statues at an ancient oak table in the center of the hall. Like the stone walls, the table looked crudely made but timeless and sturdy. The food and drink set before them lay untouched beneath a thick blanket of cobwebs and dust. After an eternity, the Gentle Pig slowly turned and looked at the Little Yellow Bear. His mouth began to open, and the Little Yellow Bear's ears were filled with a sound as furious and terrible as the howl of a hurricane wind.

The Little Yellow Bear awoke with a start. After a minute trying to rub the sleep from his eyes, he realized the meadow was obscured by thick fog. Though no wind blew, he suspecting it was the same fog that had swallowed the Fair-Haired Boy's cottage.

An odd thought occurred to the Little Yellow Bear. The fog blotted out the world, not by obscuring it, but by eating it. It was a malignant tumor infiltrating the Forest, feasting on the familiar even as it left a strange new reality in its wake. Whatever it was, the ancient and wicked thing that had come with the storm had already claimed the Wood. Soon, nothing would be left of the Little Yellow Bear's world save for the Little Yellow Bear himself.

And yet even that wasn't true. He was no longer the Little Yellow Bear who had helped prepare for the Fair-Haired Boy's party only days earlier. Like the rest of his world, that other Bear had also been stolen away. There was nothing left of that other world save in his memories, and someday even those would fade.

The Little Yellow Bear reached the Gentle Pig's house that afternoon. After burying his friend, he fashioned a tombstone from a plank. Carved into the tombstone were the Gentle's Pig's name and the simple epitaph, "Here lies my friend." He considered saying something but ended up leaving as he had come...in silence.

From there, it was a short walk home. The quietness was unbearable. The Little Yellow Bear spent the day admiring his favorite things and savoring the memories they invoked, memories of parties and adventures and lazy days that only he was left to remember. That night, he finished off every last pot of honey he had, indulging to the point of vomiting, and slept in his own bed for what he knew to be the last time.

The next day, the Little Yellow Bear restocked his supplies, then set off for the southern swamp which, to him, had already stopped being 'Melancholy Donkey's Place'. The sun was setting by the time he reached the trapdoor. With all his friends accounted for save the Curious Tiger, one last adventure waited.

After some effort, the Little Yellow Bear managed to lever open the trapdoor. Gazing down the stone steps, he squinted into the darkness. As before, the stench was horrendous. He lit the lantern and, carrying it in one hand and the spear in the other, took one step, then another. Nothing rose up from the darkness to claim him.

Pausing at the fourth step, the Little Yellow Bear looked back one last time. The Black Goat stood at the edge of the woods, watching him as it had on the morning of the Fair-Haired Boy's going away party. Maybe the storm had brought the Black Goat, or maybe the Black Goat had brought the storm. Maybe the storm *was* the Black Goat. It didn't matter. The forest belonged to the Black Goat now. There was nothing left to do but finish the last adventure. Within moments, the darkness swallowed him up and he was gone.

The Dunwich Ball

~ J.F. Gonzalez ~

When a traveler in north central Massachusetts takes the wrong fork at the junction of the Aylesbury pike just beyond Dean's Corners, he comes upon a lonely and curious country rife with backwoods rednecks and superstitious religious zealots.

It would be amiss of me to go into detail about the terrain one might come across when they enter this strange and desolate area. It should be enough for me to tell you that this story takes place in the hills of the upper Miskatonic Valley, far northwest of Arkham, and is based on two legends. The first legend is well known to most people so I won't mention it by title here; you will certainly recognize it once my tale beings. The second legend it is based on concerns what happened in Dunwich back in 1928 at the old Whateley farm.

If you haven't been to this area of New England, then let me provide some color for you: the countryside is rough and rambling with many hills and valleys. There are roads that run through great stretches of marshland that one instinctively dislikes. Indeed, there are fears that at evening, when unseen whippoorwills chatter and the fireflies come out in abnormal profusion to dance to the raucous, creepily insistent rhythms of stridently piping bullfrogs, one might think they are in another world. A fantasy world, perhaps. One that has its roots in gothic melodrama, or even the imaginative swept tales of the Brothers Grimm. Alas, this country is very real, with its ravines and heavily wooded hills and desolate roads that lead through sleepy little villages populated with structures that seem as if they are from another time. Most of the homes seem to harken back to an earlier century, for many are deserted and falling to ruin. Despite this, people still live here and they, too, seem to harken back to an earlier time, before cell phones were in wide use and computers had invaded our lives.

Strange things have always been afoot in this region. Four centuries ago there was talk of witchcraft and Satan-worship. Some of the older gentry in the village are descended from those who came from Salem in 1692. These families, the Whateleys and the Bishops, still remain in this section of the upper Miskatonic valley. The younger family members attend Harvard and Miskatonic University and, these days, they never return to the moldering gambrel roofs under which they and their ancestors were born.

This story concerns both families. The Whateley's tale has been told before, many years ago, by another New Englander who hailed from those parts. His tale recounted the terrible events that occurred in 1928 that left one of the Whateley's dead and the memory of an invisible thing rampaging across Dunwich, cutting a path through fields, trees, and ravines, leaving huge prints the size of tree trunks in its wake. This creature, whatever it was, was eventually destroyed by three professors from Miskatonic University who had been summoned to the Whateley farmhouse.

However, some say that the creature wasn't actually destroyed, that all the professors did was send it back to the world from which it came.

II

It was in the township of Dunwich, in the large and very

modern-looking farmhouse set against a hillside four miles from the village and a mile and a half from other dwellings (where, incidentally, the old Whateley farmhouse once stood back on that horrible day in 1928), where a girl named Cinderella Whateley lived with her step-mother Elizabeth Whateley and her two step-sisters, Zelma and Faye.

Cinderella wasn't her real name, of course; her real name was Cynthia – Cindy for short. Her father christened the nickname Cinderella on her when she was toddler as a token of affection. For the purpose of this narrative, we will refer to her by this beloved nickname that bears uncanny resemblance to the classic fairy tale.

Cinderella's father died, and since he left no will and was, essentially, the last in his line, the court saw fit to grant custody of Cinderella to Elizabeth, since she was legal next-of-kin due to the common laws of marriage. It should be noted that Cinderella's great-grandfather was alive at this time, and living in a small apartment located in the attic of the Whateley home. He was related to the infamous Wilbur Whateley, and it was rumored he was, in fact, Wilbur's first cousin. However, Old Whateley, as he was called in town, was too elderly and frail to properly care for Cinderella, and the court took this into consideration when granting legal custody to Elizabeth.

Cinderella was very close to her father and did not trust Elizabeth from the moment she first laid eyes on her back when she was a child. Back then, her father was absolutely smitten with Elizabeth, whose long black hair, wide, dark eyes, and her youthful figure, could entrance any man she wanted (and unbeknown to Cinderella, she had). Suffice to say, Cinderella's father was still reeling from the death of his wife, who had contracted a fatal illness and died in agony a few weeks later. When she finally passed on, Mr. Whateley was devastated. He had his only daughter, of course, but, in a way, he had lost his soul.

Cinderella, of course, tried to make things better for her father, but a twelve-year old girl can only do so much. Cinderella instinctively knew this even at that tender age, and so it came to pass that one-day her father brought Elizabeth home and introduced her to his daughter.

In time, Cinderella came to know Elizabeth's two daughters Zelda and Faye. Both were a year apart, with Zelda being Cinderella's age and Faye being a year older. At first the girls got along splendidly together, and for a short time Cinderella was happy again. In a way, it was as if her mother had never even passed on. Elizabeth would pack two large picnic baskets full of food – various meats and cheeses, bread, apples and grapes and pears, carrots and greens for salads – and they would trudge into the country for the afternoon. Cinderella's father and Elizabeth would spread out a large blanket and set the picnic baskets down and they would have a grand feast. Then, after lunch, the girls would scamper off into the fields for their own adventure while Elizabeth and Mr. Whateley reclined on the blanket. In light of how things later turned out, those times were, indeed, happy.

The happiness did not last long though. Her father married Elizabeth, and not only did she take his last name, he formally adopted her daughters. For a while all seemed well – her father continued his work at the University and Elizabeth kept house. Cinderella and her new stepsisters attended Miskatonic Middle School and later, the high school. The only people who didn't like Elizabeth were Cinderella's great-grandfather and Kevin Foster, the young man who lived closest to them.

Despite Old Whateley residing under the same roof, Cinderella had only seen him four times, and she thought he was a rather creepy old man. Tall in stature, Grandpa Whateley resembled Slenderman and The Hollowers from those creepy Internet memes she sometimes saw during the brief occasions she was able to steal away from her bedroom and log into the computer downstairs. She had no idea how old he was, but to her he was ancient. He always dressed in black, and his white hair was thinning and seemed to hang about his head like that of a mad scientist. His skin was pasty and pale, his face beaded with stubble. His watery blue eyes always sparkled with delight whenever he saw Cinderella, though. He would hold out his arms and say, "Cynthia! Come to your grandpa! Come, my child!" And Cinderella would go to him, knowing that she should, knowing it was the right thing to do, but still a trifle apprehensive about it. For whatever reason, there was something odd about her grandfather.

Kevin Foster, on the other hand, was a fairly young man. Blue eyed and standing at an even six feet tall and of medium build, Kevin favored goatees in the winter and was clean-shaven in the summer. He wore his dirty blond hair shaved close to the scalp in summer and let it grow out a bit in winter. He worked as a librarian at Miskatonic University and was lucky enough to dress casually for work. Kevin sported numerous tattoos of various corporate and sports team logos on his arms and back, which Cinderella thought were amusing – her favorite was his tattoo of a bottle of Heinz Ketchup on the underside of his left forearm, and the Monster Energy star logo on the other side. Kevin was a studious young man and he would take long walks through the woods, often winding up at the Whateley's where he would sit and talk with her father about all manner of things philosophical. He lived in a modest, well-constructed cabin deep in the woods about a mile from them. Her father casually told Cinderella one time that Kevin had a personal library that rivaled that of the Miskatonic University library.

Cinderella often imagined what Kevin Foster's house was like; to live in a house that was filled with books was something she found wonderful!

But it came to pass that one day, late in the spring of the previous year, Cinderella's father was stricken with fever and died. He died in agonizing pain in the bed he shared with Elizabeth. Cinderella tried to be at his bedside any chance she could, but was banished from the room by Elizabeth, who said, "Go! I will take care of him, for he is my husband!" Cinderella would do as she was told and wander down to the spot in the garden where she and her father had laid her mother to rest and she would cry, hoping her father would recover.

On the sixth day of his illness, Cinderella's father passed away. There was a quick and short burial service, and Cinderella spent the rest of that season in mourning, watering the graves of her mother and father with her tears.

Shortly after the court granted custody, Elizabeth took Cinderella's clothes and handed her some old clothing that was nothing more than threadbare rags. "Here," she said. "You can wear this from now on. The clothes your father bought for you will now be worn by Zelma and Faye."

When Cinderella protested, Elizabeth slapped her across the face and banished her to the basement. There was a little room in the basement that served as a storeroom. She locked Cinderella in this storeroom and wouldn't let her come out until the next morning. The next day, she made Cinderella prepare the evening meal. As Cinderella was working in the kitchen, she instructed her daughters to make up a bed for Cinderella in the basement storeroom. "That will be your new room," she told Cinderella.

It didn't matter how much Cinderella protested – she was beaten whenever she raised her voice. She tried complaining about Elizabeth to the local constable but he wouldn't hear of it. "The court has granted your step-mother legal custody," the constable said. "And besides, you Whateley's have been nothing but a thorn in our side since the inception of this town! It's about time somebody gave you a good thrashing!"

Cinderella couldn't believe what she was hearing! The town was turning against her? First her mother, then her father perishes and her stepmother not only inherits her father's money, but the family house and all its land? And Elizabeth's own daughters assume possession of those things that were once Cinderella's?

Where was the fairness in all of this?

That spring, Elizabeth and her daughters forced Cinderella into servitude. She was made to work day and night performing menial chores for them. Many of these chores consisted of back-breaking work – cleaning the floors, dusting the entire house, shaking the dirt out of the carpets, preparing all of the meals, keeping inventory of food and supplies, doing the laundry, making up the beds. After her chores were done, she would retire to the cold, barren room in the basement and curl up on the pallet that was made for her bed and cry. And as spring turned to summer, and summer turned to fall, the weather grew colder and she would curl up near the fireplace in the basement in an attempt to stay warm. By then school had started, but Cinderella was forbidden from attending. Instead, she was made to stay inside and toil at her chores all day, forfeiting her education.

Occasionally when her stepsisters were out of the house at school, and her stepmother was in town on a shopping run, Cinderella would steal away from her chores and snoop around. Most of her snooping involved sifting through Elizabeth's personal belongings, and it was how she came across receipts for arsenic in her step-mother's dresser. Shocked, Cinderella sifted through the receipts, finding not only proof of two tins of arsenic, the purchase dates corresponding to her father's illness, but another receipt which was dated three years ago – preceding her mother's death!

Was Elizabeth responsible for her parent's death?

My God! Is she planning to kill me, too?

Cinderella understood now that Elizabeth had murdered her father to gain his money, his belongings, and his house. In doing so, she had also gained a servant, the daughter of her late husband.

As the fall months turned to winter and then back to spring and then summer, Cinderella thought desperately of a means to escape, but there was none. After her chores were completed for the day, she would gaze up at the tiny window of her basement room, yearning to feel the fresh air of the lush forests. Instead, all she had was the drab, clammy basement!

When her father was alive they would get a stream of visitors every week, everybody from the delivery people, to travelers, to Kevin Foster, the man who was their closest neighbor. These people had seemed to enjoy their company. Since her father's death, their visits suddenly stopped. Cinderella had asked Elizabeth about this the previous winter. "They stopped coming around," she said, "because you're a Whateley and everybody around here despises the Whateley's."

Cinderella had almost answered, "But you're a Whateley now too. Did you forget?" But she didn't. To do so would only invite her stepmother's fury.

One day, after completing the day's work, Cinderella was chained up down in her basement room. Moping on her bed, she heard voices outside. Curious, she stood up and, craning her head, looked out the little window that was set up high on the wall.

Kevin Foster was standing just outside her prison, talking to Elizabeth.

She had to listen carefully to hear what was being said. "It's been almost a year since I've last seen Cindy," Kevin said (because the name Cinderella was one used only by her father, Kevin referred to her by her Christian name). "Does she still live here? I thought I saw somebody who looked like her working in the garden."

"That was my daughter Faye," Elizabeth told him. "Cindy no longer lives here. I sent her to live with a relative in Kingsport. I don't think you'll be seeing her anymore since she—"

Cinderella couldn't take it anymore. She was so taken aback by

Elizabeth's response to Kevin's question, she shouted out, "Kevin, I'm here! I'm down here! Look!" She started jumping up and down and waving her arms.

Kevin turned and saw her. For a moment their eyes locked, and he smiled, raising his hand to wave. For a moment their eyes locked, and he smiled, raising his hand to wave. He didn't see the look that came over Elizabeth's face, one of unbridled fury and rage.

Suddenly, Elizabeth launched herself at Kevin and brought him down. Cinderella heard him give a strangled yelp, then they were both out of her line of sight. She heard Kevin Foster give a bloodcurdling scream, which was suddenly cut off. A fountain of blood spurted into the air. Elizabeth yelled for her daughters. "Faye! Zelma! Get over here!"

There was the sound of running footsteps and Faye and Zelma joined their mother. The three women crouched out of her line of sight and all she heard was muffled grunting, the gnashing of teeth, the ripping of cloth, and what sounded like a frenzied struggle. More blood squirted. Then the struggle ceased and there was silence.

No, not quite silence.

There was the sound of chewing. The wet, slurping sounds of feeding.

Elizabeth turned to look at Cinderella. Cinderella's heart froze. Elizabeth grinned with bloodstained teeth. Her face was smeared in blood; it was in her hair, along the front of her dress. Her stepsisters sat up, also stained with blood. They looked like they'd just gorged themselves at a pig roast.

Cinderella fainted away in dead shock.

III

Afterwards, Cinderella was sternly punished – no food or water for three days and an extensive paddling by Elizabeth. Then,

Elizabeth told her she had to resume her work around the house. "The garbage is filling up and the house needs cleaning," she said. "Snap to it!"

Cinderella went about the next few weeks in a daze. What kind of monsters were her stepmother and to have killed Kevin Foster like that? This was just unbelievable. She felt bad for Kevin, and every evening at supper she was banished back to her basement room and given a supper of an awful, lukewarm stew that consisted of stringy meat, soggy potatoes and hard carrots. The broth was cream-based, not a beef-based broth at all, and the meat itself tasted more like pork than beef. Who made stew out of pork? She was forced to eat this wretched meal for breakfast, lunch, and dinner for the next three weeks. "You'll eat it even if you puke," Elizabeth said when Cinderella protested. "We made it especially for you. You eat every bit of it!"

Cinderella was too traumatized by what she'd witnessed Elizabeth and her daughters do to Kevin to even think of asking her stepmother if perhaps they had sought to get rid of their neighbor's remains by chopping him up and turning him into the stew she was eating. For that is what it was – Kevin Foster stew, with horrid potatoes and terrible carrots.

As fall turned into winter, and then into spring, and she continued to be treated horribly as her stepmother's slave, she continued to think about Kevin's horrible fate. She wondered if Kevin had any family who questioned what happened to him.

And she wondered about his great and vast library.

One afternoon, when the sisters and her stepmother were out of the house, she stole upstairs to the attic rooms where her great-grandfather lived.

Old Whateley was ancient, at least in her mind. He was still a hulk of a man, standing at the gargantuan size of close to seven feet tall. Despite his age, he was still rather strong of heart and mind. He recognized Cinderella at once and smiled eagerly as she closed the door to his rooms. "I can't stay long," she said. "Elizabeth will be home soon, but I had to see you and I've never had the chance to get up here. They hardly ever let me out of my rooms and – "

"But of course, dear," Old Whateley replied. He grinned knowingly at her. Cinderella noted that his rooms were cluttered with lots of manuscripts and books lying on tables, chairs and on the arms of the lone sofa in the center of the main room. There was an artist's easel propped in the corner with a large sketchpad on it with a drawing that contained strange, archaic shapes and symbols. Cinderella noticed one of the shapes painted on the bare wooden floor of the room and realized the entire floor was marked up by these symbols. The rumors of witchcraft she'd heard all her life from the villagers came briefly to mind.

"Tell me what troubles you," Grandpa Whateley said.

Cinderella told him. Old Whateley nodded, the smile remaining on his face.

"Pay attention to what Zelma and Faye have to report when they return this afternoon," he said cryptically. "I think you will find it most interesting."

"Why is that?"

"Have faith in your Old Grandpa." Old Whateley grinned. What remained of his teeth were blackened stumps.

A noise from outside signified that Elizabeth had returned, so Cinderella quickly left her great-grandfather's quarters and rushed back downstairs. She was dusting the living room as Elizabeth and her stepsisters entered the house.

Zelma and Faye were especially chatty, dressed in their best outfits and were positively beaming. "Have you heard?" Zelma addressed Cinderella. "Mr. Bishop is having a party at his estate – an old fashioned ball! And he's invited us!"

"He's actually invited all the girls at the high school," Faye said, her voice catcalling and mocking. "*All* the girls! I guess that would include you as well – if you actually went to *school!*"

Laughing, Zelma and Faye went upstairs, leaving Cinderella with her broom in the foyer. She hung her head in sadness. At one time, she had been friends with the Bishop family and knew all of his children, especially William Bishop, who was her age and quite handsome.

Over the next few days the two stepsisters gleefully planned their outfits for the party that was to be held at the Bishop estate. Cinderella continued with her duties and overheard much. She also caught a glimpse of the outfits her stepsisters acquired; Elizabeth had taken them to the mall in Arkham and bought the loveliest dresses for them. When the stepsisters saw Cinderella they taunted her: "Too bad you can't join us for the ball, Cinderella," Zelma said, as she posed in front of the full-length mirror in her room as Cinderella walked by carrying a large sack of garbage from Faye's room. Zelma did look rather nice in the dress, which was blue and hugged her frame beautifully. Thinking about the fun they would have, about the friends she once had who would most likely be at the Bishop estate, brought tears of shame and loss to Cinderella. She dropped the garbage bag in the metal chute at the side of the house and ran down to her basement room and cried.

The night before the Bishop's party, Cinderella couldn't take it anymore. Confident that Elizabeth and her stepsisters were asleep, she stole upstairs to Old Whateley's attic rooms.

Old Whateley was huddled over his great oak desk, which faced the large picture window that looked out over Miskatonic Valley. One gnarled finger pointed at a series of runes in the book. She heard him mutter something that sounded garbled and not intended for human speech.

"*N'gai, n'gha'ghaa, bugg-shoggog, y'hah, Yog-Sothoth, Yog-Sothoth!*

Ia! Ia! Gyaggin Cthulhu Fhtagn. Gyaggin! Gyaggin!"

Cinderella let herself in quietly and shut the door. "Grandfather Whateley?"

He turned around, and his expression changed from intense concentration to happiness. "Cinderella! You have come to me on this dark night, when the stars are almost right! What brings you here?"

Cinderella could hardly contain her emotions. Though she did not know him well, he was the only real family she had left. "I need help, Grandfather!"

Old Whateley's rheumy blue eyes appraised her from behind his thick spectacles.

"Your wicked stepmother banished me to this attic room and forbade me to leave it," he said. "But this suits me fine, for all my studies are undertaken here. She keeps me alive because she thinks that when I pass on, my wealth will pass down to her and her daughters."

"Your wealth? I didn't know you were wealthy."

"I'm not!" Old Whateley grinned. "But *they* don't know that."

Cinderella told him of the party at the Bishop estate, and her stepsister's gleeful gloating over their attendance. "It's just getting to me," Cinderella said, the tears starting again. "Ever since my father died my life has been terrible! All I do is serve these…"

"Now, now, Cinderella," Old Whateley said, a gleam in his eye. "There is no need to fret. I think I have just the solution for you."

Cinderella's cheeks were streaked with tears. "What's that?"

"You remember Master Foster who lived in the woods in that old stone house?"

Cinderella nodded. "Of course."

"He was set upon by Elizabeth and your stepsisters. I watched it happen from this very window. They *ate* him!"

"I know." Cinderella shuddered.

"I am told by the night gaunts that Master Foster's home is unattended. He had a rather large library that consisted of thousands of volumes, and holds copies of some very rare grimoires. One such book is said to be the Olaus Wormius translation of *the Necronomicon*."

Cinderella was confused. "The Necromancer? I don't know what that is…"

Old Whateley waved her concern aside. "The book itself shouldn't concern you…but it concerns me. I'd rather have the unabridged Latin edition, but Miskatonic University has it well guarded. They won't let anybody enter the room it is housed in. The copy Master Foster has will suffice, and it contains segments that are missing from my copy. Will you get it for me?"

Elizabeth nodded. "Yes."

"Good," Old Whateley said, nodding. "Here is what I need you to do."

He told her. It seemed simple enough. Cinderella merely had to sneak out of the house and off the grounds, make her way to Kevin Foster's home, locate The Necronomicon, and bring it back to the house.

"Bring it to me, and I will guarantee you will be at the ball," he said.

Cinderella was desperate to be out of the house. She was even more desperate to be among her old friends, to socialize again. "Yes!" she said. "I'll do it!"

That night, Cinderella sneaked out of the house while her stepmother and stepsisters were fast asleep in their chambers. She made her way down the narrow, unpaved road toward Kevin's home deep in the woods. The air was cool, tinged with the lingering fingers of winter that still hung on.

Eventually, she reached her destination. Kevin Foster's house was dark, the windows shuttered. The trees that grew around it were finally getting their spring leaves. Cinderella mounted the front steps to the large, heavy front door and tried the knob. The house was unlocked. Of course it was. He lived so far from town there was no reason for him to lock his house up, even if he did have an extensive library. Cinderella opened the door.

Kevin's living room was large, but was taken up by several floor-to-ceiling bookshelves. There was one sofa and one easy chair tucked in the far corner with an overhanging lamp for reading. Cinderella turned on the light – so far so good; the electric company hadn't turned off the electricity yet. Now she had to find the book.

The Necronomicon was a spell book of some kind, so she figured it would be filed accordingly. A quick perusal of the books in the living room told Cinderella that the bulk of the volumes here were fiction. She moved deeper into the house and saw another room just past the kitchen and dining room – a den of some sort. She turned on the light, revealing bookshelves on all four walls, all containing more fiction.

She checked all the rooms upstairs. More fiction, old magazines, and even more fiction, from volumes that appeared to go back to the late 18th century. Cinderella was giving up hope when she entered one of the back rooms upstairs. It held books on history, archeology, anthropology, and religions. A few titles on magic were salted in. The volume her grandfather was seeking was not among them.

She spied a small door, and opening it, found a closet with bookshelves crammed with a dozen titles, all of them old and moldering. Among them, was a package wrapped in brown paper with the word *Necronomicon* marked in black felt marker.

Excited, Cinderella pulled the book out and extracted it from the bag, verifying it was what she sought. Then she put the book back in the bag and made her way downstairs and out of the house, turning lights off as she did. She closed the door behind her, leaving it unlocked, and ran home.

The next day, Cinderella brought the musty old tome to her grandfather, who took possession of it with greedy delight. "At last!" he cried, his watery blue eyes dancing with glee. "I have it! The Olaus Wormius translation of *the Necronomicon! Ia! Ia! Cthulhu Fhtagn!*"

"The ball is tonight," Cinderella said, hardly able to contain her enthusiasm and trying to not to sound annoyed at the weird sounds coming from Old Whateley. "What can you do to get me out of the house unseen by Elizabeth?"

Old Whateley turned to her, the book clutched in his gnarled hands. "I will commence a spell for this." He regarded the book reverently. "This book has helped us Whateley's in the past; it will help us in the present!"

Cinderella tried to get her grandfather to commit to a more realistic method – she knew vaguely about her family's history and knew much of it centered on superstition. Cinderella was a millennial and, therefore, less inclined to myth and superstition. Despite her demands that Old Whateley explain how he was going to help her, he only replied cryptically. "Be ready at eight o'clock. When the sound of the whippoorwills flock to the house, you will be transported to the Bishop Ball. But you must be home at midnight – if you aren't, the spell will wear off and the consequences will be dire."

Cinderella had to leave his quarters because she heard Elizabeth's car pull up to the driveway. She spent the remainder of that afternoon doing her chores with a sense of frustration. She was going to miss out on the ball; she just knew it.

At six o'clock she took her dinner downstairs in her basement room and listened with envy as her stepsisters got dressed and made up for the ball. For the first time she wished the superstitions about her family were true and that her grandfather was right – she wished the Old Ones, or whatever they were – would assist her.

As Elizabeth herded her daughters out to the car, Cinderella stood in front of the mirror, a sense of blind hatred enveloping her. Then, she felt a change come over her. It wasn't subtle, but it wasn't as profound as she thought it would be; it was as if some force had reached down and taken her in its hand. Suddenly, she was looking at a completely different person in the mirror.

Cinderella blinked and the girl with the black hair, the kohl make-up around her eyes, the dark rouge on her cheeks, and the dark lipstick blinked back. It was still Cinderella's face – there was no denying the symmetry of her cheekbones and her chin – but the hair had gone from blond to pitch black. She wore a black dress with a wide V, her breasts supported by a black lacy bra that not only supported but also drew attention to her milky cleavage. Cinderella stepped back and examined the rest of the outfit – the dress reached mid-thigh; her legs were covered in black fishnet stockings, and her feet were encased in black heels. Cinderella bent her right leg up, her right arm braced against the wall to support herself, and inspected the shoe. It was hard, made entirely of glass, but it was comfortable, like a slipper. Unlike other high heel shoes she'd worn, they weren't uncomfortable at all.

The chatter of the whippoorwills outside drew her attention to the front of the house. Her heart fluttered in her chest. Old Whateley's words resonated in her: "…you must be home at midnight – if you aren't, the spell will wear off and the consequences will be dire."

It was five minutes past eight.

Cinderella stole upstairs and waited for the arrival of her transportation.

IV

The ride was a blur – Cinderella wasn't sure if she was driven by a black carriage pulled by several large, frothing dark steeds with fiery eyes and piloted by a rat-like coachman, or a sleek black limousine driven by a pale, cadaverous chauffeur. She didn't stop to ponder it; instead, she entered the Bishop manse by the front door, nodded at the butler, and made her way through the foyer to the large ballroom at the rear of the estate, feeling a sense of nervous excitement.

She felt alive, happy, and beautiful. She also noticed the attention she was getting from everyone as she entered the ballroom. Her outfit turned heads – she looked like a cross between a fairy princess and a Goth chick – but she remained focused and poised. She sensed that the boys all wanted her and the girls either wanted to be her – to have that power, poise, and sense of purpose – or they were jealous. And the two who seemed the most jealous were her stepsisters, Faye and Zelma.

Cinderella saw them out the corner of her eyes, but focused instead on William Bishop, standing with his friends on the other side of the room. She sensed insane jealousy coming from the sisters, but she also knew, instinctively, they had no idea who she was. If they had known, they would have raised a ruckus. Instead, they glowered at her from afar.

William Bishop did not glower. In fact, he seemed completely smitten with her. She remained calm as he tentatively approached and asked her if she wanted to dance. Until then, Cinderella had only been vaguely aware of the bland pop music pumping out of the sound system. William was dressed impeccably in a black suit, black slacks, a white shirt and a black tie. His suit coat was a slim cut, his black hair slicked back from his angular features. He looked like he could be a prince or a vampire, she thought.

Cinderella's first impulse was to turn him down – she didn't like modern pop music – but the song had changed. It was minimalist in sound – a simple drum beat, with echoing percussion, a throbbing, heavy bass line and sweeping guitar riffs, the singer wailing in an echoing, deep voice. It was at that moment that everything clicked together and she answered yes to William's invitation to dance.

And what a dance it was! She moved to the rhythm of the music she never would have thought possible. It was as if some other force was guiding her, influencing their movements. Some of the other guests attempted to dance but not everybody. Most stood around and watched as Cinderella and William danced together, completely mesmerized by each other.

At some point Cinderella found herself at the bar with William and he was getting her a drink. The music had changed again, this time to something completely different, and while other couples had taken to the dance floor, she could tell that people were sneaking glances at them. William asked her name and Cinderella gave it willingly. Whether he remembered it or not she didn't know – her guess was he didn't, he seemed so mesmerized by the overall ambience of the night.

Over the next two hours Cinderella and William talked and grew closer to one another on an intellectual level. They also grew more attracted physically to one another. They found themselves on the dance floor again, their moves becoming more suggestive, more sexual. This created a ripple affect with others in attendance, but it also sparked more jealousy in her stepsisters, who kept their distance. *They still don't know this is me*, Cinderella thought at one point. *But they're too afraid to confront me.*

Cinderella liked that.

"I think you're amazing," William said, as they stood outside on the veranda, off the main garden that opened up from the ballroom.

Cinderella looked up at him, her heart swelling. "I think you're amazing, too."

And then he kissed her and she kissed him back, and the world seemed to stop.

She melted into his embrace then, feeling content.

This moment was the happiest in her life.

The moon was large and glowed full. Curious, Cinderella glanced at her watch and was startled to see that it was ten minutes before midnight.

"Oh no," she exclaimed. "I have to leave!"

William looked surprised. "So soon?"

"Yes," Cinderella said, panicked. "I'm sorry!" She kissed him quickly, squeezing his hands, then darted away. "I'll call you!" And then she was off, dashing around the other partygoers who looked on in surprise and bewilderment as Cinderella hurried through the crowd. She ignored them as she entered the ballroom and ran through it in her haste to get to the front door and down the long driveway to her waiting limousine.

Rushing and nervous, she was dimly aware of the left slipper falling off her foot as she ran down the long driveway to the waiting limo. There was no time to stop to retrieve it – every second counted. She saw her driver, standing tall and straight. He quickly opened the door for her as she dived in the back. Before she knew it the door was shut firmly and he was behind the wheel, piloting them back to the house.

Cinderella checked her watch, her pulse racing. Eight more minutes…

Three minutes later, the Whateley home was in sight. Elizabeth's car was in the driveway. How was she going to get in without being noticed or seen?

Her vision seemed to go blurry. She felt her stomach flip, as if it was being turned inside out in her abdomen and for a moment she didn't know where she was.

Then she realized it was her basement room.

Cinderella blinked and looked down at herself. The black dress, the fishnet stockings, the lacy bra, the black glass slipper, they were gone. She was wearing her usual threadbare clothes – baggy jeans, and a stained t-shirt. She glanced at herself in the mirror – the makeup was gone, revealing her plain old self. Her blonde hair was frizzled, dirty and limp.

Cinderella sighed. She was back in the nick of time.

She could hardly contain her enthusiasm. She had to see Old Whateley. She waited until well after her stepsisters arrived home, complaining to their mother about the dark-haired Goth chick that had showed up to the ball and spoiled it for them. "William didn't even look at us!" Faye exclaimed. "He spent all his time slobbering over that whore!"

Cinderella allowed herself a brief smile as she sat in her dark basement room.

At three a.m., Cinderella stole quietly upstairs to Old Whateley's attic room and let herself in. She paused, letting her eyes grow accustomed to the dark. There was a presence here, something she hadn't felt before. And then she saw it.

The Necronomicon lay open on the floor, its pages turned to a horrible looking passage. The etched design matched the same image that had been drawn on Old Whateley's floor years ago. There was the scent of animal fat and blood in the air along with something else. Something dead.

Whatever it was, it was still in the attic room. Cinderella couldn't see it, but she sensed it watching her, waiting for her to make a move.

There was no sign of Grandfather Whateley anywhere.

And then…very faintly…she heard a noise. Whispering.

"I'm going to let you stay here," she said softly to the thing whispering in the darkness. "My grandfather called you up for a reason. He knew what was best for me, for my family. I have to trust that. He gave me a wonderful time tonight. I am going to honor his wishes."

She returned to her basement room and tried to get some sleep. Amazingly, she did.

The next morning she did her best to ignore her stepsisters, who were still smarting over their perceived treatment from William Bishop and the unknown Goth chick that had dared to steal their spotlight. Elizabeth made a crack at her expense: "At least Cinderella has no idea who you're talking about because the Bishop's did not see her fit to attend their party." That seemed to make the sisters happy, and Cinderella gave them this petty victory. She went about her chores – dusting, sweeping out the rugs, clearing the breakfast table and doing the dishes – with her usual perfunctory attitude. By noon, the stepsisters were off the Whateley grounds, embroiled in some other drama, and Cinderella finally had a moment to collect her thoughts.

The following day she overheard a rumor from Faye, who was talking to her sister outside. It seemed that William was obsessed with the Goth girl from his party and was looking for her. "I don't know why he's so taken with her," Faye remarked. "Bitch left him right before midnight and never came back. She even left one of her shoes behind!"

"Really?" Zelma said.

"Yes, really," Faye said. "William seems convinced she lives around here. You aren't going to believe what he's doing."

"What?" From the sound of it, her stepsisters were smoking cigarettes in the back garden while their mother was shopping in town, most likely spending more of her father's money.

"That shoe she left behind? William is going around to all the single girls in town and trying to see if it fits."

There was silence from Zelma on this. Cinderella listened, keenly attuned to what her stepsisters were most likely thinking about. This was confirmed a moment later. "What is he going to do when he finds her?"

"You saw how he was with her," Faye said. "He was completely smitten. Gloria Henderson said he fell in love with her and she's all he's been talking about since. If you ask me, he wants to find her. I wouldn't be surprised if he asked her to marry him."

The sisters laughed at this but Cinderella felt a flush of excitement in her. She felt her heart swell. The connection she'd felt with William was more than just genuine – it was solid, as if they were connecting on a deeper level. After hearing this, she was determined to meet up with William when he came around. After all, it was her foot that fit inside the slipper.

She tried not to let her excitement show as the day wore on. That afternoon, Elizabeth arrived home with groceries and the stepsisters told their mother what they'd heard. Elizabeth was completely supportive of her daughters and had heard the same story in town. "He'll be in this part of Dunwich tonight," she told them. "We need to make sure one of you can fit into that slipper."

"I can fit into it!" Faye exclaimed.

"No, *me!*" Zelma shot back.

The competitive tension between the sisters was obvious. Cinderella was clearing the dinner table as this was happening and it was at that moment when the sound of a car rolled up to the driveway. They all looked up and out the window – a large, white limo was parked just beside Elizabeth's vehicle and a portly chauffeur was opening the rear door for the passenger. Cinderella felt her heart stop as William stepped out of the vehicle.

While William was no longer dressed in his black formal attire, he still struck a glorious pose. His eyes watched the house as Faye and Zelma raced out of the house, their mother trailing after them. Cinderella started toward the door after them and Elizabeth whirled around, hand held out to stop her. "*No!* You stay here! This is only for girls who were at the Bishop's ball the other night!"

Cinderella wanted to say, "But I was *at* the ball," but hesitated.

To blurt this out now would only invite sudden anger and possible violence from Elizabeth. Instead, she hung back and approached the screen door as Elizabeth trotted after her daughters, who had already met William at the end of the driveway.

"You were at my party the other night?" William asked Zelma, his features curious.

"Oh yes!" Zelma exclaimed. "Yes, I was."

William gave her a quick once over and from this distance, Cinderella thought there was slight disapproval on his features. "I don't think you're the girl who was wearing this slipper." Cinderella saw that he was holding the slipper in his right hand protectively, keeping it close to his body. "The girl who was wearing it was smaller and more – "

Suddenly, Elizabeth was there, once again taking command of the situation. "Why don't you let her try the slipper on, William?"

William regarded Elizabeth for a moment, shrugged, then held the slipper out. "Okay," he said.

As William crouched down to help Zelma put the slipper on, Cinderella silently stepped outside. She closed the screen door softly, then began heading down the driveway, watching the proceeding with bated breath.

Zelma was having a hard time fitting into the slipper. She pushed her right foot into the slipper but it wouldn't fit – her pinkie toe and the toe next to it wouldn't squeeze into it. Zelma grunted in frustration as she tried to wedge her foot in another way.

"I'm sorry," William said. He took the slipper away and then turned to Faye. He glanced up at her, apprehension on his features. "You're about the same size as her," he said. "I don't think it's going to – "

"Let her try it," Elizabeth said. "It'll fit. Trust me."

Faye tried working her foot in a more careful way and met the same resistance.

William frowned. "I don't know…" he began.

And then Cinderella found herself in the throng. "Let me try it on," she said.

Elizabeth, Zelma, and Faye turned to her, looks of shock and bewilderment on their features. Elizabeth also looked angry and annoyed. "What are you doing here? I told you to stay in the house. This is only for girls who were at the ball!"

Cinderella ignored Elizabeth and stepped up to William. "Here," she said. She held her left foot out to him. "Try it on."

There was a glimmer of recognition on William's face. He bent down and took Cinderella's foot in his hands. Her foot slid inside the slipper deftly; it was a perfect fit.

There were gasped shocks from the stepsisters and Elizabeth. Cinderella's heart swelled and she felt a surge of power rush through her. She looked at William and for a moment their eyes.

"It was you," he whispered.

Cinderella wanted to rush into his arms but she maintained her composure. "Yes, it was me," she said. Then she turned to Elizabeth and her stepsisters and regarded them with a sense of triumph. "Elizabeth, you said this was for girls who went to the ball that night. Well…I was at the ball! I was the girl William fell for – and I fell for him, too. I lost my slipper in my haste to return home before midnight, as Old Whateley bade me to."

At the mention of the old man, Elizabeth gave a startled gasp. "Old Whateley! That old…"

"He's gone beyond time and space now," Cinderella said, this knowledge coming to her as if it was being fed to her from another dimension. "And the spell he used to reach it is still growing. It's going to finish what was started in 1928, when my great-grandfather first conjured it. And it's going to tear the three of you inside out and cast you into the veil!" A thought bubbled to the surface of her mind unbidden - *N'gai, Yog-Sothoth! Ia! Ia! Gyaggin* – but she did not utter it aloud.

Elizabeth and the sisters cringed in fear. Strangely, William and his chauffeur didn't seem bothered by this.

Cinderella turned to William and smiled. "You've found me," she said. "And now that you've found me, you shall have me!"

William smiled and embraced her. Cinderella hugged him back, not caring that Elizabeth and her stepsisters were speechless by this spectacle. And with that, she followed William into the limo. The vehicle sped away, leaving a dismayed Elizabeth and her daughters, reeling from the sudden turn of events.

V

Like all fairy tales, this one has a happy ending.

Of course, that depends on your definition of the term "happy".

Naturally, Cinderella was the girl William Bishop was searching for. After this bit of verification, Cinderella rode with him to the Bishop estate, where they rekindled their budding romance and, very shortly after, consummated their relationship. This pleased the elder gods.

Of course, you probably want to know what became of Elizabeth Whateley and her daughters. Very well. But I must warn you…their ending was most definitely *not* happy.

When the Bishop's vehicle retreated in the dusty gloom, Elizabeth and her daughters went inside the Whateley home. They still could not get over this sudden and huge disappointment. Elizabeth blamed her daughters of course, and they denied knowing the dark, mysterious Goth girl at the party was Cinderella. Elizabeth was so angry she broke all the dishes in the kitchen and began smashing the furniture – most of it valuable antiques. She was so worked up, and Zelma and Faye were so fearful of their mother, that neither noticed the growing presence that was now being felt throughout Miskatonic Valley.

It started up in the attic the night before, when Old Whateley completed his part of a spell that had been started by his infamous relative over eighty years before. That spell sucked him through a portal into another dimension. It had granted Cinderella the power she needed to ensnare William, and it had also let something else in.

That something had been growing in size and power ever since. It had hid among the angles of our dimension, always just out of sight. It grew until it occupied the entire top floor of the home.

While Cinderella and William consummated their long, happy life together, the majority of residents of this little section of Miskatonic Valley stayed in their homes. They felt a certain malevolence in the air. The old timers, perhaps remembering the stories their parents and grandparents told them when they were children, warned their own children and grandchildren not to go outside. They forked the sign against the evil eye and hung up signs and trinkets around their doors and windows.

And the arguing and fighting at the Whatley house suddenly ceased.

That night there was a terrible explosion from the Whateley home. Dozens of residents reported feeling – and even seeing – a large, black thing with great wings and appendages that resembled tentacles flying through the air toward the moon. By the time the volunteer fire department arrived, the fire had largely burned out at the house. Nevertheless, the state fire inspector and the state police were on hand. The local police kept residents away and when morning came they got a better idea of what had happened.

No trace of Elizabeth or her stepdaughters were found in the fire. The house and everything in it was in ruins except for one thing, found in the attic…the perfectly preserved copy of a very old book. A call was made to Miskatonic University who sent their head librarian. Upon viewing the book, the librarian took possession of it and whisked it back to the University, presumably to join its Latin-translated version under lock and key in the library's Forbidden Book section.

Cinderella and William watched all this from William's second floor bedroom window. He stood behind her, his arms around Cinderella's waist. She pressed her backside up against him as they watched the activity in the valley far below. She smiled, feeling content.

A lot of people were going to think that with Old Whateley finally dead that the Whateley line was gone for good. Of course they had not seen Cinderella since shortly after her father died, believing the rumors Elizabeth had spread that the girl had run off. They had no idea that Cinderella Whateley had remained in town after all.

That's okay. Cinderella smiled with satisfaction. *That is just what I want them to think.*

She turned to William, who smiled down at her. He embraced her, kissed her neck. She kissed him back. They stood at the window, perfectly content with each other.

Within the next day, she would feel her baby begin to kick.

<u>End</u>

Christine Morgan's previous works have appeared in several anthologies and magazines. as well as about a dozen novels in print, some self-published and the rest via various small presses; the next, His Blood, is due out from Belfire any time now. Recently she's had stories accepted for Steampunk Cthulhu, Atomic Age Cthulhu. Dark Rites of Cthulhu, World War Cthulhu, In The Court of the Yellow King, The Conqueror Womb, and Cthulhurotica II.

Jayaprakash Satyamurthy is a writer, musician and indentured servant to a vast feline horde. He has previously been published by the Lovecraft eZine, Andromeda Spaceways Inflight Magazine, Pratilipi, The Affair and Dynatox Ministeries. A chapbook of his short stories entitled 'Weird Tales of a Bangalorean' may or may not be published by Dunhams Manor Press by the time you read this.

Michael Wentela is the author of Fallen Is Babylon, a post-apocalyptic science fiction horror novel. His writing ranges from novels to short stories in science fiction, horror, crime fiction, mystery, thriller, or whatever idea sparks his creativity. He is currently a technical product support specialist for an international company. In previous adventures, he has been an award-winning journalist, a communication specialist, and an economic development professional. Among his other life lessons he lists the time he spent clearing brush from a mosquito-infested swamp, helping to build wooden steps to a bluff-top overlook and digging graves in a cemetery. Born and raised in Michigan's Upper Peninsula, Michael and his wife, Stephanie, now live in a century-old house in southwest Wisconsin with a purebred Irish setter and a cat. They have two adult children. More information about Michael and his writing can be found at www.michaelwentela.com.

E. Catherine Tobler is a Sturgeon Award finalist and the senior editor at Shimmer Magazine. Among others, her fiction has appeared in Clarkesworld, Lady Churchill's Rosebud Wristlet, and Beneath Ceaseless Skies. Her first novel is now available. Follow her on Twitter @ECthetwit or her website, http://www.ecatherine.com.

John Claude Smith originally wanted to be a horror writer; now he's not sure what it is he writes, he just knows it is dark, and he's the one holding a flashlight, shining light on those places most people want to avoid, scribbling notes. He's had over 60 short stories and 15 poems published, as well as a debut collection of 'not your average horror,' The Dark Is Light Enough For Me. His second collection, Autumn in the Abyss, was published by Omnium Gatherum in March of 2014, and is garnering much positive response and reviews. He is presently writing his third novel, while shopping around the other two and putting together a follow-up collection. Busy is good. He splits his time between the East Bay of northern California, across from San Francisco, and Rome, Italy, where his heart resides always.

Michael Griffin's short fiction has appeared in the anthologies The Grimscribe's Puppets and Mighty in Sorrow, and such periodicals as Apex Magazine, Black Static, Lovecraft eZine. His novella 'Far From Streets' is forthcoming from Dunhams Manor Press, and his story 'Firedancing' will appear in the Laird Barron tribute, Children of Old Leech. Michael blogs about books and writing at griffinwords.com, and his Twitter feed is @griffinwords. He's also an electronic ambient musician and founder of Hypnos Recordings, an ambient music record label he operates with his wife in Portland, Oregon.

B.A.H. Cameron was born in Mississippi, raised in Colorado and now lives in Seattle with his wife and five children. He writes speculative fiction with an emphasis on space opera and superhuman fiction, and works as a freelance editor, writer, illustrator and web designer. His debut novel Ordinary Villainy, will be available fall 2014.

Michael M. Hughes lives in Baltimore with his wife and two daughters. He writes fiction and nonfiction, and his bestselling debut novel, Blackwater Lights, was released by Hydra (Random House) in 2013. The second book in the trilogy, Witch Lights, will be released in October 2014. When he's not writing, Hughes performs as a mentalist (psychic entertainer) and speaks on Fortean and paranormal topics. Visit his website at: http://michaelmhughes.com.

Jeff C. Carter lives in Venice, CA with two cats, a dog, and a human. His stories appear in the anthologies DELTA GREEN: EXTRAORDINARY RENDITIONS, OH LITTLE TOWN OF DEATHLEHEM, CELLAR DOOR Vol 1, SONG STORIES: BLAZE OF GLORY, SUPER, TALES FROM THE BELL CLUB, SHORT SIPS Vol 2, AVENIR ECLECTIA Vol 1, SCIENCE GONE MAD and FRIGHTMARES as well as Trembles, Calliope and eFiction magazine. He is currently developing MECHAWEST, a steam punk RPG for Heroic Journey Publishing.

L.K. Feuerstein is a Colorado native. She moved to Northern Colorado while obtaining her B.A. in Creative Writing from Colorado State University. She's been writing stories and poems since she was ten years old and prefers to write in science fiction, fantasy, and horror genres. This is her first inclusion in a non-poetry compilation. She is currently working on two books, a horror Blood Valley and a fantasy Waterfall Mentor (both working titles), drafts expected to be completed in 2016.

Nick Nafpliotis is a music teacher and writer from Charleston, South Carolina. During the day, he instructs students from the ages of 11-14 on how to play band instruments. At night, he writes about weird crime, bizarre history, pop culture, and humorous classroom experiences on his blog, RamblingBeachCat.com. He is also a television, novel, and comic book reviewer for AdventuresinPoorTaste.com. Nick has been published in Voluted Tales, Horror in Bloom Anthology, and Nebula Rift Science Fiction Magazine. You can also follow him on Twitter at @NickNafster79, where he brings shame to his family on a daily basis.

Tracie McBride is a New Zealander who lives in Melbourne, Australia with her husband and three children. Her work has appeared or is forthcoming in over 80 print and electronic publications, including Bleed, FISH and the Stoker Award-nominated anthologies Horror for Good and Horror Library Volume 5. Her debut collection Ghosts Can Bleed contains much of the work that earned her a Sir Julius Vogel Award. She helps to wrangle slush for Dark Moon Digest and is the vice president of Dark Continents Publishing. Visitors to her blog are welcome at http:// traciemcbridewriter.wordpress.com/.

David J. Fielding is a writer and an actor, most well-known for playing the role of Zordon on the Mighty Morphin' Power Rangers television series, and voice actor for video games such as Empire Earth, Dungeon Siege: Legends of Aranna, Zeus, Poseidon, and Anvil of Dawn. His published works have appeared in Nevermet Press, Rebel ePublishers LLC, Source Point Press, and the upcoming Capes and Clockwork Anthology from Dark Oak Press and the Something Strange is Going On anthology from Flinch! Books. He is busy editing and revising his superhero novel, a series of paranormal stories and a number of other short stories.

Brian Kaufman might have been the slowest center fielder in the history of the New York Yankees, or the loudest, most abrasive radio talk show host to ever grace the airwaves. Instead, he opted for a major in cooking with a minor in fiction writing. Known for procrastination and the consumption of adult beverages, Brian managed just three novels in six decades of amateur and professional lying. The Breach (Last Knight Publishing, 2002) tells the story of the Alamo from the Mexican point of view. The Apocalypse Parable (Last Knight Publishing, 2006) follows a low-rent private eye in search of a modern-day messiah. Dead Beyond the Fence (Dark Silo Press, 2010) is a zombie horror tale. Brian currently writes textbooks for a distance-learning company. He lives in the Colorado mountains with his wife and dog. In his spare time, Brian lifts weights, plays blues guitar and tries to get the dog to do the chores.

Robert M. Price, a fan of H.P. Lovecraft since the Lancer paperback collections of 1967 appeared, began writing scholarly articles and humorous pieces on HPL and the Cthulhu Mythos in 1981. His celebrated semi-pro zine Crypt of Cthulhu began as a quarterly fanzine for the Esoteric Order of Dagon Amateur Press Association in 1981 and made it to 109 issues. In 1990 he began editing Mythos anthologies for Fedogan & Bremer and Chaosium, Inc. and still does! His fiction has been collected in Blasphemies and Revelations.

Pete Rawlik, a long time collector of Lovecraftian fiction, and is the author of more than twenty-five short stories, a smattering of poetry, the Cthulhu Mythos novel Reanimators, and it's forthcoming sequel The Weird Company. He is a frequent contributor to the Lovecraft ezine and the New York Review of Science Fiction. In 2014 his short story Revenge of the Reanimator was nominated for a New Pulp Award. He lives in southern Florida where he works on Everglades issues.

Mary SanGiovanni is the author of ten books and counting, usually involving cosmic supernatural horrors, as well as numerous short stories. Her first novel, The Hollower, was nominated for a Bram Stoker Award. She has an MA in Writing Popular Fiction from Seton Hill University and is a member of The Authors' Guild, the International Thriller Writers, and Penn Writers. More information aboutMary can be found on her website: http://www.marysangiovanni.com.

William Meikle is a Scottish writer, now living in Canada, with twenty novels published in the genre press and over 300 short story credits in thirteen countries. His work has appeared in a number of professional anthologies and magazines with recent sales to NATURE Futures, Penumbra and Buzzy Mag among others. He lives in Newfoundland with whales, bald eagles and icebergs for company. When he's not writing he dreams of fortune and glory.

Joseph S. Pulver, Sr., is the author of the novels, The Orphan Palace and Nightmare's Disciple, and he has written many short stories that have appeared in magazines and anthologies, including 'Weird Fiction Review', 'Crypt of Cthulhu', and 'Lovecraft eZine', Ellen Datlow's Best Horror of the Year, S. T. Joshi's Black Wings (I and III) and A Mountain Walked, Book of Cthulhu, Tales of Jack the Ripper, and The Children of Old Leech, and many anthologies edited by Robert M. Price. His highlyñacclaimed short story collections, Blood Will Have Its Season, SIN & ashes, and Portraits of Ruin, were published by Hippocampus Press in 2009, 2010, and 2012, respectively. He edited A Season in Carcosa and The Grimscribe's Puppets (Miskatonic River Press 2012 and 2013), issue #30 of 'Lovecraft eZine', and collections by Ann K. Schwader (The Worms Remember) and John B. Ford. He is at work on two new collections of weird fiction, A House of Hollow Wounds, and The Protocols of Ugliness, both edited by Jeffrey Thomas, and is currently editing CASSILDA'S SONG and THE LEAVES OF A NECRONOMICON for 2015 release (both Chaosium).You can find his blog at: http://thisyellowmadness.blogspot.com/

Tom Lynch is a longtime devotee of the art of the terrifying tale. He is descended from a line of family that enjoys a good nightmare, so is it any wonder he writes stories with a darker twist? Tom's first fiction appeared in Horror for the Holidays from Miskatonic River Press, and he has since appeared in the ever-eldritch Lovecraft eZine, Tales of the Talisman Volume 8, Issue 4, Undead and Unbound, Eldritch Chrome, and Dark Rites of Cthulhu. As of this moment, future appearances include When Darkness Calls, Dark Rites of Cthulhu, Atomic Age Cthulhu: Terrifying Tales of the Cthulhu Mythos, and others, but the ink is not yet dry enough to divulge details. By day, Tom is an elementary school teacher, looking to expand young minds and spends the rest of his spare time hunched over his keyboard writing scary stories devoted to giving you nightmares.

Richard Gavin is often praised as a master of numinous horror fiction in the tradition of Arthur Machen, Algernon Blackwood, and H.P. Lovecraft. His fiction has appeared in THE YEAR'S BEST WEIRD FICTION, THE BEST HORROR OF THE YEAR and has been collected in the books CHARNEL WINE, OMENS, THE DARKY SPLENDID REALM, and AT FEAR'S ALTAR. He has also published numerous essays of the macabre and the esoteric. "Echoes from Hades", his non-fiction column, can be found on the acclaimed website The Teeming Brain. Richard lives in Ontario, Canada. He welcomes readers at www.richardgavin.net

Born in Vancouver, Canada and bred on a steady diet of comics, horror books and movies, **Desmond Reddick** writes, podcasts and teaches in a small town on Vancouver Island. There he resides with his loving wife, two wild sons, a half-dozen vicious chickens and one very neurotic duck named Howard (pictured above). He has been published in two volumes of Pulpwork Press's HOW THE WEST WAS WEIRD and in THE END WAS NOT THE END: POST-APOCALYPTIC FANTASY TALES from Seventh Star Press. Find him at www.dreadmedia.com.

The art and poetry of **Morgan Griffith** appeared in numerous fantasy/horror magazines in the '80's and '90's, including Eldritch Tales; Undinal Songs; Etchings and Odysseys; Grue; Fantasy Macabre; The Arkham Sampler and Gary Crawford's Supernatural Poetry. In 2003 two pen and ink drawings were included in Leilah Wendell's hardcover volume Necromance under the name Wraith. Attempting reanimation, short fiction and art of Morgan's has recently appeared in Cellar Door and James Ward Kirk's Bones anthology. Poetry is also to come in Dead But Dreaming. She is a Californian relocated to Florida who does glass etching/sandblasting, and lives with pet rats.

Jason Andrew lives in Seattle, Washington with his wife Lisa. He is an Associate member of the Science Fiction and Fantasy Writers of America, Active Member of the Horror Writer's Association, and member of the International Association of Media Tie-In Writers.

By day, he works as a mild-mannered technical writer. By night, he writes stories of the fantastic and occasionally fights crime.

His first short story, written at age six, titled 'The Wolfman Eats Perry Mason' was severely rejected. It also caused his Grandmother to watch him very closely for a few years. His short fiction has appeared in markets such as Shine: An Anthology of Optimistic SF (Harper Collins), Frontier Cthulhu: Ancient Horrors in the New World (Chaosium), and Coins of Chaos (Edge Science Fiction and Fantasy Publishing). In 2011, his story "Moonlight in Scarlet" received an honorable mention in Ellen Datlow's List for Best Horror of the Year.

In addition, Jason has written for a number of role-playing games such as Call of Cthulhu, Shadowrun, and Vampire: The Masquerade. His most recent projects include Hunters Hunted 2 (The Onyx Path), Anarchs Unbound (The Onyx Path), and Atomic Age Cthulhu: Terrifying Tales of the Mythos Menace (Chaosium). Recently, he served as Developer for Mind's Eye Theatre: Vampire The Masquerade for By Night Studios.

Brett J. Talley is the Bram Stoker Award nominated author of That Which Should Not Be, The Void, and The Reborn, as well as numerous short stories. Born in Alabama, he now lives in Washington, D.C. where he serves as a speechwriter for a United States Senator.

Mexican by birth, Canadian by inclination, **Silvia Moreno-Garcia** lives in beautiful British Columbia with her family and two cats. She writes speculative fiction (from magic realism to horror). Her short stories have appeared in places such as The Book of Cthulhu and Imaginarium 2012: The Best Canadian Speculative Writing. Her first collection, This Strange Way of Dying, is out in 2013. Her debut novel, Signal to Noise, will be released in 2015 by Solaris.

James Pratt mostly writes in the weird horror genre with dashes of fantasy, sci-fi, and action/adventure. And monsters. Lots of monsters. He has stories appearing in a number of anthologies including Canopic Jars: Tales of Mummies and Mummification from Great Old Ones Press, Demonic Visions Vols.1, 2, and 3, Alter Egos Vol. 2 from Source Point Press, Dark Hall Press Cosmic Horror Anthology, and Mirror Mirror from Thirteen Press, as well as in a number of upcoming anthologies. He also has short story collections available for download from several vendors including Amazon.com: the creature-centric Horrible Stories for Terrible People Vol. 1 - Monsters, and Horrible Stories for Terrible People Vol. 2 - Obscura whose inhabitants include ghosts, the Grim Reaper, the Devil, and the Lord Almighty. James is currently working on two more short story collections, one fantasy and the other apocalypse-themed, and a Weird Western novel set firmly in the Lovecraft universe. James' author page can be found on Facebook as "James D. Pratt".

J. F. Gonzalez is the author of several novels of horror and dark suspense including They, Back From the Dead, Primitive, Survivor. With Wrath James White, he is the co-author of two short novels (Hero, The Killings). He is also the co-author of the Clickers series (with Mark Williams and Brian Keene respectively), of which the latest effort is Clickers vs. Zombies. Over eighty of his short stories and novellas have appeared in various magazines and anthologies and much of this is collected in four volumes which includes the latest, Screaming To Get Out & Other Wailings of the Damned. Several of his novels and short stories have been optioned for film, but nothing ever gets made. J.F. passed away in 2014. For more information on his work, visit his official website at www.jfgonzalez.com.

A very heartfelt thank you to all of our Kickstarter supporters!

<table>
<tr><td>Kirsty Spencer</td><td>Matthew Rayback</td></tr>
<tr><td>Ben Cameron</td><td>Tim Meakins</td></tr>
<tr><td>Matthew Carpenter</td><td>Gary McCluskey</td></tr>
<tr><td>Lee Moe</td><td>Chris Specker</td></tr>
<tr><td>Rhona M Tennant</td><td>Sarah Troedson</td></tr>
<tr><td>Andrew Clough</td><td>Mechanomaly</td></tr>
<tr><td>Jesse Oberes</td><td>Chris Duncan</td></tr>
<tr><td>JayHawk</td><td>Madeleine Riehs</td></tr>
<tr><td>Justin Zimmerman</td><td>Jennifer Bird</td></tr>
<tr><td>Kevin Smith</td><td>William Merrill</td></tr>
<tr><td>Scott Maynard</td><td>Thomas C McGee III</td></tr>
<tr><td>Doug Blakeslee</td><td>Marc Burnell</td></tr>
<tr><td>Kristen Hovet</td><td>Olivia Niver</td></tr>
<tr><td>Jason Andrew</td><td>Tina Jens</td></tr>
<tr><td>Brian Keene</td><td>gigglestick</td></tr>
<tr><td>Contesse</td><td>Tim Morgan</td></tr>
<tr><td>Cthulhu Commune</td><td>Larry</td></tr>
<tr><td>Lydia Helm Nafpliotis</td><td>Brian White</td></tr>
<tr><td>Heather</td><td>Jonathan Grimm</td></tr>
<tr><td>Sam Stoute</td><td>Nicholas Federle</td></tr>
<tr><td>Rhiannon Louve</td><td>Valerie</td></tr>
<tr><td>Valerie Tiley</td><td>Glade Packer</td></tr>
<tr><td>Alec Pappas</td><td>Moria Trent</td></tr>
<tr><td>Arinn Demo</td><td>Aaron Spriggs</td></tr>
<tr><td>Gnoggin</td><td>Lefebvre</td></tr>
<tr><td>Nathan Filizzi</td><td>Scott Bowen</td></tr>
<tr><td>Stephen Brent McDowell</td><td>Emilie Dionne</td></tr>
<tr><td>Chad Anctil</td><td>Deborah Bonnema Perry</td></tr>
<tr><td>Divina Johnson</td><td>Katherine Valdez</td></tr>
<tr><td>Will Hall</td><td>Joe Kontor</td></tr>
<tr><td>mike mcintosh</td><td>Kibeth</td></tr>
<tr><td>Nicholas Chavez</td><td>Brian Kaufman</td></tr>
<tr><td>Amy Lynn Messner</td><td>Dana</td></tr>
<tr><td>Ryan Anderson Dean</td><td>Aaron Nitz</td></tr>
<tr><td>Hilary</td><td>Warren Rumble</td></tr>
<tr><td>H.P. Lovecraft Film Fest & CthulhuCon</td><td>Megan Peterson</td></tr>
<tr><td></td><td>Ron Neely II</td></tr>
<tr><td>Andrea Kleihege</td><td>Karrie White</td></tr>
<tr><td>Lewis Evans</td><td>Jesper Anderson</td></tr>
<tr><td>Bob Hattier</td><td>Denise Mercer</td></tr>
<tr><td>Brianna Agnew</td><td>Andy Lucas</td></tr>
<tr><td>Mark Froom</td><td>Michelle Maxfield</td></tr>
</table>

Joseph Boutin
Serial007
Kristopher Mallory &
    J.W. Zulauf
Allan McPherson
Sebastian Ruecker
Christine M Torrez
Richard Lai
lehmann
Tad Kelson
Geoffrey Sperl
Kyle Miller
leecachu
Sean Quilty
Kris Leeke
Tyrel Fox
johne
Bryce Undy
Ian Paterson
Christopher A. Fahlsing
Marc Margelli
Will Ackerman
Russell Smeaton
Vitamancer
Mark Coole
Jax Pierson
Joseph Duchesneau
Jason Leisemann
G.S. Case
Emily Jorrey
Timothy
Alberto Lopez
Chris Johnson
Brian DeMarzo
eric priehs
Aloysius Delapore
Nancy Martin
Bride Florent
Guillaume Viveiros
Melinda Olson
Gavran
Joshua Hair
Brent Yoder
scorpiusoka7

ATH
Philip K. Sharp-Garcia
Jeff Becker
spacedlaw
Kathryn Sullivan
Diane Severson Mori
Karen Martin Nafpliotis
Ryan Brush
Michael Sims
Mark L
Tom Bither
Tommy Casapueblo
Jen Piatek
Jamie Revell
David Rains
Scott Berke
Leland Eaves
Elena
jason rainwater
Abby Witherell
Debbie Crookston
Mark Martinez
Elan Auman
Timo Zingg
Angeline Burton
Jason Aiken
Laura Trittipoe
Erin Gunderson
Jennifer Kahng
incandescens
Fae Morgan
ron aviles
Scott Bauer
Beth A Lawhead
David
Allen Drees Jr.
Dayna Jones
Amanda
Cassidy Hara
Lisa Deutsch Harrigan
Adam Alexander
Thorin
Mitchell Willie
CorrieHemenway

Jessica Schulze
Hailey Duran
Tyler Walker
Stephen Bettles
Ellen Fleischer
Joseph Fernandes
Miskatonic River Press
Araceli Ricardez
Andy Barbieri
Brian McNatt
Eben Brooks
Aoshia
ZMiles
John D
Meghan Euringer
Tim Scott
Kathryn Slater
stephanie wagner
Betsy Abbott
Sabrina Howes
Nathan Morimitsu
Dan Toland
William Mayorga
Timothy Reinhart
Callum Stoner
Danielle Holbein
Edward Sizemore
Ralph D Will
Terry Willitts
Will Hart
Laura Ahlstrom
Christina Lee
Andrew Fisher
Andrew Byers
Dan Conser
Mark James Featherston
Rich Simmons
Caity Moore
Kieran Cardoza
Ricardo Arredondo
Jim Bellmore
John Blankenship
Mark Barnett
Lea Zukas

shadow
Jake Johnson
Kari Ramadorai
Tara Moeller
Dan Alban
Christopher Hackney
Ethan Chiang
Paul Cardullo
Kimberly McField
Will Childs
Heather D Bechard
Robert Biskin
Antonio A Rodriguez
Liz Westlake
travis a neisler
Neil Mahoney
Monique
Morgan Markowski
Patricia A. Duplantis
David Zelasco
Michael Moore
Skarsnik Larsen
James-Henry Holland
Clancy Cunningham
Sean McGrath
John OConnor
Brittany Phillips
Steven Zuber
Raven Daegmorgan
Cathy Betchel O'Malley
Wouter Dhondt
Chris Miles
Chris Jarocha-Ernst
Chris
Angela Keeley
Chris Heath
Travis Chapa
Yosef Maayan
thaumaturgan
Ronny Anderssen
Eileen Hendriksen
Chris Smith
Patrick Burdell
Riccardo Sartori

Snarkodile
Charles Wilkins
Damien Walters Grintalis
Aaron Vanek
Tymothy
Adam
Lauren Phelps
Georgia Michelle Yoder
Heather
Andrew Jack
Patrice Mermoud
Annie Donaldson
Kevin Foster
Tony Southcotte
Courts Towns
Rebecca Romney
Charles Meyer
joe
Vanessa A. Miller
Jaime Will
Abigail R. Gordon
Connie Theodoropoulos
T.K. Cvetkovic
Michael Feldhusen
Lori Nicole Evans
Marc Severson
Jason Williams
Matt Wiseman
  John Martin

Craig Hackl
Elizabeth Barrial
 Ian McFarlin
Tim Ellis
LK Hart
Wibble!
Lorenz Thor
Benet Devereux
James Pratt
Ross Payton
Jeremy Butler
Aaron Lile
Lester Smith
curtana
Fraydog
 Brett Talley
Eric Helgeson
Sven Wiese
Scott Glancy
Sarah Helstrom
Harley Jebens
 Paul Richardson
Simina A
Sara & Chris Martinez
Jenna Venker Weidenbenner
Richard Lantz
nyarly23
SwordFire

www.ingramcontent.com/pod-product-compliance
Lightning Source LLC
Chambersburg PA
CBHW051207120726
47905CB00004B/1010